PRAISE FOR *FOUR-LETTER WORD*

"Raw, real, and impossible to put down. *Four-Letter Word* tackles fitting in, sexuality, and friendship. Without a doubt, this is Christa's bravest, best work yet."

—JENNIFER MATHIEU, AUTHOR OF
THE TRUTH ABOUT ALICE AND *MOXIE*

"Tender, gripping, and deceptively haunting, *Four-Letter Word* reminds us just how necessary, dangerous, and potentially life changing some friendships can be. This novel is a startling jolt to the heart."

—BRENDAN KIELY, *NEW YORK TIMES* BESTSELLING COAUTHOR OF
ALL AMERICAN BOYS AND *THE LAST TRUE LOVE STORY*

"Christa Desir's bold and edgy *Four-Letter Word* will leave readers breathlessly turning pages. . . . A MUST READ."

—GAE POLISNER, AUTHOR OF *IN SIGHT OF STARS*
AND *THE MEMORY OF THINGS*

"*Four-Letter Word* is a mystery, a psychological thriller, and a searing look at what happens when we make a game out of other people's pain."

—ELANA K. ARNOLD, AUTHOR OF *INFANDOUS* AND
NATIONAL BOOK AWARD FINALIST *WHAT GIRLS ARE MADE OF*

"Refreshingly sex-positive . . . Chloe's strong voice and perspective, as well as the warm, healthy friendships she ultimately cultivates, are eye-opening and rewarding."

—*BOOKLIST*

Also by Christa Desir

Fault Line

Bleed Like Me

Other Broken Things

Love Blind
(with Jolene Perry)

FOUR-LETTER WORD

Christa Desir

SIMON PULSE

New York London Toronto Sydney New Delhi

SIMON PULSE

An imprint of Simon & Schuster Children's Publishing Division

1230 Avenue of the Americas, New York, New York 10020

First Simon Pulse paperback edition July 2019

Text copyright © 2018 by Christa Desir

Cover photograph of scissors copyright © 2019 by Mohamad Itani

Cover photograph of paper copyright © 2019 by iStock.com/robynmac

Also available in a Simon Pulse hardcover edition.

All rights reserved, including the right of reproduction in whole or in part in any form.

SIMON PULSE and colophon are registered trademarks of Simon & Schuster, Inc.

For information about special discounts for bulk purchases, please contact Simon & Schuster Special Sales at 1-866-506-1949 or business@simonandschuster.com.

The Simon & Schuster Speakers Bureau can bring authors to your live event.

For more information or to book an event contact the Simon & Schuster Speakers Bureau at 1-866-248-3049 or visit our website at www.simonspeakers.com.

Cover designed by Tiara Iandiorio

Interior designed by Mike Rosamilia

The text of this book was set in New Caledonia.

Manufactured in the United States of America

2 4 6 8 10 9 7 5 3 1

The Library of Congress has cataloged the hardcover edition as follows:

Names: Desir, Christa, author.

Title: Four letter word / by Christa Desir.

Description: First Simon Pulse hardcover edition. | New York : Simon Pulse, 2018. |

Summary: Sixteen-year-old Chloe's isolation is relieved when she is drawn into a high-stakes game with potentially dire consequences by a new student, also called Chloe.

Identifiers: LCCN 2017008155 (print) | LCCN 2017034321 (eBook) |

ISBN 9781481497374 (hardcover : alk. paper) | ISBN 9781481497398 (eBook)

Subjects: | CYAC: Games—Fiction. | Friendship—Fiction. | Secrets—Fiction. | Dating (Social customs)—Fiction. | Identity—Fiction. | Family life—Iowa—Fiction. | Iowa—Fiction.

Classification: LCC PZ7.D4506 (eBook) | LCC PZ7.D4506 Fou 2018 (print) |

DDC [Fic]—dc23

LC record available at https://lccn.loc.gov/2017008155

ISBN 9781481497381 (pbk)

To the extraordinary women of the world.
May you know them, may you support them, may you
raise them, may you be them. ¡Viva la vulva!

1

Chloe Donnelly transferred to our high school the day Melissa McGrill miscarried a baby none of us knew about on the floor of the disgusting locker room showers. It wasn't like I didn't notice a new girl, of course. It was after spring break, and who starts in a new school after spring break? Particularly small, boring Grinnell High School, which had little to show for itself beyond a decent baseball team and a state-recognized antibullying poster slogan. But still, any interest I might've had in a new student was sidelined by the mental image of a blood-covered baby gasping its last breath on unclean, scuzzy tiles.

Most of the morning I couldn't shake the picture in my head. I had to ask Mr. Meyers to repeat his question about *As I Lay Dying* twice before I finally could answer correctly. By the time I got to lunch, the miscarried baby in my mind had grown extra hands and a mouth that opened and closed like a hungry fish.

"Did you hear about Melissa?" Eve asked as soon as she slid onto the bench across from me in the cafeteria. It was burrito day, and I couldn't stand the wet-dog smell of the school's cafeteria burritos. Eve always got two of them.

"Yep," I answered, and shoveled a handful of pretzel sticks into my mouth, trying not to breathe through my nose.

Eve squinted at me, then adjusted her headband so her zit-free forehead was on full display, all that flat-ironed light-brown hair framing her face. She waited a few seconds and then huffed, "Is that all you have to say?"

Things with Eve had been pretty crappy since spring break. Even before that, really. I hated seeing the side of her that was so impatient with me, but it'd be a lie to say that side didn't come out more and more frequently every day. I'd been trying everything I could to be more what she wanted, but it never seemed to be enough.

"Did you want me to say something else?" I tried, going for teasing, but maybe sounding snippy because the burrito smell was bad and my stomach already hurt thinking about that dead baby.

The first two years of high school Eve and I had been best friends, barely able to make it through class without texting each other. But that was before Holly. Holly with her beautiful face and her perfect dancer body, and her insistence that Eve ditch me over spring break.

"A girl miscarried at the Catholic school last year," Holly said, setting her tray of burritos down and squishing on the bench beside Eve. Always beside Eve, never sliding in next to me. "But not during gym class. Gross. I can't even imagine. . . ."

Neither could I, was the thing. Or rather, I didn't want to imagine it anymore. That was part of the reason why I didn't have anything to say about it. Because everything my imagination was conjuring up was horrible, and I couldn't reconcile that with what I knew about Melissa. Melissa, who helped me run a lemonade stand during new student orientation at nearby Grinnell College when we were in elementary school. Melissa, who was the person I'd told about my own mom's miscarriage when I was thirteen years old and how for a while I didn't think my family would survive it.

"It's not that big a deal," a voice said next to me, and before I could look up, I was being shoved down the bench by a large canvas messenger bag and a girl whom I'd never spoken to before. Half of one of my butt cheeks was hanging off the side of the bench, but I was too shy to push back. "Abortions are way bloodier than miscarriages. I'm Chloe, by the way. Chloe Donnelly."

I dropped my head and studied her through my curtain of hair—my bangs were taking way too long to grow out, but my

3

forehead was a mess of acne so I didn't mind so much. Plus, my hair was the perfect two-way mirror. No one could see in, but I could see out.

There was nothing interesting about the way Chloe Donnelly looked; she was plain, dark hair to her shoulders, and a basic face with slightly too much makeup, including bright-pink lip liner, which I thought made girls look trashy. I almost dismissed her altogether as not really worth getting to know in the two months we had left of our junior year. But then she pushed my hair from my face and tucked it behind my ear *like we were friends,* and studied me with her wide, light-blue eyes. They looked practically white, and I couldn't decide if they were creepy or angelic, but they made her look less average.

I shifted my butt back onto the bench and shook my hair back to its curtain position. Chloe Donnelly's clothes were dark and a bit New York arty for being in Grinnell, Iowa, but not exactly drastic or extreme enough to make her stand out. Except the longer I studied her, the more she *did* stand out. And not just her eyes. It was as if the atoms around her were all sucking in their stomachs to give her more space.

"I just started here," she said, pulling a recycled lunch sack from her messenger bag. The sack was faded green and had an Earth Day logo peeling off the side. She had rings on every finger of her left hand, and a single ring on the pointer finger of her right hand, a thick silver band that almost covered her first knuckle with a purple stone embedded in it.

Eve and Holly stared at her—no curtains of hair to hide their full-on gaping—before Eve finally said, "I'm Eve, this is Holly, and her name is Chloe too." She swatted the air toward me like I was a fly circling her wet-dog burrito, hoping to eat it and then barf it back up. Hurt must have registered on my face because Eve crossed her eyes and gave me a goofy smile like she used to when the two of us were being stupid. I laughed and Eve did too until Holly nudged her.

Chloe Donnelly looked at me, taking in my hockey shirt and dress-code-regulation-length jean skirt. "Another Chloe, huh?"

I wanted to say I was the *first* Chloe, but my tongue felt too thick in my mouth, so I resigned myself to nodding and hoping people wouldn't start calling me Chloe S. like they did in elementary school when Chloe Brockenrick was in my class.

"So you've had an abortion?" Eve leaned forward and asked, because this was what she would ask. Eve was extremely curious, always wondering aloud what stuff would be like. *What do you think it's like to have a pierced tongue? Do you think the principal still has sex with his wife? Would you ever let anyone tie you up?* I was the opposite of curious. Thinking about those things scared me a little. Or maybe more than a little.

The thing with Eve, though, was that as curious as she was, she usually never did anything about it. Her curiosity was all just out-loud speculation. Freshman year, when everyone was doing all those "challenges" on social media that involved shot glasses or cinnamon or marshmallows, Eve would endlessly tag people for them but never actually participate. She was the last one to ever try anything, and not only because of her hovery mom, who always seemed to be popping up at school events for one reason or another. Eve was as unadventurous as me, stuck in a tiny town in the middle of Iowa. It was one of the things that made us friends, being perpetually bored and not quite willing to change that.

"Of course I've had an abortion," Chloe Donnelly answered, lifting a bony shoulder as if she was used to these sorts of lunchtime conversations. "I'm from Chicago."

"Is Chicago an abortion hot spot?" I blurted out, going red as soon as the words dropped from my lips. *That* was the thing with me: I was a blurter. I had this humiliating habit of saying something inappropriate as soon as I was pushed out of my comfort zone.

Eve used to think it was hilarious—she'd even egg me on—but like everything else, she seemed embarrassed for me now. "Chloe. Oh my God."

Chloe Donnelly turned to me. "No, Other Chloe, Chicago isn't an abortion hot spot. But we are firmly a blue state, which is more than I can say about the mercurial, often-red-state status of Iowa."

Mercurial? I blinked once, twice, then blurted, "Chicago's not a state." Jeez, what was wrong with me?

"Chlo-e," Eve said again, holding out the final *e* like a whiny note of judgment and intolerance. I looked at her, hoping for the goofy eye-crossing face to spring up again, but that wasn't happening.

Holly touched the bracelet on Eve's wrist where she wore her half of their BEST FRIENDS charm. "Don't you mean . . . 'Other Chloe'?"

Eve touched Holly's bracelet like it was some secret signal, then looked at Chloe Donnelly, totally ignoring the no-doubt-defeated expression on my face. "Yeah, that's what I meant. *Other* Chloe."

So within ten minutes of wet-dog-burrito lunch, I got to watch the Wonder Twins activate their best-friend superpower, I became "Other," and Chloe Donnelly was launched onto a pedestal for Holly and Eve to fawn over. Another crap day in my life.

I'd completely lost my appetite, which no one seemed to notice, but Eve offered to share her second burrito with Chloe Donnelly. She passed, but then made us all exchange numbers with her. Though she did ask me first, and told me she thought my penguin phone case was "adorably retro," so at least there was that.

         ❖   ❖   ❖

"Did you hear about Melissa?" I said, as I sat next to Mateo in the back row of Spanish class, last and *best* period of the day. I always got there as early as possible because Señor Williams was a total hard-ass about during-class chatter and I didn't want to squander even thirty seconds with Mateo. "Melissa McGrill? In gym class?"

Mateo raised his dark eyebrows so they made this upside-down V. And the tiny balloon of hope inside me that always surrounded talking to Mateo deflated. I hated his disappointed look. *Hated* it. "I'm not one to follow gossip, Chloe," he said in this way that wasn't exactly judging, but more a statement of fact about his character. I shoved my left ring fingernail into my mouth to gnaw at it, trying to figure out if there was a way to regroup.

He *wasn't* a gossiper. I knew this. And he wouldn't see this as an opportunity to ask about me and my life; he'd see it as me spreading rumors. Which sucked. It was a stupid thing to bring up with him, and I should've planned out a better conversation topic. A different way for him to get to know me. To *see* me.

Mateo wasn't like anyone else in our high school. He was quiet and thoughtful and mysterious in an almost shy way. He'd moved to Grinnell the summer before this school year started, and I'd spent six months doing everything I could to get him to like me. Though I wasn't completely sure what I'd do if he ever really did. Somehow my fantasies of us always stopped with him smiling and holding my hand and asking me out—wanting to spend time with me for real.

He didn't *dislike* me, I didn't think, but he didn't say a whole lot either. I didn't know if it was because he was Mexican American in a really white high school and felt out of place, or if he was just not chatty. Lots of guys weren't. At least they weren't chatty with me.

"Sorry," I mumbled, tugging at a thread on the pocket of my skirt and trying to swallow down my embarrassment.

He nodded and flipped open his notebook. I peeked at him through my hair, zeroing in on his lip ring and wondering what it would feel like when I kissed him. *If* I kissed him. The thought of it ratcheted up a gas bubble of anxiety in my stomach, but it definitely seemed less like panic and more like excitement. Like the buzziness that comes from a *maybe*.

"I used to be friends with her. Melissa, I mean," I blurted. Again. "I wasn't trying to gossip. I have some experience with miscarriage." Oh God. Did I just say that? "I mean, not mine. But . . . anyway, I had no idea she was pregnant. I didn't even know she was dating anyone."

Mateo didn't say anything about my miscarriage experience, only shrugged. His shoulders were big—man shoulders—and I wondered if he lifted weights on his own or if it came from playing baseball or working. I'd heard he'd spent some of the summer helping his family on a farm where they lived, though I hadn't gotten up the courage to ask him. Everything with Mateo felt a little like prying.

"It was a long time ago . . . when we were friends, me and Melissa. Elementary school and most of junior high. I haven't hung out with her in forever. I see her in church, though. And I did see her once in town with a guy in an army outfit, or navy, or whatever. How do you even tell? Maybe he's the dad."

"This seems like gossiping," Mateo said, and my cheeks burned hot.

"No. It's not, though. I . . . I mean, I'm just worried, I guess." The blood-baby in my imagination did another lap around my brain, and I slammed my eyes shut. What was I doing talking about this?

"Other Chloe," a voice called, but I didn't need to open my eyes to look for who it was. "Who's your friend?"

I blinked the spots out of my vision and turned to Chloe Donnelly. "This is Mateo."

She stood before him and eyed him like she had a lot of experience sizing up guys. Not that she was necessarily interested in him so much as she could quickly read and catalog attributes. I wished I was good at that, but I always got hung up on one thing. The way a guy's ears stuck out or how he had a patch of acne along his chin or how one tooth tipped in front of the others.

"Mateo. Huh. So are you Latino?" she asked, as if her

question was totally normal, not a million kinds of awkward and invasive and a little racist, particularly at GHS, where 92 percent of us were white kids. At least I'd never blurted-asked about his family's background. Instead, I just waited, listening and memorizing everything he said, including him mentioning once that his mom grew up in Mexico City.

I shoved my fingernail into my mouth, gnawing the thumb this time, and let my gaze ping-pong between him and Chloe Donnelly. When Mateo—unsurprisingly—didn't answer, Chloe Donnelly grinned wide as if she'd won something. Then she turned to me and said, "Can you hang out this afternoon? I need to get some stuff from Walmart and don't feel like going alone."

I dropped my thumb from my mouth and answered, "Yeah. Definitely." I probably agreed too quickly, but I hadn't gotten any texts from Eve all day and the idea of going home alone right after school—again—seemed too depressing to even consider.

I used to play hockey. I started at the Grinnell Community Center when I was really young, playing every chance I got, including making my parents build a backyard skate rink every winter. But then two years ago, after my parents concocted their bucket-list plan of joining the Spirit Corps—a nonprofit organization for whole families to do humanitarian service abroad—we all moved to Burkina Faso. I lasted eight weeks before I begged and pleaded to move back home and live with my grandparents, Nan and Pops. It was a stressful few weeks after that, when my parents tried to figure out if they could get out of their Spirit Corps commitment—they couldn't without some serious financial repercussions—and they tried to convince me to stay. When I went on a hunger strike, they agreed to send me back as long as I spent summers and winter breaks with them.

Nan and Pops lived in Grinnell too, so presumably it should've been a fairly smooth transition. They did open their house to me without complaining or making it seem like a hassle at all. And my grandparents were pretty okay, but they weren't the type to cart me all over the state to play travel hockey, and GHS sadly wasn't big enough for a hockey team. So I pretty much had no extracurricular activities.

"Walmart is great. I love Walmart," I said to Chloe Donnelly, which . . . sounded ridiculous.

"You sure you don't have other plans?" Chloe Donnelly asked, her voice a little soft and concerned. "I don't want to mess anything up for you."

I peeked at Mateo again, wondering what he thought of my overenthusiasm, and then said as normal as I could, "No worries. I can rearrange things."

"Great," she said, slipping into the empty seat in front of Mateo as the bell rang. "It'll be so pink."

2

For the rest of class I tried to figure out what *It'll be so pink*
actually meant. Señor Williams snapped at me for mixing up
the preterite and imperfect tenses. Mateo didn't participate
in class at all—again—but did wave at me when he took off
after the bell. I pulled my phone out after class to see Eve still
hadn't texted, then I searched Google and Urban Dictionary,
but neither had any compatible hits for how Chloe Donnelly
used *pink*.

I considered asking her; if it was Eve, I would have and
wouldn't have cared—much—about looking dumb. But Chloe
Donnelly wanted me to go to Walmart with her. Just the two
of us. And I was determined not to screw things up by looking
like I didn't know anything.

I headed toward my locker, mostly ignoring the hallway

speculation still swirling about Melissa McGrill's miscarriage, and packed my bag up for the day. My bag was overly full and cut into my shoulder so I dropped it at my feet. I waffled for a few minutes, wondering if I was supposed to go find Chloe Donnelly or text her or what, but before I could decide, she walked down the hall toward me.

"Ready to go?" she asked. She somehow looked fresher than she did five minutes ago in Spanish, and I wondered if she was one of those girls who applied a new layer of mascara after school. Then I felt small for not being one of those girls myself, particularly when I had a bunch of makeup in my too-heavy bag.

"You know it's just the Walmart," I said, hitching my bag on my shoulder and pulling my skirt up a little.

Chloe Donnelly laughed. "I know. Do you have a car?"

I nodded. Nan's crappy "errands" car that was about a hundred years old and involved windows you had to manually roll down. But Nan let me drive it to school some days and it was more than most kids had, so I wasn't above using that in my favor. "Yeah, it's in the parking lot."

"Great. Let's go."

She hooked her arm in mine *like we were real friends*, and I didn't know if I should be uncomfortable with how fast she glommed on to me or excited that this new girl in black clothes with rings on six of her fingers wanted to hang out with me. I thought about my textless phone in my jean skirt's back pocket and Holly's and Eve's BEST FRIENDS bracelets, and allowed myself a small grin at what Eve would think if she saw me.

The Walmart in Grinnell was noteworthy only because it was the sole superstore within a five-mile radius of Grinnell College. It was one of the bigger stores that also sold groceries, though my nan said buying Walmart groceries was like shooting all the local farmers' puppies, so we only shopped there for the things we'd otherwise have to go to Marshalltown for. The entire store smelled like beef and starch. But it was usually busy—Grinnell College kids seemingly had no end to reasons why they needed to make a Walmart run.

"What are we looking for?" I asked Chloe Donnelly as she pushed a cart with one squeaking wheel down the aisle. Her dark clothes looked less fancy and more garage sale-ish under the Walmart fluorescents. I kicked the annoying wheel three times and it stopped squeaking. Chloe Donnelly grinned, and I tried not to look super pleased with myself. She seemed so easy and confident. I got the feeling she could make friends with anyone, and if I was being completely honest, I couldn't figure out why she'd choose me.

"I'm mostly just looking for stuff to decorate my room."

"When did you move in?"

"A few days ago. My mom got a position at the University

of Iowa, and my dad's law firm agreed to transfer him to the Des Moines office. Grinnell is sort of right in the middle; plus, my parents liked the college being here. Liberal politics are like meth to them, and the opportunity to relocate and make a real difference in a state that maybe could swing left again was too hard to pass up."

Whoa. This girl *knew* stuff. A million questions zipped through my brain, but I tucked them all away. If there was one thing I'd learned from Mateo, asking too-personal questions was the quickest way to shut down a conversation. So instead, I said, "My parents are on their second year in the Spirit Corps, which is like a volunteer service nonprofit for families. They were assigned to Burkina Faso. In Africa. They're pretty political too. I live with my grandparents right now."

"Burkina Faso, huh? That's cool. How come you didn't go with them?"

I scratched my cheek with my stubby nails, thinking about how much I was willing to tell this girl, whether it would make me look more real or more needy. "I did, at first. But it was different from what I thought it'd be. My parents were really busy and I was lonely and . . . I don't know. It wasn't a great fit for me."

I hated admitting that. It made me feel like I couldn't handle hard things. But the truth was, I couldn't. Ten weeks in Burkina Faso nearly killed me. I was alone and scared and it felt like I'd been dropped into another world. The first night we were there, the villagers killed three chickens in celebration of our arrival. My parents said it was a huge deal since the people were so poor and any meat was a rare commodity. But I couldn't eat it, because the celebration feast was about twenty feet from where they'd slaughtered the chickens. The blood and the flies and the smell, it was all too much. Plus, at the end of the meal, they gave my dad the talons and beak to eat, which I guess was supposed to be a huge honor. He ate it without grimacing, but I threw up, and since there was nowhere to do it in secret, the whole village saw me. My parents were furious with how rude I was about it all. It only went downhill from there. Every day of those ten weeks, people stared at me constantly. Even now, when I went to spend my school breaks with my parents, the villagers looked at me as if I didn't have any business being there.

Chloe Donnelly nodded as if she'd react the same way I had, and my stomach bubbled a little at the idea that she might actually understand not wanting to give up my whole life for Burkina Faso. Eve had never really asked about my experience, though she was completely thrilled sophomore year when I told her I'd be returning to GHS after all. She'd gone on and on about how hard it had been without her "bestie." Of course, that had all been before Holly.

"Do you miss them? Your parents?" Chloe Donnelly asked, her voice soft and sounding interested.

I missed them terribly, but I knew enough not to admit that. Especially not to someone like Chloe Donnelly, who seemed a bit above needing parents. "Well, my grandparents are pretty low-key so it's nice not having anyone hover. I webcam with my parents every week. And I spend holidays and the summers with them. They'll be home for good this summer."

Chloe Donnelly nodded and grabbed a set of polka-dotted bedsheets for a twin-size bed before steering us toward the women's accessories section of the store.

I let my hair fall and studied the way she dragged her ring-filled left hand over the scarves and purses, her nonbitten nails rubbing the fake-leather handbags. She held scarves up and wrapped them around her neck as if they were already hers. Her pale skin and dark hair made her have that winter-sickly coloring that all of us usually got by January, but her eyes were bright enough to make her almost pretty.

"You should get this one," she said, thrusting a blue-green silky scarf my way. "It goes with your eyes, and it'll help keep your hair off your face."

I refolded it carefully and said, "It's not really in my budget. My grandparents are on Social Security and the Spirit Corps only pays a stipend. I mean, we're fine. My parents planned and saved for it and everything. My mom used to run an organic coffee shop in town and my dad worked for the Iowa Environmental Council, but still, we're not rich. I just feel bad spending my allowance on stuff I don't totally need when my parents are . . ." I waved vaguely.

What in the hell was I doing telling her all this stuff? She didn't care about my mom's coffee shop or my grandparents' Social Security checks. A bubble of shame filled my stomach. I was such an embarrassment when I got nervous.

"I get it," she said with a nod. She glanced around quickly and stuffed the scarf into her messenger bag, then pushed the cart toward the home goods section all casual like.

"What are you doing?" I whispered. "You're going to get caught."

She looked at me and shook her head. "I'm not. Don't worry. I've done this before. And before you start stressing over the ethics of shoplifting, I would point out that this is *Walmart*. Walmart, which notoriously underpays its employees and which is currently the largest seller of firearms in the nation."

"Is that true?" I asked.

Chloe Donnelly didn't even blink. "Yes. Definitely." She sounded so certain, like this was something everyone should know. "Trust me. Stealing that scarf is an act of subversiveness," she said.

An act of subversiveness, I repeated in my head. I fisted

my hands to keep from biting my nails, and then, taking a deep breath, I lifted my chin the tiniest bit and let myself be proud. *I* was being subversive. My parents would probably high-five me. Maybe.

Once she realized I was on board with shoplifting, she continued down the aisles. The farther into home goods we got, the less it smelled like beef and the more it smelled like starch and Styrofoam. "The Walmarts in Chicago are so crappy. All picked-through stuff with no one bothering to put it back in place so you can barely find anything."

"When I was little, I used to think that inanimate objects moved when no one was around, and so if I'd see one out of place, I figured it was trying to make its escape and I'd move it a little closer to the exit," I said, then I looked down because maybe that was stupid. I mean, I didn't do it anymore— much—but it probably sounded ridiculous.

Chloe Donnelly just laughed and swatted my arm. "That is the best. What a smart little kid." Then she plucked up a picture frame and moved it down the aisle, closer to the exit. "I'm so glad you came with me today. It sucks being new."

"You think? I mean, you seem to be doing fine."

She twisted the ring on her right hand, and I wished my nails weren't so wrecked so I could wear rings too. "I guess. But this late in the year, everyone's friendships are already set. How am I going to get in on that? I fought so hard with my parents when they said we were moving. I begged them to let me finish the school year in Chicago."

I understood. I'd done the same with my parents in Burkina Faso, even knowing that it killed my mom a little to say good-bye to me. Chloe Donnelly's voice sounded so sad that I wanted to squeeze her shoulder or hug her or something, but I didn't. "It's better you came with them, though. It would've been hard living in Chicago on your own without anyone. Even if there's more fun stuff to do there."

She blinked and gave me a funny look. "Well, I wouldn't have lived on my own. I begged for them to stay in Chicago too. For all of us to stay. But their jobs and their *goals* were more important."

I swallowed the large baseball of saliva in the back of my throat, shushing the tiny voice that always wondered *why* my parents couldn't have stayed in Grinnell and waited a few years before joining the Spirit Corps, and nodded. "Oh, right. Of course."

Then, as if Chloe Donnelly could hear the tiny voice, she asked, "How come your parents decided to go into the Spirit Corps while you were still in high school? Couldn't they have joined after your senior year?"

The answer was on the tip of my tongue, an avalanche of an explanation about Mom's miscarriage and subsequent depression, and how none of us thought she was going to ever

21

care about anything again until she'd heard a podcast about Burkina Faso and finally found a reason to get out of bed. But I stopped myself. Things were too new with Chloe Donnelly, and I wasn't sure if she could understand it. So instead, I said, "Well, someone offered to buy my mom's coffee shop and my dad's position at work was being phased out because of funding issues, and they really wanted to do volunteering as a family, so the timing worked out for us to go." Which was true, but not exactly right.

"Except you didn't end up volunteering as a family."

I swallowed. "Yeah. Because I didn't want to stay in Africa."

"Hmm," Chloe Donnelly said, but didn't ask anything else. Instead, she rolled the cart, whose wheel had started squeaking again, toward the front of the store.

We got in line for the cashier and I remembered the scarf shoved in Chloe's bag. I tried to stay cool, but *act of subversiveness* didn't sound as great now. The cashier rolled her eyes in disgust at the white dude with dreadlocks in front of us, and I couldn't stop my grin at her annoyance. Somehow white guys with dreads always smelled like they bathed in dumpsters. None of the black guys with dreads from the college smelled like that. Were the white guys too embarrassed to ask for tips on hygiene? It was bad enough they were hijacking a traditionally black hairstyle, but they couldn't even do it right. I could almost hear my mom's lecture about the difference between honoring a culture and shaming it with your own stupidity.

I glanced at Chloe Donnelly and stopped myself from blurting any of that out loud. She may have been the arty type with left-wing parents, but that didn't necessarily mean she'd understand my parents' strange fascination with other cultures, particularly considering their choice to live in Grinnell after college.

The cashier looked relieved by the time we got to the register. She rang up Chloe Donnelly's bedsheets and didn't look at us with any kind of suspicion. The whole transaction was almost underwhelming for my first criminal act.

We pushed the squeaky-wheel cart toward the cart corral with the others and left the store. Then Chloe Donnelly pulled the scarf out of her bag—while we were still in the parking lot!—and wrapped it around my head, pushing my hair out of my face. She was too touchy and fussy, really, particularly for a girl I'd just met. But it reminded me a little of how my mom used to be when she braided my hair, so I didn't say anything, just let her do her thing. When she was done adjusting the scarf, she said, "Let's see what Holly and Eve are up to."

I nodded and tried not to care that it took less than an hour for Chloe Donnelly to already be bored with me. "I think Holly has dance team, but I'll see what Eve is doing. She might be busy."

Too busy to have wanted to hang out with me.

I'm with Chloe Donnelly, I texted. What are you up to? Wanna hang out with us?

Less than a minute later, Eve texted back. Definitely. Can you guys come to my house? Mom is all over me to catch up on homework but I'll tell her we're doing a group project.

"We've got to go to Eve's if we want to hang out," I told Chloe Donnelly. "Her mom's a bit . . . involved."

She grinned at me, as if we were in on some secret. "Sucks to be her." I grinned back. "But tell her fine, we'll be there soon."

I texted Eve back, then we climbed into Nan's car, and I took the long way to the Jacobsons', letting Chloe Donnelly talk the whole time about her old friends, and hoping the slight insecurity in her voice meant that she was trying really hard to be friends now with *me*.

Eve's house was cookie-cutter cute from the outside. Not massive or fancy, but adorable and well-kept. Her mom gardened and put up holiday decorations for every single holiday—including St. Patrick's Day—and generally really bought into the whole small-town vibe of Grinnell. As I pulled into her driveway, I noticed all the Easter decorations had been taken down and replaced with more WELCOME SPRING plaques.

Chloe Donnelly laughed when she saw it. "You didn't even need to tell me her mom was involved. Those wooden flower placards speak for themselves."

I laughed too. "Yeah. My grandparents can barely pull off

getting a Christmas tree up and there are two of them who aren't working. Eve's mom is sort of a force."

Almost to prove my point, her mom had opened the front door, wearing a dress and high heels like she did every time I saw her, and was shoving a plate of something in our faces before we even rang the doorbell.

"Chloe," she said in a sort of pinched singsong voice, "it's been too long."

"Hi, Mrs. Jacobson. It's good to see you. Did you make a new recipe?" I asked, plucking one of the chocolate-drizzled Rice Krispies Treats from the plate.

"Yes. Eve refuses to try even one because she saw the amount of butter I put in, but you girls are growing and need the calcium."

And that was Eve's mom, convinced that butter was a good source of calcium. I once overheard my mom say she was a few IQ points short of a bag of hair but meant well, which was particularly cruel for my mom, who always emphasized people's strengths. I chewed a bite of Rice Krispies Treat and then nodded to Chloe Donnelly. "This is Chloe Donnelly. She's new to Grinnell."

Mrs. Jacobson's face split in half with her smile. "Oh, a new GHS student? We've had a few this year, which is unusual for us, but very welcome. Does your mom know about Grinnell Boosters? We can always use extra help."

Chloe Donnelly made her face mirror Mrs. Jacobson's. It was kind of amazing how she could go all teacher's pet like that. "That's so nice of you to think of her. She's starting her new job, so I think she's going to wait until next year to get involved. But I'll mention it in case."

"She works?" Mrs. Jacobson asked, a tiny frown of disapproval on her face. I wanted to roll my eyes at how dumb she was about working moms, and maybe even say something about how my mom always worked, but I never had that much courage with grown-ups, so I shoved in another mouthful of Rice Krispies Treat.

Chloe Donnelly paused for a second, then said, "Yes, she works. Though I wish she were home more. She used to be and it was so much better. She was a room parent in my elementary school and volunteered at the book fair and stuff. It's hard not having her around as much."

Mrs. Jacobson lifted her chin and smiled big, a tiny bit of lipstick caked on her front tooth. "Well, not everyone can be as present for their children as they'd like to be. You're welcome here anytime." She held the plate out to her.

Chloe Donnelly did not take a Rice Krispies Treat, and it made me want to put my half-eaten one back, but I didn't, because it was delicious and for all I might put up with from my friends, skipping out on food wasn't one of them.

"I'll pull together some Booster pamphlets and send

them home with you," Mrs. Jacobson told Chloe Donnelly. "And I could stop by this weekend to talk to her about it, to answer any questions she may have. She might be able to help with behind-the-scenes stuff like some of the other working parents."

Chloe Donnelly's eyes went wide for a second—not that I could blame her since Mrs. Jacobson dropping by always meant endless conversation about how great the GHS parents were—but then she said, "We're still getting settled with unpacking. But I'll let her know to reach out to you."

Eve came downstairs and huffed at her mom. "Leave them alone, Mom. God. We have a group project due."

Mrs. Jacobson looked embarrassed for a second, but then shook it off and said, "All right, you three should get to work. Remember what your dad said about getting your grades up, Eve. You can't go to volleyball camp this summer if you're in summer school."

Mr. Jacobson was the hard-ass of the family. The grouchy bad cop to Mrs. Jacobson's parental cheerleader. Even seeing Mrs. Jacobson try to be serious about Eve's schoolwork was a little hilarious, because more than once I'd watched Eve talk her mom into writing notes explaining why she needed an extension on some assignment. She did the same thing for Eve's younger brother, Jamie.

Eve curled her lip and said, "Yeah. Dad already told me

this morning. By-e." Then she dismissed her mom with a swat of her hand.

The whole interaction was pretty harsh. When I used to spend more time at Eve's, I always tried to soften the blows of her rudeness. I knew it was just how they were with each other, how they'd always been, but sometimes I felt like Eve didn't really appreciate what she had. Her mom was *really* into both of her kids. I couldn't imagine what it must be like for her to have nothing to show for herself beyond the flair covering her house and her parental involvement in Jamie's junior high, GHS Boosters, and Eve's volleyball. *Always have something that belongs to just you, Chloe*, my mom had told me once when I asked why she opened an organic coffee shop that barely broke even. *Don't co-opt your children's lives as your own. That will only leave you with nothing when they eventually rebel.*

We followed Eve upstairs, past Jamie's room with the loud video game sounds spilling out beneath the door, to her room at the end of the hall. She'd had a passive-aggressive fight with her mom over being able to decorate however she wanted, but ultimately relented to her mom's interior design vision as long as her mom agreed to never clean or tidy it in any way. Which meant that Eve's room looked like a closet exploded all over Martha Stewart's "simple bedroom" model. The walls were robin's-egg blue, and the room had white furniture and little china figurines on various surfaces. And the bookshelf looked perfectly ordered—probably alphabetical—because Eve never read so she didn't touch it. But there were clothes and makeup and hair stuff everywhere. Nan and Pops would kill me if I kept my room like Eve's.

Chloe Donnelly glanced around before pushing a pile of laundry over on a chair and sitting. "You have some amazing clothes. You should hang them up."

Eve looked stung but then plopped on the bed and said, "You think my clothes are amazing?"

Chloe Donnelly nodded and held up a jersey dress. "Yeah. I mean, I saw this dress at Tillys and totally loved it, but they didn't have my size."

Eve lit up. "Did you try online? Grinnell sucks for clothes, obviously, but you can get such good deals online. I have an app that lets me know when certain things are on sale."

Eve didn't used to be so into clothes, not until Holly showed up and they started sharing a wardrobe. It was horribly clichéd, but I was barely holding on to my friendship with Eve so I never said anything about it. Though I couldn't stop myself from blurting out, *That's how people get lice,* when they went through their share-winter-hats phase.

Chloe Donnelly said, "Yeah. I should do that. Walmart isn't exactly bursting with fashion options. Though we did get that scarf for Other Chloe."

Eve narrowed her eyes and looked at me. Skepticism was written all over her face, and she said, "You bought that?" almost like an accusation. She'd been pissed when I didn't go back-to-school clothes shopping with her at the end of last summer, but I hated shopping and was too embarrassed to tell her I promised my parents to only buy secondhand because it was better for the environment. Holly shopped with her now.

Chloe Donnelly twisted her purple-stoned ring and said, "We didn't buy it. We relieved Walmart of some of its stock, gratis."

Eve blinked a few times and I swallowed a snort, which I knew was mean, but sometimes my frustration at her bled out and I wanted her to feel like I did every time I wasn't included in something. "Huh?" she said.

"Shoplifting," Chloe Donnelly explained.

Eve's mouth dropped open. "Really?" She swiveled to face me. "You stole something? What was that like?" Her eyes blinked fast with curiosity, and I felt a hundred feet tall. I wanted to lean in and tell her every detail of my afternoon, but I couldn't in front of Chloe Donnelly, not without looking like I had some sort of girl crush.

So I said, "Well, technically, I didn't steal anything."

Chloe Donnelly shook her head. "She covered for me. She's totally badass and subversive. Completely cool about it so the cashier didn't give us suspicious looks or anything."

"It wasn't really hard," I admitted.

Eve scrunched up her face for a second, then said, "Oh. Well, the scarf looks good on you." Though it sounded a little grudging and maybe jealous. She must have heard the tone in her voice too, because she knocked her knee into mine and said, "Really. I'm not lying. I've always said you should show off your face more."

Chloe Donnelly leaned forward and fussed with the scarf—touching me again!—and said, "It's the perfect color, right? That shade of blue totally pops her eyes."

It'd been so long since I'd been the subject of such intense speculation that my cheeks burned like they were on fire.

Eve said, "Yeah, it's a good color." I hoped I didn't look like I'd been chosen for homecoming court, even if that was totally how I felt.

Chloe Donnelly picked up one of Eve's bottles of nail polish and shook it. "Manis?"

For a second I felt like I was in a time warp. We were going to do our nails together. Something Eve used to ask me to do for her. Then she'd flat-iron my hair since my nails weren't ever long enough to be painted. But it had been almost a year since we'd done that. The grin she gave me made me feel like she remembered how we used to do this too. And for a little while I thought we were going to be okay. Maybe Chloe Donnelly was exactly the thing that would make Eve start really liking me again.

Eve hopped up from her bed and sat at Chloe Donnelly's feet, presenting her nails, her dumb BEST FRIENDS charm bracelet slipping down her forearm. "Yes. Fire-engine red, please."

Chloe Donnelly looked at me, then at my nails. A small frown appeared between her eyebrows and I tucked my fingers into fists. "We'll do facials after," she offered, and I knew she was trying to include me. For the first time in too long, someone wanted to include me. Eve looked between the two of us and smiled.

"Yeah, facials as soon as we're done," she said, and I smiled back.

Chloe Donnelly twisted the cap off the bright-red nail polish and asked, "So what's the deal with the girl who miscarried?"

"She used to be my best friend in junior high," I blurted. God, why did I have to try so hard? Stupid, stupid, stupid.

"Really?" Chloe Donnelly asked.

"Yeah."

Eve's brows furrowed. "Yeah, I forgot about that. You guys hung out a lot."

And then we didn't, and I had Eve. Until Holly. Though maybe I still had Eve a little. "Yeah. But I didn't know she was pregnant."

Eve shuddered. "Me neither. Who do you think the dad is? Some older guy from the college?"

I wanted to tell them we shouldn't gossip. I could hear

Mateo's judgment as if he were standing next to me, and I didn't think it was fair to Melissa, even if I hadn't really hung out with her in years. But I was too chicken and didn't want to ruin things with Eve when we were just getting on solid ground again, so instead, I said, "I don't know. My mom miscarried when I was in eighth grade. Do you remember when I told you about it?"

Chloe Donnelly looked at me like she was hurt I'd left this fact about my mom out when we'd talked earlier. Not that she could know how tied Mom's miscarriage was to their decision to join the Spirit Corps. And not that I wanted to talk about that part. I couldn't really say why I brought the miscarriage up now, except that it felt safer to mention it with Eve there, and it kept me from feeling horrible about gossiping over Melissa.

"Yeah, I remember," Eve said with a nod. "You said it was pretty late in the pregnancy, right?"

I shrugged. "Yeah. Twenty-three weeks. It kind of wrecked her. She made my dad get a vasectomy after that."

Chloe Donnelly twisted the cap on the nail polish and leaned forward to touch my shoulder. I wondered if she knew how her touching was almost too much. "I'm sorry. That sucks."

"It did," I said, my voice cracking a little, but I didn't offer any more.

She took a breath like she was going to say something, but then untwisted the nail polish and started on Eve's nails again.

"I didn't know you still thought about all of that," Eve said to me in a low voice. "You could've talked to me about it."

"I know."

"I thought we didn't have secrets," Eve said, and I couldn't mistake the hurt.

A million responses flooded my brain, but I bit my tongue on them. Eve and I didn't used to have secrets, but now it seemed like she and Holly had tons of them, always whispering in the halls and doing that thing where they stop talking when I walk up to them. Their special charm bracelets they'd gotten over spring break making me feel like I was never invited to the party when it came to them.

"Sorry," I mumbled.

"Eve," Chloe Donnelly said, "where do you keep your facial stuff? I'm going to teach Other Chloe a guaranteed acne-prevention trick."

I tried to smile at her, I tried to be appreciative of what she was doing for me, but I couldn't help feeling crappy about needing acne prevention, in the same way I felt crappy about not being able to do manicures.

"Actually, I'm going to take off. I have to be home for dinner," I said. I got up and pretended not to see the concerned look on Chloe Donnelly's face and the slightly stung expression on Eve's.

"You sure?" Chloe Donnelly asked.

"Yep. You guys have fun."

Eve's face changed again, and she waved her painted fingers dismissively like I was an acquaintance who'd stopped by, unnecessary and unimportant. I wished I hadn't said anything about my mom. Eve had no right to be mad that I didn't talk to her about how much the miscarriage still seemed to cast a shadow over my life. She had only called me one time over winter break when I was with my parents in Burkina Faso, and she'd spent most of that call talking about how she and Holly had gone drunk sledding on cafeteria trays down Hamburger Hill.

I slipped out of the room, hearing Eve's whispered, "So tell me what shoplifting is like. How do you do it?" as I shut the door.

Before I got home, my phone vibrated in my pocket. I pulled into Nan and Pops's driveway and glanced at the text. It was from Chloe Donnelly.

Thanks for taking me to Walmart today. It was totally pink. Let's do facials sometime later this week, k?

I quickly typed back, Definitely.

So I apparently had a new friend.

3

At school the next day Melissa McGrill was absent. I'd dreamed of her last night, her and Chloe Donnelly. A strange dream where the two of them were sisters and both pregnant. But neither of them wanted their babies and kept doing things to put them at risk, stuff like drinking bleach and punching their stomachs. I woke up sweating and wanting to throw up, with a whisper of my mom's voice in my ear. *We don't always get what we want, Chloe. But maybe sometimes what we get is the right thing anyway.*

Chloe Donnelly slid in next to me again at the lunch table, this time without pushing me so far over that my butt was half off. She hugged me, and even though her lack of personal space made me feel all kinds of awkward, I could see Eve's envy when she let me go. Eve was wearing the jersey dress Chloe Donnelly said she wanted, and her fire-engine red fingernails were even more prominent because she had a ring on every finger of her left hand. And, of course, the charm bracelet on her wrist. I shook my head when I saw all of it and shoveled my sandwich into my mouth so I wouldn't say anything stupid. Holly showed up five minutes later, slamming her tray down and shoving Eve over on the bench. Only Holly could look pretty when she was pissed. As if anger was just another pose she'd practiced in dance.

"What's up?" Eve asked.

"Coach decided we couldn't do my routine at the dance show because she's worried it's too provocative. *There'll be parents there, Holly.* As if there haven't been parents at every football halftime show where we've done way more racy stuff than my routine. She's just being a prude because the principal got a call from a parent who said our routines make us look like strippers and that we're compromising the values of our town."

I shut down my blurting mechanism hard because I didn't think Holly would appreciate me agreeing that their last half-time routine of the season had resembled a pole/lap dance. I mean, chairs were involved—chairs!

Chloe Donnelly tsked like some sort of mother hen, then said, "That sucks. Is there any talking your coach into it? Like, do you think maybe you could change some stuff in your routine to make it less racy?"

"It's not racy, though," Holly whined.

"It's totally not. I've seen it," Eve added, always so quick to defend Holly. Freshman year, Eve and I had both gone on and on about how dance wasn't a real sport, no matter how all the girls pretended it was a hard workout. With me having done hockey and Eve on volleyball, we both had seen plenty of bruises, and dance seemed soft in comparison. But as soon as Holly started at GHS and made the team, Eve changed her mind, telling me I was *part of the problem*, whatever that meant.

"I'm sure it's not bad, but this is small-town Iowa, Holls." *Holls?* "Maybe you can do your routine for me after school and I can help come up with some suggestions?" Chloe Donnelly said.

Eve got all fidgety with excitement. "Wait. Do you dance? Because you could probably do dance team. I've been to a lot of their practices. They could use more good dancers."

For a minute Holly's face flashed hurt. Then she looked at Eve how she always looked at me—like she was playing chicken on a tractor and was ready to gun it—but before she could say some snippy thing about Eve not knowing jack about dance, Chloe Donnelly said, "Oh God, no. I don't know how to dance like Holly, I'm sure. I just had a friend at the Academy for the Arts in Chicago, and she showed me how to switch up things so you could make dances be more PG. It's only an offer to help."

Holly glanced between Eve and Chloe Donnelly, as if she were calculating, then said, "Sure. I mean, like I said, it's really not racy, but if you want to come see us practice, you totally can."

Chloe Donnelly made this approving noise in her throat, and suddenly the sandwich I was eating tasted of cardboard and mayonnaise. I wanted to stomp my foot and say Chloe Donnelly was *my* friend, but I knew I couldn't, and I felt dumb for even thinking it.

"I'd love to come see you guys. It'll be totally pink," Chloe Donnelly said, then turned to me. "We should all do pizza afterward."

"We could go to Beau's," I said. *Blurted.* Mateo worked at Beauregard's in town and the built-in excuse of seeing him while I was with my friends—friend?—was too good to resist.

Eve rolled her eyes. She was well acquainted with my frequent drive-bys of Beau's to see if Mateo was working. But Chloe Donnelly said, "Yeah, sure, whatever. We'll text you when we're headed over. Eve, will you come to watch the dance team with me?"

Eve put on a pouty frown, the same one I'd seen her use with her dad whenever he told her she needed to get homework done before she went out for the night. "I can't. I have to meet with Mr. Meyers about some missing English assignments."

"Come after." Chloe Donnelly leaned forward and squeezed her hand. Eve shifted. Maybe she thought this girl was a little overly touchy too.

But maybe not, because then Eve smiled and said, "Yeah. Sure. Of course."

I got to Spanish class early, but Chloe Donnelly was already in my seat talking to Mateo. His face was as unemotional and guarded as always, and his hair looked floppy and a little damp, like he'd actually taken a shower after gym class, unlike most of the guys in our school. She said something as I approached and then laughed, brushing her ring-covered hand against Mateo's forearm. He moved his arm back and smiled at me. Well, half smiled, maybe.

"Hey. Chloe."

"Hey, Mateo. Hey, Chloe."

"Other Chloe. I was just telling Mateo how you stole a scarf from Walmart yesterday."

Mateo's mouth dipped a bit, and I blurted, "I didn't. I mean, not really. Chloe stole it. I was just there with her. Walmart sells a lot of guns, did you know? And they're horrible to their employees."

I dropped into the seat on Chloe Donnelly's other side. There was an awkward silence between us before Mateo said, "I hadn't heard that."

"It's true."

He did the eyebrow-raise thing. "Probably you shouldn't trust everything you hear or read. That sounds like a fake internet story."

My cheeks heated and I dropped my head so my hair fell in front of my face. Dang. I *knew* all those liberal college students wouldn't shop there all the time if it were as bad as Chloe Donnelly said. Crap. Crap, crap, crap. I swallowed and shifted in my seat before finally mumbling, "Yeah. I guess you're right. It was stupid."

"Don't let him make you feel bad, Other Chloe. It was an act of subversiveness. And Walmart totally sucks. Your parents would be proud." She pulled my desk closer to hers and her fingers dug into my forearm a little. Not hard so much as a reminder that we did it together. But somehow our *subversive act* seemed a little stupid today, babyish.

Señor Williams entered and called Chloe Donnelly to the front to speak with him for a minute. He was frowning and held out his attendance book. I turned to Mateo. "I usually only shop at thrift stores. Actually, I don't really shop. I'll pay for the scarf. It was not cool."

Mateo shrugged. "Not really my business."

"Still." I wanted to lean all the way over and touch his forearm too. So much. But I wasn't Chloe Donnelly. "I know better. Punishing Walmart really just punishes the employees."

Mateo smiled a little, the lip ring moving in this distracting way, and my stomach flip-flopped. "Yeah. At least you get that."

Chloe Donnelly was laughing at the front and Señor Williams had on a face like he'd just won Teacher of the Year. I strained to hear what they were talking about, but all I caught was him saying, "It's fine. Just try to get it cleared up soon so I don't keep getting flak from the administration."

Then the bell rang and we were trapped in a forty-seven-minute discussion with Señor Williams about this weird magical realism movie we saw called *The House of the Spirits*. A discussion we had all in Spanish. I glanced at Chloe Donnelly a few times during class, but she was twisting her rings and didn't seem to be paying much attention. I wondered how much Spanish she actually knew or if she was ignoring everything because she hadn't watched the movie. It didn't matter; Señor Williams liked her well enough. My brain hurt by the time class ended, and I couldn't pull myself together quick enough to do anything but wave good-bye to Mateo as he bolted from the room.

"So I'll text you about Beau's later, right?" Chloe Donnelly asked, gathering up her notebook and sliding it into her bag.

"Yep." I couldn't decide if I wanted her to ask me to join her at Holly's dance team practice or not, but she didn't say anything, so I waved and headed out.

I stayed at the media center after school because I didn't

want to have to lie to Nan's and Pops's faces. It was bad enough I bailed on family dinner, which they insisted I be part of, with the weak excuse of studying for an English test at Eve's. Pops was no fool, and he'd mumbled more than once that I shouldn't be modeling study habits after "that dim Jacobson girl," but luckily I got Nan on the phone and she agreed to it after extracting a promise from me to help her with housework this weekend.

The media center was filled with people and it was hard to concentrate on real work. I flipped through my precalc book and tried not to listen in on other people's conversations, most of which were about Melissa's miscarriage and if she would ever come back to school.

Then two freshman girls sat at the study table next to me and started talking about some movie they saw that had a bunch of male-stripper sex in it, which made not listening in practically impossible. One of the girls said the whole thing was so crazy hot she thought she'd come, which I was pretty certain could not happen merely from watching male-stripper sex. At least nothing like that had ever happened to me, though my experience with strippers was nonexistent. Then they started to talk about this issue of *Cosmo* one of them had read in the dentist's office that had an article about how women could have a fifteen-minute orgasm. I dropped my book and the girls dropped their voices. Fifteen minutes!

I wished Eve was with me so we could talk about how bananas it was that these girls were having this conversation in the media center. And I could ask her if she thought the fifteen-minute orgasm thing was real. Part of me wanted to find that issue of *Cosmo* and read it, but I'd been instructed by my mom never to trust magazines that catered to the male gaze when it came to female orgasms. Still, I couldn't help but wonder if either of these girls had ever had real orgasms, if they'd even know if they had. If I ever would.

I didn't want to be alone with all my questions. I probably could've showed up at Holly's practice and even avoided having her comment on me being such a shadow because I'd have the protective shield of Chloe Donnelly and possibly Eve when she got there. But I didn't want to give Holly the satisfaction of thinking I'd ever give up my plans to watch her dance. Even if I technically didn't have any plans beyond homework and eavesdropping. So probably it was good Chloe Donnelly hadn't asked me to join her.

I flipped through my precalc notes again and considered going to Beau's early, but what would I say if Mateo saw me there alone? Then I ditched precalc for my chem book, trying to memorize which compounds were made with covalent bonds and which were ionic so I'd be ready for tomorrow's quiz. The girls next to me had finally pulled their homework out and stopped talking. I stared at all the letters on the page, but before I could make any progress, my phone pinged with a text from Chloe Donnelly.

We're heading to Beau's. Meet you in fifteen.

It hadn't taken her very long to figure out that you could get everywhere in Grinnell in fifteen minutes or less. I texted back. Great. See you there. And then I worried that sounded like I was trying too hard. But texting again would be even worse. Wouldn't it? God, I was such a case.

After Spanish I'd transferred the scarf Chloe Donnelly stole for me from my locker to my bag, but I couldn't get up the nerve to wear it. There were too many ways for that to be interpreted, by her and by Mateo if he was working at Beau's tonight. And I'd never feel good about the scarf until I somehow paid for it. I wished for one second that my brain wasn't always calculating what people would think, but I'd learned long ago it was no use trying to shut that function off; it never went away.

I left school and glanced toward the baseball field like I always did, in case the guys were magically there. I knew they weren't. Mateo played on the varsity baseball team, and I had his practice and game schedule memorized. They'd had a late away game last night, so there was no practice today. Which meant a fairly decent chance Mateo was working.

Beau's was pretty empty when I got there. It was the less popular of the pizza places in town, with most of the college

45

crowd preferring Pagliai's for their superior breadsticks. Plus, it was too early for the college students and not exactly the kind of place where Nan and Pops's five-o'clock-dining geriatric pals liked to eat. I looked around the dark interior for Mateo but couldn't see him anywhere. The bartender was an older woman shining glasses and talking to one of the busboys. She laughed and it ended in a hacking cough, which reminded me to dig out my hand sanitizer and scrub up. I might have been a nail-biter, but I tried to be as germ-free as possible.

Chloe Donnelly, Eve, and Holly were in a corner booth, laughing and whispering. I braced myself to walk up and have them stop talking, but it didn't happen. Chloe Donnelly merely slid over and patted the seat next to her, then went on with her story. ". . . and then I told him if he ever wants to get laid again, he'd better show up with real condoms, not the Magnum XLs."

Eve squeaked in laughter, and even surly Holly seemed charmed by the whole thing. I laughed a little too, because what else was I going to do, but I didn't really get why Magnum XLs were funny. Mom had given me the sex talk early and often when I was little, and it damn near traumatized me into never wanting to consider sex as an option for me at all. No seven-year-old needs to hear about gonorrhea. As I aged, Mom's full disclosure sex ed agenda got even worse, with her sticking Planned Parenthood pamphlets in my backpack and making the Scarleteen website the home page for the family computer. *When I was nine.*

"How was dance practice?" I asked when their laughter died down, hoping the subject change wasn't too obvious.

Holly was still a little sweaty and flushed, but she grinned at Chloe Donnelly and said, "It was great. Chloe totally agrees my routine isn't racy at all and it's just the general prudishness of this dumb town making everyone nervous. She even talked to Coach about it and mentioned her friend in Chicago at the Academy for the Arts, and get this, Coach changed her mind and said we could do my routine at the dance show!"

Of. Course. I didn't want to be salty about it, but I couldn't help feeling like it was just another example of how Holly always got what she wanted in the end. Which was bratty of me, but I didn't care. "That's great," I choked out, but it must have been obvious I did not think it was great, because Eve frowned at me.

"Yeah," Chloe Donnelly said. "I could've shown them how to push it into PG territory even more, but it definitely didn't need it."

"Wish I could've been there," I mumbled.

I didn't know what to do with my hands, so I pulled out my sanitizer again and offered it to Chloe Donnelly, who tilted her head and looked at me for a second before taking the tiny bottle and liberally squirting some out. She twisted her rings as she spread the sanitizer and said, "Thanks." Then she handed the bottle over to Eve and Holly, who both sanitized without giving me grief about my cleanliness like they usually did. Score one for Chloe Donnelly.

Mateo's best friend, Josh, came up to our table and pulled out a pencil. "Who's this?" he asked, glancing at me first, then Chloe Donnelly, while smoothing his hand over his waiter apron, as if pulling out the pencil caused him to get all disheveled.

My favorite thing about Josh was how tidy he always was. With red hair and freckles and what my mom called "Irish good looks," he was the oldest of six children, and from what I could tell, the nicest. He was shy and sweet, and best of all, he stepped in a lot when someone was being bullied. It made complete sense that he and Mateo were best friends.

"This is Chloe Donnelly. She's new. Chloe, this is Josh."

She smiled and did her quick-gaze full-body assessment, and because it was Josh, who was pale and always self-conscious and maybe not used to being checked out much by girls, his cheeks burned red in about two seconds.

"Josh is Mateo's friend. He goes to our school too."

"Cool. Nice to meet you," Chloe Donnelly said, holding out her hand for him to shake, which to me was a little weird, but maybe Chicago people did that. "Can we get some Cokes?"

"Actually, I'll just have water," I said.

"You already have water. Cokes for everyone, Josh," Chloe Donnelly said. Which I guess settled it. Eve didn't drink Coke either; she'd told me it made her break out, but she didn't say one word as she looked between Chloe Donnelly and Josh.

When he left, Eve asked her, "How do you do that?"

"What?"

She fussed with the little BEST charm on her bracelet, then said in this shy way, "How do you figure a guy out and get him all flustered in five seconds like that? Is it a Chicago thing?"

I shut my eyes for a second, trying not to snap at Eve that assessing guys wasn't regionally specific. I didn't want to be mean, but I was rattled by that dumb bracelet. I inhaled a long breath through my nose. Eve at her best was a sweet friend who would do anything for you, but sometimes, particularly when I was feeling left out and hurt, I thought her curiosity bordered on idiotic.

Chloe Donnelly nudged my knee under the table, but she folded her hands and said, "No, Eve, it's just something I figured out, I guess. You probably could do it too."

I snorted but covered it with a cough and quickly gulped down some water as Chloe Donnelly nudged me again under the table. I loved being a conspirator with someone, even if I felt a little bad that it was directed at Eve.

Holly gulped down the water the busboy had put on the table in front of her and said, "I still can't believe we'll get to do my routine at the show. Thank you so much, Chloe."

Chloe Donnelly shrugged. "It's not a big deal. Your dance is amazing. I bet Other Chloe would've agreed it wasn't that provocative either."

"Just Chloe is fine." I shoved my hair behind my ear and sat up as tall as I could.

"Hmm?"

"You don't have to call me Other Chloe. Chloe is fine."

"No," Holly said, shaking her head and offering a small smirk only I could see. "That's too confusing. Other Chloe works better."

I shut my eyes and imagined hockey-slamming into Holly on the ice while she wasn't wearing any pads. I took another deep breath and opened my eyes. "Whatever."

"You should've worn your scarf today," Eve said, then I noticed her looking at the acne constellation on my forehead. Not completely obvious, but enough that I suspected she was feeling grateful not to have the same problem. I let my hair fall forward so my forehead was less noticeable, even more glad I'd decided not to wear the scarf.

Chloe Donnelly rolled her eyes. "She's feeling guilty about it. Mateo got all judgy on her."

"No, he didn't," I said, immediately regretting it. I did not need to call attention to my crush on Mateo any more than I already had.

"It's no big deal," Chloe Donnelly said, her ringed hand flickering. "I don't care if you want to pay for the scarf now because of Mateo. You wouldn't believe the stuff I did for my last boyfriend. Do you know that he got me to go to church? Shudder."

No one said anything for what was a painfully long thirty seconds. We all went to church. Most people in Grinnell did. But apparently no one had explained this yet to Chloe Donnelly.

"So what do you all do around here for fun?" she asked, pushing past the silence as if she didn't notice it at all.

I sipped my water. "Hang out. Go to the Dari Barn. See movies. Sometimes the college has things we can go to, but a lot of times they're weird and kind of boring."

Chloe Donnelly stared at us and her eyes narrowed slightly. She flicked her black-polished thumbnail, then twisted each of the rings on her fingers. It looked strange and a little contrived, as if any second she'd start stroking her chin thoughtfully. Or maybe I was struck by the slightly-too-sophisticated package of her, so out of place sitting there with us in Grinnell.

"Do you know any guys?" she asked us when Josh returned with our Cokes. He blushed again.

Eve sipped her Coke and made a face. "Of course."

Holly leaned forward, boobs shelving on the table so we couldn't help but notice them in her tight dance leotard. "I have a boyfriend. He's a twin."

I held back a snort at how she said *twin* as if that leveled him up to some über-boyfriend status.

Eve said, "She knows. I told her about Cam last night when we were doing manis."

Holly looked huffy, pissed at Eve for stealing her thunder, or maybe pissed she hadn't been there for manis. It was the second time I'd noticed tension between them in the past day, and the small and petty part of me wanted to do a victory lap.

"You told her about Cam?"

Eve looked at Chloe Donnelly, then at Holly, then at the table. "Yeah."

Chloe Donnelly placed her hands flat on the table. "Yeah, I heard all about Cam. It's weird you didn't say anything, Holls. Is it supposed to be a secret?"

I also couldn't believe Holly had waited *this* long to mention Cam, but maybe she wanted him to be there so she could prove it. Or maybe she was feeling a little cagey and territorial about him. Holly's motivations for practically everything sort of baffled me.

"No, it's not a secret," Holly said. Her nostrils flared, but then her face smoothed out to normal again. Apparently, having a boyfriend was enough not to be too crabby about Eve filling Chloe Donnelly in about it first.

"Anyway, twins are great. And Other Chloe knows Mateo. And Josh goes to our school, so that's four. Perfect."

"What are you talking about?" Josh asked, not even hiding that he'd been sponging off a nearby table way too long so he could snoop on our conversation. Before anyone could respond, the front entrance door swung open and Mateo walked in.

My breath clogged in my lungs for a second when I saw the small nod he gave me as he crossed to our table. At least I was pretty sure the nod was for me. Maybe. I hoped.

I nodded back and squeezed my legs together. Guys probably shouldn't look as pretty as he did, with full lips and round cheeks and soft dark-brown eyes, but he really was beautiful. My dad, a science-obsessed father to his core, would point out all the facial traits in Mateo that were symmetrical or divided in thirds perfectly to make me feel this way, but I didn't really care. I wanted to figure out a way for Mateo to like me, not figure out why I liked him so much.

"What's up, guys?" he said, dropping the pizza-warming delivery bag at his feet, not even glancing at Holly's boob shelf.

"Mateo. Perfect timing. I was just about to explain Gestapo to everyone," Chloe said.

"Gestapo? The Nazi secret police?" I asked, feeling my forehead scrunch and then trying to relax it so the zit constellation wasn't as obvious. "Is that starting up here now?" I tried to joke, but it fell flat. What was wrong with me? Always with the awkwardness. No wonder Eve was constantly ditching me.

"No, Other Chloe. Not the real Gestapo. Gestapo the game."

4

"What's Gestapo?" Eve said, almost bouncing in her seat. Her Tigers T-shirt was too small, though not so much in the chest as in the arms, as if she'd gotten a children's small instead of an adult small. It suited her little-kid enthusiasm but made the difference between her and Holly's bra-cup sizes very obvious. The two of them sharing a wardrobe was not always the best idea, though Holly didn't seem to mind too-small-in-the-chest shirts.

"It's this game we played in Chicago," Chloe Donnelly said. "You need at least four guys and four girls. Two teams. Girls against guys. Each team has a captain who picks a four-letter word—"

"Wait, wait," Josh said, sliding into the booth next to Holly as Mateo pulled up a chair at the end of the table. I glanced at the bartender to see if this little employee break was a problem, but she was wiping the bar and ignoring us. "This is a word game? Called Gestapo? Do you play it in school?"

Chloe Donnelly sighed like Josh's questions were a big hassle and said, "No, of course not. You play it outside. At night. I was trying to explain."

Josh tugged his ear self-consciously and said, "Sorry."

"Anyway, how it works is the captain of each team picks a four-letter word that only he or she knows. And then whispers a different letter from the word to each teammate. Then everyone goes and hides. Or goes on the offensive. The object of the game is to get the letters of the other team and figure out their word without giving up your own letter. It's sort of like capture the flag, only the flag is whispered letters. And we each have to protect our own."

"Girls against guys?" Josh asked, his face looking a little pale with those freckles popping like they'd been made with an orangish-brown Sharpie.

Chloe Donnelly nodded. "Yeah, usually."

"And it's called Gestapo?" I said, still hung up on that one thing. Was this a joke?

"Yes, Other Chloe, I believe that's already been established," Chloe Donnelly said.

"How do you get the other team's letters, though?" I asked.

Chloe Donnelly grinned and looked around the table again. "By any means necessary."

By any means necessary. I let this sink in for a second, puzzling out what that might mean, then I glanced at Holly's boob shelf. Dread balled up in my stomach, making the too-sugary taste of the Coke I'd just sipped feel like I'd ingested battery acid. A game named after a group famous for torture? Girls against guys, where you win by any means necessary? Crud. I could see exactly how this might play out. As I looked around and saw Eve and Holly's intrigued faces, it seemed they had figured it out too. And it didn't seem to be a problem for them.

"By any means necessary? Is this game for real?" I asked. There was no way anyone could have missed the weirdness in my voice.

Chloe Donnelly nodded. "Yeah, of course. It's super fun. I mean, think of all the possibilities." My stomach twisted and the battery-acid Coke taste hit the back of my throat. I swallowed it down hard. Holy crap. Holy, holy crap.

"So four girls and four guys each get a whispered letter to a four-letter word the captain picks, right? And you hide or you look for people, trying to get their letters while protecting your own, so you and your team can figure out the other team's word? And you do that by any means necessary? Like, however you want?" Eve asked, breathy with excitement and curiosity, like she wanted to make sure she got it exactly right. Like we were actually going to play this game.

"What's to stop the captain from lying about their word or a

56

team member from lying about their letter?" Holly asked, her head tipped to the side so her dark hair fell forward slightly, not like a curtain but like an ad for conditioner.

Chloe Donnelly shrugged. "Well, two things. First, the captain writes the word down on a slip of paper and keeps it with them until the end of the game when the other team guesses. And second, there's an honor code we all agree to. If you're good enough to get someone else's letter and not give up your own, we all assume it's the actual letter. Liars automatically lose."

Lose what?

I shoved a fingernail in my mouth, waiting for Chloe Donnelly to look disgusted or disappointed in me for being obviously anxious about this, but instead, she offered a small smile that felt too much like pity. I dropped my finger.

"And what's to keep someone from hurting you to get your letter?" I asked, balling my hands and sliding them under my thighs.

Chloe Donnelly pointed to Mateo and Josh. "Don't you trust your friends, Other Chloe? Do you really think these two would hurt you to win a game?"

I didn't even need to look at them. I was sure they wouldn't. But they weren't the ones I was worried about. Holly's boyfriend, Cam—the *twin*—was a walking bad-boy cliché in every sense of the word. He was always in trouble at school for one reason or another. The only time I saw him regularly was either as I was passing the after-school detention classroom or in the parking lot after lunch with his tongue down Holly's throat.

When he and his brother, Aiden, were little, they were both really clever and smart. In early elementary Cam would build this incredibly cool stuff all the time. But somehow he gave up on school as if it were impossible to have two smart twins. He acted out in class and never could sit still. In fifth grade Cam decided to run for student council president against his brother and lost, badly. That was sort of the beginning of the end for him, and he became dedicated to being bad. Every year he got in more fights, spent more and more time in the principal's office. I'd heard rumors he was a dealer now, but that might have just been part of the mystique. Regardless, he was hardly the most trustworthy guy.

I looked directly at Mateo and said, "I trust my friends. But still . . . a game where you win by any means necessary seems a little sketchy."

Eve clapped her hands and said, "No. It sounds like fun."

Chloe Donnelly studied me. "You can always hide. It's not as fun that way and you won't have the chance to get any of the guys' letters, but at least you'll keep your own letter a secret."

I nodded, but the knot in my stomach wasn't going away. A game called Gestapo. Did my friends not listen in world history, about how neo-Nazis were actually a thing? The entire prospect was a giant red flag wrapped around warning bells.

Holly had her phone out and was madly texting, I assumed to tell Cam about the game. Mateo's face was thoughtful and guarded, but not exactly skeptical, more resolved or . . . resigned? His dark eyes landed on me for a second, held, and then moved away. I glanced at Josh, whose expression seemed to be full of a million questions. Thank God. He was my only hope of getting out of this, and I silently prayed he'd make everyone realize how badly this might go.

"So we try to get letters and not give up our own, by any means necessary, but how does that really work? You said we were outside. I mean, are we all hiding in the cornfields and waiting for someone to find us?"

Chloe Donnelly shook her head and then looked at Holly. "Are Cam and Aiden around?" It was strange how she talked about them as if she already knew them. Eve must have dished out a lot during the manicure last night.

Holly answered, "Cam's home. I don't know about Aiden."

Josh said, "He's home. I'm supposed to do American history review with him after I get off my shift."

"And when are you off?"

"We're both off at seven tonight," Josh said, nodding to Mateo.

Chloe Donnelly grinned. "Perfect. Let's do pizza and then we'll head over to Cam's."

"What for?" I asked, even though I was 100 percent sure I knew the answer.

"It's too hard to explain the game. It's easier if you just play. We'll do a practice round."

I glanced at Eve, seeing my own uncertainty reflected back. *Finally.* We weren't the type of people who went for things out of our comfort zones. It was what we most had in common. Eve asked questions, but she never acted on her curiosity, and I mostly watched and didn't do anything. But before I could take her aside and point out all the problems with the game, Holly leaned forward, drawing attention again to her boob shelf, and said, "Yes. Totally. Practice game. This is going to be amazing."

Eve's face changed, and suddenly she was full of courage I'd never seen in her when we were best friends. And it confirmed for me that Holly being up for anything was what made Eve like her, and probably why Eve had slowly stopped liking me over the past year. I hated myself for not being able to be brave. And not saying no to this practice game was just one more example of that.

It's one night, it's one night, you can get through one night of anything, I repeated in my head like a mantra as I walked to Cam and Aiden's. Holly had changed at Beau's from her dance clothes into a T-shirt and short jean skirt that kept riding up as she walked in front of me. She and Eve were listening to another one of Chloe Donnelly's "Chicago" stories, and I trailed behind them, breathing through my nose with deep inhales and exhales and trying not to completely freak out. Josh and Mateo were a few minutes behind us because Josh wanted to stop at home to change.

I put my thumbnail into my mouth and started biting at the cuticle.

"Other Chloe, stop biting your nails. This will be completely pink, I promise," Chloe Donnelly said, turning around as if she'd been aware of me the whole time. "And it's not even going to be a real game. I just want to show you all what it's like."

I dropped my hand from my mouth and got out my hand sanitizer. I scrubbed my hands thoroughly, focusing on that so I wouldn't keep thinking of all the ways Gestapo could go badly.

Cam and Aiden's house was near the end of Pearl Street, a smaller ranch-style in need of new siding. It took us less than fifteen minutes to get there from Beau's. Both the guys were outside working on Cam's car when we got there—an old Volkswagen Golf with a hundred thousand miles on it that their parents had found on Craigslist. It was a dumb, gearhead thing to be doing, and I'd almost think it was them showing off, except I knew Cam lived and died by that car, and was always fixing one thing or another on it. Even though he sort of gave up on school, he was still good with his hands and building stuff. Though Holly complained he was obsessive and so focused all the time on it that he'd lose track of other stuff. One time for a joke sophomore year, someone had sent him crappy school-sponsored carnations on Valentine's Day with a note that said, "Love, Your Car." He'd laughed with everyone else, but I didn't think he thought it was funny. For the past year and a half, when he wasn't working on the car, I'd see him driving around town constantly in it, and part of me wondered if one day he'd take off altogether.

Now he slammed the hood shut and crossed his arms, his black shirt tight across his chest and biceps. He shook his head to push his hair from his eyes even though it wasn't much longer than Aiden's. Probably a lot of girls would think the move made him super hot, but it seemed like such a cliché to me.

Aiden stood next to his brother and scanned us quickly when we walked up. Scanned and dismissed us. He was nothing if not efficient. He had on a long-sleeved T-shirt, his dark hair and way-too-good looks and super-serious face making him seem as if he didn't belong in Grinnell. The best way I could tell Aiden apart from his identical twin brother was how he held himself—rigid and straight, at military ease. His hair was slightly shorter than Cam's, but not enough for it to make a huge difference. However, his shoulders thrown back and lifted chin were nothing like Cam's perpetual give-zero-fucks slouch. Aiden had been talking about being a pilot in the navy since we were little kids. I kept thinking he'd eventually grow out of it, the way we'd all gotten over wanting to be a ballerina or firefighter or the president, but Aiden was determined still. Nearly everything he did was a step toward getting into the Naval Academy.

Which was why I was so surprised when he was the one who said to Chloe Donnelly, "Explain to me again how this game works."

I looked between Chloe Donnelly and Aiden, and noticed she didn't do her quick-gaze guy assessment, like maybe they'd already met. Confusion settled in. It didn't make sense that they knew each other. She'd only been in school two days. Chloe Donnelly couldn't have told him about the game already. Could she? A weird shiver ran up my spine and I shook my head to clear it.

"Gestapo, Aiden. It's called Gestapo. You can say it out loud. No one is going to put it on your permanent record or add you to a list anywhere," Chloe Donnelly said.

So they *did* know each other. Why hadn't she said something when Holly mentioned dating a twin? Chloe Donnelly must have had a class with Aiden because she seemed to have already figured out his deal. And she was comfortable enough to tease him about it, which I would never do with soldier-serious Aiden.

He stepped forward. "You do need four guys, right?"

Eve slipped next to him and put her hand on his arm—so obvious—then said, "It's so cool you're playing. This is going to be really pink."

Then she blushed because *pink* sounded dumb coming out of her mouth, and Aiden had shaken her hand off and was looking at her like she was a few cards short of a full deck, as Nan liked to say.

I glanced at Cam, who had a hand hooked around Holly's hip with two fingers slipped into the waistband of her skirt, his oil-stained thumb smearing over her. I almost blurted, *Leave room for Jesus*, but didn't think anyone would appreciate my joke. Probably Holly liked Cam's possessiveness and how he groped her in public all the time. But to me, it looked more sleazy and as if he was trying to prove something—about himself or her, I wasn't sure which.

Chloe Donnelly pursed her lips and then said, "It's not that hard, Aiden. I'm captain and I pick a four-letter word and write it on a slip of paper. Then I whisper a letter from the word to each of the girls. You guys pick a captain who won't likely give anything up and do the same thing. Then we go find you and get your letters and figure out your word. Or you try to find us and get our letters. First team to figure out the other side's word wins."

I'd heard the same spiel three times and it still gave me the creeps.

"What are the boundaries? How far can we go?" Cam asked.

"Let's just play on both sides of this block tonight. No going inside, no going out of bounds. It's a practice game, so we'll play for half an hour. You all should be able to figure out how it works in that amount of time."

Before anyone could ask any more questions, Josh and Mateo walked up. Josh was in jeans and a tucked-in T-shirt, and Mateo had taken his work shirt off for the plain white tee underneath. Mateo nodded at us all and Josh fist-bumped Cam and Aiden, though it looked sort of unnatural for him. Chloe Donnelly repeated the parameters and rules of the game, pulling out a slip of paper and two pens. Then she said, "Okay, guys, pick a captain and have him choose a word and give you your letters. I'm huddling with the girls."

I shoved a finger back in my mouth, ignoring the hand-sanitizer taste, and tried to figure out what in the hell I was doing there. Chloe Donnelly ripped the paper in half and handed a piece to Cam along with a pen. Then she pulled me closer to her, Eve, and Holly, and patted my arm like I was a skittish animal. I spit my nail out and straightened up. I was being ridiculous. It was a dumb game, not that different from ghost in the graveyard, and I was treating it like a prison sentence. These were my friends. Breathing slowly through my nose again, I told myself I could do this.

Chloe Donnelly cupped her hand around her slip of paper and penned something we couldn't see before tucking it in her pocket. Then she said, "Okay, I have the word. I'm whispering your letters and then you all take off and hide somewhere on the block. Don't go after the guys unless you're sure you can get their letters." She looked pointedly at me, but it wasn't necessary. Going on the offensive was not in my game plan.

She leaned in to each of us and whispered letters in our ear so only we could hear. I nodded when she gave me an *E*, and she added in a low voice, "Don't worry, Other Chloe. There're a few bushes a half a block up. Hide there. The guys won't be able to see you."

Then she squeezed my bare, charm-bracelet-free wrist and called out to the guys, "Okay, we're going to hide. Give us a three-minute start and then come looking for us. Or you can try to hide. Meet back here in thirty minutes."

I made sure my bag was tucked away beside Cam's car and readied myself for the game. I took one last look at Mateo, but he was huddled with the guys. I couldn't help but notice how cute his butt looked when he leaned over, so maybe male-stripper-sex movies weren't enough to press any buttons inside me but . . . Chloe Donnelly coughed and I glanced at her, my cheeks on fire.

"I'm so obvious," I whispered.

She squeezed my shoulder—again with the touchiness.

"Obvious and adorable. It'll totally work in your favor. Particularly with this game. Trust me."

I nodded, then booked it down the block and hid in the bushes she'd mentioned. I was certain any minute the people who owned the house were going to come out or call the cops because someone was lingering near their window, but when I glanced in, I saw an older couple watching *Law & Order* on the TV so I felt a little safer on that score.

I squatted behind the farthest bush from the house and pulled out my phone to check the time. We'd be done by seven forty-five. This wasn't a big deal. I was freezing but I could wait the game out. Thirty minutes was nothing.

I scanned the parts of Pearl Street in my view, but I didn't see anyone hiding. I heard a guy's laughter at the end of the block and then a high-pitched squeal. Definitely Eve. Caught already. I took a deep breath and counted seconds in my head. The scrape of shoes drew my attention to the right. Josh. I held perfectly still, but it didn't matter.

"Chloe," he said. "I knew you'd be in the bushes somewhere."

Panic mode. I could either bolt and try to lose Josh—not likely—or I could pretend I didn't hear him and hope he went away. Neither seemed like a workable option. I curled my fingers into my palms and took a deep breath. I couldn't imagine the old couple watching *Law & Order* wouldn't notice *two* people in their bushes. Which left me reluctantly stepping out of the bushes and onto the sidewalk.

Josh laughed when he saw my face. "You look like someone stabbed your kitten. Come on, this is supposed to be fun."

"Josh. No one else is here. You don't have to pretend. I saw your face when we were at Beau's. The game's sketchy and you know it."

Josh shrugged. "Well, at first it sounded that way. But you guys are my friends. No one is going to force anyone to do anything. We're not on a spy mission going across enemy lines. We're playing a *word game.*"

"A word game called Gestapo."

He shook his head. "With high school kids in the middle of Iowa. Come on."

I studied him for a second, taking in the ease with which he was standing, like this was nothing, like he'd spent the time between Beau's and Pearl Street convincing himself this was nothing. He had a sort of puppy-dog look on his face, hopeful and optimistic. A face I'd known for most of my life. Finally, I laughed. "It is kind of dumb, right?"

"Totally."

We stood there for another thirty seconds, both of us not saying anything. "So . . . um, what's your letter?" I tried.

Josh laughed again. "It doesn't work that way, I don't think. You need to talk me into giving it to you."

And that was the problem. I had no idea of a way to talk Josh out of his letter that wasn't either sleazy or would leave me owing him some huge favor. And I was pretty sure he'd never go for anything sleazy with me.

"Or I could talk *you* out of your letter," he said, but then looked down. It was dark but I knew for sure he was blushing. Which made me laugh. We were both completely out of our league trying to play this game in any real way.

"How about we rock-paper-scissors for it?" I said.

"What?"

"Well, I don't see either of us getting the other person's letter any other way. Rock-paper-scissors seems legit."

Josh grinned wide and held up his hands. "Deal. Best out of three."

Thirty minutes later I was back in Cam and Aiden's driveway, smiling a little to myself. I'd won two of three rock-paper-scissors games, and Josh had reluctantly given me his letter, mumbling that Cam was going to kick his ass but grinning like we had a secret. Which we sort of did.

Chloe Donnelly called the girls over. "How'd you do?"

"I got Cam's letter. It's *B*," Holly said, wiping her mouth in an obvious way, which I hoped to heck was fake because . . . gross.

Eve grinned, all smug and self-satisfied. "I got Aiden's too. *A*."

I looked at her and for a second wondered if she'd picked up more than I thought from Holly's influence, but then she blushed and whispered, "I offered to bring him a plate of Mom's chocolate Rice Krispies Treats."

I laughed and so did Eve. We high-fived, and for a second we were back in our freshman year, trying to learn the "Thriller" dance in gym class and bumping into each other every single time. Chloe Donnelly crossed her arms. "Well, I guess that was inventive. It's fine for a practice game."

"You said, *By any means necessary*. Eve's way was genius. You should've tried those Rice Krispies Treats yesterday afternoon. We probably could've even got the word from the guys if we offered them a month's supply," I said.

Chloe Donnelly's fingers drummed, but she was shaking her head and laughing a little. "Well, Other Chloe, when we play for real, I'm not sure Rice Krispies Treats are going to cut it, but whatever." Then her face got all serious and she looked right at me and said, "I got Mateo's letter. *N*."

I froze, waiting to hear how she'd done it, what tactic she'd used to get quiet Mateo to give up his letter, but she didn't offer an explanation. Instead, her face went all bright and friendly again, and she asked, "You didn't happen to get Josh's, did you?"

She was looking at me, but I couldn't choke out an answer. My mind was too busy clicking through all the ways

Chloe Donnelly might've gotten Mateo's letter—simple things like offering to do his Spanish homework, and much grosser things like hand jobs—but my brain couldn't settle on one that seemed feasible. I couldn't picture him giving up his letter easily. God knew he didn't give up anything else about himself.

"Other Chloe? Hello?"

I blinked. "Oh. Sorry. Yeah. I got Josh's letter. It's *K*."

Eve clapped and high-fived me again. "Oh my God, this is so great. We all got letters. I *love* this game."

I wasn't sure I totally shared her enthusiasm, but Josh's words knocked around in my head. *We're not on a spy mission going across enemy lines. We're playing a word game.* Yes. I was with my friends. Playing a word game. And after flipping through the catalog of options for how Chloe Donnelly might've gotten Mateo's letter, I decided that he probably gave it to her because it was friends playing a game, and who really cared anyway. This was the first time I'd been fully included in something in so long, the first time I felt like a real part of anything. My whole body hummed and buzzed with excitement. And maybe it was dumb how I'd won Josh's letter from him, but Chloe Donnelly didn't need to know how I did it.

"Yeah," I agreed with Eve. "The game is fun."

Chloe Donnelly stared at me for a long minute, then finally said, "So you like the game after all? That's unexpectedly pink.

I wasn't sure you had it in you to get someone's letter. Way to surprise me, Other Chloe." She turned to Eve and Holly. "*B. A. N. K.* God, the guys are so dumb. They didn't even pick an anagram."

"What's an anagram?" Eve asked, and I winced a little. She really needed to brush up on her vocab if she was going to do well on her ACTs, which was maybe a little judgy of me to think, but she had parents who would get her extra tutoring and she wasn't taking advantage of it. How did she not see that?

Chloe Donnelly patted Eve's arm. "Don't worry about it, sweetie. Leave the big words to the grown-ups."

I blinked. Ouch. It was one thing to think she was squandering a chance to do well on her ACTs, but this? Chloe Donnelly's words were cruel and harsh, and Eve looked stung. I felt stung on her behalf. I took a small step back, glancing at Chloe Donnelly. Her face didn't seem plain anymore, it seemed meaner and older. Way older than us, and for a second I wondered if she was different from what I thought she was, if she wasn't a girl who understood me at all, but someone who only pretended so she could get what she wanted. But then she pulled Eve into a hug and said, "Oh my God, I'm kidding. Do you really think I'm that bitchy? We're on the same team. I told you where Aiden was. I was totally messing with you. Anagrams are when you can mix letters up so they form different words, like *team* can also be *tame* or *meat*. Captains don't have to pick an anagram for their word, but it makes it harder for the other team."

Eve looked mollified and hugged Chloe Donnelly back, but I couldn't completely shake the strange kick in my gut. Something felt off. But I ignored it when Eve grabbed my arm and squeezed. "We won. We won. We won," she singsonged. "I can't believe you got Josh's letter. We won!"

The guys walked over to us. Josh and Cam were smiling, but Aiden and Mateo both seemed serious. Of course Aiden would hate to lose; he was so competitive about everything. But Mateo's expression troubled me. Maybe Chloe Donnelly had gotten his letter in some sketchy, underhanded way. I should've asked her, but it made me feel inexperienced and childish, and I didn't want Chloe Donnelly to think of me that way.

Mateo's gaze landed on me, and after a second his face changed into a warm smile. A real one, like maybe his serious expression was because he was worried about me. Though probably that was just a lot of wishful thinking. I wanted so much from him.

"*Bank*, guys. Really? So easy," Chloe Donnelly said.

Cam shrugged. "You said it was a practice game. I don't know about anyone else, but I don't give a shit that we didn't get any letters. I feel like I won here." He pulled the zipper of his fly—double gross—and I wanted to bleach my brain.

I couldn't figure out how someone like him could be related to someone like Aiden. And the worst part was that Holly seemed to like the attention, to like that she was Cam's sex toy or whatever. She walked right over to him and wrapped her arms around his neck and kissed him, with tongue, like we all weren't standing right there!

Holly had started dating Cam her third week at GHS. It was as if she was looking for a way to scuff the shiny Catholic school vibe she'd carried with her, and Cam was perfect for scuffing. Holly's older sister had gone to the Catholic school and was now on a full-ride scholarship to Michigan State. Holly told us she hated every minute of her Catholic education and begged her parents for an entire year to let her go to the public school, claiming there'd be no commute and her school friends would actually live in the same town. They finally agreed after their divorce went through and they were both stuck with lawyer bills too high to afford private school.

She'd told me and Eve all of this her second week at school. At first I thought it was something we'd had in common, me not wanting to be in Burkina Faso and having to beg my parents to let me live with Nan and Pops so I could go to GHS. But when I mentioned it to Holly, she flared her nostrils and told me our parents were *nothing alike*. Then she decided Eve was the only one worth being friends with and I was a sad sack to be ignored.

If I were a better friend, I might've sat Holly down and explained that no guy was worth how Cam treated her, that being liked wasn't worth sacrificing yourself. But the whole lecture would've been a bunch of platitudes I'd been told by my mom, capped off by Nan's succinct *No one is gonna buy the cow when they can get the milk for free*, and I was certain Holly would ignore me. I wasn't her friend. And anything I had to say about Cam would likely ostracize me from both Holly and Eve even more.

So I kept my mouth shut when Cam's fingers slipped down to Holly's ass during their ridiculous kiss. Though I internally cheered at Mateo smacking Cam on the arm and muttering, "Don't be such a douche," which thankfully ended the PDA.

"So you guys get how to play now, right?" Chloe Donnelly asked.

Mumbled *yeah*s and a bunch of nodding.

"Good. Because we need to make it bigger and better for our real game."

"What does that mean?" Josh asked.

Chloe Donnelly tightened her lips and put on a weird smile. "We play longer. And we set up boundaries for the game that are wider. Maybe the college campus. And"—she paused, building the anticipation enough so we all seemed to be holding our collective breath—"each person on the winning team earns one platinum favor from someone on the losing team."

"What's that?" Eve asked, her eyes lit up still from our victory.

"A platinum favor is a favor asked that the loser cannot say no to. No matter what."

"Wait . . . what?" I said, hating how my voice sounded sort of squeaky.

"A favor where the loser has to say yes." Chloe Donnelly enunciated her words slowly.

My gaze skidded to Mateo. A million scenarios erupted in my brain. God. What would I do if I had a guaranteed yes from him for anything? It would be like a perfect song that came on at just the right time. *Yes, Chloe. Sure, Chloe. Of course. Yes.*

Josh's face went from smiling to concerned. "I don't know. That seems a little intense."

"That's the point. And since you guys were the losers tonight . . ."

"What?" Cam started. "No way. You didn't explain what the stakes were. I wouldn't have given up my letter."

Chloe Donnelly lifted a shoulder, her bright eyes almost dancing. "Whoops. My bad."

"I'm not agreeing to anything."

She crossed her arms. "It's not that hard. Cam, will you give me a ride to Walmart tomorrow? I need to return a scarf." She glanced at Mateo and then tipped her chin slightly at me. I stuck my pinkie in my mouth and gnawed on the nail.

"What?" Cam asked.

"Will you give me a ride to Walmart?" She did that slow-enunciation thing again.

"Sure. I guess."

She spread her arms wide. "See? Platinum favor completed. Easy."

I looked at Mateo. *Will you take me to prom?* I whispered in my head. *Will you hold my hand? Will you walk with me to my classes? Will you ask how I'm doing? Will you ask me to come see you play baseball? Will you call me your girlfriend?* So many yeses I wanted from him, so many I didn't think I could ever ask for, even with a platinum favor dangling between us.

"Come on," Chloe Donnelly said. "What else do you all have going on? Seriously. Ice cream at the Dari Barn? The game is fun. Didn't you guys have fun tonight?"

Aiden stepped forward. "Yeah, it was all right. But a platinum favor? Really?"

Eve laughed. "Imagine how many unlimited desserts you could get from my mom. You'd have to run twice a day to keep your six-pack abs."

Holly said, "Unlimited desserts are a terrible platinum favor, Eve. The poor baseball groupies will be devastated if he doesn't maintain his deep investment in that six-pack."

It was cheesy, but everyone laughed. Even Aiden. And like that, things were casual again. The atmosphere flipped and we were all just people who went to high school together, people who understood what it was like living in Grinnell. Chloe Donnelly and her *bigger and better* didn't really understand how we worked. But I felt it and knew it would be okay because we were definitely a *we* again, including me. And that made all my nerves disappear.

"Come on, Aiden, pretty please with Rice Krispies Treats on top," Eve pleaded.

Her Aiden crush was long-standing and well established but, from what I could tell, on a fast track to nowhere, same as all the baseball groupies. Aiden was way too focused on his studies and a future at the Naval Academy to mess around with dating. We all knew that, probably even Eve. I was surprised he'd agreed to play with us in the first place, though we did sort of just show up and not give him much of a choice.

Aiden glanced at each of the guys and it looked like he had a definite *no* about to come out of his mouth. Cam leaned forward and mumbled something that made Aiden's expression turn hard and a little angry. He scrubbed his face, all put out and annoyed, then finally said, "Sure. Fine."

"Yay. I'll be in charge of game refreshments," Eve said, though I wasn't sure if she meant alcohol or her mom's pastries.

I looked around the circle. Josh was staring at Mateo. "Do *you* want to do this?" he asked Mateo as if we weren't all standing right there.

Mateo was quiet for too long. I held my breath. I wasn't

going to play if he wasn't, that was for sure. He had the same face he'd had on before, not fear but resignation. He glanced at me and there seemed to be something there, a request maybe, or an out, but I wasn't sure which. Finally, he shrugged and looked at Chloe Donnelly. "Sure, let's play for real. It could be fun."

Then he met my gaze for another second and it felt as if he were looking inside of me. As if all the things I wanted and all the things I was afraid of were right there out in the open for him to pull apart and study. As if he'd say yes to every favor I asked. As if he wanted me to say yes to him. My cheeks warmed and I looked down, letting my hair drop in front of my face again.

"Perfect. This is going to be so pink," Chloe Donnelly said. "Are you both working on Friday?"

"I'm off," Mateo answered, at the same time Josh said, "I'm working till eight thirty."

"Okay, we'll meet in front of the college library at nine," she said.

Mateo smiled at me again, and for a second I thought it'd be okay. We'd had fun playing. I'd rock-paper-scissors'd myself into Josh's letter. Gestapo was different and I needed different, something to break up my loneliness and a way to hold on to my friends. But when I saw the strange glance Mateo threw toward Chloe Donnelly, I couldn't shake a hint of dread at what exactly *bigger and better* could mean.

5

The girls all walked up Pearl Street together. The guys were staying at Cam and Aiden's for some sort of video game marathon. Holly pouted when Cam wouldn't drive her home, but he shrugged and countered with, "Babe, I've still got to replace the clutch on the car." *Babe.* It sounded so gross when Cam said it.

"My mom is gonna freak that I'm out this late," Eve said as we turned onto Third Avenue. "And I left my book bag at school so she'll for sure know we weren't studying."

"It's not your mom, it's your dad," I said.

Eve spun around. "I know, Other Chloe. You don't need to remind me."

I flinched. Sometimes it seemed everything I said to her hit the wrong note. "Sorry," I mumbled.

Holly nudged Eve's shoulder. "Ignore her. I'll go in with you and tell your parents I was having a crisis and needed you."

"Really?" Eve's puppy-dog look made me feel like I should've done that, covered for her with her overbearing parents.

"Yeah. My mom won't care," Holly said. "She'll lie for the both of us if your mom asks."

I'd seen Holly's mom at a few of her dance performances; she looked like an older and much heavier version of Holly. I'd never seen her dad, but I didn't exactly blame him for wanting to bow out of a dance show with his ex-wife. Holly's parents' divorce didn't seem very amicable when she'd first described it.

"You're the best, Holls," Eve said, and I looked at my feet.

Chloe Donnelly stepped toward me and linked her arm with mine. I had to shift to counter the weight of my bag. "That was totally pink tonight. I can't wait to play with you again."

"What'll you ask Cam for when we win the platinum favor?" Eve asked Holly, linking their arms too, and making a big deal out of touching their charm bracelets. As if everything weren't completely clear.

Holly grinned. "I don't know. There are so many possibilities. I mean, you have no idea how many times I wish Cam would have agreed to something I asked him for." She laughed in this innuendo way, but it was ridiculous and too show-offy for me to believe. Probably he said no to lots of basic stuff, too busy working on his car or doing whatever else he did that kept him from agreeing to Holly's demands. For a second I felt bad for Holly that she didn't have the kind of boyfriend who would just do her a favor because he was a nice guy, that she *needed* a platinum favor to get what she already deserved.

Chloe Donnelly chimed in. "When we played in Chicago and my team won, I made my boyfriend do his homework in only his boxers every time we were studying together at my house."

"No. Way," Eve said, but she sounded slightly thrilled by this possibility. To me, the thought of it was a little horrifying. As much as I wanted to see Mateo's chest, and maybe even see him in only boxers, I couldn't imagine casually studying with him while he sat next to me in his underwear. The blurting that would happen in that scenario . . . God.

Chloe Donnelly laughed. "Yeah. It's a good thing our team won, because he would have had me doing homework with him in no clothes at all. Although both ways we ended up naked."

I gasped. I'd been thinking so much of Mateo's unconditional yes, I hadn't thought enough about my own. I squeezed my eyes shut and willed myself not to blurt. Would any of the guys ask for nakedness? No. They were my *friends*, it was fine. They weren't those kinds of guys. I didn't think.

As we walked through the main part of town, I saw Melissa McGrill coming out of the pharmacy with her mom. She wasn't wearing any makeup, just baggy pants and a fleece, her hair in a low ponytail. I wanted to call out to her, maybe jog over and have an acquaintance conversation with her like we sometimes did in church. Nothing big or serious, but maybe something dumb about how much it sucked that Grinnell still didn't have a Starbucks. But she was hunched in on herself, and her mom had her arm around her like she was a little kid again.

Eve looked back at me, her eyes shifting to Melissa like maybe she thought I should go say hi too, but Chloe Donnelly tightened her hold on my linked arm and started in on another story about when she'd played Gestapo in Chicago. And before I could do anything, Melissa was in her mom's car and gone.

The one slice of pizza I'd managed to choke down at Beau's earlier was a deadweight in the bottom of my stomach by the time Chloe Donnelly finished her stories about platinum favors she'd won, and I left the girls and turned onto my street. When I got to Nan and Pops's house, all my good feelings about Mateo had been pushed aside by worry. I couldn't stop thinking about a guaranteed yes and how it might change the intensity of the game. *By any means necessary* seemed different now, less of a joke. A platinum favor was actually something worth playing for, and rock-paper-scissors wasn't going to work. The entire thing made me panic a little, even though I kept remembering the way Mateo looked at me like maybe he wanted to play *because* of me.

"Nan. Pops. I'm home," I called, dropping my house keys into the little handmade pottery bowl on the table.

Nan and Pops had an obscenely clean house. It wasn't

fancy or anything, but it felt like a museum, albeit one without anything expensive in it. Nan was vigilant about her housework agenda on Saturday afternoons and usually bugged me or coerced me into helping her, which I felt I owed her, considering she was putting up with me for two years. I slipped my shoes off and tucked them in the front closet, hooking my bag on the side of the closet where Pops had installed a series of evenly spaced hooks.

"We're in here, honey," Nan called over the twenty-four-seven sound of Fox News. Even when we were leaving the house, they kept it on as if their houseplants couldn't be deprived of the Republican agenda.

Considering my parents were practically socialists in the Spirit Corps, I couldn't believe they agreed to let me stay with Nan and Pops when I begged to come home after that first summer in Burkina Faso. Mom did everything she could to remind me of "our values" when we chatted online, and she always asked if I'd changed my mind and wanted to come live with them in BF, to which I always answered no. The truth was, I did share my parents' politics, and I did think the world was worth saving, but I'd been with my grandparents for more than eighteen months, and it was hard to argue with them when they started in with political talk—when they talked about how we needed to "protect" our country, but really meant we needed to keep out anyone who didn't look like them . . . us. Usually, I nodded and bit my tongue and reminded myself how grateful I was to them for taking me in, then I'd go online and donate the tiny allowance I was given to the ACLU.

"You missed chicken and stuffing tonight," Nan said. "Can you still smell it? I used rosemary this time."

"Yeah, it smells amazing," I called out. "I'll bring leftovers for lunch tomorrow."

I made sure the stolen scarf was tucked at the very bottom of my bag, not wanting to get into a bunch of questions from Nan and Pops, still feeling ridiculous for ever being talked in to stealing it. I should've handed it to Chloe Donnelly when I left tonight, but I felt stupid. She *said* she was going to return it when she asked Cam for a ride to Walmart, but I couldn't tell if that was for my and Mateo's benefit only, an easy platinum favor that she'd never really ask for.

Nan came out from the family room, her brassy blond hair newly done at the Grinnell beauty salon, and smiled wide. "There's also Neapolitan ice cream for dessert if you're still hungry. Did you have a nice time with your friends? How's the project?"

I tried to smile back. "It's good."

"Your mother called on the computer when you were gone. Sorry you missed her. She says hello and they'll try calling again in a few days. She said she'd send you an email." Nan fussed over my hair and patted me a little awkwardly, as if she'd been holding all these words in and wanted to get them right.

"She asked all about you, and I had to give her the whole play-by-play. She worries too much. As if your grandfather and I aren't handling things. But I know it's just because she's so far away and misses you."

I let her words sink in and then choked out, "I can't believe I missed Mom and Dad's call."

I blinked back tears that pushed against my eyelids. I missed a conversation with my parents. It shouldn't feel like that big of a deal, but it *always* hollowed me out if I couldn't talk to them. The lack of regularity of their calls and the fact that I sometimes felt so lonely I wanted to die made every call feel like a lifeline. And it was a million times worse knowing it was a lifeline for them too, that they were desperate for me to join them in Burkina Faso, that it killed my mom a little not to have her only child with her and she'd give anything for me to change my mind about staying in Grinnell. I took a deep breath and reminded myself they'd be home soon.

"I'm sorry I wasn't here when they called," I said, trying to steady my voice. Then I kissed Nan on the cheek. "I'm going to get some more homework done."

Nan squeezed my shoulder. "Okay, sweetie. Pops and I are going to watch *Two and a Half Men* in a bit if you want to join us."

"Thanks," I said, then went to give Pops a kiss before heading to my room.

"*Two and a Half Men* in twenty-two minutes, doll," he called after me.

It was a nightly ritual. Fox News interspersed with reruns of a crap TV show that more often than not involved Charlie Sheen. I could almost hear my mom's voice in my head muttering about misogyny and privilege and the pedestalization of bad boys. That voice made the choking tears diminish. It reminded me that Mom was always with me, in some way.

How she sprang from the sperm-egg combo of my conservative, Charlie Sheen–loving grandparents still baffled me. Though I suspected her politics had a lot to do with going to Grinnell College—the pinko school, as Pops liked to call it— and meeting my socialist dad there.

In my room I fired up Pops's old Dell computer, saying a silent prayer that the rumors about GHS giving all students their own laptop next year were true. It was nice that my grandparents let me keep the one family computer in my room for homework, but it also meant no real privacy, as Pops randomly busted in to use it for fact-checking *some damn thing* he'd heard in town. Sadly, he never used it for fact-checking Fox News.

Because of the lack of privacy and the fact that Nan and Pops were doing me a big favor by opening their house to me, I didn't decorate my room or let it get trashed like Eve's. It was a tidy, light-yellow guest room when I moved in, and it remained that way almost two years later, with a bedspread of tiny blue and yellow flowers and a small bookshelf of Nan's books. I checked my books out from the media center and mostly kept them in my schoolbag.

By the time the computer was humming, my phone had buzzed with a text from Chloe Donnelly.

So excited to play again. I know you're worried but it'll be pink. I promise.

Pink. Sure.

I took three deep breaths, then texted back. I'm not worried. I got Josh's letter, remember? See you tomorrow.

Then I pulled up my email and clicked on the note from my parents.

Chloe,

Sorry we missed you, but your nan said you were doing a group project with friends. I hope that little spring break drama with Eve blew over. Girls can be so hard, but we believe in you and know you'll work it out. Dad and I did an HIV/AIDS education presentation for the girls at the school this afternoon. I fall in love with these kids more every day. You wouldn't believe the questions they asked and how little they know about sex and contraception! I keep telling myself you're lucky to be going to school in the States with so many resources at your fingertips. Although that's probably me looking for something good about you being away from us.

Real talk (as the kids say!): As far as I'm concerned, there is nothing good about you being away from us. We both miss you like crazy. You know, if you lived here, I'd give you all the sex ed you'd need. LOL! (Your dad thinks I'm traumatizing you, but he doesn't know how hard things are for teenage girls. No one tells them anything.)

Anyway, we can talk more about this the next time we chat live, but Dad and I wanted to float the idea of us extending our stay here in Burkina Faso and what that would mean for you. Nothing is set in stone, but we're making such real progress with this community and we feel like they're really starting to trust us now. We'd hate to leave before we established something meaningful. Part of the problem in countries like this is so many NGOs are bandaging problems without putting in the infrastructure for sustainability, which leaves the people so vulnerable. We want this school to be able to run without us; the girls are so desperate for education. But for that to happen, we need to put in the work and the time. We won't extend without you agreeing to live here for the duration of our stay (which we're thinking will be another year, starting after this summer). We know that might cause some complications with school, but maybe you could look at it as a gap year taken one year early? You could return to Grinnell with us after we're done and finish up your senior year then, or we could unschool you in BF and you can say good-bye to public high school altogether a few short months from now. Tempting, right?

Again, nothing has been determined yet, and we should all talk about this. It's a family decision, but think about it. We'll try to get our webcam going on Friday night, so I hope, hope, hope you're around and our connection allows us to call.

Love and miss you so much,
Mom

P.S. Dad says that I'm monopolizing the computer too much and he's going to write you his OWN note later. Men!

I stood on numb legs and crossed to my door, closing it as quietly as I could, even though I was sure my grandparents heard it. Nan and Pops didn't like closed doors, said it was shutting out the family. They also insisted on tucking me in every night and giving me a hug before I left for school every day, which I didn't mind so much. But the doors? I wished for closed doors a lot. Thankfully, this time, they let me have one.

I stretched out on my bed and let the tears come. Extending their Spirit Corps stay wasn't a family decision. Not after my parents let me get away with living with Nan and Pops for two years. Mom and Dad would explain all the reasons why it was imperative for us to *Be the change we want to see in the world*, and in the end I would agree, because what else could I say? They'd given me a two-year pass, but all along they'd been coaxing me back over holiday-break trips when I got to see them in action at the village school, and peppering every conversation we had with heavy guilt about how much they missed me. Asking them to come home would be selfish, and I'd already maxed out my selfish card. I knew it and they knew it.

My parents had raised me to think of others first. Though the bitter side of me wondered why they couldn't have waited a few years, I also knew my mom might not have ever come out of her miscarriage depression if she'd stayed in Grinnell. There'd be no argument about extending, just a *necessary sacrifice on all our parts*.

I allowed myself ten minutes to cry, then scrubbed my face against the yellow-and-blue quilt, opened my door, and moved back to my computer to type a response.

Mom and Dad,

Sorry I wasn't around when you called. I miss you too. The HIV/AIDS thing sounds incredible. I'm really proud of all the work you're doing. I know big global change is important, and it sounds like you're making real progress. And I'm glad you're connecting with the girls (though, Mom, it's probably better to ease them into all the sex ed stuff).

I'll be around early on Friday night, but I'm going to hang out with Eve and Holly and a new friend I just made (Chloe Donnelly from Chicago) later, so it'd be great if you could reach out around dinnertime.

Things are going pretty well here with Nan and Pops, but I know how much you guys want me with you. I'm not sure about school and what to do about that, but if they need you in BF still, we can talk about options for extension.

I love you and miss you,
C

My finger hovered over the mouse, and I almost, almost hit send, but I couldn't. I was being horrible and selfish, but spending a whole year in Burkina Faso scared me. Mom and Dad would be working, and I'd have no friends and be alone even worse than when Eve and Holly blew me off over spring break. And that was one week, not fifty-two.

So I saved my note as a draft and shut down the computer. I took three deep breaths and stood just as Pops called out, "Come on, Chloe doll. *Two and a Half Men* is starting. It's a Charlie episode!"

The next day, over my lunch of leftovers and Chloe Donnelly telling us a twenty-minute-long story about her best friend from Chicago dating a guy who'd burned the family house down and then later overdosed after the two of them ran away together, Eve asked me if I wanted to hang out after school.

"You're not going to watch Holly practice with the dance team?"

"No," Eve said, glancing at Holly as she sneaked out of the cafeteria early so she could meet Cam in the parking lot for what would no doubt be another PDA make-out session. "She's not practicing today because she's going to see her dad."

The way Eve said it made it sound like Holly's dad was in Wisconsin instead of in the next town over, but I wasn't about to point that out when this was the first time Eve had asked to hang with only me in months. "Sure. My house or yours?"

Eve scrunched her nose. "Mine. I need to clean my room to get on my mom's good side so she lets me play Gestapo tomorrow night."

Which was how I found myself after school, folding Eve's clothes and shoving them into her dresser while she organized her makeup and hair stuff.

"So, how'd you get Josh's letter?" she asked as she tossed all her nail polish into a tiny plastic bucket under her desk.

I smiled kind of goofy and said, "Guess."

She rolled her eyes. "Well, I know it didn't involve tongues."

"Ew. Gross. You're definitely right about that." Whether she knew this because of me or because of Josh was anyone's guess.

"So how'd you do it?"

"We played rock-paper-scissors and I won two out of three times."

She laughed so hard she snorted. "For real?"

"Yeah. I mean, what else were we going to do? It's just a game." The mantra I kept telling myself every time I thought about playing the next night.

Eve fussed with her charm bracelet and was quiet for a long time. It wasn't the good quiet, like how we used to hang out and know so much about each other that we could have almost-silent conversations. It felt painful and awkward and loaded with questions I was too afraid to ask.

"It's not that bad, you know," she said finally, pulling at pieces of her hair to begin braiding it. The bracelet slid down her forearm and she knocked a bunch of hair bands to the ground as she separated hair, but she didn't pick them up. Apparently, she was done with cleaning her room.

"What's not that bad?"

"Kissing. Tongue stuff. Sex."

I blinked slowly and paused in folding her shirt. "You've had sex? When?"

"No, I haven't, but I thought about it. You know Holly's always talking. And she told me what it's like in detail, and I almost did it over spring break."

She kept braiding her hair as I stared at her. "With who?"

She glanced at me in the vanity mirror. "This guy at the college who showed up to Cam's one night when Aiden and his parents were gone."

"A guy from the college?"

"Yeah. But I was pretty hammered and Holly said I'd regret drunken first-time sex, so she had Cam take me home."

"A guy at the college? Someone you don't even really know?"

"Um, yes."

"Over spring break?"

"Yes, I said that."

My brain stalled on that point. Spring break. This had all happened over spring break? The spring break when Eve wasn't answering my texts except to say she was *too busy* to hang out. The spring break when I'd gone to see three matinees with Nan and had even let Pops teach me bridge because I was so lonely and bored. "Eve . . . ," I said, and my voice sounded all hurt accusation.

"It wasn't a big deal and it's not like I actually did it. I'm not sure why you're being so weird about it."

I looked down at the shirt clenched in my hands. I wanted to bite my nails so bad, but Eve would say something about it. I inhaled deeply. Sure, I knew that a good chunk of the world was having sex, so it's not like I thought it was rocket science or anything, but still, part of me felt so betrayed. Not just that it had taken Eve this long to tell me, but that sex was something she was seriously considering at all. This wasn't speculating about fifteen-minute orgasms promised by *Cosmo*, this was the real deal and Eve apparently was down for it.

"I don't think I could be so casual about it," I said finally. It was like she didn't remember anything about me, or maybe didn't care.

Eve turned around and looked at me hard. "Why? It's only monumental if you make it that way. The whole idea of popping cherries perpetuates a bullshit virginity myth that punishes girls."

I blinked slowly. "Who told you that?" This wasn't exactly information garnered from GHS sex ed. If anything, our health teacher made it seem like a hymen that wasn't intact on your wedding night was like being born with a cleft palate.

"Chloe Donnelly did."

I released a loud sigh. Of course she did. "Well, it's a big deal to me. You *know* it is."

"Still? God. Our health teacher was full of shit. Seriously. Why are you still hung up on it?"

I didn't know how to explain without sounding dumb—it wasn't our health teacher; it was my mom. Eve wouldn't get it. So instead of answering, I blurted, "Don't you think Holly and Cam are sleazy? I mean, all the PDA and him messing with his fly after the practice game."

Eve sniffed and turned back to the mirror. "She's a lot different from you."

I couldn't tell if it was a condemnation or an explanation, and I was too scared to ask. Too scared to know the answer. I used to think Eve and I were so much alike, with all the things we agreed on or were afraid of, but she changed more every day. And I seemed to stay exactly the same.

"She didn't really give him a blow job for his letter, did she?" I asked.

"Probably. But she would have done it anyway, so it's not like the game made her do it."

I hoped not. "Would you have . . . with Aiden?"

She ran her fingers down the braid in her hair and smiled in that conspiratorial way she used to when just the two of us knew something. "What do you think?"

6

When Friday night's game time rolled around, I was a nervous mess. I kept reminding myself it was no big deal, that we'd all had fun the first time. But *platinum favor* kept echoing through my mind, followed by the image of me studying in front of any of those guys without clothes on. Or doing anything else they might ask of me. And what would they ask? It was hard to imagine rounding all the bases as a platinum favor when I'd never even been up to bat. And it was even harder to imagine any of them asking it of me, which was the only reason I was still playing.

I changed my outfit three times before settling on leggings and a stretchy T-shirt over a cami, with a tiny purse strapped across me to hold my keys, hand sanitizer, and phone. My chest was mostly flat and underwhelming and the cami didn't help, but a padded bra seemed like I'd be trying too hard, like I wanted the guys to think about my boobs.

As I walked along High Street on the way to Burling Library, I passed a bunch of college housing and then saw Melissa McGrill's house. She was outside on the porch with a blanket wrapped around her, even though it was not at all cold. It'd been a bizarrely warm early April in Iowa, and I couldn't help but think of my dad's fears about our changing climate, fears that so many people had pushed aside as a "conspiracy." I stood in front of Melissa's driveway, waffling.

"Hey," I called out finally, lifting a hand to wave.

She looked at me and kind of half smiled. "Hi, Chloe." Then she pulled the blanket tighter around her.

She seemed so sad. I didn't know what to say. I didn't want to pry, and she hadn't confided in me about being pregnant in the first place. I didn't even know if the rumors were true, though the only time I'd seen her, she was coming out of the pharmacy and she'd missed the whole rest of the week at school.

"You okay?" I asked. My mom's miscarriage had left her basically bedridden for two months. Not just because she'd gotten an infection from the D&E they did after they found no heartbeat in the baby, but because every time she got out of bed, she'd burst into tears again. Dad fell apart too, climbing in bed with her more often than not, and leaving me to figure out my own meals. It took even more months for my mom to recover from the debilitating depression, and when she finally did, she explained everything that had happened to her. *In detail.*

Melissa shrugged. "Sure."

"Do you need anything?"

"No, thanks."

I couldn't figure out what to do with my hands, having no back pockets to shove them in and not wanting to start biting them, so I waved again and said, "I'll see you in church."

The one thing my grandparents insisted on—in spite of Mom's declaration that I should choose my own spiritual path—was that I attend their Episcopal church every Sunday. I was happy to see Melissa there the first time I'd had to go, even though we didn't say much more than hi to each other. It was weird how someone could be so important to you for so long, and then . . . not.

Melissa blinked, adjusted the blanket again, then nodded. "Yeah. See you then."

Melissa and I didn't ever sit together in church. I sat in the front with my grandparents' friends, and Melissa and her mom sat in back. Melissa's dad was in the army, stationed in the Middle East, and only showed up between tours. Part of the reason Melissa and I had grown apart in junior high was I didn't ever really know what to say to her about her dad always being gone. I knew she and her mom could've gone and lived on a base and seen him more, but her grandparents lived here, same as mine, and they were dug in. So after a while, I stopped calling Melissa as much, letting our friendship fade because of my own fear of saying the wrong thing. How does a twelve-year-old ask her best friend if she's worried about her dad dying in a country so far away?

Of course, now, with my parents nearing their two-year mark in the Spirit Corps in a politically unstable country, and me deciding to stay here instead of live with them, I knew exactly what to say. I just wasn't good enough friends with Melissa anymore to say it.

Walking onto the college campus was almost like entering a movie set. Mostly because all the students seemed like they had money. I knew this wasn't true—had heard unendingly about the college's unique need-based financial aid from my parents—but the buildings and the grounds and the way people were always outside with laptops or playing Ultimate Frisbee, it seemed rich in a way I'd never known. Most of the campus was filled with beautiful stone and brick buildings, a little like how I'd imagine one of those small East Coast boarding schools.

Eve, Holly, and Chloe Donnelly were already on the square in front of Burling Library when I got there. I ignored my jealousy over knowing they'd all been together at Eve's house first, but I couldn't meet them there because I'd been waiting for an internet chat with my parents that hadn't happened. Whether it was because they couldn't get online tonight or because I'd never sent the letter to them letting them know when to call, I wasn't sure. I felt guilty as hell for not sending that email, and even guiltier wondering if they would try to call when I was out playing this game because they'd assume I'd be home. Either way, it left me in a shame spiral I couldn't quite shake.

"Other Chloe!" Chloe Donnelly called, running up to me and hugging me hard *like we were best friends*. Were we? She'd sat next to me at lunch again today, entertaining the three of us with more stories about her Chicago friends, who all sounded a bit like characters from a TV show, but I wasn't about to say that.

Her arms were vise-tight around me, and when I finally stepped back, I could see she was a little tipsy. She was wearing a short T-shirt dress with pockets that made it flare out. And she had on Converse sneakers and no socks. Didn't seem like the easiest thing to run in, but at least it was better than the platform sandals Eve and Holly wore. The *exact same pair* of sandals, as if they'd bought them together over spring break and planned outfits around them, which I was sure they had. Probably got them along with the BEST FRIENDS charm bracelets, sometime before Eve decided sex with a random guy from the college wasn't *that big of a deal*.

Chloe Donnelly did a quick-gaze assessment of me and said, "You're dressed to run, huh? Even after getting Josh's letter in the practice game?"

I shrugged. What did she expect? I certainly wasn't going to go on the offensive when a platinum favor was at stake. I cleared my throat and asked, "Could the guys really ask for anything if they won? And we couldn't say no?"

Chloe Donnelly laughed, kind of tinny and a little fake sounding. "Of course. That's the definition of a platinum favor."

They would have a guaranteed yes. And so would we if we won again. I had to remember that or I'd never get through the night.

I glanced at the brightly lit library behind her. I'd looked up the hours online and knew it would close at ten. It was basically empty already. The activity around that part of campus on a Friday night was minimal since the buildings were academic, a fact I knew from all the reunion weekends my parents made me attend with them as a kid. The few people passing by the library to get somewhere tonight didn't seem to care about us at all.

Eve and Holly tottered closer, dumb platform sandals keeping them from being able to walk steadily. Eve handed me a plastic party-shooter syringe of amber liquid.

"What's in it?"

"Jack Daniel's. Liquid courage. We've each already had two, so you need to catch up."

I handed the syringe back. "I'm going to skip it tonight."

"Other Chlo-e," Eve whined. "Don't be weird."

"Let her do what she wants," Chloe Donnelly said. "It's probably smart to be sober the first time she plays for a platinum favor."

The first time. As if this was going to become a regular Friday night activity, which a big part of me hoped it wasn't. Although the other part of me held on to our practice-game win and how easy it had been, and how I'd been part of that. Part of *something* with my friends. If winning were as easy this time, I'd have a platinum favor from Mateo. The idea made me kind of shivery and flushed.

Will you kiss me in the hallway every morning? Will you have dinner with my grandparents? Will you write me if I have to move to Burkina Faso? So many favors spun through my head. And maybe Mateo would laugh and do all those things and tell me, "You didn't need to waste your platinum favor on that. You just had to ask."

"Yeah," I said, trying to sound casual. "I hate the taste of Jack Daniel's."

Eve rolled her eyes. "Everyone hates the taste of Jack Daniel's. That's not the point." Eve could be a mean drunk, and all the softness from the previous night seemed to have seeped out of her, leaving her judgmental and harsh. The Eve from the past few months instead of the one from our first few years as friends.

I wasn't straight edge or anything, but there was no way I wanted to drink. Particularly because I was possibly an even worse drunk than Eve. Alcohol made me paranoid, and I was grappling with enough of that without a push from Jack Daniel's. I could tell Holly wanted to say something snotty to me too, about not taking the syringe, but before she could, all four guys walked up.

Mateo was wearing jeans and a light-blue T-shirt that said SO? All the other guys were in a variation of the jeans/T-shirt combo; Aiden had a hoodie on too, and Josh's shirt was tucked in to jeans that looked new. With six kids in his family, I knew they wouldn't be new, but Josh wasn't the type to have holes in his jeans or wear the same pair five days in a row like he couldn't be bothered going beyond the top layer of the laundry basket. He wasn't into dirt biking or playing touch football in the fields like most of the guys in our school. I even once saw him use a napkin at lunch instead of his pants. The tidy thing was pretty cute.

"So tell me again how you're going to make this bigger and better," Cam said to Chloe Donnelly, like he hadn't been there when she'd explained about the platinum favor. It was hard to tell if Cam never listened or if he pretended not to listen because it went so well with his general apathy about everything.

She shrugged. "It's not that different from how we played before. Just longer and with more area to cover. We'll meet back here at ten thirty. The boundaries are the blocks surrounding the immediate college campus: Park, East, Sixth, and Tenth. You're not allowed to go inside any buildings, and the big gym complex and all the fields and courts north of Tenth are out of bounds."

"The gym complex is called the Bear," Eve put in, but then looked embarrassed for interrupting.

Chloe Donnelly barely looked at her. "Yeah, I know. Anyway. The Bear's too big, with way too many dark corners and hidden pockets. There are enough spots to hide without including it in our boundaries." Then, looking at me, she said, "Overall, we've got plenty of places to transact in private."

"Speaking of transacting," Cam said, pulling a handful of foil squares from his pocket, "a bunch of people were giving these out in front of the health center on my way over." He started to pass them around to the guys.

I leaned forward to look at what they were. Oh God. Condoms. He was seriously passing out condoms. I couldn't decide if I was scared to death or mad at Cam for being so disgusting when there was no need. It was like he was intentionally being a jerk to show off.

Chloe Donnelly smirked. "That's a little presumptuous."

Cam grinned. "They're safety condoms. Emergency use only. You never know when you may need one."

I couldn't stop myself from looking at Mateo as Cam

handed him a condom. His jaw was locked and he looked a little angry, but he didn't say anything, just pulled out his wallet and shoved the condom inside.

My stomach felt gurgly and full of acidic ire, and again I considered bailing on this whole thing. But then I thought of Chloe Donnelly sitting next to me at lunch this week and the way Eve and Holly looked at me as if I was suddenly relevant. How Eve had invited me to her house for the first time in months. How Mateo talked more in Spanish class because Chloe Donnelly kept dragging him into our conversations. How when we'd played at Cam and Aiden's on Wednesday, we'd had fun. Together. All of us. *We're not on a spy mission going across enemy lines. We're playing a word game,* I reminded myself. And the only one who'd need a safety condom was probably Cam.

I peeked at Mateo and caught him staring at me, maybe checking to see what I thought about Cam being such a dick. I rolled my eyes to indicate Cam and his safety condoms were dumb as hell. Mateo grinned a little, his lip ring glinting in the lights from the library. I picked at the cuticle on my thumb, trying not to be too obvious about how fluttery I felt when he smiled. He shook his head and grinned wider, like my nail picking was adorable and not this gross, nervous habit.

"Okay, everyone exchange phone numbers if you don't have them," Chloe Donnelly said. We plugged them into our phones, and I hoped my flush when I added Mateo to my contacts wasn't totally obvious. I'd been wishing for his number for almost a year, wishing for any way to connect with him outside of class, but I didn't know how to ask. Didn't think he'd give me a way in if I did ask. Even now, he looked a little put out by everyone having access to him in this way.

When that was done, Chloe Donnelly pulled out a small square of paper and handed it to Cam. He was apparently their default captain. "Do you have a pen?"

"No. They weren't giving those out at the health center." He winked and it looked so dumb.

Chloe Donnelly rolled her eyes and handed him a pen. "I brought an extra one."

Then she stepped away and wrote something on her slip of paper before tucking it and the pen into the pocket of her flared dress. She hooked an arm around me and said, "Eve, Holly, come over here with me and Other Chloe so I can whisper your letters."

She waved a hand at Cam as if to say *get to it* and then pulled each of us away to whisper a letter.

"*T*," she said, soft and low in my ear. *T.* I thought of all the possible four-letter words that included a *T* in them and was glad I wasn't the captain protecting our word—the one thing standing between us and an unconditional yes to the guys.

I looked at Cam, all cocky and shoving Aiden, and imagined myself trying to get his letter or the guys' word from him. What would I do? Could I sneak the paper out of his pocket without him noticing? Not with it tucked into his back pocket by his butt. Maybe I could get it another way. My neck felt all weird and splotchy, not in a good male-stripper-sex-movie way, and I put a different fingernail in my mouth. A game of rock-paper-scissors wasn't going to seal the deal with someone like Cam, especially if he was passing out safety condoms.

"Okay, girls," Cam called out after he'd whispered into each guy's ear. "You'd better go hide because we're coming for you."

Chloe Donnelly said to him, "Wait here for five minutes while we get ourselves in position. And then we start. Don't forget, stay outside, stay within bounds, and get letters by any means necessary!" Then she let out a dumb horror-movie laugh, and the girls all took off in different directions.

I glanced back as I headed for the dorms on the south side of campus and saw Mateo's gaze tracking me. I stopped myself from fidgeting or adjusting my underwear, which had ridden up my crack beneath my leggings. Faking calm, I looked at the other guys and saw Cam with his arms crossed and a smirk on his face, watching Mateo watch me.

"Run and hide, little girl," Cam yelled. "Your life is about to get a lot more interesting."

7

The thing was, my life didn't get interesting. At all. I planted myself behind a tree in the quad near the corner of South Campus, close to the fancy-looking dining hall that apparently the college didn't use much anymore.

There was more activity on this side of campus, college students popping in and out of the dorms, but after twenty minutes of sitting, I was bored out of my mind. A guy came down the street wearing a North Face jacket with no shoes on and his hair in a bun, then ducked into the loggia. I played Candy Crush on my phone and waited. Another twenty minutes and I decided I needed to move or I'd freeze. Maybe I could find Josh again. A cold and steady breeze had picked up, and I couldn't imagine Chloe Donnelly in her skimpy T-shirt dress or Eve and Holly in their sandals and short skirts. I'd be pissed if they'd broken the rules and gone inside, though the sane side of me wouldn't blame them.

I walked north along the quad and came to Eighth, which split the middle of campus. Grinnell was such a weird place for a college. We didn't have things like Thai food restaurants or twenty-four-hour pizza places or anything else college students might find useful. We had Walmart and the Dari Barn. I couldn't imagine the appeal of staying in this town like my mom did. She'd graduated from GHS too, and then started at the college a few months later. Maybe that was why she was so desperate to join the Spirit Corps. For a dozen different reasons, she was finally ready to get out. I'd lived here seventeen years, and that was enough for me. No way would I end up at Grinnell College.

More students were on Eighth, but none of them seemed to notice or say anything as I passed. Did they think I was just another college student? That was sort of an excellent thought, knowing my basic outfit made me blend in with older people instead of stand out.

The JRC was lit up brighter than the library—one of the newer buildings my parents said "squandered the endowment," though from what I could tell, all campus activity seemed to circle around it. Three guys were messing around out front, tossing a football beneath the streetlights.

The tallest one, dark-skinned with his hair shaved close, caught the ball and looked at me. "Hey, girl. You lost?"

My cheeks burned and I shook my head, quickening my steps to pass them and find the safety of the shadows again. Guess I didn't look that much like a college student after all.

I turned left on Park Street at the academic buildings. Almost two blocks down, when I reached the dark shadows outside the arts building, I saw Eve teetering on her platforms on the sidewalk at the corner of Sixth and Park. Her pale skin almost glowed and her hair bounced on her back as if she hadn't used any product at all in it, as if it was *naturally bouncy*, which I knew for a fact it was not. My hair, like my skin, was an endless source of frustration. No bounce, too thin and too straight, not lush like Holly's or glossy like Eve's. It was the products they used, I knew, but I could never imagine asking my grandparents for any fancy hair stuff. As it was, it was pretty much a miracle I'd talked them into switching from 2-in-1 Head & Shoulders to two different bottles of Suave.

I nearly called out to Eve, worried she'd finished the last syringe off herself and was wasted and lost, but then I realized someone was in the shadows she was stumbling toward. It made me feel a little pervy and weird, but I ducked into the bushes on the west side of the arts building and sneaked closer until I was just around the corner from where they were standing. I slid to my butt, back pressed against the outer wall, and took three breaths to calm my rabbit-fast heartbeat.

"You've got to be cold, Eve." Cam's voice. Or Aiden's.

I peeked around the corner. Gray hoodie. Aiden. Good news for Eve. I ducked back to my hiding place.

"It's not so bad. Jack Daniel's has helped warm me up."

"Do you have any more?"

Weird. Aiden wasn't a drinker. Though maybe he was tonight; maybe he needed liquid courage too. What kind of platinum favor would he ask for? Maybe he would ask Eve for unlimited desserts, though that seemed highly unlikely. Maybe he would ask her to leave him alone, though that level of cruelty wasn't his style either.

"Maybe," Eve teased. "I might be able to give you a syringe if you give me your letter."

I almost snorted. As if it could be that easy. Could it? Maybe it had been that easy when she'd offered him Rice Krispies Treats. Aiden laughed, which was weird and not something I'd heard very often.

"Nice try, sweetheart. How about I give you something you want and you give me your letter?"

Sweetheart. God. Eve had to be dying inside. Aiden calling her sweetheart would probably go in their family Christmas letter. I could already imagine the debrief between her and Holly. God, I missed our debriefings, when she would tell *me* every single thing Aiden had said to her and we would try to decipher all that it meant.

"Something I want . . . ," she echoed, and sort of hummed.

Then things got quiet. I peeked around the corner again, and Eve and Aiden were pressed tight against the wall of the building, making out. My lungs froze. They were actually kissing. After all this time of her pining away for him, they were kissing like it was nothing. No buildup or anticipation or acknowledgment of Eve's relentless campaign of flirting. Jesus, this game made things go from zero to sixty fast. So much for Eve offering up baked goods.

Goose bumps pebbled along my skin. Apparently, everyone was taking the game more seriously. The platinum favor had made Aiden bold. And Eve was right there with him, motivated by Jack Daniel's or her long crush or her assertion that sex wasn't a big deal or the promise of Aiden having to say yes to something she wanted from him.

I for sure felt pervy and gross now and stood to sneak away, figuring out if I could slink around the building toward Goodnow Hall. But then I heard Eve say, "Aiden, slow down." Her voice sounded small and scared.

Cold dread prickled down my arms and up my neck. I peeked around the corner a third time. Aiden's hand was up Eve's skirt. Oh God. Oh God. I slammed my eyes shut. What the very hell?

"Aiden," she whisper-cried. "Stop."

It was everything I feared but had convinced myself wouldn't happen, because we were friends, because this was Iowa, because it hadn't happened the first time. At least not with anyone but Cam and Holly, who were like that anyway. But this? No. I didn't want it to be like this. And for all her bravado, I knew Eve didn't want it to be like this. God. My legs were rubbery sticks and I wasn't sure if I could take more than two steps, but I had to bust this apart. I'd be sealing my fate as a social pariah for the rest of high school, but it didn't matter. Eve's voice definitely sounded not okay, and she'd said *stop*. This was not okay. I opened my eyes again, ready to move, but Aiden had dropped his hand.

"Don't pretend you don't want this, Eve. That you haven't wanted it every time you've seen me and Holly together. I can give you a hell of a lot more than my brother can."

The air whooshed out of me. Eve stumbled back. "Cam? Cam! I thought . . ."

Cam grinned. "I'm surprised you'd let a hoodie fool you, considering your devotion to my brother."

"But I . . . But he . . . You . . ."

"It's okay, sweetheart. We can keep this between us. Aiden would never go for my sloppy seconds, but he doesn't have to know."

Eve released a stuttering breath. "Okay. Yeah. Thank you. I'm kind of drunk. I wouldn't . . ."

"Yeah. I get it. You'd never slum with someone like me."

"It's not that. It's just . . . Holly. . . . And Aiden is . . . I mean, I've always wanted—"

"I said I get it. Anyway, what's your letter?"

Eve jerked back. "What?"

"Your letter. Come on, sweetheart. How do you think this works? I'll keep this from Aiden if you give me your letter."

The *sweetheart* sounded horrible now. Rehearsed. Too polished. Like he'd watched old Zac Efron movies and decided that's how you talk to girls. Cam was gross. Disgusting and gross. Him and his dumb safety condoms. No wonder. I wanted to punch him even harder now.

I stepped forward to say something. To put a stop to it, but before I could, Eve whispered, "*E.*"

Then she pulled her platform sandals off and hugged them to her chest before dashing away toward Park Street. Cam took two steps back, away from the bushes and out of the shadows, far enough to see me. He looked as if he'd known I was there all along, which upped the whole ick factor even more. "Your turn, little girl?"

Little girl.

I bolted, ran past the academic buildings through the center of campus, headed for the science building. My tiny purse banged against my hip and I shoved it back. The air was cool on my face, hair whipping my cheeks as I ran as hard as I could. My eyes started to water from the cold, or maybe from how completely overwhelmed I was. I needed to find Eve and make sure she was all right, but more, I needed to get out of there.

I wanted to throw up. I wanted to take an endless hot shower that Pops would complain about. I kept picturing Cam's hand shoved up Eve's skirt and how she'd said *slow down* and *stop*.

Ragged breaths escaped my lungs. Gestapo was a dumb game. I should've figured *bigger and better* meant more sleazy and horrible. What was I thinking agreeing to this after I heard what was at stake? After I saw Cam pass out condoms like they were toothpicks following a meal at the Cracker Barrel? I needed out.

I kept going past the science building and crossed the tracks until I got closer to the South Campus dorms. Then I slumped down on a bench. I pulled out my phone to text everyone and tell them I was quitting, to call Eve and see if she was okay, but before I could do either, I felt a hand on my shoulder.

"Chloe?"

I looked up. Mateo. Mateo with a soft, concerned face and eyes that made me want to crawl inside of them and never leave. Mateo looking at me like I'd wanted him to look at me all year—like we were real friends and he actually cared. The air whooshed out of my lungs.

"What's happened? Are you okay?"

I shook my head and Mateo sat beside me, wrapping an arm around my shoulder as I took deep breaths and tried to sort out all the things I was feeling. He was warm, so warm.

And he felt so solid, like everything before this was a nightmare and he was the only real thing. I had no idea why he was being so nice; he'd never acted this open with me before. But I was so grateful for the anchor of him that I tucked myself deeper beneath his arm.

"I don't want to play this game," I choked out. "I . . . I can't do it."

"Do what?"

But I couldn't say it out loud. I couldn't explain what I was afraid of. It would be juvenile and make me look dumber than I was certain I already did.

"Easy, Chloe. Calm down. Tell me what happened."

A few college students came out of the first dorm and headed our way. I looked at my feet, not wanting a bunch of older girls to see the shape I was in and say something about it. I leaned in closer to Mateo and his arm tightened the smallest bit around me. I picked at the cuticle on my thumb until it bled as I waited for the girls to pass.

"It's the game?" he said. "Did something happen with the game?"

"Have you ever had sex?" I blurted, and then I wished for a giant hole to swallow me up. I jerked away from Mateo and stood. "Forget it, I'm sorry. That was a stupid question."

Mateo huffed out a soft laugh. "You're giving me whiplash here, Chloe."

I stood and started to pace. Back and forth three times. "I should be okay with sex. I've had so much sex education thrust at me. Ugh, *thrust*. God. My mom took it upon herself to explain everything about sex. In vivid detail. And then she got pregnant and lost the baby really late in the pregnancy. And it was horrible. Eve and I said we were going to wait until we were sure. We swore. But then she said she almost did it over spring break. God, I can't believe I'm telling you all of this. I'm babbling so bad."

"Yeah, you are. It's okay. But I'm a little lost, to be honest. Did you give up your letter? Is that what this is about?"

"No. I just . . ." I inhaled slowly, quieting down my brain until I could calmly say, "I'm not the same as other girls. I'm scared all the time. You'd think I wouldn't be. I should be fearless, like my parents out in the dangerous world making a difference, but everything terrifies me. Everything. Do you know what I mean?"

"Not really."

God, I sounded like an idiot. I jammed my bleeding-cuticle thumb into my mouth. Mateo watched and didn't say anything. His lip ring seemed all out of place with his soft face and concerned eyes. I dropped my hand and took a deep breath.

"Sex scares me. A lot."

His eyes widened. "Did someone ask you to have sex?"

"No." I slumped back next to him and put my face in my

hands. "Nothing like that. I haven't even talked to anyone tonight but you. This game, though. I feel like no one is worried in the same way I am. But . . ."

"But?"

"Gestapo is about sex, right? I mean, I wasn't as sure after the practice game, but now? With Cam and his safety condoms? And everything else. It is. The platinum favor means too much to everyone. You have to see that, don't you? Sex stuff is how people get letters."

Mateo laughed, but it wasn't mean, more startled. "Well, that wasn't the first idea that came to mind."

"It wasn't?"

"No, Chloe," he said, putting his hand on top of mine, his rough fingers making me shiver a little, though I wasn't sure if it was good shivering or bad shivering. "Those dumb safety condoms were just Cam fronting. I thought you knew that. He's trying to rile you all."

"But if it's not with sex stuff, how else do you win the game?"

"The way to win Gestapo is with secrets."

8

"What do you mean?" I asked, turning toward Mateo and crossing my legs on the bench so I could face him. My thumb stung, but I kept picking at it with my pointer finger anyway. The only other option was to lean forward and trace the letters of SO? on Mateo's shirt, and I didn't think that would be helping me any on the appearing-stable front.

"Your thumb is bleeding," he said. And I felt dumb all over again. I shook my hand out and propped my elbows on my knees, folding my hands together tightly.

"How do you win with secrets?"

He mirrored my pose. "Think about it. It's like the real Gestapo. If you've got something to hide and someone knows about it, then that makes you vulnerable. They could leverage your secret to get your letter."

I laughed. I couldn't help it. "This isn't a movie. We're high school students in Grinnell, Iowa. What kind of secrets do we have that someone could 'leverage'?" I threw air quotes on *leverage* to make my point. Because, honestly, this level of strategy seemed ridiculous. The sex thing seemed way more likely, and I'd seen it firsthand.

Mateo's face was steady and serious. "Everyone has secrets. Small ones, like they cheated on a test, and bigger ones. Things they'd hate for anyone to know about them."

I thought about how closed off and guarded Mateo had been since he moved to Grinnell last summer. How I'd learned not to ask too many questions, because otherwise it would result in an abrupt end to our conversation. I wondered what he could be hiding, what he'd hate for someone to find out about him. Maybe Chloe Donnelly knew and had used it against him in the practice game. But I didn't want to ask. I didn't want to ruin the comfort of this moment with him. The relief that sitting across from him gave me. How my breathing had slowed and I'd calmed down so easily just being with him.

"I don't have secrets," I said, and I was pretty sure that was true. There was really nothing about me that would spin me into a panic if someone found out about it. If anything, I wished more people would ask about me. I wasn't certain if that made me the least interesting person in the world or someone who was way too honest about everything.

Mateo smiled. "Now *that* I believe. But I think you're alone on that front. Most people would prefer not to have others stomping around in their business."

"Do you think I'm boring because I don't have secrets?" I blurted. God.

That drew a full laugh out of Mateo. One I loved to hear because it was so rare from him. He tapped my knee twice with his pointer finger. His nails were perfect, strangely clean, like he'd gone out of his way to scrub them and cut them with nail clippers. "No. I think it's cute how easy you are to read."

I pulled back a little, feeling childish again, and let my hair drop in front of my face.

Mateo leaned forward and tucked the hair back behind my ear. It should have made me feel weird, the way he was touching me *like we were dating*, like he knew me well enough to treat me with that level of familiarity. And I was a little scared, but not because I thought he was pushing, as much as because I felt like I wanted him to push a little more. I was such a mess of contradictions.

"Don't hide behind your hair," he said. "I see you anyway and I don't want you to hide around me."

It was too much, how he was being with me, as if he understood I'd been waiting for him all year, wanting him to notice me. As if he'd sit there and listen to all my fears and make them go away.

"Mateo . . . ," I started, but my words felt roadblocked in my throat.

He touched my cheek, the shell of my ear, the bottom of my chin. It was different from how Chloe Donnelly touched me when she barged through my personal space. There was a question in his eyes, and even though I was still scared, I couldn't help but think: *Ask me.*

"Chloe. Let's get you out of here. You don't have to play anymore. Give me your letter and I'll tell everyone you had to get home."

Give. Me. Your. Letter.

My breath left me and I reeled back as if he'd slapped me. "What? You're . . . you're just looking to get my letter? That's why you've been doing . . . this?" I flapped my hand between the two of us, then jumped off the bench.

"What? No," Mateo said, following me. "That's not what I meant."

I paced in a circle, tucking my thumbs into my fists so I wouldn't pick at them. "Then why did you say, *Give me your letter?*"

"I was going to play for you. Be on both teams."

I stopped pacing and stared at him for a second. "You were?"

"Yes. Look at you. You're trembling and I found you sitting here scared half to death. I know you don't want to be here."

I started pacing again, then stopped. Start, stop, start, stop. Like my silly heart. I flinched when he stepped closer to me. "You were going to play on both teams? How would that work?"

He scrubbed a hand through his hair. "I don't know. I was just trying to help. You said you didn't want to play. I hate seeing you like this. I don't want you hurt."

My head was spinning. Was he really trying to help me?

"I'm sorry, Chloe. I didn't mean to . . . I don't have an agenda. I swear."

But how could he not? I'd just seen Cam try to pull this same thing. *Give. Me. Your. Letter.* I slammed my eyes shut and thought about all Mateo's sweetness over the past fifteen minutes, the way he'd tapped my knee and tucked my hair behind my ear and touched my face. It couldn't have been real. I wasn't someone anyone cared about. He'd only been interested in my letter. And I'd been dumb enough to fall for it. My shoulders slumped and the knowledge of my own stupidity settled in the bottom of my stomach.

"It doesn't matter," I said. "This is stupid. All of it. My letter is *T*. Go tell the guys."

"Chloe," he said, his voice sounding weird and a little crackly. "That's not why—"

But I held up a hand to stop him. "It's got to be almost ten thirty. The game will be over soon."

He took a step toward me, but I stumbled back. I was right

to be scared. I didn't have the first clue what I was doing when it came to guys, and this game seemed to make it a hundred times worse. This wasn't rock-paper-scissors and promises of desserts; it was serious, and everyone was apparently playing for keeps. I turned away from Mateo and headed toward the South Campus loggia, ignoring him as he called out after me. I pulled my phone from my small purse, the penguin case looking now as if it were laughing at my stupidity. I swiped my finger to check the time. Ten fifteen. Thank God the game was almost done.

9

I walked on stiff legs along South Campus, gnawing at each of my nails like they were a row of kernels on an ear of corn. I peeked inside the loggia and read some of the signs hung up on campus: WE NEED EDITORS FOR THE GRINNELL REVIEW, PRACTICE RANDOM ACTS OF KINDNESS DAY, PASS OUT RIBBONS FOR TRANS DAY OF REMEMBRANCE! I wasn't sure I'd ever quite understand the workings of "the college," even with having two parents who'd gone there. I turned and headed west toward the library, passing a group of students, guys all arguing about a basketball game, but they thankfully ignored me. By the time I crossed the tracks, my other thumb cuticle was bleeding too.

I thought about the call from my parents that didn't come because I'd been too chicken to send them the email, and I missed them with a swift and fierce pain in my chest. Not that

I would ever tell them about the game. I could only imagine what my mom would say about a game called Gestapo. *Making light of the organized cruelty and torture of marginalized people by Nazi secret police is hardly my idea of a good time on a Friday night, Chloe. Aren't all the neo-Nazis around the world enough? Why would you do this?* Guilt swept through me because she wouldn't have been wrong. Which made me too ashamed to ever mention the game to her. Still, I wished I could tell my parents about Mateo. About how I wanted to believe he was real and not lying, but I couldn't. And whether that was because I'd spent the better part of the past year watching my best friend turn away from me, or because I thought most teenage guys had some ulterior motive, didn't really matter. I was still defeated.

Eve and Holly were already in the square in front of Burling Library when I walked up. I tried to catch Eve's eye, make sure she was okay, but she was sucking down another syringe of Jack Daniel's and any kind of silent girl communication wasn't in the cards. Holly looked bleary eyed too, but she waved me over and motioned to the seat on the bench next to her as if we were suddenly the best of pals.

"Other Chloe," she said, too loud and too chipper. "Any luck with the letters this time?"

"No," I said, letting my curtain of hair fall and slumping next to her.

She patted me on the leg, her self-polished French-manicured nails as perfect as the rest of her. Only her pat on my leg was more like a slap. Too hard, too enthusiastic. It was like being fouled in hockey in a way the ref couldn't recognize. "It's okay," she said. Slurred, really. "None of us was counting on you. You couldn't get lucky with Josh twice."

Eve laughed and I hated her a little. And I hated myself for hating her after what she'd been through tonight. I'd heard her say *stop* and I hadn't done anything. Sure, I'd thought about it, but in the end, I hadn't intervened right away when I should have.

Cam, Aiden, and Josh arrived, crossing from the arts building. Cam smirked at me, but I looked away and sucked on my bleeding thumb cuticle.

Eve stood on wobbly legs and said, "Has anyone seen Chloe or Mateo? I'm freezing and want to get inside."

I didn't say anything about Mateo or my letter. No need for Eve to hold that humiliation over my head just yet, not that she didn't have one of her own. Stupid, stupid game.

"We're here," Chloe Donnelly called, dragging Mateo behind her. "I found this guy on my way over. He claimed he was heading home. Can you believe it? Before we even officially ended the game."

Heading home? Was this another trick? Mateo glanced at me for less than a second, then moved to stand with the guys. I got out my tiny bottle of hand sanitizer. It burned when I rubbed it in, my cuticles not loving the alcohol in the stuff, but there was comfort in being germ-free.

"Okay," Chloe Donnelly said, rubbing her hands together as if she had just sanitized too. "Circle up with your teams and let's see if we can figure out our opponents' word."

I dragged myself toward Chloe Donnelly's little huddle. The energy and excitement of the practice game were nowhere to be found. Holly seemed blurry and bummed out—had Eve told her what Cam pulled?—and Eve seemed overly peppy, like her mom when she was pitching the benefits of the Booster Club. Maybe she wasn't as horrified about how Cam got her letter as I thought. Maybe her new attitude about sex made her think Cam's gross trick wasn't that big a deal either. Chloe Donnelly wrapped an arm around Holly and Eve, and for a second I considered walking away. Not saying anything, but taking off in the other direction, running until my legs hurt and I was far from there. But then Chloe Donnelly looked up, dropped her arm from Holly's shoulder, and put it around me instead, drawing me in closer.

"So did either of you get anyone's letter?" she asked, scanning Holly's and Eve's faces. Hard to miss I wasn't included in the question. *None of us was counting on you.*

"No," Holly whined. "I couldn't find anyone and I looked everywhere. A couple of college guys asked me to a party at Fairgrounds later, though."

I had no idea where Fairgrounds was, and from Eve's facial expression, neither did she. But then she recovered and quickly grinned, saying, "That's cool. We should go."

Holly's face registered shock. "Are you for real? You never want to go to college parties."

Eve's eyes flashed toward me for an instant. Had she told me the truth about almost having sex with a college guy over spring break? She looked strange and guilty, but there were so many reasons for her to seem that way after tonight. I used to know everything she was thinking, but now I didn't have the first clue.

"I'd totally go," Eve said. "But I forgot that my mom expects me home by midnight because we're delivering plants tomorrow."

Holly shook her head, but I didn't know if it was because she thought Eve was lying or if she felt bad Eve had to be part of her mom's early Saturday morning plant delivery. "Of course she does. Maybe I'll go to Fairgrounds on my own. I mean, a party's a party, right? I need to find out what Cam wants to do."

Eve looked hurt but then perked up again. "Whatever. I'll go with you next time for sure, okay?" She touched Holly's charm bracelet. BEST FRIENDS. God, all the posturing was so exhausting.

"Eve? Did you get anyone's letter?" Chloe Donnelly asked, evidently seeing the whole Fairgrounds thing as a distraction and opting to ignore it.

Eve shook her head. Chloe Donnelly raised an eyebrow but only said, "I guess people are taking the game more seriously now, not going to be swindled by a plate of Rice Krispies Treats and a pretty face. Don't worry, Eve, I got Aiden's and Mateo's letters. *B* and *T*. So at least we can guess."

She'd gotten Mateo's letter again? My shoulders got tight and I had to work hard to relax them. Was it before or after I'd seen him? It had to have been before. But he hadn't said anything. Maybe that was why he'd asked for my letter. He was embarrassed about losing his. Though I couldn't help but wonder how he'd lost it. If it was about secrets, how did Chloe Donnelly know any of his? She'd just moved to Grinnell. Which meant it was more likely about sex. My stomach went acid-fire hot and my shoulders tightened again. I should've asked her, put myself out of misery and found out what she did to get the letter, but I stopped myself. I didn't want to know. I didn't want Mateo to have been with her and then been kind to me, even if it was just about my letter. I *needed* him to be a good guy.

I put my thumbnail in my mouth, but the gross taste of hand sanitizer made me pull it back out. Mateo said sex wasn't the first thing he thought of when it came to winning the game. But it could've been the first thing Chloe Donnelly thought of.

I looked at her T-shirt dress, wondering if it had been as wrinkled before. Or if she'd been doing sex things and it had gotten wrinkled. Sex things with Mateo. Or maybe he was groping her to find the slip of paper that contained our word. I didn't care about the gross sanitizer; my thumb was back in my mouth. I'd determined I wasn't going to ask her what she did, but that didn't mean my brain wasn't going to continue spinning out all the scenarios it wanted.

"What words have B and T in them?" Chloe Donnelly asked.

Words. Right. Focus on the words. This is a dumb word game. That's all.

"*Boat*," I said, dropping my thumb. What was I even doing? I didn't care about any of this. I wanted to get home.

"*Boat* is stupid. Cam wouldn't have picked that word. We live in Iowa," Holly said. Apparently, she'd sobered up enough to remember she found me mostly intolerable.

"What does living in Iowa have to do with anything?" I snapped back.

Eve stepped closer to Holly. Always choosing her side. "*Boat* really isn't the first thing that comes to my mind. Holly's right. It's probably *bent* or *boot*."

Chloe Donnelly crossed her arms. The T-shirt dress definitely looked more wrinkled around the boobs, sort of stretched out at the neck. "He's your boyfriend, Holly. You guess."

Eve's cheeks turned pink at the word *boyfriend* and she looked down. Now I felt bad for being upset when she sided with Holly. It wasn't her fault Cam tricked her. She'd said *stop*. I didn't know why she wasn't explaining what happened. Maybe that was why I was no good with secrets. It seemed more logical to be honest.

"*Boot,*" Holly said with certainty. "Cam would choose *boot.*"

Chloe Donnelly nodded, but glanced at me and raised her shoulder slightly as if she thought I might be right. She bumped my arm and smiled at me. We were friends still, apparently. I looked down and said nothing, emotions churning too much about this girl who was friends with me one minute and playing a game I hated the next.

All the things from the night overwhelmed me and there was no sorting through them until I was home, so I kept my eyes trained on the ground. The platform sandals Holly and Eve were wearing were kind of crappy looking up close. Like they'd been made cheap and wouldn't last very long. Eve must really be in trouble with her parents if they weren't lavishing the best stuff on her. Not that they were super rich, but her mom never skimped on quality because she always said, "The good stuff lasts longer, and how you present yourself reflects on your whole family." I wondered if Eve's mom thought Holly "presented" as a higher-quality friend for Eve than I was.

"*Boot* it is then. Okay, guys," Chloe Donnelly called toward the huddle of guys, pulling out her folded slip of paper and holding it over her head. "Come on over and let's hear your guess."

Nerves twisted inside me and I clutched the tiny purse I wore across my chest to keep from attacking my nails again. I had nothing but stubs to gnaw at after the night, and I could only imagine what Nan would say when she saw them at breakfast in the morning.

The guys had two of our letters. They had as much of a chance guessing our word as we did theirs. Which meant they could win a platinum favor. I gripped Chloe Donnelly's free hand. "The platinum favor. Is it . . . ? I mean, can the guys ask anyone if they win? Does each winner get assigned a loser on the opposite team to ask the favor of?"

She laughed. "No. If they win, they get four 'can't say no' favors from our team. They can each ask any one of us. That's what makes it so completely pink."

"But then they might all ask the same person. And she'd have to say yes no matter what. Four times."

Chloe Donnelly nodded. "Yep. That's how you play. But don't worry, Other Chloe. It's not that hard to say yes after the first time."

Cam laughed from where he was standing a few feet away. Oh God. I was going to barf. My eyes went wide and the image of his hand up Eve's skirt spun around my head on an endless loop. *Please, God, do not let them guess our word.*

135

"So let's hear your guess, Cam," Chloe Donnelly said.

His smirking face changed into one of frustration and irritation. I'd seen that face before, when he'd lost to Aiden in the fifth-grade student council election. It was the face that said *I can't believe I have to deal with such amateurs.* "Well, I was the only guy who got a letter from anyone. . . ." He glanced at Eve and her neck got splotchy, but she didn't look away. "So I've only got a guess, but I'm going to go with *easy*."

Wait. Wait wait wait. He was the only guy who got a letter? My gaze shot to Mateo. He didn't tell Cam my letter? So he *was* telling the truth all along. I couldn't stop the smile from taking over my face. I probably looked like a grinning doofus, but I didn't even care. Mateo didn't tell anyone. He wasn't trying to trick me. He was trying to help me. A half grin pulled up the left side of his mouth, but then he looked back to Chloe Donnelly, the girl who had taken his letter from him. Both our smiles disappeared.

"*Easy? Easy?* Puh-lease. As if I'd ever pick a word with a Y. Our word was *dent*. An anagram." She opened the slip of paper and showed it to them. "Too bad for you guys."

They didn't get the word right. Thank God. Relief pounded through me. They didn't win. Maybe because Mateo hadn't said anything about my *T*. I bit the inside of my cheek to keep from smiling this time. I wouldn't be doing any platinum favors for anyone.

Chloe Donnelly waved at Holly, this sort of queenly wave as if she was really above all of us. Holly tottered forward and smiled at Cam. "Okay. Our guess is that your word is *boot*."

Cam's shoulders dropped a fraction. "Close, baby, but our word was *boat*." He pulled out his crumpled word and a safety condom dropped out. He left it on the ground as he held up his slip of paper, and it took everything I had not to point out that he was littering. "See? *Boat*. So it looks like no one wins."

Boat. I raised my told-you-so eyebrows at Holly, but she only sneered at me.

Chloe Donnelly strummed her black-polished fingernails on her crossed arms, the rings on every finger glinting in the light from the street lamp. She glared at Holly for a second, but then smoothed out her face as if none of this mattered and turned back to the guys. "Technically, you're right, no one officially wins. But we did get two of your letters and you only got one of ours."

"Hold on," Aiden said, stepping forward, all stiff and almost angry. "That's not how you explained the rules. You said a team had to correctly guess their opponents' word to win."

Josh stepped next to him. His shirt was wrinkled, untidy. He must have been hiding in a balled-up position. "Aiden's right. You can't change the rules after the fact. I'm not giving up a platinum favor when you didn't really win. The practice game was a fair win, but this . . . no."

Aiden looked at Josh and nodded, some secret guy communication happening that once again I didn't really understand. I studied Aiden and wondered how Chloe Donnelly got his letter from him. He was always so uptight and put together. I couldn't really believe he had secrets, not with his path to the Naval Academy lit up like a landing strip toward his future. Maybe an easy hookup was all he wanted. Something without the clingy strings of Eve Jacobson.

All the sex-stuff speculation made my skin crawl. I was so far out of my league with this game. I didn't know Chloe Donnelly well enough to guess if she'd offer herself up for a letter. And the more I did get to know her, the more I guessed her stories about abortions in Chicago and her outrageous friends weren't completely true. She did get two letters, though. So maybe sex was involved. It seemed gross and trampy, but maybe this was how they played in Chicago. Cam certainly seemed to be inclined to play that way. Although I couldn't imagine Mateo would have gone for that. Especially after he'd kept my letter to himself. So maybe she had some sort of leverage on Mateo. But how?

None of it made sense; my brain hurt from all the speculation. I'd watched Cam get Eve's letter, and still I wasn't completely sure how to play the game that would work for *me*. Not with what was on the table for the winners.

I thought again about asking Chloe Donnelly how she

got Aiden's and Mateo's letters, but something kept holding me back. Partly it was not wanting to seem like I had no idea what I was doing, but more, I was afraid of finding out. My mom would call it the bliss of ignorance, but I'd hardly consider myself in a state of bliss. The only thing worse than all the speculation would be finding out my fears about the game were right, and then what would I do?

"Okay, okay, you big baby rule followers," Chloe Donnelly said. "No one won this time. We all get to hold on to our platinum favors. Which is super boring, but whatever. Everyone needs to try harder next time we play." She turned and stared directly at me before saying, "And maybe we could make more of an effort at offense instead of choosing to hide. I know you have it in you."

I didn't say a word, just shoved my pinkie in my mouth and gnawed off the last sliver of nail there. It didn't matter that Chloe Donnelly was disappointed. Or that in all likelihood Holly and Eve would go back to Eve's house for a sleepover— something Nan and Pops had long ago cut off discussion about with a succinct *You have a bed here*—and discuss how worthless I was at Gestapo. None of it mattered. Because there was no way I was going to play this game again.

10

It was ridiculous to have wanted Mateo to walk me home, too much to ask for after he already didn't tell the guys my letter. But still, I wanted the chance to ask him *why* he didn't. I walked slowly toward High Street, hoping he'd catch up with me, but I saw him turn the opposite way down Sixth, and I was left alone.

When I slipped in the door, Pops made the snoring-snort sound he did whenever he was lightly dozing on the couch. He'd waited up for me.

"Chloe?" he asked, heaving himself and his stomach pooch up and heading my way with a cautious stride, as if I might be someone else. His thinning gray hair stood out at all angles, and I felt bad he'd had to stay up.

For all Nan and Pops talked about the "safety" of small-town Grinnell, I happened to know Pops kept a gun in his nightstand drawer for intruders, and he was always worried about me. The irony was that it was the gun thing more than anything else that made my parents very anxious when it came to me living with Nan and Pops.

"Yeah, it's me," I said. "You didn't need to wait up."

Pops hugged me, his sweater smelling like Nan's beef stew and Suave. "What else do I have to do? I'm retired."

Pops had been a structural engineer for the state of Iowa most of his life. Now he played bridge twice a week and watched TV and went to church.

"Still. It's pretty late."

"And you're a seventeen-year-old girl," he said, giving me his shrewd look, which meant he was checking to see if I'd been drinking. "I'm always going to wait up for you."

I considered letting my hair curtain fall, but Pops would pick up on it in the same way Mateo had. *I don't want you to hide around me.*

"Well, it's late. We should both go to bed."

Pops nodded, hugged me one more time, and then headed down the hall to their bedroom. I wanted to take a shower, but with us all on one floor, there was no way that wouldn't result in a whole lot of questions at breakfast from Nan and Pops. They monitored showers in the way most parents monitored their kids' social media accounts. Showers at the wrong time,

141

more than one shower a day, showers that steamed up the hall too much or lasted too long—they all resulted in a third-degree grilling. Eve used to think it was cute how old-fashioned my grandparents were, but it'd been ages since she'd been to our house, and I knew Nan and Pops noticed and didn't think much of her because of it.

I paused in front of the bathroom, and Pops asked, "Everything okay, doll?"

I swallowed. "Yep. Just tired."

"Well, get to sleep then. And don't stay out so late next time," he said with a laugh. "Nothing good happens after nine o'clock."

So, no shower in the cards for me. I'd have to suck it up and wear the filth from the night along with my pajamas.

Nan and Pops had gone off to do Saturday errands—Hy-Vee, post office, sandwiches at Subway—when Eve showed up at my door the next morning. As if I'd somehow willed her there by thinking about how long it'd been since she'd come over. She wore yoga pants and a hoodie and looked like a plate of warmed-over crap.

"Hey," I said, holding the door open for her. It felt awkward and too formal with her standing on the threshold instead of waltzing in and putting her shoes in Pops's fussy closet. "Everything okay?"

"Are your grandparents still running errands? I need to talk to you."

That was the thing about having a best friend who knew everything about you—she also knew when you'd be alone.

"They're at the Hy-Vee. Come in. You want some water?"

Her skin was pasty and sick looking, the post–Jack Daniel's wilt obvious enough I was surprised her mom didn't ground her.

"Water would be great." She followed me to the kitchen, without taking her shoes off first—had she forgotten Nan's rules about shoes?—and hopped up on the counter while I got her a glass.

"Where's Holly? Didn't she stay over last night?" I asked, not that I actually cared about her whereabouts, but I'd learned to fake interest in Eve's plus-one.

"She said she had pointe class this morning so she left early."

I handed the water to her—room temp, no ice, how she always drank it—and she gulped down the entire glass before putting it to the side and saying, "I need to tell you what happened last night."

She adjusted her hair band—acne-free forehead, even after three shots of Jack Daniel's—and took a deep breath. The pause was long enough to give me a chance to come clean, to admit I'd witnessed the whole thing. But my tongue seemed to have swollen a hundred sizes because I couldn't speak. I worried I'd lose Eve completely if I admitted I not only watched her like a creepy stalker but also didn't do one thing to help her. So I just nodded and let her tell me the entire story about Cam, and pretended I didn't know the part of the story she'd left out—the part with his hand up her skirt.

"I don't know what to do," she finished, dropping her elbows on her knees and her face into her hands.

"It wasn't your fault. Cam tricked you. Holly will understand."

Eve jerked up and looked at me with wide eyes. "Holly will not understand. She wouldn't even believe I was tricked. She'd think I was trying to steal her boyfriend on purpose. She'd never speak to me again. You have to promise not to tell her. Swear."

I wanted to ask her why she'd be best friends with someone who didn't trust her. But then I thought about Chloe Donnelly, and how she'd dazzled all of us in a way, and how even as I remembered the things I liked about her, I wasn't completely sure I trusted her. So instead, I shrugged. "I won't tell her. I mean, why would I? She's not really my friend."

Eve swatted the air. "Don't be stupid. Of course she is. We're all friends. Anyway, you have to tell me what to do about Cam. He's gonna use this against me the next time we play."

I shoved my pinkie in my mouth and bit the cuticle for a

few seconds before saying, "Well, we could just not play again."

"What? No. No way. Chloe would be so pissed. And she's just starting to be friends with us. We're *this close* to being officially pink."

So Chloe Donnelly remained firmly on a pedestal. And evidently being pink was our new life goal. "I don't know, Eve. I don't think I want to play again. I mean, I like Chloe, but . . ."

Eve stared me down. "You should have heard her the night you guys came over for manis and you left early. She said all these really nice things about you. How amazing and strong you were for choosing to stay in Grinnell without your parents. How smart she thinks you are. I can't believe you're considering backing out. She thinks of you as her new best friend."

I scanned Eve's face to see how she felt about that. To see if it bothered her at all that I was well on my way to getting a BEST FRIENDS charm bracelet with Chloe Donnelly. But all I could read was relief with a hint of guilt. Eve, happy to be rid of me, and guilty about how happy she was. "How can she say all that? I've known her a week," I said.

Eve shrugged. "Holly was my best friend in that amount of time."

Ouch. "Then probably you should tell her the truth about Cam."

She played with the BEST charm on her bracelet. "I sort of

want to keep her as my best friend, so there's no way I'm telling her I hooked up with her guy. Even accidentally."

"I think she would understand."

"She wouldn't. I told you, she's different from you." *Then why stay with her?* I wanted to scream. I didn't understand the Holly mystique. Who cared if she was brave and up for anything.

"Whatever," I sighed. "You guys can figure it out without me. I'm not playing again."

Eve hopped off the counter, the color returning to her pale cheeks—whether it was from the water or her sudden pissy-ness at me was hard to tell. "You're for real? Even after what Chloe Donnelly said about you? Chlo-e, come on. You have to play. You'll ruin it for everyone if you quit."

"I don't matter. You could get someone else."

Her mouth dipped into a frown. I wanted her to say I did matter. I wanted her to say it wouldn't be the same without me. I wanted her to say she wouldn't play if I didn't. I wanted her to care that I was bailing. Her eyes narrowed and she licked her lips in a way that seemed contrived and a little weird. "*We* could find someone else, but I don't think *you* could. I mean, Chloe, not to be harsh, but I've been carrying you for most of this year, going out of my way to make sure you're included. And it hasn't always been the easiest with your gross nail biting and how you always seem so prudish and you barely say anything unless you're blurting out some random awkward thing. But we have a history together. We've been friends for a long time. Do you really want to let go of that?"

It was the most calculating thing I'd ever heard Eve say. It didn't even sound like her. At her worst with Holly, she'd never made me feel like I was nothing, easily replaceable. I felt like I'd been butt-ended with a hockey stick. Evidently, opting out of the game was opting out of our friendship. God. Why was she doing this? My mom would tell me I didn't need friends who gave me ultimatums. She'd tell me to break up with Eve and find a best friend who saw me as more than just an obligation. But my mom was fifty-seven hundred miles away. Eve's words sank in like tiny stones falling into Rock Creek. If I quit the game, I'd lose *all* my friends. What did I really have to offer anyone else in terms of friendship? I lived with my grandparents and didn't do any after-school activities. I bit my nails and got patches of acne on my forehead. I blurted. None of these things was a strong selling point.

I clenched my hands to keep from biting and looked at my bare feet, allowing the hair to drop in front of my face.

"I could play maybe one more time," I said, my voice sounding like I'd single-handedly caused my team to lose a hockey tournament. I hated myself for being this weak. I hated Eve for putting me in this position.

Eve clapped her hands as if she hadn't just ultimatumed

me, and then said, "Yay! It'll be so pink next time. I am determined to get at least two of the guys' letters."

I went to the cabinet and got myself a glass for water—crushed ice in half of it and as cold as the tap could get. "You'll have to find out how Chloe Donnelly got Aiden's and Mateo's letters." Because God knew I couldn't find it in me to ask her.

Eve filled her glass at the tap again and hopped back on the counter. "How do you think she got Aiden's? I mean, she wouldn't do anything. She knows I've liked him forever. I mentioned it at lunch. And it's not like she can cook better than my mom, so she didn't ply him with baked goods."

I shrugged. "I'm not sure. I don't know how she got Mateo's letter either."

I almost told Eve about what happened with Mateo by the South Campus dorms, about giving him my letter and him not telling the guys. I wanted to tell someone, to find out if it meant what I hoped it did, but Eve gave me such a pitying look. And she'd proven that any weakness of mine was fair game to get what she wanted.

"Chloe has a lot of experience," she said, as if that explained everything. "Do you know I heard she has her labia pierced? God. I wonder what that feels like."

"Labia?" I whispered. "Do you know where that is? It's down in her . . ." I pointed vaguely to the area between my legs—what Mom insisted I call my vulva—feeling a little sick.

"Yeah, I know. Did she mention it to you? Can you imagine spreading your legs for someone with a piercing gun?"

My mouth dropped open. "Why would she pierce her labia?"

Eve kicked her feet against the cabinet—thank goodness Nan wasn't home or she'd throw a fit—and said, "I guess it makes orgasms better."

Well, this was not something Mom had ever told me. "Really? How would that work? I feel like you'd either be stimulated all the time or become totally desensitized so you never had orgasms."

The whole thing was so unimaginable that I almost forgot about how Eve had been so crappy to me and essentially blackmailed me into playing Gestapo if I wanted to still hang out with her. And yet this whole conversation proved why I wanted to keep her as my friend. I missed having Eve around to talk about all this stuff with.

"I know, right? She's so advanced, she probably even owns a vibrator or whatever. Though maybe that wouldn't work with the piercing. My God. I'd never be able to get anything down there pierced," Eve said, her voice a mixture of fear and awe.

This was the Eve I knew. Curious and a little afraid. Always speculating but never willing to get hands-on experience. Not until Holly. And now because of the game, she had even more hands-on experience. With Cam.

My gut churned again at the mental image of his hand up her skirt and her choked out *stop*.

"Chloe might be a little *too* advanced for me," I said.

Eve set her glass down and jumped off the counter, getting herself ready to take off. "Don't worry. You'll catch up. The game will help."

I didn't say anything, but I decided if I had to play Gestapo again, I was going to spend the entire time hiding in a tree.

At church the next morning I bumped into Cam and Aiden and their parents on the way into the sanctuary. Their parents were friendly and chatty; they had been as long as I'd known them. They were the type of couple who'd complete each other's sentences because they'd been living and working together so long. Or rather, their mom completed their dad's sentences. The twins' dad was handsome in that way older guys who worked out and spent a lot of time outdoors could be. Their mom was tiny—tiny bones and tiny face—but she had a big voice. They had a handmade furniture company they ran together where they custom built stuff that looked like it belonged in the Amana Colonies. Neither of their sons really seemed anything like them, with the exception of Cam's skill at building stuff.

I dropped my hair and choked out a hello when I saw them. Cam leered at me. Aiden elbowed him and then offered a stiff "good morning" to me and my grandparents. Then they followed their parents into the church.

Inside the sanctuary, I saw Melissa McGrill sitting in the back with her mom. I turned to Nan and said, "I think I'm going to sit with Melissa today."

Nan worked her mouth like she was chewing on a fatty piece of meat. "Not today, Chloe. Let's let that die down a bit before we put on our Good Samaritan hats."

Small-town Grinnell: where even my seventy-year-old nan had heard about Melissa's miscarriage.

"The Good Samaritan didn't wait a few weeks before he helped that guy on the side of the road," I mumbled.

Nan's lips tightened even more. "The guy on the side of the road hadn't been having sex with God knows who before he'd gotten ill and asked for aid."

And that was Nan and Pops's helping philosophy in a nutshell—help others, but only if they're family or they're "worthy" of receiving help. I'd heard countless battles as a child between my parents and grandparents about this. Arguments about welfare and the homeless, with my parents throwing out words like *unconditional mercy* and my grandparents countering with words like *enabling*.

"You helped me when I needed you," I offered.

She patted my hand. "And we always will. You're our family and we'll take care of you the best way we can. But we know you'll always make good choices because we've instilled those values in you. We can't be responsible for other people's lack of morals or poor parenting."

I could only imagine what Nan and Pops would say about my choices with respect to playing Gestapo. But I didn't want to fight with her, so I dutifully followed her to the front pews, where her octogenarian friends all sat. I waved to Melissa as I walked down the aisle and told myself I'd make sure to cross the sanctuary to find her during the passing of the peace.

Only we didn't end up doing the passing of the peace because it was Youth Sunday and the Sunday school kids were running the service. Which meant mass chaos, a skit at least half the sanctuary didn't hear a word of, and a bunch of toddlers singing "This Little Light of Mine."

Near the end of service, our priest got up and said, "It has been a wonder to see our church youth put together such an incredible program. God is good all the time, indeed. We have one last special treat from a member of our senior high youth group. Campbell Ahers, will you please come up?"

I said a prayer of gratitude my grandparents only insisted I attend service and didn't mandate my participation in any of the youth programming. Then I watched Cam settle into a chair, cradling his guitar in his lap. Of course Cam played guitar. No skirt-lifting bad boy was complete without a dumb guitar to round out the image.

I glanced at Aiden, who was staring impassively at his brother. Then Cam started to play and sing Psalm 40. I was probably one of the few people who recognized the U2 version of the psalm—Dad being a U2 addict, though preferring their early albums like *War*, when they were still pissed-off Catholics—but it didn't matter. No one moved when Cam sang. His voice filled the sanctuary and it wasn't smirky or sleazy or *sweetheart*-y. It was beautiful in this way that made me so sad. I couldn't really even explain why. He looked so happy, so content, like this was what he was meant to be doing and all the rest of the dumb stuff he did was just killing time while he waited to sing like this. It was a voice someone who hadn't been leered at could fall in love with.

Crossing the street to the parking lot after church, I saw Holly sitting on the hood of Cam's car. Of course Cam never drove with his parents, even if it was a huge waste of gas for him to take his car too. Holly's lean, muscular legs dangled over the side of the Volkswagen hood, her heels bouncing against the tire. I had no idea how she got out of going to Catholic mass. Her parents had obviously been devout enough to send her to parochial school in another town for most of her life. Maybe she'd been to one of the Saturday evening masses.

I squinted and lifted my hand to wave at her, feeling like I should make an effort since she had such a crappy boyfriend. But she either didn't notice me or chose to ignore me. She kept her eyes trained on the door behind me, and as soon as Cam exited the church and crossed the street, she bolted for him. He slid his guitar behind his back and lifted her up to kiss her. If I hadn't watched him do the same thing to Eve, I'd almost think he was being romantic, but I couldn't believe that. Then he put her down and touched her face. I was too far away to see, but from where I stood, it looked like he was wiping away tears. Did she know about what happened with Eve? But then why would she be coming to Cam for solace? He hugged her and tucked her beneath his arm as he led her to the passenger side of the VW and helped her inside. His hand lingered on her shoulder and he leaned in to kiss her forehead.

I didn't know what to think except: What was I supposed to do with this version of Campbell Ahers?

11

After church, during Sunday brunch—egg, sausage, potato, and cheese casserole on Nan's "good" china—I told my grandparents about Mom and Dad wanting to stay in Burkina Faso if I agreed to move there with them for the extension.

Nan folded and refolded her napkin before saying, "I don't know why your parents feel the need to do all that. They've served and done enough. They've given up two years of their life."

I swallowed. "I know, Nan. But the work they're doing is really important. It's making a difference."

She huffed and added too much salt to her casserole. "Yes, yes, fine. It takes a village and all. Though they've somehow elected themselves president and vice president of the whole village."

"Nan . . ."

"What? I'm being honest. I saw a thing on the news about all the humanitarian aid in Haiti that never even got to the people. There were cases of water bottles stacked in government offices that weren't distributed!"

I blinked. "But they're not in Haiti."

Nan tsked as if every third world country was the same. "You know what I mean. I'm not sure those people want all this assistance. People don't like others doing things for them. They want to help themselves."

"They've started a school, Nan. I can't imagine that anyone in the village is upset the girls there are getting an education."

Nan stared at me and asked, "Do you want to go live with them, Chloe?"

I looked at my lap and heard Pops, who'd been eating silently the whole time, shift in his seat. I cleared my throat. "I've already been away from them too long. They miss me a lot. I know they do. And I miss them too."

Pops leaned forward. "That's not an answer, doll. We know you miss them. Summers and winter break aren't enough. But this traipsing about the world? You know I love your mother, but running away doesn't make problems go away. No matter how long you're gone from home."

And there it was, the thing none of us ever talked about: Mom's broken heart after the miscarriage. How I had to go live with Nan and Pops for a few weeks back then when Mom's crying started to scare me, and Dad thought she might need to go to the psych hospital in Newton. How Mom spent a full month after the baby died talking to her as if she were in the same room. I cleared my throat again. "She seems better, though, Pops. She has all these girls there who need her and it's made her better."

"She has a girl here who needs her too," Nan said.

"Yeah, but it was my choice not to stay with them. I know she'd love for me to be there with her. Plus, I have you guys." I offered them a shaky smile.

"Of course you do, doll," Pops said, shoveling little pieces of sausage to one side so he could eat them all in one large bite. "But I worry about your mother. When she was a teenager and went through a hard time, I told her, *Nothing is so bad that you can't change it by moving.* She seems to have taken that to heart too much. If you don't want to go to Burkina Faso, then you need to tell them."

I sighed. "But those girls at the school . . ."

Nan waved a hand. "Enough. The weight of the world shouldn't fall on your shoulders or your mother's. All this do-gooding. There is plenty of good to be done *at home.* No one needs to go to Africa to save the world."

I knew Mom and Dad would disagree. They'd explain about global responsibility and what those of us who are privileged can and should do to redistribute that privilege. It would be a big fight and Nan and Pops would blame my dad for turning their daughter into a socialist.

I shoved a bite of casserole in my mouth and barely chewed before swallowing, then said, "Thank you again for letting me live with you. I know I don't say it enough, but I'm glad I'm here. I'm really lucky."

Which was true. Even with my grandparents' overly simplistic view of life and the world, I felt grateful I got to spend time with them and that they offered me an alternative to my parents' plans in Africa.

Pops blew his nose into his napkin. "We're the lucky ones. You can stay as long as you want."

Monday morning, Eve was waiting for me at my locker before first period—another thing she hadn't done in a while—but when I got there, all she did was adjust the slightly see-through blue T-shirt she was wearing and say, "Remember you promised not to say anything about Friday?"

I nodded and yawned, having stayed up way too late thinking about everything going on in my life—my parents, Chloe Donnelly, the game, Mateo. "I remember." I looked at her hands, rings on every finger of the left one. Again. But she wasn't wearing her BEST FRIENDS charm bracelet, which I tried not to wonder about.

"Good. So I talked to Chloe yesterday, and we're playing again on Friday."

"Even Aiden?"

Aiden was the hope I glommed on to the moment I agreed to play one more time. I couldn't believe he'd ever go for it again, particularly after he lost his letter to Chloe Donnelly. I thought if anyone would put a stop to the game, it'd be super-serious Aiden. Mateo might also pass, but he wasn't really one to rock the boat and make a fuss. Aiden had no problem declining anything that detracted from his agenda.

"He's playing. I texted him yesterday and he said he would."

Eve smiled smugly as if she was the reason he'd agreed to play again, which I didn't believe for a second was the case. Chloe Donnelly must have talked him in to it. Which meant she probably found out something about him. Or maybe they were hooking up on the sly, and she had him pussy-whipped or whatever that absolutely gross term was for when a guy did everything a girl said.

Part of me hoped the hookup theory was true, if only because it would mean Mateo didn't do sex things with Chloe Donnelly. He hardly seemed the type to go after another guy's girl, and I had to believe that Aiden would've staked some sort of claim on Chloe Donnelly to the other guys, even if it all was in some sort of mumbling guy way. The other part of me couldn't believe a guy like Aiden, who'd shot down Eve's relentless flirting for the past three years, would be lured by an arty girl with bright eyes and a hand full of rings.

God, my head hurt. I wished I could have seen Chloe Donnelly in action during the game. It couldn't be much worse than what I'd imagined happened. I knew I should just ask her how she got the guys' letters. I'd thought about it all night and braced myself to hear whatever response she'd give me.

"Other Chloe," Eve said, impatience ringing through her voice, even though I wasn't sure what I was supposed to say. On Saturday, when she was freaked out and feeling guilty, I'd been Chloe again. She must have gotten her confidence back over the past two days.

"Hey," a voice called from down the hall, drawing the word out until the few people near us turned to look. Chloe Donnelly walked toward us wearing the exact same ultrathin T-shirt as Eve, only in black instead of blue.

My gaze bounced between them both. "Nice shirts."

Eve beamed. "Thanks. Chloe gave me this one because she said it brought out my eyes. I swapped for my Tillys dress."

Eve's eyes were brown. The shirt did nothing for them. If anything, the shirt probably looked better on Chloe Donnelly, her bright-blue eyes popping even more from that shade of blue. The Tillys dress likely cost way more too. The jealous part of me that wanted someone to swap clothes with relished how gullible Eve was. Then I felt bad for being a crappy friend.

"Those shirts are pink," I tried, but cringed at how stupid it sounded.

Eve and Chloe Donnelly laughed and I felt even dumber. They were coconspirators now, which explained everything about why I'd been downgraded in Eve's eyes back to "Other Chloe."

Chloe Donnelly did her quick-gaze assessment of me and grinned. "Your legs go on forever. I wish I had legs like yours."

I didn't want to blush, but my cheeks weren't cooperating, same as always. I let my hair fall in front of my face, and Chloe Donnelly laughed and tucked it back behind my ear. Again. "Don't be shy, Other Chloe. Take a compliment already. Girls are the worst with taking compliments. It's a societal problem. We're raised never to expect anything but crumbs, so when someone actually acknowledges us, we're left with an inability to accept it as a true fact."

I laughed and tugged at the skirt I'd picked out to wear that morning. "You sound like my mom." Though my mom would never compliment a girl on her looks. *I'm not perpetuating an attractiveness-based value system. It breeds unnecessary competitiveness between women, who should be building each other up, not tearing each other down.*

Chloe Donnelly nodded. "Good. I hope your mom gives you lots of compliments." And then her face changed as if she'd just realized what she'd said. "I'm sorry. I didn't mean . . ."

I swallowed down the choking feeling I got when any of my friends mentioned my parents in that pitying voice, and shook my head. "No big deal. I heard from my parents last week. They're doing great. There's this program they're implementing at the girls' school—"

"Other Chloe," Eve cut me off. "You're rambling and the bell is about to ring."

I blushed again, but Chloe Donnelly squeezed my hand and whispered, "Tell me the rest at lunch. I'll save you a seat."

Then she and Eve headed down the hall toward their first periods. I watched them until the first bell rang, realizing I hadn't gotten the chance to ask Chloe Donnelly about how she played the game. Instead, I stood puzzling over all the sides of her, the ones I liked and the ones that made me feel out of sorts.

I ended up in a chem study session at lunch, so I didn't see any of my friends until I bumped into Holly in the bathroom between sixth and seventh periods. She was covering up a hickey on her neck, her charm bracelet jingling on her wrist. The hickey was big and dark, like it hadn't been an accident but Cam going to town without giving the first shit. I rolled my eyes and muttered, "Classy."

She put down her cover-up and said, "Jealous much?"

"Of you? No."

For a second she looked hurt, but then she threw back

her shoulders and said, "Yes, you are. Tell me again how many times you've made out with Mateo? What's that? None. Yeah, I thought so."

I inhaled deeply through my nostrils and channeled my mom, saying, "It doesn't have to be like this with us, Holly. I don't have any problems with you."

She shoved her cover-up in her bag and turned to me. "Yes, you do. You hate that Eve is my best friend. You've been horrible and cold to me ever since I started going to school here."

"What? No, I haven't."

"You have."

"I didn't mean to be. . . ."

"Sure you did. You and your perfect parents, who are out saving the world and telling everyone how to live their lives. As if it's all so easy. As if worrying about normal things is beneath you. Eve told me how cool your parents are, how smart and progressive and friendly they are. She envies you so much."

"Me? You think I'm perfect? What are you even . . . ?"

She held up a hand. "Save it, *Other* Chloe. You made your choice when it came to me. But it was stupid to be so clingy and insecure. You didn't want anyone wedging in on your death grip on Eve, and surprise, surprise, she dropped you as soon as she could breathe again. Guess you're not so perfect after all."

"I never said . . ."

"Whatever you seem to think I did to break up you and

Eve, I'd look at yourself first. No one wants to be friends with someone who's so needy they suffocate you."

Then she grabbed her cheap Walmart bag and walked from the bathroom all full of dancer grace, as if she hadn't just stomped on my self-esteem and made me feel greedy and oppressive with Eve. And what was all that stuff about me and my perfect parents? The conversation was overwhelming, leaving me reeling.

I considered going after her, trying to hash it out, but then Chloe Donnelly stepped out of the last bathroom stall and washed her hands. I flinched when I saw her pitying face in the mirror. She dried her hands on her jeans, then turned and tucked my hair behind my ears, saying, "She doesn't know what she's talking about. Don't let her make you doubt yourself. You're a good friend. She's the one who's been suffocating Eve. Do you see how clingy she is with Cam? It's the same with Eve."

"Did you hear what she said about my parents? She doesn't even know them."

Chloe Donnelly tipped her head slightly and then shrugged. "I'm not sure what that was about, but it sounds like a *her* problem, not a *you* problem."

I nodded, but I didn't really believe her. Not when a little part inside of me kept shouting that Holly was right about me and Eve. That I had been needy and insecure, that I'd even given up some of myself because I was afraid to lose Eve as a friend. Would I still be playing the game if Eve hadn't insisted? I wouldn't. I knew I wouldn't, but it didn't matter, because I *was* playing, to hold on to her.

By the time Spanish rolled around, I was itching to talk to Mateo. But when I got to class, Chloe Donnelly was already there in deep conversation with him.

My steps faltered and I paused at the door. Chloe Donnelly looked up, her thin black shirt going see-through with the afternoon sunlight. "Other Chloe," she said. "We were just talking about you."

I caught Mateo's eye and his mouth curved into a rare full smile. A distracting, flustering, beautiful, full smile. The lip ring probably didn't stop him from being a great kisser. Or maybe it only caused him a problem if he kissed someone else with a piercing.

"Do you really have your labia pierced?" I blurted to Chloe Donnelly. "Oh God. Sorry. That was . . ."

Stupid. Inappropriate. Awkward. Humiliating.

Chloe Donnelly cackled. "You are so random! It's excellent and refreshing."

I glanced at Mateo to see if I could read his face, but it was completely expressionless. Did he know about the labia piercing? Did he have firsthand experience with it? Was the thing about easier orgasms actually true? Maybe he didn't even know what a labia was. I probably wouldn't have if my mom hadn't insisted I read Natalie Angier's *Woman: An Intimate Geography* when I was thirteen. Not that I really remembered much more than having a solid grasp of anatomical part names and a near certainty that lots of women book clubs spent a box wine–filled evening talking about the struggles of periods and menopause because of that book.

Before any of us could say anything else, Señor Williams came in, followed by a bunch of students. He told us to move our desks into a large circle for the day's interactive discussion on Latin American literature.

Chloe Donnelly planted herself between me and Mateo, cutting off any chance of me talking to him about what had happened at the game. Señor Williams asked Chloe Donnelly a couple of questions during the discussion that she obviously couldn't answer—what was she doing in such an advanced-level Spanish class?—but she flirted with him to deflect. Flirted! And it seemed to work. I caught Mateo's eye after, and he raised his eyebrows in this way that made my heart want to explode, and made the bottom of my stomach swoop and feel sort of warm. God. I liked him so, so much. But when the end-of-class bell rang, he bolted for the door with nothing more than a quick head nod and wave.

Chloe Donnelly offered a little shrug. "He told you he had baseball practice, didn't he?"

My shoulders slumped. Of course he didn't. But he'd told

her. I only remembered because I'd memorized his schedule. Like a lovesick puppy. I checked my phone. No texts. I looked at Chloe Donnelly, ready to have a conversation with her about how she'd gotten letters at the game, but she'd already gathered up all her stuff. "I'm meeting my mom in Iowa City," she said, with a hint of pity when she glanced at my phone. "But I'll text you later, okay?"

"Sure."

Then I headed to the media center and spent the next two hours doing my homework. When the clock read five thirty, I packed up my gear and headed for the baseball field. Dinner with Nan and Pops was at six thirty every night—right after the first daily airing of *Two and a Half Men*—but I figured I'd have enough time to quickly talk to Mateo and thank him for not giving me up during the game.

Only, when I got to the baseball diamond, the field was empty. Coach Sykes must have ended practice early. My whole body wilted. I shuffled toward the locker rooms, noting a new sliver of nail growing on my pointer finger and thinking maybe I should try growing my nails out. The field house was a ghost town. I shouldered my bag and turned the corner to a rarely used side exit. My breath caught in my throat.

Josh was pinned to a wall and Aiden was kissing him. Seriously kissing him. Their hips were pressed together and Aiden's hands were planted on both sides of Josh against the wall. And Josh was making these little moaning sounds and scraping his fingers along Aiden's lower back as if he was trying to drag Aiden closer.

I gasped, and Aiden must have heard me because he pulled back and turned himself to block Josh from my view. His cheeks were scratchy and red—razor burn?—and his mouth was reddish purple and slick with spit.

"I'm sorry . . . ," I stammered. "I was looking for Mateo. I . . . uh, I don't care that you're gay." Blurt, blurt, blurt. Stupid, stupid, stupid.

Josh's arm reached around Aiden's waist and he buried his face in Aiden's back. I'd wondered about Josh's sexuality more than once, and suspected part of the reason I never saw him with girls was because he wasn't into them. But I knew never to ask him. My parents had drilled into me to keep my questions to myself, and that people should be allowed to talk about their orientation when *they* wanted to.

Aiden scrubbed a hand through his hair, shook his head, and mumbled, "Another fucking Chloe."

Another. Fucking. Chloe.

Suddenly, everything became totally clear. Tumblers on a lock clicking into place in my mind. Chloe Donnelly knew about Aiden and Josh. She knew about them and used it against Aiden. That was her leverage. That was why he'd lost his letter and that was why he was playing again.

"Oh," I said. "No. I wouldn't. . . ."

Aiden let out a disgusted huff. He swiveled to face Josh. "I'm not sure why we're bothering, babe. We should just come clean. It isn't worth this."

Babe. Josh's face softened, and I suspected they'd had this conversation before. Probably not in front of an audience, though. He touched Aiden's cheek in almost exactly the same way Mateo had touched mine. In the same way Cam had touched Holly's. It made me want to help these two, but I didn't really know how.

"No, Aid," Josh said. "You're not going into the Naval Academy as a marked guy. I don't care how progressive they claim to be. You know how things are in the military right now, hell, in half the country. Plebes at the Academy go through hazing, and I'm not going to be responsible for you being inundated with fag jokes and constant harassment. We said we were going to wait. It's a few years. We can suck up anything for a few years."

Aiden looked so sad and defeated. "Maybe I should forget about the Naval Academy. I mean—"

"No." Josh shook his head. "No no no. You've been working your whole life for this. It's what you want."

"You're what I want," Aiden said back, softly, maybe thinking I couldn't hear. Or maybe I was as invisible as I suspected.

I felt gross for interrupting the intimacy of this conversation, and even worse for making them feel like they needed to have it at all. I cleared my throat and said, "I swear I won't say anything. And I wouldn't use it against you in the game. I don't even want to play Gestapo."

Josh gave me a sad smile. "None of us wants to play Gestapo, Chloe. Not anymore. Turns out it's a little more than just a dumb word game."

Chloe. Not *Other Chloe.* Just *Chloe.* I returned Josh's smile, trying to offer a little hope. We all might have been stuck playing the game, but for the first time I didn't feel so alone. I felt like I had allies.

12

When I got to school the next morning, Mateo was sitting on the floor in front of my locker. The light from the windows at the end of the hall created an almost halo around him. I wished I had on a see-through shirt like Chloe Donnelly's instead of the dumb I SPEAK HOCKEY shirt I'd put on this morning. I didn't know why I bothered pretending I still had hockey as an interesting thing about me. I hadn't been on the ice for more than just Open Skate in a few years.

"Hey," he said, pulling himself up and leaning on the locker next to mine. He wore faded jeans and a gray long-sleeved Henley-type shirt stretched across his built chest. "I heard you were looking for me."

Josh must have told him. Did Mateo know about Josh and Aiden? I couldn't imagine it. Even with Mateo and Josh being best friends, it didn't seem like something that would come up at Beau's while they were sitting around waiting to make a delivery run. Mateo wasn't the type to judge, but he also wasn't the type to pry.

"Yeah," I answered. "I was."

"You okay?" he asked.

"You didn't tell the guys my letter at the game," I said. "I gave it to you and you didn't tell them."

He rubbed the back of his neck with his hand. The first thing I ever noticed about Mateo was his hands—strong looking with a few cuts and scars and calluses that he probably got from working, deceptively big for him being only a few inches taller than my own five-five.

"I told you I was trying to help you," he said. "It's a game, Chloe. I'm not about to compromise our friendship for a game."

Friendship sounded like way too inconsequential a word for how I felt about Mateo, but I still was pleased about what he said. About how he wanted to help me.

It was more than a game, of course. If Eve manipulating me into playing again didn't make that obvious, then the look of utter defeat on Aiden's face when I discovered him and Josh certainly did.

"Thanks," I said, then stopped myself from letting my hair fall forward. "It would have been pretty terrible if we'd lost."

He leaned forward the littlest bit, or maybe he was just shifting and I thought it was a lean. "Why? Are you worried about losing that platinum favor? You're so nice, I can't imagine there's much you'd say no to, regardless if it was a platinum favor or not."

My eyes went saucer wide. "There's a *lot* I'd say no to."

Mateo laughed and touched my arm for a second, definitely leaning. "Guys aren't as bad as you think. None of them would ask for something you didn't want to give."

I remembered how Eve had said *slow down* when Cam had his hand up her skirt, then *stop*. Would he have asked her for more if she couldn't say no? I wanted to think the guy who sang "40" with the voice of an angel wouldn't have, but he also tricked her into thinking he was Aiden. Cam might very well ask for something a girl didn't want to give.

Mateo lifted his hand like he was going to touch my face, but then he dropped it and stepped back. "You worry too much, Chloe."

But the low-key tone of his voice didn't match up to his eyes. Chloe Donnelly got *his* letter too. And maybe it was because he didn't care that much. Maybe it really was just a game to him and it didn't cost him anything to give up his letter. But somehow I doubted that was true. I needed to ask Chloe Donnelly to find out for sure.

Melissa McGrill was back in school, sitting by herself at the end of the far right table in the cafeteria. The table by the large garbage can where all the guys tried to slam-dunk their half-eaten lunches. An untouched turkey wrap sat in front of her, and her gaze was locked on the large windows across from her. It was the kind of gray outside that made me feel like going home and binge-watching Netflix under my covers.

I wanted to sit by Melissa, let her know that even if we weren't really friends anymore, she wasn't an outcast. Let her know that I would listen if she wanted to talk. But Eve was behind me in the caf line, and she steered me toward our table on the opposite side of the room.

She slumped down and said, "I am so screwed in English. I have to read six chapters of *Moby-Dick* tonight and write an essay on it. And my mom volunteered me to work the Boosters concession stand at the baseball game."

"What time's the game?" I tried to sound casual, but Eve knew me as well as I knew her.

"JV's first. Mateo isn't playing until five thirty. Which I know you know." She gave me a teasing smile, but then said, "You won't be home for dinner if you want to see the game."

Skipping dinner was a nonoption in Nan and Pops's house, particularly after I'd just missed one. They made a big deal of family dinner. All of us together at one table. Every night. No exceptions unless they were school related, and that didn't include extracurricular activities. I'd originally thought I could convince my parents to go to bat for me in creating some flexibility with that, but Mom sided with Nan and Pops. *Girls get eating disorders because they don't learn good habits like having family dinners.* It was ridiculous logic, plenty of anorexics had faked their way through family dinners just fine, but Mom was unbending.

Holly slid into the spot at our table next to Eve, a salad and cheese fries on her plate. Holly was the strangest eater—subsisting on only Swedish Fish for the week before her dance performances, but then eating platefuls of mac and cheese right after it was finished. It seemed to me that eating healthier overall would be in her best interest as an "athlete," but I was sure she didn't want to hear my opinion on the matter.

"Cam is bailing on having dinner with my mom and sister tonight. Again," she said, instead of *hello*. "This is the third time he's backed out at the last minute. I mean, I've met his parents tons of times, since they're almost always at his house working, but he's never once met anyone in my family."

Eve threw me a *remember your promise* look, as if she hadn't reminded me every chance we were alone together, then turned to Holly. "That sucks, Holls. Did he say why he couldn't make it?"

Holly curled in on herself. "No. He said he had a thing and needed to rain check. My mom was going to make lasagna."

"He's really never met them?" I blurted.

"I just said that, Other Chloe. Keep up."

175

"What about when he dropped you off after church?"

Holly's eyes narrowed. "Were you stalking us?"

"What? No. I saw you after church. I even waved at you. I wasn't stalking you. That's my grandparents' church." I hated that we couldn't even have a regular conversation. I didn't understand what her problem with me was.

Holly's gaze shifted right and then back to me. "My family wasn't around when he dropped me off."

The hitched tone of her voice made me think that there was more but she didn't want to discuss it. It *must* have been tears Cam was wiping off her face after church. But what in the world would Holly have to be upset about? She had *my* former best friend and a good-looking boyfriend—albeit kind of a crappy one.

"Sorry, Holls," Eve said, leaning toward Holly.

Holly looked at Eve's wrist. "Where's your bracelet?"

Eve went guilty red and stammered, "Oh. Crap. I must have forgotten to put it on this morning."

I studied Eve through my hair, watching her shift uneasily. I felt bad for her. She was probably right about her certainty that Holly would get pissy over Cam's bait and switch. Holly was obviously territorial. It sucked. Cam being a douche wasn't Eve's fault. And it was ridiculous she couldn't explain every-thing to Holly. What kind of friend wouldn't understand the girl had been manipulated?

"Maybe he can't come over because of something with his singing," I said to Holly.

"Excuse me?"

"Cam . . . maybe he's singing. I heard him sing at church. I'm surprised you didn't come inside to hear him. He sounded really good. He's got a really good voice."

Holly's eyes narrowed and her nostrils flared. "Cam sang for you?"

I shrugged. "Well, not just for me. For all of us at church. Why doesn't he sing with the school choir? I mean, he could really do something with his talent."

Holly's facial expression got even stormier. I wasn't sure why she was getting so hostile until she said, "Well. I wouldn't know. He's never sung for me before."

"Really?" Chloe Donnelly said, coming up and sliding on the bench beside me. "I heard him in the orchestra room last week. Other Chloe's right, his voice is totally pink. Weird that you've never heard him."

Holly's neck got splotchy, and for a second I thought she was going to implode. But then Eve reached out and squeezed her arm and said, "He's probably too shy to sing in front of you because you really mean something, you know? Your opinion actually matters to him."

It was a dig at both me and Chloe Donnelly, but it was exactly the right thing to placate Holly. She smiled and said,

"Probably. He doesn't even play guitar around me all that often. He gets adorably self-conscious about it."

Cam and *adorably self-conscious* seemed paradoxical, but I wasn't about to say anything. Chloe Donnelly tapped my thigh and rolled her eyes when I glanced at her, but otherwise she didn't say anything either.

Eve smiled. "I'm sure he'll make up dinner to you. If not, you can always have him meet your family as a platinum favor when we win against the guys on Friday."

Holly grinned back at the same time my stomach plummeted into my Converse high-tops. I couldn't believe I'd have to play Gestapo again. I opened my mouth, thinking maybe I should suggest an alternative, but snapped it shut again as I recalled Eve's words: *I've been carrying you for most of this year, going out of my way to make sure you're included.* Chloe Donnelly eyed me as she pulled out her green lunch sack, but she didn't say anything. Instead, she carefully arranged her apple and yogurt and ham sandwich, then started asking Eve how things were going with her *Moby-Dick* paper.

I wanted to bring up the game again, casually ask how she got Mateo's letter, but now that I knew how she got Aiden's, I couldn't. Not in front of Holly and Eve, at least. So I ate my carrot sticks and kept my mouth shut until I could figure out a way to ask her without anyone around.

❀　❀　❀

Spanish was a bust again that day because Chloe Donnelly hijacked me into a conversation about Holly and Cam before I could even say hi to Mateo. *Don't you think it's weird he's never sung for her? . . . Do you think he's one of those guys who "doesn't do" parents? . . . She told me he's only ever seen one of her dance performances, that they spend most of their time alone.* I felt a little gross even as I speculated with Chloe Donnelly, because I worried Mateo would overhear us and think I was gossiping again. Which was also why I couldn't ask her about how she got his letter.

Then Señor Williams put a Spanish film on, which was sadly not an opportunity to talk but rather an opportunity for him to walk around and ensure we were paying attention. My Spanish was solid because my parents had insisted I start lessons with one of the Spanish-major college students when I was five—*Chloe, it's absolute laziness not to master Spanish with forty-one million native speakers in our country*—but films were always hard to follow with all the rapid-fire dialogue. Plus, Señor Williams had an affinity for these bizarre, existential Latin American movies that all seemed to be saying there was no reason to carry on. Maybe that was his act of subversiveness in Iowa.

Mateo bolted right after class with another quick wave, and I headed to my locker with little more than a rushed "I'll text you later" from Chloe Donnelly. The busy halls and usual buzziness of GHS after school felt different today. It was a little like the first time I'd gotten drunk, doing shots in Eve's room the night of her dad's company holiday party while everyone downstairs talked about the state of Iowa's economy and if they'd be able to get out of town for Christmas.

The speed of all the kids in school felt like it had been adjusted slower, and the air was heavy. I thought maybe people were looking at me, but there wasn't really a reason for it. Sometimes it seemed that the whole world was staring at me, and sometimes it seemed like the whole world was staring through me. It was always extreme like that, ever since I left Burkina Faso and returned to GHS, at least. I couldn't find my way back to normal.

I walked past the gym on my way out of school and saw Holly practicing some elaborate dance move for the GHS Dance Team. She didn't look flawless when she was practicing dance. She looked sweaty and out of breath and like she was trying super hard. It was really the only time I liked Holly— when it was obvious that everything didn't come easy for her. Even her lamenting at lunch about Cam bailing on her mom's lasagna made me like her more. I was horrible for wanting her to fail, but her words from the bathroom about me suffocating Eve still stung.

I stepped out of the side entrance and into the parking lot. Eve was leaning into the window of Cam's car. I'd never asked why Cam was the twin who got the car, whether it was because Aiden cost his parents money with all his activities on the road to the Naval Academy and Cam didn't do anything so the least they could do was buy him a car. Or whether Aiden was fine with his brother driving all the time and didn't want his own car. Cam's car was an extension of him, so maybe it was as simple as that. Maybe his parents could see how much he needed it and how much he obsessed over it. A different way out than Aiden's, but still a way out.

Eve pressed her elbows on the rolled-down window and leaned farther in, creating a lesser variation of Holly's boob shelf at Cam's eye level. My feet cemented to the ground. I had no idea what they were talking about, but the creepy feeling from the game slithered up my neck all over again. I forced myself to move and ducked back into the glass double doors at the side entrance. Less than a minute later she'd rounded the hood of his car and was sliding into the passenger seat.

What in the hell did she think she was doing? I couldn't imagine her hooking up with Cam behind Holly's back, but I didn't know what else it could be. Maybe Eve was the "thing" Cam had to do so he couldn't make dinner at Holly's house. Gross. The whole situation made me feel itchy and unsettled.

After the car pulled away, I stepped back out of the side entrance, trying to compartmentalize what I'd just seen, but it wouldn't fit with any explanation I came up with. It didn't fit with the Cam I saw tucking Holly into that same passenger seat after church. And it didn't fit with how scared Eve had sounded when Cam had his hand up her skirt.

Halfway across the parking lot, I paused and looked back at the school. There, in the upper window of the science wing, stood Chloe Donnelly. She held up the hand with all the rings on it, and I waved back, but I couldn't shake the feeling of absolute dread that followed me home.

13

That night, after dinner and *Two and a Half Men* with Nan and Pops, I walked into town to see if Mateo was working at Beau's following his baseball game. It was after nine thirty when I got there, so the place was pretty cleared out, except for two tables shoved together of college students who were in some kind of debate over the dismissal of a professor and the need to diversify the faculty.

Josh was sitting on a stool at the bar alone, counting his tips and evidently waiting for the college students to close out their check. He once told me half the reason he worked at Beau's instead of Pag's was so he could avoid the hassle of the college crowd. Obviously his plan wasn't foolproof. The bartender was nowhere in sight.

"You should work here," he said when I sat on the stool next to him. "You're in here enough."

I blushed and picked at the cuticle on my thumb. "My parents don't want me to work during high school. They think it's too much extra pressure." I didn't mention that they encouraged me to volunteer as much as possible and reminded me there was plenty of work to do in Burkina Faso if I wanted to move back there. I was still stung after Holly's comments about my perfect, progressive parents.

Josh shrugged. "I've figured out working while in school. So has Mateo, and he plays baseball on top of this."

"Yeah. It's dumb. I know. But my parents are sort of hard to argue with."

A soft look crossed his face, and I stuck my thumb in my mouth to chew on the nail. I hated pity so much. Particularly when my parents were doing something good and worthwhile. Pity felt like my constant companion over the past two years.

I grabbed a cocktail napkin and put my nail in it before wadding the thing up and shoving it in my pocket. I pulled out my hand sanitizer and focused on cleaning while I asked as casually as I could, "Mateo didn't come in after his game?"

"No," Josh said, shaking his head and tucking his tips into the pocket of his waiter's apron. "He's not on until tomorrow. But Aiden texted. Varsity won."

Josh's blush and the way his freckles popped gave away the ease with which he said Aiden's name. He didn't used to get flustered mentioning Aiden, but maybe he was embarrassed now because I definitely knew what was up.

"Is it hard having to hide who you love?" I blurted. "I mean . . . not that . . ."

He waved off my stammering. "I know what you meant. And I guess it isn't any harder than watching my family try to hide who I am."

"So they know, and they don't approve?"

"Yeah." He pressed a hand down his shirt to smooth it out, even though it didn't have any wrinkles. "I told my mom when I was pretty young. At first she said it was a phase, but then when she realized it wasn't going away, she started on the Catholic guilt and said all this stuff about what God wants for me. She even considered one of those conversion places, but my siblings didn't want me to leave. When nothing else worked, my parents decided to ignore it."

"Your siblings know too?"

"Not exactly, but they're young. I don't know how to tell them, how to let them know that if they . . . if they want something different for themselves that doesn't fit into Catholicism, it's okay. I walk on a lot of eggshells at home, but I do my best."

"Does that bother you? Always having your parents act like you're not gay?"

"I don't know. I mean, it's better than them actively despising my choice and trying to convert me, I guess."

"It's not a choice," I said, remembering every lecture my parents had ever given me on the matter. *You don't choose who you love, Chloe, any more than you choose your hair color.*

Josh smiled. "I think they assume the choice comes when I act on my feelings instead of trying to make them go away."

"So they know about Aiden?"

He shook his head. "No. My mom might suspect, but I doubt it. Look at him. Nothing about him even hints at him wanting to be with someone like me."

The way he said *someone like me* broke my heart a little. As if maybe he wasn't even worthy of anyone's love, let alone Aiden's. I couldn't imagine growing up in a strict Catholic family in the middle of Iowa and being gay. I wished my parents were around so I could invite him and Aiden for dinner and they could see what parental acceptance looked like. But instead, it was me and Nan and Pops and Fox News. Not exactly a recipe for "embracing the gay."

I shoved my hair behind my ear and looked him in the eye. "I don't know, Josh. I think you're pretty great. I've always thought that. Aiden is lucky to be with you."

"Thanks, Chloe. I think you're pretty great too."

Silence sat between us and Josh eyed the tables of college students, who appeared ready to camp out for the rest of the night.

"I'm going to have to go tell them we're closing soon," he sighed. "I hate having to get into it with the college."

"The college." It was how most of us in town referred to people associated with Grinnell College. As if they all universally were to be tolerated, though most of "the college" was suspect and "too liberal" to be trusted. My parents were outliers, but I always felt a hint of suspicion lobbed at us when I was younger. One of the perks of living with Nan and Pops was being wrapped in a blanket of town acceptance in a way I never had been before with my parents.

Josh's whole tone was a little ironic considering "the college" would be way more accepting of him and Aiden than the majority of our town. "You want me to go tell them to move it along?" I offered.

He shook his head again. "No. I got it. You really should work here, you know. You'd be great. And it'd probably make Mateo happy too."

"Really?" I couldn't help perking up like a needy puppy, but then Josh just shrugged.

"I mean, I guess. I don't know for sure. It's hard to tell things with Mateo. That guy is more closed off than Aiden, and that's saying something. . . ."

"How come he's your friend then?"

His eyebrows went up. "Aiden?"

"No. Mateo."

He pressed his apron flat. "I don't know. He seemed like he needed someone and I have a thing for strays."

Then he crossed to tell the college students they were closing. A chorus of groans and shouts about whose turn it was to buy followed Josh back to the bar.

"I should let you finish up here."

"Yeah," he said. "You want me to tell Mateo you stopped by?"

"No. I already probably look like a stalker. I'll just see him tomorrow."

Josh squeezed my shoulder. "You don't look like a stalker. You look like you care. Keep showing up. He could use someone who cares."

I wondered if Josh knew whatever it was Mateo was hiding. Then I wondered if Mateo was hiding anything at all. Maybe he was one of these what-you-see-is-what-you-get types. Maybe the reason he didn't share a bunch of stuff about himself was that he was pretty basic and didn't have much to share.

"Stop thinking so hard, Chloe," Josh said, walking me to the front entrance. Cars outside slid past, full of high school guys who didn't have anything better to do at night than scoop the loop. Nan said they were all roosters vying for attention from disinterested hens.

"I'm not thinking that hard," I said.

Josh laughed. "Sure, you're not. Look. If you keep trying to dissect Mateo, you'll work yourself into a problem that doesn't exist. Be yourself with him. It's enough. And one good thing about Gestapo is it'll give you another chance to hang out with each other."

"Oh." My dumb cheeks heated again. "Did he tell you about the last game?"

Josh pulled the door open. "Yeah. He mentioned you gave him your letter, but that it was sort of an accident and he didn't mean to get it. Don't worry, I won't tell Chloe. Or Cam."

The mention of Cam's name brought the image of Eve slipping into the passenger seat of his VW back into my mind. Did Josh know what was going on with that?

"Do you like Cam?" I blurted.

He lifted a shoulder. "He's my boyfriend's brother."

Not exactly an answer. "Does he know about you?"

Josh looked down. "I'm not sure. I haven't asked Aiden."

It seemed weird that they wouldn't have talked about that, but then I had no idea even how much time they got to spend together. If all they got were furtive kisses outside the base-ball locker room. Josh worked and had five siblings, and Aiden played baseball and did whatever he needed to be ready for the Naval Academy, and I didn't think the two of them could pull off a lot of alone time at either of their houses.

"I think Cam—" I started, but he held up a hand and shook his head.

"I know absolutely nothing about Cam and I don't really want to."

"Nothing?"

Josh looked back at the table of college students, arguing about the breakdown of the check, and sighed. "Aiden doesn't talk about him and whenever I even say his name, I get hostile one-word answers. They are *nothing* alike. I mean, could you imagine Aiden passing out safety condoms?"

"Definitely not."

"For whatever reason, there is no love lost between those two. I feel weird even talking about him with you. Like I'm betraying Aiden."

Josh evidently didn't like gossip either. I should have been happy he'd admitted anything about Cam, but my dumb mouth couldn't help blurting, "Do you think Cam pressured Aiden to play again after the practice round? It seemed like he did."

"Maybe. I mean, it was fun the first time. And Aiden got those Rice Krispies Treats, but this game . . . not really his thing."

"So whatever Cam mumbled that night was . . . ?"

Josh blushed. "Okay. I wasn't going to say this, but I don't want you to keep poking or say anything to Cam. Aiden didn't spell it out to me completely, but it's possible I forgot to clear the history from their computer one day and Cam stumbled onto some websites I'd been checking out."

His cheeks burned even redder, and mine probably

matched them. Even thinking about Josh surfing the twins' computer for the no doubt copious amounts of gay porn available on the internet made me want to bolt out the door. I mumbled, "Oh. Okay then, yeah, that might explain it. So . . . um, I guess I'll see you."

"See you Friday, Chloe." And the embarrassment I'd been feeling switched to dread. Friday. The next time we were going to play Gestapo.

"Yeah. See you," I choked out.

I was half a block away with my head down when I bumped into Melissa McGrill. She looked tired, but not wrecked. All in all, she seemed okay. Part of me wanted to hug her, but I knew that would end up being awkward.

"Hey," I said.

"Were you just at Beau's?" she asked.

"Yeah."

"Still think it's better than Pag's?"

"Totally. Who cares about breadsticks. The crust is better at Beau's."

"You're wrong, but I know there's no arguing. That place . . ." She let out a soft laugh. A truck honked and three guys screamed out the window, but whatever they said was lost in the breeze.

I shifted between feet, wondering what to say, but Melissa surprised me and spoke again. "Remember when we were in first grade and you got yelled at by the hostess?

Your mom freaked out at her and made the manager write her up."

I squeezed my eyes shut and wanted to die. I couldn't believe she remembered that. When I was little, I used to rub up against the edges of tables and the sides of furniture because it felt good. I called it "tickling myself" and Mom told me it was natural for girls to want their private parts—vulvas!—to feel good. She never stopped me or told me there was anything wrong with it. But people sometimes gave me weird looks when I did it in public, and then the hostess at Beau's told me I needed to "stop masturbating because it's making the other customers uncomfortable," and my mom lost it on her. It was the first time I realized how different my parents were from most people in town. How different I was too.

"Yeah," I choked out. "Thanks for bringing up that exercise in humiliation."

Melissa smiled. "Oh, Chloe, it was forever ago and it wasn't a big deal. Your mom was pretty fierce. I remember wishing she were my mom."

"Nuh-uh. You totally had the superior mom with stuff like that. Your mom would have quietly told me that we do these things in private, not in public, instead of letting everyone in the restaurant know I'd found my clitoris as a six-year-old."

Melissa laughed, then said, "No. My mom would've told you to stop doing it."

I thought about that and then shrugged. "Maybe."

"No, she would have. She would've been embarrassed. Your mom has never been embarrassed about you. Even when you were humping tables."

We both snorted laughter then, because what else could I do? I was kind of pervy as a kid, or at least pretty interested in my vulva, until my mom basically ruined it all.

"Are you heading there now? Beau's? Because they're closing soon, you know. They aren't open as late as Pag's."

She glanced at the restaurant behind me. "Yeah, I know. I'm just picking up. I'm running kind of late because I got a phone call. . . ."

It was an opening, though an opening for what, I didn't know. Was I supposed to ask who she was talking to? We weren't friends like that anymore, I didn't think. We were people who shared memories. But I wasn't completely sure who she was friends with. Freshman and sophomore year, she'd played soccer and mostly hung out with teammates. But this year she'd given it up, and I rarely saw her with anyone who went to our school. What would my life be like if I started hanging out with the girl who miscarried in gym class? The impact on my social status was a dumb thing to worry about, and I knew my mom would be disappointed in me, but she hadn't had to deal with watching her best friend turn away from her for someone else, someone who didn't bite her nails and blurt and live with her grandparents because her mom couldn't handle it in Grinnell.

So instead of taking Melissa's opening, I said, "Well, I'll let you go. It was good seeing you." Then I took off before she even had a chance to say good-bye.

Thursday night, Chloe Donnelly invited herself over for dinner and to "help" with my Friday night wardrobe. I thought her arty Chicago attire would put off Nan and Pops, but she showed up in jeans and a long-sleeved shirt with no rings on her left hand.

Then she talked to Pops about decentralizing the federal government and told Nan her meat loaf was the best she'd ever eaten, asking for the recipe and describing the Ina Garten variation she'd tried that was also delicious but took too long to make. I blinked in surprise. What seventeen-year-old knew about this stuff? She acted like she obsessively watched the Food Network and listened to conservative talk radio.

Chloe Donnelly crossed and uncrossed her legs so many times during the meal I decided there was no way she could have her labia pierced. I stopped myself from asking for confirmation—thank God—but I felt better chalking it all up to the Grinnell rumor mill.

After dinner she helped with the dishes. Nan beamed as if this new Chloe was exactly the kind of Chloe she'd been hoping for all along. I was stacking up reasons to resent Chloe

Donnelly—not the least of which was her using Aiden and Josh's relationship to her advantage in the game—but then she told Nan, "I'm lucky to have a friend like your granddaughter. She's been so sweet since I moved here. It's been hard and lonely with my parents adjusting to their new positions, and I'm so grateful to Chloe."

Nan said, "Oh. That's so nice to hear. We're doing our best by her while her parents are gone for so long."

Chloe Donnelly nodded. "I can tell. She talks about you all the time and how much you mean to her."

She seemed to be spreading it on awfully thick, but then she said, "Would it bother you if she slept over at my house tomorrow night? My parents will be out late at this Des Moines GOP fundraiser my dad is helping with, and I hate being alone."

Apparently, *GOP fundraiser* was the golden ticket into dismantling Nan's hard-and-fast no-sleepovers policy. And I knew it was a total lie after Chloe Donnelly had told me about her parents' liberal politics, but she'd said it with so much conviction I wanted to give her an Oscar. Nan *hmm*ed for a minute, glancing at Pops, and then they crumbled. I didn't even know if I wanted to stay at Chloe Donnelly's house after the game, but that she'd turned it into a viable option with my grandparents was amazing. When I'd first moved in, I'd begged for months to have sleepovers with Eve, then later with Eve and Holly, but they'd never agreed, and I always felt like it made me look even weirder, more of an outsider.

When we got to my bedroom/guest room, I sat on the bed while Chloe Donnelly went right to the closet, pushing aside Nan's ironed tablecloths to look through my clothes. She pulled out things that were ridiculously fancy and totally unworkable for a Friday night game of Gestapo.

She held a deep-purple dress up to her that made her eyes go even brighter, and made me want to drown in my hair curtain, humiliated by how plain I was. She tossed the dress at me, saying, "You should wear that tomorrow."

"It's my confirmation dress. I'm not wearing this to hide in trees."

"Other Chloe"—back to *Other*, even though I'd been *Chloe* throughout dinner—"you aren't going to hide in the trees this time. You're going to play offense, like you did during the practice game. I'll bet your legs look totally pink in that dress."

Maybe this girl *liked* me, liked me. What with all the touching and the leg talk. But then that was dumb. I flushed, then braced myself for the question that had been burning in my gut all week, and blurted, "How did you get Mateo's letter?"

She lifted a shoulder, then went back to riffling through the closet. "I asked him for it, same as I did in the practice game."

"Nuh-uh."

"Yeah. It wasn't even hard. He saw me and gave it to me, like he didn't even care. I think he was more interested in finding you."

"Really?"

She lifted her shoulder again. Everything Chloe Donnelly did looked like she'd practiced it. Was I supposed to practice gestures? Maybe working on things like that would make me confident like Chloe Donnelly. "Yeah. At least I think he was. I mean, he wasn't bothered about giving me his letter. Just sort of . . . distracted and anxious to leave."

So Mateo *was* easygoing and unconcerned about the game. I'd read his initial hesitation and questioning looks at me all wrong. He *did* only see it as a game and didn't really care about losing his letter. It explained a lot, but it also made me realize he didn't know anything about how Chloe Donnelly had gotten Aiden's letter.

"What about the platinum favor?" I asked. "He didn't care about that, either?"

She waggled her eyebrows. "Maybe he doesn't *want* to say no to you."

The idea was a flare gun of excitement to my stomach. "You think?"

She turned back to me. "Definitely. You should be the one getting his letter this time. And leggings and a big T-shirt aren't going to get you there. I bet you could sleep over at his house after. I mean, my place is fine, but it's not Mateo's. If you play the game right, he'll ask you over. And I just got you a free pass from your grandparents."

"Sleep over at *his* house?"

"Sure, we used to have coed sleepovers in Chicago all the time."

"I don't want to use sex to play the game," I blurted. Again. God.

Chloe's eyebrows shot up, and I thought maybe she should use a little less pencil on them, but I didn't say anything. "Are you a virgin?"

I shoved my pinkie in my mouth and shrugged noncommittally.

"Oh my God. You are. Really?"

I spit out part of the nail, not even caring how gross that was. "Who cares? It's not a contest. I . . . well, there could be some pretty serious consequences to sex. Look at Melissa. And it seems dumb to make that kind of commitment with someone I don't like just to get it over with."

"You haven't liked anyone but Mateo? Even before he came to Grinnell? You didn't have a crush on anyone last year or anything?"

"No." I'd lived vicariously through Eve's Aiden crush and actively tried not to like anyone. High school relationships seemed like a hassle I wasn't ready for. And it wasn't like every-thing Holly had been describing to me and Eve for the past year was a big selling point.

"Why not? You're so pretty. Surely guys have been all over you."

I flushed again. Mom always said pretty was a bullshit compliment, but no one called me pretty, unless it was Nan telling me how pretty I *could* be if only I wore better clothes.

"I'm not pretty."

"I've seen guys checking you out. You're pretty, and I'm sure at least a few have hit you up."

I couldn't tell her about being afraid. I couldn't tell her how my mom's brand of sex education coupled with her miscarriage made the cost of being with a guy too high. Until Mateo. "I don't know. I guess there weren't really any I thought would be worth the drama."

"So you really haven't had sex?"

"No. I really haven't."

For a little while during freshman year, I thought *maybe* I'd just get it over with. But when I'd gotten really drunk with Eve at a party that spring, I hadn't been able to follow the GHS wide receiver up the stairs. He'd had his hands all over me and whisper-slurred it wouldn't hurt *too much* and I knew I should've just gone with him upstairs, but I couldn't. Not without thinking about my mom in bed for weeks after her miscarriage, sobbing and calling for my grandparents or my dad to deal with me.

"I haven't ever had sex," I repeated, stronger now, less embarrassed.

"Have you ever had an orgasm?"

I blinked. This girl went right for it, not blurting, but more as if she had a right to know. I swallowed too much spit in my mouth and said, "I don't know. Maybe. But I think it was accidental."

"How do you have an accidental orgasm?"

I sat on my hands and stared at my feet, blinking, blinking, blinking, then said, "I don't know. I mean, haven't you sometimes been washing down there or had a loofah or whatever and sort of rubbed yourself enough that you got a little warm and tingly?"

God, I was calling it *down there*. My mom would be so salty about how shy I was being, but come on, I didn't have much to go on when it came to girl talk and orgasms. Holly always sounded like she was lying, and Eve had as little experience as I did, or at least I'd thought she had until I found out about the spring break thing.

Chloe Donnelly laughed and I felt as humiliated as I had when my mom called out that hostess at Beau's. "Um, no, my hot button clearly is defective if you can get yourself off with a loofah. But good for you."

I took a deep breath and sat up straight like I was doing the mountain pose in one of my mom's yoga videos. "I've never had an orgasm with someone else, and that's fine. I'm seventeen."

Chloe Donnelly studied me for a long time, her thumb twisting the single ring she'd kept on her right hand. Finally, she shrugged. "Whatever. You don't have to use sex to play the game."

I almost blurted that Cam did, that sex was the only thing I had if I was playing offense, because I didn't want to use secrets and I didn't know how to win a platinum favor otherwise. That rock-paper-scissors best-out-of-three wasn't going to position me into an unconditional yes from Mateo, not with the guys' team playing to win. And now I wasn't even sure I wanted an unconditional yes from Mateo anymore.

But it was too many words and they clogged in my throat, especially with the echo of Chloe Donnelly's laughter at my expense still ringing in the room. I didn't trust her, even if we were on the same team. For all her attention—and kindness—to me, I couldn't shake the broken sound of Aiden's voice when I'd discovered him and he'd said, *Another fucking Chloe.*

I wondered if I was being immature. If Chloe Donnelly using Aiden and Josh's secret wasn't that big of a deal, if maybe it really was just about the game and never something she'd hurt them with. I'd spent too much of the year stressing over Eve and was probably making a bigger deal of everything

Chloe Donnelly said and did than I needed to. But I felt the weight of our town on my shoulders, and knew that "outing" Aiden or Josh could leave them exposed and unsafe. Secrets were not something anyone should play with, particularly in a game called Gestapo. Everyone should be able to see this. So why was I too afraid to say it?

I cleared my throat. "If you don't expect me to use sex to play, why do you keep pulling out dresses and talking about my legs as if they're an invaluable asset?"

Chloe Donnelly crossed to my bed and sat next to me, taking my hand in hers so I felt the purple stone on her ring. "Other Chloe," she sighed. "The game is a device to get what you want. It strips away all the things people are hiding and leaves everyone honest. Think about you and Mateo. You've been crushing on him for a year and nothing has happened, but after Friday night's Gestapo, suddenly things are different between you two."

"How do you know?" I pulled my hand from hers, fisting it to keep from chewing on my nails when she sat so close to me.

"Because I've seen you. I've seen *him*. Something changed and it was because of the game. So why not use Gestapo as an opportunity to figure out what you want and how to get it?"

"Is that what you're doing?"

"Of course. I'm new and the game helps me be less alone because I get to know people. Especially you girls."

It was a little weird how she said *girls* like we were her

children, but there was truth in her words, a starkness that made me certain that she'd been lying about her abundance of friends in Chicago. That maybe why I was drawn to her was the same reason she'd been drawn to me—loneliness.

"I . . ."

She stood. "Trust me. People don't want to pretend and hide who they really are. They don't. They're just stuck most of the time. They love this game because it allows them access to everything they've ever hoped for, everything they've dreamed of. That's why I love it. It's fun."

I wanted to roll my eyes at her dumb line about accessing dreams—it sounded like a commercial for a cruise to the Caribbean—but I couldn't help thinking about the chance to kiss Mateo, the chance to go out with him, the chance to be his girlfriend, all with just one platinum favor. *Will you walk me home every day? Will you text me when you're falling asleep? Will you answer when I call? Will you ask me to stay in Grinnell?*

I looked at my feet, letting my hair fall and taking a few deep breaths. Finally, I said, "I'm not wearing my confirmation dress, but I'll consider wearing a skirt."

Chloe Donnelly smiled wide and pulled me off the bed, wrapping her arms around me in a slightly too-tight hug. "You're going to be unstoppable tomorrow night. It will be so pink. Wait and see."

14

Señor Williams sent us to the media center to do research for our upcoming oral reports on Friday afternoon. He assigned us to tables, and even though Chloe Donnelly stood next to Mateo like she assumed they'd be together, Señor Williams put her with a girl with a pixie cut and large eyes who also couldn't speak Spanish nearly as well as the rest of us. Chloe Donnelly huffed, but Señor Williams crossed his arms and said, "¡Ni modo!"

Then he pointed me and Mateo to a table near the windows. Me and Mateo. For a second I thought I saw Señor Williams give me a wink, but I couldn't be sure. I felt ridiculously giddy and I couldn't really express why. Maybe Chloe Donnelly was right. Maybe something big had changed between us.

"What are you going to do your research on?" Mateo asked, when I'd dropped my bag and sat across from him.

"Glaciar Perito Moreno and how it's able to maintain equilibrium with its icebergs in spite of climate change," I said.

He laughed in this startled way. "Ambitious project."

"I know. And I'm not even sure how I'm going to pull it off in Spanish, but it's an area of interest for me. I mean, my dad got me into environmental stuff."

"Oh yeah?"

I nodded. "Yeah, a little. He majored in biology with an environmental studies concentration at the college."

Mateo looked at me but didn't say anything. So I said, "What's your dad do?"

I immediately saw the shutters drop over his eyes. He shrugged. "He works on a farm." Then he stood and moved toward the computers. Stupid, stupid, stupid. Hadn't I learned by now that Mateo didn't like invasive questions?

I sighed and dragged myself to the computers, pulling a list of books to check out on climate and the Argentinian glacier. When I returned to the table, Mateo didn't even look up from the book he was reading. I sat and mumbled, "Sorry."

He glanced up. "I'm not really a sharer. It's not you. My family is complicated, and mostly I feel like people who ask about them are digging."

"Digging for what?"

"You tell me."

My pits got sweaty and I was certain my cheeks were all

pink. Was I digging, or was I just trying to be nice? I thought it was being nice, but maybe it read as nosy. "You don't have to tell me anything about your family."

"Okay."

Then I opened my book and we didn't say anything to each other for the next twenty minutes, though every once in a while our eyes met and I smiled a little. Chloe Donnelly kept looking at the two of us, but she must have figured out there was nothing to see, because she asked for a pass to the bathroom and then disappeared. As the end of class neared, I saw her standing outside the media center door staring at Mateo in this way that made me think she liked him as more than a friend. But how could that even be after she'd helped me pick out clothes for him? Her gaze turned to me and it looked both lost and envious, like she wanted something from me she wasn't getting. But then her expression dropped into a sly grin, fake and a little jaded and too old for anyone from high school. She tipped her head at me and then took off down the hall, evidently not worried about bailing on Spanish for the rest of class.

The bell rang and I got all flustered and beelined out without saying good-bye to Mateo. I bumped into Aiden standing outside the door of the media center.

"Mateo in there?" he asked.

"Yeah. He's putting books away."

Aiden pocketed his phone. "Okay."

I studied him and he seemed to stand a bit taller. I wanted to say something about him and Josh, but I couldn't. I didn't know Aiden that well, and he wasn't warm like Josh. He was serious and somber.

"You guys have practice, huh?" I asked, trying to linger so maybe I could see Mateo and diffuse the weirdness that my invasive question and abrupt departure had created between us. Why couldn't I have tried to patch things up earlier, apologized for my nosiness?

"Yep," Aiden said.

"Then we all play the game tonight," I said, and my voice definitely sounded a little pathetic. His expression went angry.

"Gestapo," he practically snarled. So maybe I wasn't the only one who felt horrible. "The game is called Gestapo."

"I wish . . . ," I started, wondering if I could tell Aiden how sorry I was, how it was stupid to play, how I thought it was gross too and had from the first, and maybe there was a way out of it, but Mateo exited the media center before my words could form.

"Did you need something, Chloe?" Mateo said, and there was no warmth there. He was a closed book, and part of me wanted to scream in frustration. We hadn't taken a step closer, like Chloe Donnelly said. It was exactly the same as we'd been all year, with him being guarded and mistrustful and me being nosy and bumbling.

"No," I choked out. "Just wanted to say sorry again. I'll see you."

Then I turned on the heels of my Converse and left. I wanted him to call me back. I wanted him to catch up to me and maybe tell me he was being illogical and suspicious. But then I didn't know if he had a reason to be. Chloe Donnelly said he'd just given her his letter, but I couldn't really believe it now. Unless giving her a letter was easier than answering any personal questions.

I spotted Eve talking to our English teacher. She had tears in her eyes, but Mr. Meyers didn't seem to be in a forgiving mood for whatever she was asking for. Eve's shoulders slumped and she walked away. I considered catching up to her, but I stopped myself. I didn't want to fix something for Eve right now. I couldn't even fix my own life.

I turned to the right at the end of the hall and couldn't stop glancing back to where Mateo and Aiden still stood talking outside the media center. Mateo looked at me and the expression on his face seemed to be asking me a question. I had no idea what the question was, but I tried to put everything I felt on my own face so that he understood whatever he asked, I would answer yes. He didn't even blink, just led Aiden in the opposite direction.

When I turned the corner feeling like the saddest sack in the world, I saw Melissa McGrill at her locker tossing books into it with way more force than was necessary. A pang of guilt crept up my back. I should've walked with her to Beau's that night, kept her company on the way home, asked her if I could do something for her, but I'd chickened out. I always chickened out.

I stopped a few feet away from her and said, "Everything okay?"

She turned. No smile for me today. "Yep. I hate this school."

I laughed. "That bad?"

"It's like no one has anything better to do than gossip or talk about other people."

I nodded, and she stopped her book throwing to say, "They talk about you too, you know."

I opened my mouth to ask what they said, but the soft voice of my mom filtered into my head. *Chloe, don't spend your time on people who won't discuss things with you to your face. Don't give them that kind of power over you.* I shoved my finger into my mouth and shrugged.

Melissa laughed and it was as if suddenly her bad mood lifted. "Don't ever change, Chloe." Then she grabbed her hoodie, slammed her locker shut, and took off with a wave over her shoulder, not bringing one book home with her.

15

My legs were covered with goose bumps and I was shivering as I walked toward Burling Library on Friday night. We'd started earlier tonight so the temperature would be warm from the day still, but April had gotten cold again, and I didn't know whether I should curse Mother Nature or Chloe Donnelly for the fact that I was freezing my butt off.

Eve rushed over and hugged me when I arrived. She had on the see-through shirt again and a super-short mini that looked more like a cheer skirt than something to wear for a night out. She must have been even colder than I was. She smelled like curry, and I knew her mom had been experimenting with what she called Iowa-Indian fusion for dinner again. "I thought you were going to bail," Eve whispered, like she hadn't blackmailed me into playing again.

I was late because I'd lingered outside of Melissa McGrill's house, hoping by some miracle she'd come out and save me from the game, that these half conversations we'd been having could turn into something more and I wouldn't care about Gestapo or any of this. As if she had that kind of power. As if she had any power now that rumors were flying that she'd intentionally caused the miscarriage, something I'd heard after she'd taken off today.

I'd stood on the sidewalk of High Street for ten minutes, but she didn't come outside. It was barely sixty degrees, hardly a night for hanging out on the front porch. And though I knew all I had to do was walk twenty feet to her front door and she'd probably let me in, I couldn't do it.

"Sorry I'm late," I said, loud enough for everyone to hear.

Chloe Donnelly eyed my outfit and smiled. She had on a long-sleeved shirt and a just-above-the-knees flowy skirt with bobby socks and Converse low tops. Weird, but it worked on her. I, on the other hand, felt naked. "You look ready," she said with approval.

I glanced at Mateo and saw his lip piercing shift up with his half smile. The air gushed out of me. One look and I knew he forgave my nosiness. Whatever had happened in Spanish class today, he understood that I wasn't trying to hurt him. We were okay.

His lip ring had two silver balls on it, which was different.

Was that how guys got "ready" for someone they were interested in: switching piercings? Did he think about his THIS IS THE END T-shirt when he put it on tonight? I hoped it all meant what I thought it did, but maybe I was projecting. I felt dumb suddenly for wasting so much time wardrobe scheming with Chloe Donnelly. It didn't matter now. I was ready. Or as ready as I could be.

"So," Chloe Donnelly said, spreading her ring-covered fingers wide. "Same rules apply. I'll be captain of the girls. Cam?"

Cam stepped forward and grabbed Holly around the waist, draping his arms around her and tucking her into him. "Yeah. I'll be the captain for the guys."

I thought he was going to pass out safety condoms again, but instead, he slipped his hands under Holly's shirt to encircle her hips. She blushed as if being manhandled in front of everyone was the most charming thing in the world. I remembered what she'd said in the bathroom, about being new and how she thought I'd been cold to her, and then she accused me and my parents of being perfect. It made me wonder about Holly, about how hard she was trying to fit in and be liked too. Maybe it was what we were all after.

I glanced at Eve and saw her cross to Aiden's side. Her too-short skirt popped up with each step, but at least she was wearing Converse instead of platforms. Same color Converse as Chloe Donnelly. Though her BEST FRIENDS charm bracelet was back on her wrist. Eve leaned in to Aiden, and because I was studying his expression, I was probably the only one who saw the flinch. I shifted my gaze to Josh, and his nostrils flared a little like he was smelling wet-dog burritos. Maybe I wasn't the only one who'd noticed the flinch.

"Aiden," Eve said, pulling out her most seriously flirty voice. "Don't hide so well this time. I was so bummed not to find you again last Friday."

Her words sounded forced and awkward, and for a second I couldn't believe we'd ever been best friends. But then I remembered how she'd taken me home after that drunk wide receiver got pissed I wouldn't have sex with him freshman year, and covered for me with my parents—who later told me they knew I was wasted but felt I was *exploring my own adolescent rebellion in a healthy way*, which translated to: *We're planning for the Spirit Corps and can't be bothered*—and I knew the version of Eve hanging on Aiden was really just as scared and insecure as me. I wished we could admit that stuff to each other like we used to.

Aiden fake-laughed and said, "Yeah, sorry, Eve. It's too bad you had to deal with my brother instead. I heard you offered him treats too."

It was like dropping a flare in the middle of a dark forest. Eve stepped back. Cam snorted. Holly looked confused. And Josh grinned. But when Aiden caught my eye, my feelings must have shown on my face, because he looked immediately repentant. He may have been an ambitious guy who was hiding a secret that could compromise his future with the Naval Academy, but I'd never heard him be outright cruel before.

"Well," Chloe Donnelly said, dousing the flare and directing attention back to her by strumming her ring-covered fingers on her thigh. "Hopefully tonight someone will actually win the platinum favor. It's sort of a waste if no one wins. So let's huddle up, girls. I have your letters."

She held a folded slip of paper up and tucked it in her bra strap with a giggled "oops, no pockets." Then, she pulled each of us to the left of the library entrance, ducking into the shadows to whisper in our ears. When she said, "*E*," in my ear, I started to walk away, but she pulled me back toward her. "Don't forget what I said. Go get what you want."

Mateo was too far away for me to see his face, but it almost felt like his gaze was on me. I let my hair curtain drop, and Chloe Donnelly laughed. "Good luck, Other Chloe."

When Cam had his word in his back pocket and everyone had their letter, Chloe Donnelly told the guys to give us a five-minute head start again. "We'll meet back here at ten. My parents took my cell phone because I got a D on my first English paper, so no one can text me, but I promise I'll be here at ten, grinning pink with the rest of my winning team."

Her parents took her cell but let her go out? I hadn't ever

been to her place, so I didn't really have any idea what they were like, but it seemed like screwed-up logic. Though maybe Chloe Donnelly got a lot more use out of her phone than I did. And what did "grinning pink" mean? I kept grasping to get myself onto Chloe Donnelly's level, but I was constantly reminded how out of my league she was. Did she really tell Eve we were best friends?

The girls broke off, and I followed Holly and Eve toward the academic buildings, not wanting to venture out on my own, until Holly turned and glared. "Do you mind, Other Chloe? It's a little hard to play when we've got a creepy shadow hovering around."

Eve gave me a look of pity but didn't say anything. I shook my head, anger pulling my shoulders back and making me want to lash out, but instead, I turned in the opposite direction, heading for the train tracks.

I walked up and down the tracks for twenty minutes, equally hopeful and terrified someone would see me. Trains rarely came through Grinnell, so I wasn't worried about getting hurt. When they did come through, they were freights that moved at a snail's pace and caused everyone in town to stop and watch them. My dad told me he knew a guy when he went to college there who used to hop the freights and travel all over the country hitching rides on various trains. I couldn't imagine having the courage to hop onto one even once.

I bit one of my nails to take my focus off how cold I was getting, but after a while, even that didn't help. I needed to warm up somewhere, whether it was against Gestapo rules or not. No way could I last till ten standing outside dressed like I was. I headed along Eighth to the entrance of JRC. At least maybe there I could blend in.

Two steps into the building and I spotted Holly sitting at one of the tables. She stood and walked toward me, all dancer graceful even with her face looking mean like it did.

"You're not supposed to be inside," I blurted.

"Well, no one would even know if you weren't stalking me."

"I'm not stalking you."

She folded her arms, staring at me as if I were twice-baked garbage on a plate and she'd just eaten a four-star buffet. "Then why are you here?"

"I got cold."

She huffed. "Not here, here. Here . . ." She arced her arm in a wide circle. "Playing the game with us. We could find a way better girl for our team than you. I told Eve she should've dropped you from the start. You're a gross third wheel that brings down all of our worth."

My mom always told me that anger and venom—particularly from other girls—were usually rooted in insecurity. That I needed to approach an angry girl with compassion because I had no idea what she was going through and hadn't walked in her shoes. But Holly's words felt like a body blow, and I couldn't muster up an ounce of compassion.

"What happened to all your accusations about me and my perfect parents?"

She practically sneered. "Perfectly boring and a big fake. You don't fool me, Other Chloe. You're plain and uninteresting and a cling-on."

Holly had always been little more than a notch above horrible to me, but this was worse. She was off the rails, and I wasn't completely sure why all that rage was directed at me.

And she kept going. No end in sight. "You're Eve's pity project and it's about time she shook you off and realized what a lost cause you are."

The truth of her words burned through me. I snapped, "Oh, really? You told your *best friend* Eve that I was a lost cause and to ditch me? The same Eve who had her tongue in Cam's mouth during the last game? The same Eve who took off with him after school on Tuesday? *That* best friend? You know what? You two deserve each other."

Then I slammed out of the JRC and into the freezing night air, which felt colder and even more biting after being inside. I ran toward the North Campus dorms, pulling oxygen into my lungs and kicking myself for lashing out like that. I usually was so much more patient and tolerant of Holly. Even when she was being catty, I tried to remember when she started at our

217

school and wasn't so horrible, when she was obviously insecure and messed up about her parents' divorce or whatever it was that made her treat me so terribly. But she had never been so blatantly harsh to me before, and all Mom's "insecure girl" platitudes didn't work when I was pushed against a wall of cruelty. I kicked myself for letting her get to me. I knew I was on edge and should've considered the fallout of my words. Crap. Crap, crap, crap.

I needed to find Eve. I needed to throw myself on the altar of our past friendship and apologize for what I'd told Holly and explain how it'd been an accident. A blurt.

I pulled out my phone and texted her. Where are you? I need to talk to you.

Then I waited, staring at the unanswered text. *Another* unanswered text to her. Just like spring break. Maybe it served her right if Holly found her first and blindsided her. But that was an ugly, horrible thought. That was the game talking, not me.

I headed back toward South Campus, staying visible beneath the sidewalk lights, not worried if anyone would see me. Sort of hoping someone would and whoever it was knew where Eve was.

A girl and a guy were walking—stumbling—toward one of the dorms.

"Where did you say your room was again?" she said—slurred.

218

The guy laughed. "James, honey. James. Like my name." He laughed again. "Oh, Jesus, we started drinking too early and are way too wasted already to be doing this." Then they both laughed and stumbled into the loggia.

I texted Eve again. Hello? Where are you?

No answer. A dozen different scenarios played out in my mind. Maybe she was with Cam again. Maybe Holly had already texted her and found her. Maybe she was with Chloe Donnelly. Maybe she'd found Mateo.

My feet froze as if they were controlled by someone else. Would Eve do something with Mateo? No. *No.* I was being ridiculous. Paranoid. She wouldn't look for him. She knew how I felt about him. She was the one who pointed him out to me in the beginning of the year. *He seems like good boyfriend material for you, Chloe.* She'd said it like she meant it, before Holly had totally poisoned her against me.

I started walking again, staring at my phone. I headed back toward the library. My heart jackhammered in my chest, and I wished I had a Jack Daniel's syringe to make all of this go away. Where was Eve?

I crossed over from the library to near where the old bookstore used to be, frustration and worry rolling off me, making me forget about the cold. How many minutes had it been since I'd seen Holly—ten, fifteen? I stepped out of the shadows and into the light from the street lamp, and felt a hand on my shoulder. I spun and screamed at the same time, but the sound died in my throat.

Mateo. *Mateo Mateo Mateo Mateo.* I collapsed into his chest and he wrapped both arms around me. Tight.

"Whoa, Chloe, what's going on?"

16

"Oh, Mateo, this is such a mess."

"What is?" he asked, arms still banded around me like I might fly away if he let go. Like he actually cared and wanted me to know it.

I peeked up at him, his face serious with concern. "I've screwed everything up. I don't know if it's the game or me, but so much has gotten out of hand."

He touched my hair and shifted my head to look at him. He was so beautiful. All those words I'd thought were dumb and overdramatic when describing guys poured into my brain: soulful, intense, protective. God, my stupid brain could *not* be reasonable around him. And he still held on to my hair. It had to be a move; I knew better than to think it was real because what guy actually gripped a girl by the hair, but I liked it. I wanted to sniff him and lick him and do dirty things I'd never considered before. Things that had scared the crap out of me when Holly mentioned them or when Mom had gone all scientific in describing the mechanics of them to me when I was younger. The longer Mateo stared at me, the more my stomach muscles got tight and my legs squeezed together and I wanted to squirm, closer or farther away, I wasn't sure.

"It's the game," he whispered, his low voice seeped in defeat. His Adam's apple bobbed as if he had something stuck in his throat. He swallowed and I waited for him to explain, but he just said, "Come on."

He let go of my hair, probably realizing it was a bit much too, and pulled me toward the benches by the academic buildings.

"How did Chloe Donnelly get your letter? Was it sex stuff?" I blurted, too wrecked and too raw to clamp down on the racing thoughts that wanted to escape my brain and be dealt with in the open. "She said you just gave it to her, but I don't believe that anymore. Tell me."

He laughed once, a sharp and bitter bark.

"I didn't just give it to her, but it wasn't sex stuff." He shifted closer to me and I could feel his warmth. He was my own personal outdoor space heater, like the ones they had on the patios in the fancy restaurants on cold nights in Iowa City or Des Moines.

"Does she . . . does she know something about you? Something personal about your family?"

He looked down and leaned toward me even more, so his thigh pressed against mine, the soft denim brushing my bare knees. "It's complicated. I'm complicated. I've wanted to tell you. . . . I know I can trust you." He looked up and his eyes had almost gone totally black. My heart beat so fast and so loud. I felt like a frog pinned to a dissection board. Three more deep breaths. "My family, me, we work here, but there're issues with our status."

My face scrunched up. "Your status?"

"Yeah. Our paperwork. Documents. . . . You know."

My eyes went wide. He was undocumented? "But . . . but . . . you work at Beau's."

He shrugged. "We've been doing this a long time. I've been in the country since I was two. My family, people like me, we do things a certain way. We know *how* to do things a certain way to stay under the radar. Even in a small town like this."

"So you have a Social Security number?" Everything my parents had ever told me about the plight of the undocumented flooded my brain. *They can't report crimes, Chloe. Not really. It's difficult for them to go to the hospital without risk. They can't ever fly out of the country. So many things we take for granted leave them exposed to deportation.*

"I have a Social Security number that works for Beau's. It

might not hold up under intense scrutiny if the ICE guys came sniffing around, but I don't usually stay working at one place for longer than a year. I don't want to put Beau's at risk, so I'll find something else soon."

I nodded. "You're a good worker."

He raised a shoulder again, but I could tell he was a little proud. Or maybe it was because I believed in him. Hopefully.

"And Chloe Donnelly somehow found out about your status?"

He raked a hand through his hair. "Yeah. I don't know how. My family is guarded. I haven't told anyone, not even Josh."

"But she found out?"

"Yeah. And she used it against me for a game. A goddamn game named after Nazi police. I'm not even sure what she's playing at, but you can't trust her. None of us can."

I thought about Aiden and Josh. About how she'd manipulated them. Then I thought about Nan and how Chloe Donnelly had so smoothly ingratiated herself to my grandparents. How she'd worked her way into the circle of Eve and Holly and me. God, she was good. I could almost admire her if I didn't think she was so terrible. How could she do that to Mateo? I could only imagine what my parents would think about something like that.

"How come you agreed to play the game in the first place?"

He lifted a shoulder. "It was a calculated risk. I figured I'd draw more attention to myself by refusing to play. Plus . . ." He shifted and I looked at him. "You were playing."

I thought back to how he'd been about the game, how breezy and casual, but also how he looked at me as if trying to tell me something. "You played because of me?" I squeaked out.

"A little, yeah."

I bit the inside of my cheek to stop a stupid grin from erupting on my face. It wasn't the time. I didn't know what to do with this information, and it didn't seem like Mateo was going to do anything about it either, so I asked, "Do you think Chloe's lying about everything? Do you believe her Chicago story? I mean, who starts junior year at a new school after spring break? And all that stuff about her friends . . ."

". . . Sounds made up," Mateo finished. "I know. At first I thought she was just posing, wanting to make friends, but now . . . It's more than that. I don't trust her."

"She knows a lot of secrets. I don't know how, but she seems to be very tuned in to everything that's going on. Always in the right place at the right time, as if school and her life come secondary to discovering secrets to use for the game."

"What do you mean?"

I studied him, wondering if I could trust him with what I'd seen between Eve and Cam. I wanted to trust him, same as he'd trusted me. He didn't give up my letter, after all. He didn't trust Chloe Donnelly and seemed legitimately worried

225

about me. Yes. I was positive he was on my side. I inhaled and counted to five, then blurted out everything about Eve and Cam.

I told as much as I could about the first Friday of the game—I blushed when I explained the part about me watching Cam and Eve make out from around the corner of the arts building—then I finished with, "I'm not sure how much of that Chloe knows, if Eve's told her anything, but she did watch Eve get into Cam's car on Tuesday. I saw her standing in the second-floor window at school. Standing there like she was waiting for something. Or maybe like she was a queen looking down on all her subjects. That sounds dumb, doesn't it? But *I saw her.*"

Which maybe made me look really stalky, so I added, "I wasn't following Eve or anything. I was going home late that day and happened to leave through the side exit."

"There's something off about that Chloe," Mateo said, leaning back now so I couldn't feel his warmth as much. But he said *that* Chloe, which made me smile a little, as if she was the other one instead of me.

"I know. There's definitely something off. And the game is pretty horrible. It didn't start that way, really. Not during the practice game. But with the platinum favor? It's bringing out all the grossest parts of everyone. Or maybe she is." I gnawed on my nail; Mateo reached out to pull my hand away from my mouth. I blushed again. "Sorry. It's a really bad habit."

"I don't mind it. It's part of you, like all your blushing, but you stop talking to me when you're biting your nails and I don't want you to stop talking to me."

My breath caught and wheezed out of me on a soft "oh."

"I like you, Chloe. I trust you. I don't tell anyone stuff about me and I told you. I don't even know why I did, except I know you wouldn't use it to hurt me. I saw it in your face this afternoon."

I looked at my hands, then back up at him. "Of course I wouldn't. Ever. I can't imagine how hard your life has been. And . . ." I started to put my finger back in my mouth but stopped myself and slipped both hands under my thighs. "I like you too. Which I guess you probably already know."

He smiled and my gaze moved to his lip piercing, two little silver balls nested up against his lip with a ring connecting them. I wanted to see the inside of his mouth to see how it looked. I wanted to feel the inside of his mouth. The little cocoon around us made me excited and flustered at the same time. Afraid I'd do something stupid to ruin it, pretty sure I would, but still so hopeful about things with Mateo. Not scared. In that way, Chloe Donnelly was right. The game did make things better between me and him.

"Yeah, I already know you like me," he said, but it wasn't cocky like a lot of guys could be. Would be. It was him clearing the air so everything was honest with us.

Silence drew around us like a pulled-tight rubber band and it took every muscle in my body to resist biting my nails or hiding behind my hair curtain. He leaned forward again, halving the twelve inches between us. He smelled like earth and sweat, but not in a gross way, in a way I bet tasted salty and the right kind of tangy.

"I don't have a lot of experience," I blurted. "And I'm sometimes nervous. But I'm not nervous . . . with you. Or, at least, not nervous in a bad way."

He grinned wider. "Shh, Chloe. I know this is all new to you. You told me it scared you."

Oh God. He'd probably talked about how much of an amateur I was to Josh. Maybe the whole baseball team talked about it. My cheeks burned, but he rubbed his thumb along my jaw and then kissed me. *Kissed* me, kissed me, the real way. With his whole mouth and the press of his whole body against mine. He definitely had a lot of experience. Or maybe he was naturally good at it.

Soft lips and a wet tongue and just the right pressure and tilting my head. And his lip ring was this tiny bit of cold metal contrasting with all his warmth. Holy crap, Mateo could kiss me forever. I wanted him to. I considered moaning, but that seemed dumb and fake and I didn't think I could make any noise because I was concentrating so hard on what his tongue and teeth and lips were doing. He used all three in tandem, this perfect balance. Mateo was a varsity-level kisser. All I did was open my mouth and try to do exactly what he was doing without tugging too hard on his piercing. I kind of wanted him to touch me other places besides my face, but at the same time I was not ready for his hands to move. That would require some Zen-level meditation for me to be ready for.

He sucked on my tongue then pulled back and licked his lips—licked his lips!—and said, "Chloe." Sort of breathless. *Chloe.*

"I more than like you," I said, blurted, licking my lips too because they felt all raw and tingly like my fingers sometimes did when I'd just bitten the cuticles and then put my hand in a bag of salty chips.

He laughed then and curled his hands around the base of my neck and tipped his head forward so our foreheads were touching. I tried not to think about how oily my forehead was or wonder if he could feel the acne up there. His smell seemed to be all over me, like I'd taken on his scent as my own. It felt all swoony and soap opera-ish, and I thought this was maybe how all varsity-level kissers did stuff. "I more than like you too," he said. "But . . ."

I pulled back and took in the pitying look on his face. Oh God. Oh God. Oh God. It couldn't be, could it? That look. This was part of the game. Again. He wanted my letter. How could I be so stupid? His varsity kisses were meant to stun me, manipulate me. "Don't even say it." I stood.

"What? Say what?"

"Say that you want my letter. That I can have you. This." I waved my hand between the two of us. "*If* I give you my letter."

I was ready to bolt, but he stood and grabbed my arm. "Chloe. Chloe. Look at me."

I turned, bracing myself for that pity look again, but instead, his expression was hurt. "That's what you think of me? You think I'd do that? After everything I told you."

"Umm . . ." I bit the inside of my lip, the one he'd just been licking, and tried to unfog my brain.

"This isn't *my* game. I don't want your letter. That's not what this is about. Hell, you can have my letter."

"Then why the *but*?"

"The *but*?"

"Yes. The *but*. The *I more than like you too, but . . .*"

He pulled me back down on the bench and took my hand. "I more than like you too, but I don't need Chloe Donnelly using this—*us*—against you."

"She's on my team. How could she?"

"I don't know. Maybe it's not always girls versus guys. Or maybe she uses you as another thing against me. Or maybe she wins the platinum favor and asks me for something I don't want to give her. Regardless, she's collecting secrets about all of us and it's dangerous. What you and I have together leaves both of us exposed."

"What we have *together*?"

He laughed in this sort of shy way. "Yeah. I mean, that was you kissing me back, right?"

I looked down. "Right."

"So now it's a point of vulnerability for her to use."

It was ridiculous and so full of drama I almost couldn't believe it. All this over a game. But the secrets Chloe Donnelly had were serious—more than I'd even told Mateo—and if they got out, they could affect people's futures. A whisper in the back of my head, my mom's voice: *This is how it starts. You play a game called Gestapo and this is what you get.*

I pulled my hand away from his and crossed my arms, careful to keep my fingers from straying to my mouth. "Fine. I just won't play anymore. Then what we have *together* won't be a problem."

He dragged a hand through his hair and it stuck up in a bunch of different directions, and then he said, "I don't know if you quitting the game will help. She still knows about me. I'm kind of stuck."

I looked at his THIS IS THE END shirt and wanted to cry.

I hated this. Hated how so many of us were somehow trapped by this game and this girl. I wanted to forget Gestapo. I wanted to go back to kissing Mateo and having him tell me he more than liked me. Which was maybe stupid and junior high, but I'd been waiting for him forever.

And now I knew why he was so guarded and closed off. He was protecting his family and himself. But he'd let *me* in. He'd told me the truth. And it made all the fear I'd had wrapped around me ease. It felt like an assurance that he wouldn't leave.

I was about to tell him all of this—maybe brainstorm how we could have the game over and done with for good—when my phone pinged with a text from Eve.

I'm at Burling. What's up?

No explanation of where she'd been and who she'd been with. I could almost hear the irritation in her text. I looked at Mateo. "I have to go. I have to fix things with Eve."

His brows went up. "I thought *she* was the one who was hooking up with Cam. What do you need to fix?"

"She was, but I bumped into Holly and blurted everything out. About Eve and Cam."

"Chloe." And there it was, the tone of voice that told me he didn't approve.

"I know, I know. But I wasn't gossiping. Holly was just being such a bitch"—I winced when I said the word, my mom's stern voice in my head reprimanding me about perpetuating sexism through my linguistic choices—"and she's always been a little awful to me, though tonight was really bad. It's like she's determined to get Eve to drop me as a friend completely. And, yeah, I get that she has stuff of her own she's dealing with, but her parents are divorced, not dead, and it's hardly a reason for her to treat me like crud."

My phone pinged again.

Other Chloe?

God. Now Eve was texting my otherness. Part of me wanted to let her stew and deal with the Holly fallout on her own, but there was no way I could ignore the mom voice in my head if I did that. *Sisters before misters.*

I kissed Mateo fast—that earthy smell, so yummy—and said, "I've got to go. We'll figure this all out. I promise."

Then before I decided to climb on his lap and camp out there forever, I forced myself to jog back in the direction of Burling Library, wondering if he was watching me the whole time but too afraid to look back and check.

17

I arrived at Burling Library to find Eve and Holly in what the dumb guys at school would call a "catfight." Though no actual claws were out, Holly's fists were clenched at her side and her hair was a little messed up and wild. Both their charm bracelets were broken on the ground. Eve held both hands up like she was waiting to be smacked.

"What do you mean you didn't know it was Cam when you kissed him? How could you not know?" Holly screeched.

"I was drunk. He had Aiden's hoodie on. He was trying to trick me," Eve whined. She glared at me when I stepped into the light, and I immediately dropped my hair in front of my face. "Why would you tell Holly I was hooking up with Cam?" she snapped, her voice full of so much hate I flinched.

"I didn't say you were!" I protested, though I as good as implied it and my denial was a weak foundation to stand on.

"Tell her exactly what you saw," Eve hissed. "Tell her how he tricked me." *What you saw,* not *what I told you.* Oh crap. So Eve somehow knew I'd been there that night. That I had watched and not done anything to stop Cam. Did she know the whole time she sat at my grandparents' house drinking room-temp water? Was that a test? God, maybe I deserved her ultimatum and her wrath.

I looked at Holly's furious face then back at Eve and then to Holly again. "He did trick her. She didn't know. She thought he was Aiden."

Holly raised her overly plucked eyebrows and then said to Eve, "And what about getting into his car after school on Tuesday?"

Eve gave me an even worse death glare. Our friendship was done. There was no way she'd forgive me now. She turned back to Holly and her voice changed, all soft and innocent sounding now. "Other Chloe is lying. I didn't get into Cam's car on Tuesday. I was with Aiden, watching his baseball practice. He drove me home afterward."

I swallowed down a *yeah, right.* She hadn't been with Aiden. Aiden had an away baseball game that day, not practice. And he never drove Cam's car. But there was no way I could point this out. If there was any chance at all to have Eve forgive me, it was by me telling a lie here. I closed my eyes for a second, considered if it was worth it, knowing that Eve was all I had left as a friend. I breathed deeply through my nostrils and blurted, "I might have gotten that part wrong. It could've been Aiden. I didn't see them up close."

Lie. Lie. Lie.

Holly huffed. She tried to curl her lip in disgust at me, but it looked weird because her lips were big to start off with and looked even bigger now, as if she'd spent the last half hour chewing on them. "You're trying to stir up trouble, Other Chloe. That's awful. What kind of friend are you?"

And just like that I was back to being a plate of crap that no one would ever want to dine on. Eve ignored me completely and said to Holly, "I'm sorry I didn't tell you about Cam tricking me last Friday. It was stupid. I was so drunk. And he was just trying to win the game."

I took a step forward. "Wait a second. Hold on. You're giving Cam a pass here? After he . . ." More dagger eyes from Eve with a *shut the hell up* wrinkle line popping on her zit-free forehead. "I mean, it was sleazy and unethical. How can you let him get away with this when he's treated you both like garbage?"

Holly crossed her arms. "You can spare me the lecture on ethics, Other Chloe. Cam was playing a game. He's competitive. You're hardly a model for how to treat people."

"Oh my God. You're serious? He handed out safety condoms to the guys. How do you see him being innocent here?"

Where the hell was the girl code? Cam cheated on his girlfriend by lying to her best friend and somehow *I* was being called out for not knowing how to treat people. That was rich.

"This is Cam's fault," I said, slower, like maybe it would sink in this time.

"He was playing a game," Holly said again, with a finality that made me realize no dirt would ever stick to Cam, at least not when it came to her. He was untouchable. The whole thing made me want to claw his eyes out with my stubby fingernails. I wondered for a second if he had a secret that Chloe Donnelly could use against him—he almost deserved it—but then I shook myself for being stupid. I didn't want to deal in secrets anymore. I was carrying too many of them and they were dragging me down. I just wanted out.

"We should quit the game," I said. "It's causing all this tension. No platinum favor is worth this. Look what happened with Cam. It almost tore you two apart."

I thought I was being generous, magnanimous even, all things considered, but Eve said, "*You* almost tore us apart."

So that was how things were going to be. I was the scapegoat. God, I should have given up her Tuesday rendezvous with Cam, but it didn't matter anymore. Holly wouldn't believe me. I snapped my mouth shut and tried to think of Mateo. I shoved my thumb into my mouth and tore off the newly healed cuticle, tasting a little bit of blood on my tongue. Then I released my thumb and tucked my hair behind my ear. I tried again. "We should still quit the game."

"She's right," Holly said, and I blinked. Could she actually be agreeing with me? "I'm kind of done with Gestapo. It's wasting time when Cam and I could be hanging out just the two of us."

Eve's shoulders drooped and her eyes got wide in relief. Thank God. She was done with Gestapo too. "Yeah, maybe we should quit. It hasn't really been as fun as I thought it would be. The practice game was so much better than how it's actually turned out."

Understatement of the year.

"We need to find Chloe and tell her we're done," I said.

"Let's call her."

"She doesn't have her cell. Remember?"

Holly shrugged. "Well, she can't be that hard to find."

Eve nodded, then leaned down and retrieved the broken charm bracelets. Probably they couldn't be repaired, but I was sure they'd get replacement ones by next week. "Yeah, we'll split up. Holly and I will take South and East Campus; you take North Campus, Other Chloe."

"Stop calling me Other Chloe," I snapped.

"No," Eve said with barely a pause. "Now go on. North Campus."

I shook my head, completely baffled. I couldn't believe I felt guilty about giving her up. All her worry about what Holly would think and they were tight again after barely a scuffle. And we were splitting up, so I could be the odd one out. Again.

"Fine," I said, hoping at the very least I'd bump into Mateo and tell him all the girls were bailing on the game so he wouldn't have to worry about Chloe Donnelly anymore.

I didn't even wave good-bye before I took off for North Campus. Not only was I done with the game, I was done with my friends. Not one of them was worth the headache of all of this. Maybe I would stop by Melissa McGrill's house tomorrow and start working on mending fences with her. I had to have more in common with a girl who'd miscarried on the locker room floor than with Holly, Eve, and Chloe Donnelly.

I searched for Mateo by the place I'd left him, but he wasn't anywhere near the old bookstore location. I pulled out my phone and texted.

Where are you? Have you seen Chloe Donnelly? I need to find her.

He didn't respond, which bummed me out more than it should have. He didn't live on his phone like a lot of guys did. Probably he didn't even have it powered on. Maybe. I ignored the sense of dread curling in my stomach. Chloe

Donnelly couldn't have found him in such a short amount of time, could she?

I walked faster, past the dorm where my parents told me they'd met, past a group of college students in the loggia sharing a joint between them, past the place where my parents said there used to be a nonfancy, North Campus dining hall before the big one in JRC replaced it. I made my way toward the one ugly dorm on the very north end of campus and then stopped at the covered end of the loggia near the bike racks when I heard Josh's voice.

"Will you just listen to me?"

"Josh." Aiden was with him. But his tone wasn't warm and sweet and protective like it had been the other day when I'd caught them kissing. And he wasn't serious and somber like he'd been with me. But exasperated. Almost angry.

"If you can't be who you are, then maybe you shouldn't go to the Naval Academy. Don't you want to be somewhere you're accepted?" Josh's words sounded strained with frustration and defeat.

I wanted to announce my presence, but they were clearly in an argument, and I didn't want to interrupt and make things worse.

"Where is this coming from, babe? You told me a few days ago I should wait to say anything. You said plebes have it hard and you didn't want me to be hazed any worse than I already would be. You reminded me that being a pilot in the navy is something I've wanted more than anything else in my life. You told me not to give that up."

I ducked behind the bikes, far enough away that they couldn't see me. I felt like a creeper again, but I didn't know what else to do.

Josh moved closer to Aiden. "I know. I did say that. But . . . I don't know now. I guess I've just been thinking and this all feels so heavy and I'm not sure it's worth it."

"I'm not giving up the Naval Academy," Aiden said, his tone hard and uncompromising. "It's everything I ever wanted."

"I thought I was everything you ever wanted."

"Don't be dramatic and turn this into a thing. I love you. You know that. But this isn't an either/or situation. I can make both work."

Josh slumped down on a bench and Aiden moved next to him. "They're going to change you," Josh said, his voice low enough I had to strain to hear him. "You're going to come back different and I'm still going to be here in this crappy town. Still going to be the same me."

"You're not still going to be here. You have other options."

"My family doesn't have a ton of money. You know that. I don't know if I'll be able to swing college. Even with scholarships and loans, I don't know if it's in the cards for me. I don't want to lose you."

"You're not going to."

But even I understood that the likelihood of them staying together through Aiden in the Naval Academy wasn't very realistic.

"Couldn't you go to college somewhere else? Somewhere closer? Chloe told me the LGBTQ community at the University of Iowa, where her mom works, is really amazing. It's not here, but it's close and—"

"Chloe? Chloe Donnelly?" Aiden bit off, his good-looking face going cruel like I'd seen Cam's sometimes do. "The girl who's blackmailed me into playing a dumb game? The one who threatened my entire future? That Chloe?"

A weight dropped in my stomach as scenarios spun around in my brain. Chloe and her games. Was she playing Josh too? Trying to break him and Aiden up? I couldn't stand the thought of it. It made me want to scream and scratch her eyes out.

I couldn't listen to this anymore. I backed away, stumbling when my leg bumped one of the bikes and making my location obvious, but it didn't matter. Aiden and Josh were too loud to hear me.

"It's not like she's wrong, though," Josh argued. "Iowa City is progressive. And close enough to Grinnell that we could see each other every weekend. We could be together."

"I'm going to the Naval Academy. This isn't up for discussion. You can stand by my decision or not, but I'm not giving up everything because of something Chloe Donnelly told you," Aiden countered.

I froze where I stood, unable to walk away even as I felt like the worst human being ever for witnessing this. Josh stood with his hands fisted at his side, looking more wrinkled and out of sorts than I'd ever seen. "No, you're not giving up *every-thing*. Just me."

Then he turned and strode away. Aiden jerked both hands through his hair and swore for a full forty-five seconds before stalking off after Josh.

Hatred for Chloe Donnelly and the lives she'd been playing with coursed through me. She was horrible, an example of the absolute worst kind of girl—selfish, mean, and uncaring about people's futures. My phone pinged with a text from Mateo.

I saw Chloe heading toward the basketball courts on East Campus. You okay?

Yep.

I wanted to ask him if he talked to her, but I didn't really want to know. Not over texts when I couldn't see his face. I needed to find her and end this.

18

I headed back toward the field in front of the Harris Center, the sadness over Aiden and Josh's fight getting mixed in with my anger at Chloe Donnelly. This dumb game. My phone clock read a little after nine. Still almost an hour until we were supposed to meet back up. I was exhausted from all that had already happened that night. I passed the Harris Center, ignoring the shouting and music pouring out from some big campus party, and made my way across the tracks toward the basketball court, the bright lights from the Bear glowing from the other side of the street. I felt like I needed an hour-long shower without Nan or Pops saying anything about it. I waffled again between bailing and finding Chloe Donnelly, but I kept remembering Mateo's face and the way he said she would use *us* against him. I wanted her to know without any doubt that this was over.

I veered a little north to step under a street lamp, pulling out my phone to send Mateo a text asking if he wanted to help me look for her, but before I could, I noticed two figures on the side of Rathje Hall, the northernmost East Campus dorm. The couple was half in shadow but hard to miss from where I was standing—a guy grinding into a girl against the outer wall. I took a step closer. It looked awkward as anything, him trying to hold her up and bend his knees at the same time. It couldn't be comfortable. I leaned forward and peered into the shadows. Then I realized why he was bending his knees.

I slammed my eyes shut. They were having sex. *Sex!* Outside. Against a wall. I peeked out of one eye. God. Gross. Who did that kind of thing? I never wanted to go to college if it was all sex against the sides of buildings or being too wasted to remember a guy's name when you were going to his dorm. Jesus, what was wrong with people?

Then I heard the girl's voice. "That's all? Really? I expected you to last a little longer, Cam. But I guess you didn't realize me coming was part of the deal. I probably should've been clearer up front."

Holy crap. Cam. And Chloe Donnelly. Outside. Against the wall of a dorm.

Oh. My. God.

"I would've lasted longer if I didn't have to hold you up."

"Well, if you want my letter, you're going to need to work

harder. Do a good enough job and maybe I'll even give you our word. But I'm not giving you anything if I don't come."

If she didn't come? As in, have an orgasm against the outer wall of a dorm? What in the very hell? Who talked like this? This wasn't male-stripper-movie giggling in the media center, or me and Eve wondering about labia piercing, or even admitting I might have accidentally had an orgasm with my loofah, this was a girl demanding a guy make her come—while having sex against the side of a building! I was so not prepared for this. It was the most horrifying thing I'd ever witnessed and made all my ambivalence about sex ratchet up to infinity. Chloe Donnelly was terrible. She was like a thirty-year-old in the body of a seventeen-year-old girl. We were out in the cornfields and a little behind the times, for sure, but I couldn't believe that Chicago had given her this level of experience. *Work harder.* Ick.

Cam laughed. "Jesus, you're a bitch."

"Uh-huh. A bitch who has something you want tucked in the strap of my bra. So get with the program."

My skin crawled. I tried to turn away but couldn't. I fumbled with my phone to call Mateo and tell him I was quitting. Now. I needed out of there, but it was as if my whole body were frozen in ice. On the outside of everything, watching. It was too much and still I couldn't look away. Cam on his knees with his head under Chloe Donnelly's flowy skirt and one of her legs up on his shoulder. Was that how guys did oral? I blinked a bunch of times. This was gross. I was gross for looking. This had nothing to do with me. I needed to turn away and go home. Someone inside the dorms switched on some music loud enough to get me to unfreeze and turn away, but before I could escape, I heard running from along the sidewalk.

"What in the hell are you doing?" a voice shrieked, and I flinched.

Holly, with Eve right behind her. Oh God. I wished I could disappear, but still my dumb legs wouldn't move. Holly raced forward and pulled an already-shifting Cam backward and away from Chloe Donnelly. Then Holly whirled on her and slapped her, the crack resonating so loud that even the music pumping from inside the dorm didn't cover it.

For a brief second I internally cheered at the shocked look on Chloe Donnelly's face, but then I wondered why Cam wasn't being slapped. Cam, who was stumbling up from his knees after doing oral on Chloe Donnelly in order to get her dumb letter. Cam, who'd hooked up with three different girls in a week.

Eve moved to tug Holly away from Chloe Donnelly, but as soon as she did, Chloe Donnelly struck back, a deep scratch forming on Holly's cheek. My feet uncemented and I ran forward, stepping between Chloe Donnelly and Holly, and gripping Chloe Donnelly's shaking shoulders with my stubby fingernails.

"He's *my* boyfriend, you stupid bitch," Holly shrieked.

Chloe Donnelly looked over my shoulder and glared at her. "You can keep him. He bones like a thirteen-year-old virgin and can't give head to save his life." Then she shook me off and turned to Cam. "You're not getting my letter after that weak-sauce performance."

Cam sneered at her. "You taste like old Miracle Whip. I wouldn't lick your vag again if I won platinum favors from every girl in school."

I spun and shoved his shoulder, wishing I was brave enough to slap him. "What is wrong with you? You're disgusting. You're a complete waste of space. Stop talking. Stop messing with girls. Do something with your pathetic life."

Cam narrowed his eyes at me, then looked at Holly and Eve and Chloe Donnelly. "You're all dumb bitches. None of you are worth the steam of my piss."

"Cam," Holly cried—*cried!*—as if she wanted him to stay, to still be her boyfriend. As if him walking away from her wasn't the best possible thing that could happen to her.

Cam shook his head and stalked off. From behind I saw him scrub his mouth with one hand while he lifted his other hand high and flipped us all off.

I turned back to Chloe Donnelly. "We're done with Gestapo. None of us wants to play anymore."

Chloe Donnelly crossed her arms, rings on her left hand

glinting as she drummed her fingers against her bicep, way too relaxed and practiced. "You don't, huh? Are you sure about that?"

"Of course we're sure. The game has turned terrible. All of this is terrible. We're done." I almost added *you're done*, but it seemed dramatic and unnecessary. Chloe Donnelly would find out soon enough how few friends she had. How no one was going to let her get away with being so awful.

She tilted her head and looked at Holly, completely calm like she hadn't just been smacked after having sex against a wall. "Can I talk to you alone for a minute?"

It seemed like a death wish considering Holly was about to claw her eyes out, but it was on her and I wasn't going to protect her from Holly's wrath.

Holly snapped, "Sure. It'll only take me a minute to take care of things."

Chloe Donnelly walked toward the parking lot by the basketball court with Holly on her heels. I looked at Eve, who'd been too quiet this whole time. "What's wrong? Did you think Cam would end up with you?" It was mean, but I was still pissed about how she'd treated me with Holly. Still pissed that she'd given Cam a pass.

Eve frowned. "I never thought you'd be like this. Your parents would be really disappointed."

I gaped at her. "First, I'm not 'like' anything. *I* didn't hook up with Cam. I'm actually the only one at this point."

"He tricked me. You *saw* that, remember? You spied on us."

I swallowed down my guilt and deflected. "What about Tuesday? That wasn't Aiden you got into the car with."

Eve crossed her arms—just like Chloe Donnelly had—and said, "That wasn't anything. I wasn't hooking up with Cam on Tuesday."

"Then what were you doing?"

She shook her head. "Like I'd tell you. Little Miss Innocent turned into Little Miss Tattletale. I know you don't want to play the game anymore, but you might want to consider some self-reflection before you go accusing Chloe of anything."

My breath grew choppy and my blood heated. I was seething, overwhelmed, and still grossed out. "What's that supposed to mean?"

"Look at you. How long were you standing there watching Cam go down on Chloe? How much of Cam and me did you watch from around the corner of the arts building without making a single peep? And what about how you *happened* to see me getting into his car on Tuesday? It's creepy how you watch all of us through your hair as if we don't know. What else have you seen, *Other* Chloe? Who else have you spied on?"

I reeled and stumbled back as if she'd physically punched me. It was a below-the-belt accusation and something I'd never have imagined Eve saying a year ago. And the worst part, the part that made it hurt like a physical ache, was that she wasn't completely wrong. I'd been looking for Chloe Donnelly. I had watched Eve and Cam, had watched Josh and Aiden. Oh God.

We stood and stared at each other, me coming up with things to hurl at Eve but not saying any of them. Her waiting to lay into me. Both of us torn apart and mired in the bloody remains of our friendship.

"Let's go," Chloe Donnelly shouted from where she and Holly stood. Holly's face no longer registered fury but now was a mixture of defeat and fear, something I'd never seen from her. Jesus, what the hell had happened? "Game's over. The guys are all waiting for us. It's time to see if anyone has won."

19

We headed back to Burling without saying a word to one another. I kept peeking at Holly through my hair, but she didn't look at me once. The pastiness of her skin made the scratch on her face stand out even more. Something was definitely wrong. I should have left. I'd said what I wanted to say and didn't need to watch the rest, but I kept walking, wanting to make sure the final nail was hammered into the coffin of Gestapo. Wanting Mateo to see that we'd be free of this.

I started in on biting my nails as soon as we crossed Eighth Avenue. The college around us suddenly felt out of place. Too pretty, too perfect. Or maybe we were out of place. I'd spent most of my life popping in and out of this campus world with my parents, but now it was as if I was a kid at a museum full of things I couldn't touch and didn't understand.

The campus was fairly deserted, with all the usual activity moved indoors to dorm lounges or Harris Center or off-campus parties. The people we did pass looked through us, as if we were completely irrelevant. It reminded me of the first time I'd wandered the streets of Iowa City by myself. Invisible and unremarkable in such a big city. Or at least big in comparison to Grinnell. I couldn't decide if our irrelevance on campus was because we were obviously too young to be part of college life or if it was because we weren't recognizable to anyone we passed. It made me feel smaller than I usually did. Or maybe that was because of the game and all that had happened in the past forty-five minutes.

I had no nails left to bite by the time we reached the library, and two of my cuticles were bleeding. My face cracked into a big smile when I saw Mateo leaning against the bike rack—relief, something good had come out of tonight—but he barely acknowledged me, still protecting himself and us from Chloe Donnelly. My hatred for her grew like slow poison spreading through me, toxic enough that it was easy to ignore my mom's voice in my head telling me how girls' meanness was often borne from the bitterness of being unwilling or unable to surrender to the patriarchy.

"No one got any letters," Cam said. "This game blows."

It was the perfect opening for me to announce the girls were bailing, but before I could open my mouth, Chloe

Donnelly said, "You guys need to stop hiding and start try-ing harder. When we played in Chicago, there was always a winning team. Do you even understand what a platinum favor could get you? Guys, all four of you could ask *me* for something and I couldn't say no."

The air seemed to go cool and still. There it was, a dangling carrot that caused a tiny shift in Aiden and Josh and Mateo, the possibility that a platinum favor from Chloe Donnelly would allow their secrets to stay hidden forever. The implication was clear, or maybe it was just what I heard. For all her manipu-lation, she took the game seriously. This was her olive branch, her assurance that all anyone had to do to protect themselves was to win. Could a win for the guys guarantee her silence? I had no idea, but all sorts of bells were going off in my head and I was seriously skeptical.

This girl knew what she was doing. She was a master game player. With everyone but Cam, though I supposed in a way she knew how to play him too. At least she certainly did pressed against the wall of Rathje.

"Who gives a crap?" Cam said, though his voice sounded like more bravado than certainty. "A platinum favor isn't worth all this hassle. Plus, it's freezing outside. I'm tired of running around this campus in the cold. I'm done with this stupid game."

"Cam," Holly croaked out, and stepped close enough to

whisper something into his ear. His face grew hard and he glared at Chloe Donnelly.

Oh God. What the hell now?

"We don't want to play either," I blurted out, trying to stop this train before it annihilated everyone. "The girls don't." I gestured to Holly and Eve, making sure to catch Mateo's eye. "The game is stupid."

Mateo's brows went up, but he didn't say anything. I wished he could, but I understood why he was staying mute. He had more to lose than anyone.

Chloe Donnelly stepped forward. "No, Other Chloe, the girls still want to play. Don't you, Holly? Eve?"

Holly stepped away from Cam and nodded. "Yeah, I'll play again."

Oh jeez. Crap, crap, crap. What had Chloe Donnelly said to her at the basketball court? Another secret? Maybe it had something to do with Cam. I didn't understand how Chloe Donnelly could know all this stuff about everyone. She arrived in Grinnell a few weeks ago. It'd been less than a month!

Chloe Donnelly smirked at me, then turned to Eve. "Eve?"

Eve's gaze bounced between me and Holly and finally landed on Cam. He gave the slightest shake of his head and Eve turned back to Chloe Donnelly. "I'll play too," she whispered.

I sputtered. "Are you kidding me? An hour ago you both wanted to quit."

"They changed their minds. They realized how much fun it could be," Chloe Donnelly said, then winked at Cam—winked!—but he just glared at her.

I couldn't believe what was happening. "She's got something on all of you?" I blurted. "You're all stuck playing this game?"

"Careful, Other Chloe. You're starting to sound like a paranoid freak. I thought you'd be more fun to play with, but I guess not. No worries. We'll find someone else." Chloe Donnelly looked at her polished fingernails as if I'd been dismissed, but it was hard to miss the anger in her voice. She did not want to be derailed. If only everyone would stand up to her, if only it wasn't just me fighting here.

"You're serious? You're *all* still playing?" My voice was raspy and screechy.

No one would meet my gaze, not even Mateo. I'd never felt so incredibly alone. Gutted. All my mom's lectures about integrity and standing my ground against bullies meant absolutely nothing when there was no one to stand with me. This was ridiculous.

"Run along," Chloe Donnelly said, and I shook my head in disbelief. This was the girl who'd stolen a scarf for me because she said it matched my eyes, who'd talked Nan into letting me have a sleepover, who'd helped me pick out clothes to win over Mateo, who'd said I was pretty and told Eve I was her best friend. And now she was looking at me like I didn't exist.

I lifted my chin and dragged my hair away from my face. "Fine," I said, glancing one more time at Mateo, who finally looked at me with fear in his eyes. Fear of Chloe Donnelly. I looked back at her one more time. "Interesting way you have of making friends." Then I turned and headed toward the arts building.

I was done.

I didn't hear from Mateo until Saturday night, and then it wasn't a text but him stopping by Nan and Pops's house before dinner. They'd been lecturing me about how I was avoiding calls from my parents, and the doorbell was a welcome relief from the guilt. My face practically cracked in half when I opened the door and saw that lip ring.

"I texted you last night," I said as I led Mateo into the living room, trying not to wince when he looked at the perfectly folded throw blanket and the cross-stitch pillows on the sofa. My house couldn't scream *Old people live here!* any more. Nan and Pops were puttering in the kitchen, pretending they were finishing cooking dinner, even though I was 100 percent certain they were eavesdropping. I turned up the volume on the TV so all they'd be able to hear were muffled voices.

Mateo shrugged. "I lost my phone sometime after the game. I went back to the college to look for it, but I couldn't find it anywhere. I'll probably need to get a new one. Sucks."

I tried to look bummed out, but I was secretly pretty psyched there was a good explanation for his text silence. I could barely sleep last night thinking maybe we weren't going to be a thing after all.

"Why are you smiling?" he asked, pressing his thigh against mine as he sat next to me on the old-people sofa, Fox News a buzzing din in the background.

Busted. My face was total crap at hiding my emotions. "Nothing," I said. "Just glad you're okay. *We're* okay."

He took my hand. "We're okay. But how come you backed out on the game? It's going to make things with us hard."

I sighed. "Holly and Eve were supposed to back out too. I thought if we all bailed, it would be over with Chloe Donnelly. That she wouldn't be able to find three other girls to play."

He squeezed my hand, his thumb pushing into the fleshy muscle between my thumb and pointer finger. "But they didn't back out."

I squeezed his hand back, feeling like our hands were having a whole conversation that my grandparents didn't know about. "No. Chloe said something to Holly. I don't know what it was, but Holly was all pasty and weird after they talked. And then Eve . . . I don't know. I guess she would never side with me over Holly and Chloe Donnelly."

"Yeah, and something happened with Cam too. He was so pissed when I first got back to the library."

My pits got sweaty and my face burned hot. No way was I going to tell him about seeing Cam on his knees in front of Chloe Donnelly, particularly with my grandparents one room away and able to butt in at any time. Mateo touched my cheek with his thumb.

"You're blushing."

My cheeks heated even more. "I do that so much. I want the game to be over. I want Chloe Donnelly to disappear so you and I can . . ."

I couldn't finish. I didn't even really know what he and I could do. Was *everything* too much to ask? Because for the first time, I thought I might like to do everything. I wasn't scared with Mateo. He'd taken my fears and smoothed them out with his own trust, so all that was left of me when I sat next to him was want, want, want.

"I wish she'd go away too," he said, his lip ring inching up with his smile. "We just have to ride it out until she's sick of it. Maybe her parents will decide to move back to Chicago."

"Do you . . . ?" I swallowed and started again. "Who do you think she'll replace me with?"

He shrugged. "I don't know. Depends who she has dirt on. Maybe she won't replace you at all. Maybe she'll keep two letters herself. She certainly acts like she's untouchable."

Untouchable. Was anyone really untouchable? If Chloe Donnelly had proven nothing else, it was that everyone had something that could be used against them. Except me. Which I guess was what made me expendable rather than untouchable. I was completely unnecessary to this girl and this game.

"Maybe."

"Listen," Mateo lowered his voice. "All that's happened with us . . . I'm glad about it. I like you. I told you that. But we need to be careful."

I nodded. "I know. We can't risk Chloe saying anything about your status. I get it."

And I did, mostly. Mateo and I wouldn't be able to hold hands in the hall or kiss good-bye outside the baseball diamond. It was bad enough Chloe Donnelly already knew I liked him, if she found out he liked me back, who knew what she would demand from him. But even as I understood all of this in my head, my stomach felt weird at the idea that I'd become another one of Mateo's secrets. That we were now in the same position as Aiden and Josh. That almost every platinum favor I'd thought about asking him for would be answered by no.

Mateo tightened his linked fingers along mine. "Walk me out."

I squeezed my legs together. "Sure."

He said good-bye to Nan and Pops. Nan asked him to join us for dinner, but he declined, and frankly, I was glad. Awkward and uncomfortable were not the easiest for digestion. I told my grandparents I'd be back in a minute to set the table.

The butterflies in my stomach burst into a flurry of movement when Mateo pressed me up against the side of the house and kissed me. I thought I was kissing him better this time, less like a novice and more like I wanted him to enjoy it. I even swiped my tongue over his lip ring and managed not to giggle at how it made me so giddy. When he pulled back, we were both a little splotchy and out of breath.

"Be patient with me," he said in a low voice, then turned and started down the street, his hands shoved in his front pockets in this cool way that made me feel a little out of my league with him too.

Late that night, after I heard the sounds of Nan and Pops brushing their teeth and then calling out good night to me, I put the Spanish book I was unable to concentrate on reading to the side and pulled out the book I'd had hidden under my bed. I'd found it at the college bookstore before winter break when I was buying WHERE THE HELL IS GRINNELL? bumper stickers to bring to my parents. The book contained a bunch of stories of girls' first-time sex. I nearly died of embarrassment when I bought it, but luckily the girl ringing me up had four face piercings and shaved blue hair, so I didn't think she'd really judge. I'd tucked the book away when I got home, making sure to slide it under the mattress where even housekeeping-obsessive Nan wouldn't look.

Every time I considered reading it, I decided against it, because it felt too much like something my mom would be *thrilled* about. But now, when every time I was with Mateo fear slipped further away from me and something new and a little hungry replaced it, I couldn't stop myself from pulling the book out. I flipped through the introduction and read the first essay. It was about a girl who'd lost her virginity when she was twelve. Twelve! I wasn't even wearing a bra yet at twelve. I read the next essay, which seemed kind of dirty and interesting all at once because it had to do with blow jobs. The third essay was about a lesbian, and even though I'd never wanted to be with a girl, I read it with just as much interest. I read all of them, flipping page after page, feeling like these writers were my friends and they were giving me advice. Some of their stories were kind of sad, but none of them was as terrifying as I thought they'd be. They were honest, and not in the way Mom had been too honest, almost emphatic, before she'd lost the baby and turned a little broken. I read through the question-and-answer guide at the end of the book, and as I turned the last page, I felt another tiny part of me uncurl just a little. Maybe I could. Maybe, maybe, maybe.

Before I went to sleep, I fired up the computer and sent my parents a short note.

Mom and Dad,

I'm sorry I haven't been around to talk and I didn't respond back
to your email about extending in BF. The truth is, I'm still thinking
about it. Can I have a little more time? I love and miss you.

Chloe

It was a stall tactic, but it was honest. I couldn't think about
spending next year in Burkina Faso—I'd been patently ignoring it every chance it swam into my brain—when the only thing
that was on my mind was how to end the game for good so I
could be with Mateo.

20

Monday morning I passed Holly and Eve on my way to first period, and they didn't even look at me. They turned away from my "hey" and ducked their heads together in the same way Eve and I used to freshman year. They were both wearing leggings and too-small hoodies over too-small tees. Different colors and styles, but it was hard for me to miss how they blended together. Particularly when their brand-new replacement BEST FRIENDS charm bracelets were on full display. I looked at my own jeans and Blackhawks shirt. I don't think I ever blended, even when I had friends. I lifted my chin and pretended I didn't need them. I tried to channel my mom. *An empty house is better than one filled with people who aren't worthy of you.* I didn't really believe that. Who would ever choose to be alone? Being an only child was bad enough.

My parents hadn't responded to my email, and I didn't know if their silence was pointed or if they hadn't gotten my note yet. Probably I'd have to decide about moving sooner rather than later, but my skin itched when I even thought about making the decision. What if I went to Burkina Faso for a year and when I got back things were different with Mateo? He might not even still be in Grinnell because of some complication with his status.

Chloe Donnelly was at his locker when I passed there between first and second periods, and his face flashed in panic when he saw me, so I put my head down and walked by, my guts twisting in knots. By the time I got to lunch, it was 100 percent clear that I'd been frozen out. Even people in my classes seemed to be avoiding me. Chloe Donnelly's reach was far and deep for someone who'd just started at our school. I kept wondering about that, wondering if she had someone at GHS telling her all this stuff about us, but I couldn't imagine who. Everyone seemed to have something to lose.

I glanced at Holly, Eve, and Chloe Donnelly as I got my tray of crappy cafeteria food, but they'd picked a table with no extra spots. They were even sucking up sitting with the student council crew just to keep me from joining them. Not that I wanted to sit with them anyway. I walked over to where Melissa McGrill was sitting with her sack lunch, listening to something on her headphones. She hadn't been at church yesterday, but I was happy to see her now.

She looked up when I approached and pulled one earbud out.

"Can I sit here?" I asked, my voice scratchy and pathetic sounding.

She raised a shoulder. "It's a free country."

Hardly the enthusiasm I was hoping for, but not a no.

"What're you listening to?"

"A podcast about the military."

I shoved my hair behind my ear so I could see her more clearly. "Are you thinking of enlisting?"

"No."

She didn't offer any other explanation; she just pulled the other earbud out and wrapped her headphones around her phone before tucking it away. She was wearing a hoodie too, but it was big like her clothes had been the past few times I'd seen her and it made me wonder if she'd gained weight with her pregnancy or if she just didn't care in any way how she looked.

I took a bite of overcooked mac and cheese and considered the possibility that it had been too long since I was friends with Melissa, that half conversations were the best we were going to be able to do, and there'd be no hope for a real reconciliation.

"I know you're curious. Go ahead and ask me," she said.

I tipped my head and said, "Ask you what?"

"Ask me if I miscarried in the gym showers. I assume that's why you're over here, actually sitting with me where everyone can see. Some fact-finding mission your squad sent you on."

"I don't have a squad."

Melissa glanced past me to Chloe Donnelly's table. "Oh. So you're here bottom feeding then? Your girls broke up with you, and I'm the consolation prize?"

I wanted to tell her no. I wanted to explain that she was nothing like that, but the truth was, she might have been. A week ago I'd bolted from her outside of Beau's because I was afraid what being friends with her would mean for me. Now I had nothing to lose. I hated admitting it, but a small part of me had chosen to sit with Melissa because she seemed worse off than me.

"Sorry," I whispered. "I wasn't trying to hurt your feelings."

She looked straight at me, pinning me so I couldn't move. "No. You were lonely."

I nodded and gripped my tray to stand and find somewhere else. The mac and cheese coated the back of my throat in a way that made me think I might not keep it down. Melissa tapped the table and pointed. "Sit down. I didn't say it was a problem. Just wanted to clear the air. I like you, Chloe. I always did."

Chloe. God, the relief of shedding the "other" was so enormous that I wanted to reach over the cafeteria table and hug her.

"I like you too." There was a long pause and it seemed like Melissa was waiting for something, so I said, "I don't know what happened when you were gone from school a couple of weeks ago, and it's not my business, which is why I haven't asked, but if you ever want to talk . . ."

She nodded. "I'll keep it in mind."

Then she dug into her brown bag and pulled out a baggie full of Doritos. "Want some?"

The rest of lunch was filled with stupid talk about teachers and classes and her plans for the summer. Melissa said "we" a lot and it took me a while to realize she had a pretty serious plus-one. But I was too afraid to ask her about him, too uncertain about the tentative state of our reconciliation.

When the bell rang and we got up from the table, she said, "You're welcome to sit here tomorrow if you want."

Which was pretty much the only positive thing that happened all day.

Tuesday after school, when I still hadn't heard from my parents, I stayed late to do homework in the media center. I knew there was no way I could be home every day by three thirty without a good explanation for Nan. Nan had always been a social butterfly, and she found my small number of friends and activities "troubling."

I was also secretly hoping Mateo would get home from

his away game early. I texted him the location where I'd be studying but hadn't heard back. I wasn't sure if he'd gotten his phone replaced yet or not, but I hung on to the possibility that he hadn't as an explanation for my unanswered text.

Two hours of doing chem and Spanish and precalc and my brain was completely fried. I pulled off my headphones and glanced around. Most people had cleared out already, and I knew the librarian would be kicking me out in a few minutes. I shoved my books into my bag and wrapped my headphones up. Down the hall from the media center the band practice room door stood open with someone plucking at a guitar inside. I shouldered my bag, avoiding the janitor with his bleachy-smelling mop bucket, and moved farther into the hallway.

It took less than ten seconds for me to recognize the tune the guitar player was strumming. "40." I shut my eyes and listened. Cam's raspy deep voice flooded the hallway. The music swirled inside of me, and for a full minute I let myself forget everything. I moved to the side of the open practice door and tipped my head back against the wall to let the song push the last month, the last year, out of my brain.

When Cam held the last note, I released my breath and shouldered my bag again. So much wasted talent in this guy.

"Better now?" he asked.

I froze. Someone was in the room with him.

"Yeah, I'm better." Holly's voice, soft and a little croaky.

"No more tears. It fucking kills me when you cry," he said.

"All right. No more tears. But no more girls, okay?"

There was a long pause, then Cam finally said, "Yeah, okay."

"I love you."

"Me too, Holls."

I bolted down the hallway, not wanting them to see me when they came out of the room. Thoughts flickered through my mind like pages in a book but I couldn't settle on one. I didn't know how to reconcile gross Cam with this Cam. I didn't know why Holly needed him so much, why she was willing to stay with a guy who'd cheated on her. I didn't want to feel soft toward either of them, but I did. And maybe that was the right thing. Maybe Cam and Holly were just a messed-up couple, and not my business.

I pushed out the doors to the main entrance and texted Mateo again.

I miss you.

I got home to a short email message from my dad.

Chloe,
Take some time, but don't shut us out. That kills your mom. And me. We're webcamming you this week. We don't have to talk about extending then, but we miss seeing your face, so answer! We love you and will work something out.
Dad

On my way out of school on Wednesday afternoon, I bumped into Eve's mom, who was carrying two large Tupperware containers full of cookies.

"Oh, Chloe. It's good to see you, sweetie. Help me bring these to the office for Teacher Appreciation Week."

"There's a Teacher Appreciation Week?" I asked, grabbing one of the containers.

She frowned. "Of course there is. Surely your mother did something for the teachers when you were younger, before she left?"

She said *before she left* as if my mom had abandoned our family and run off with a scarlet *A* on her chest in pursuit of Reverend Dimmesdale. "No. Mom appreciates teachers, but baking really isn't her thing."

Mrs. Jacobson pursed her lips even more. "I'm aware."

I placed the container on the secretary's desk in the office and turned to say good-bye, but Mrs. Jacobson was looking at me strangely. "Eve told me you had a falling-out. Was it over a boy?"

I shook my head. "No."

She stacked her container on top of mine. "She's been very upset all week. I don't want to interfere, but I think you need to make amends. You girls need to be looking out for each other, not fighting."

My mouth dropped open. *I* needed to make amends? God,

if only she knew everything that Eve had pulled in the past few weeks. But there was no way I was getting into it with Mrs. Jacobson, of all people. "We'll work through it, I'm sure," I gritted out.

"She needs to be focusing on her studies, Chloe. All this girl drama is keeping her from buckling down."

No, what was keeping her from buckling down was Eve didn't really like doing work. The volleyball season was over and she didn't have anything else going on after school right now, but the idea of homework always bored Eve, who would rather be doing almost anything else. Not that I could explain that to Mrs. Jacobson.

"Okay. Thanks for the feedback. Good-bye, Mrs. Jacobson."

"There's no need to get snarky, Chloe. It's an unfortunate trait you inherited from your mother and one that won't serve you well."

I stopped myself from rolling my eyes and turned to leave. The school secretary, Ms. McVoy, had returned to her desk, and Mrs. Jacobson was all smiles again, calling out to me as I exited, "Come see us anytime, Chloe. You know our door is always open."

Thursday in Spanish class—after three days of Chloe Donnelly completely monopolizing Mateo so that it was impossible to even say hi, and me finally getting a midnight text from him saying he got a new phone and he missed me too, but also reiterating the need to be patient—we had to present our oral reports on Latin America. Oral reports were a much-needed reprieve to me being persona non grata in class.

Mateo went first, dressed in jeans and a black T-shirt with the word NOT in white lettering. He explained to Señor Williams that he'd decided to change his topic at the last minute. Señor Williams grumbled about responsibility and commitment and entitlement and a bunch of other things that made no sense, but finally he nodded.

Mateo gave a presentation on the Mothers of Plaza de Mayo, the mothers of Argentina's "disappeared." The way Mateo explained it was sad as hell, a reminder of all the pain that comes from losing someone you care about. Though I'd heard about it before from my dad—U2 had written a song about it on their *Joshua Tree* album—hearing it in Mateo's low voice, full of emotion and sorrow over the thirty thousand children lost to Argentina's "Dirty War," made me choke up.

When he was done, he looked right at me, and I felt the connection between us draw even tighter. *Mothers who had lost their children.* Like my mom did. Like his mom might. It was as if Mateo was sending me a direct message about why he had to sit next to Chloe Donnelly in class and ignore me completely. It could be *his* mother, *his* family, if anyone found out about his undocumented status.

I did my report on Perito Moreno and then left without saying a word to Mateo or Chloe Donnelly, but my shoulders were pressed back and my steps felt lighter than they had all week. I could be patient. Mateo wasn't going anywhere. I would help protect him.

That night Mateo didn't text, but I got a middle-of-the-night internet call from my parents. I almost sobbed when I saw their faces filling my computer screen.

"I miss you guys so much," I said the moment our connection went through.

Mom laughed through tears. "Well, that is an excellent greeting. We miss you too. So much. I hated not talking to you. Don't ever do that to us again."

"I'm sorry I didn't reach out earlier."

"Water under the bridge," Dad said with a wave of his hand, his way of telling me that the extension discussion was tabled for now. "How are things, sweetie?" he asked, peering at me through his glasses as if he needed a new prescription—which he likely did.

"Good," I choked out. I wanted to blurt everything, lay down all that happened in the past few weeks and all that I was afraid of. But I couldn't tell them about the game or Chloe Donnelly or even Mateo. It all seemed dumb compared to their life and would take up too much time. Plus, I knew my parents would use it as a reason for me to move with them to Burkina Faso, where I could find my way back to the values they'd instilled in me or some other ethical guilt trip they'd spout. And then I'd have to tell them I didn't want to go. I couldn't take the idea of them being disappointed in me. Not when I was already feeling so alone. "How are you?"

"Well," Mom said, inching Dad to the side. "Today we did a workshop for some female torture survivors, and I will tell you that these women are absolutely astonishing. You'd think they'd be completely broken, but really they're the kindest, most optimistic people. So grateful to us for giving them time to tell their stories. So happy to be alive."

So happy to be alive. It was like the death knell on my trivial problems. My parents were working with torture survivors. Why would they care a thing about a mean girl who was making everyone play a gross game that none of us should have agreed to in the first place?

When my mom finished describing all the horrifying things these women and girls had endured, my dad cleared his throat and said, "That might have been TMI, Charley." Charley, Dad's nickname for my mom since she'd insisted on playing rugby with the men's team in college after realizing they got more fans to come to their games. To everyone else, she was Charlotte.

My mom laughed. "Sorry, Chloe. Sometimes I forget you're not here with us, seeing everything in the day to day."

"It's okay. It's good I know about what's going on in the world."

"Are you okay, honey?" Dad asked. "Is it just too late or is something else going on?"

I swallowed and shoved a finger in my mouth, attacking a nail that had grown a millimeter after I had endeavored for the past two days to stop biting.

"Chloe," Mom said. "Your nails."

Even living in Burkina Faso, my mom had prettier hands than me. The nail biting was a habit I picked up from Dad, though he gave it up as soon as he went through his first bout of a germ-borne illness in BF. Not a lot of antibacterial soap in their village.

"Sorry," I muttered after I dropped my hands into my lap. "I'm fine, Dad. Tired. Things at school have been a little weird with my friends, but I'll work it out."

Dad nodded. "I'm sure you will. You're a great girl."

I laughed. My dad could bust out the sitcom dad when he wanted to, though both of us knew he had no clue how to navigate social situations very well. I inherited the awkward blurting thing from Dad too.

"Chloe," Mom said, "all you need to do is be a person of integrity and the rest will sort itself out. If your friends don't respect that, then they aren't very good friends in the first place. I know we said we weren't going to talk about you coming here, but—"

"Charley," Dad said.

"I know. I'm sorry. I just miss you, and I think you would get so much out of being here. All that school drama will disappear. You've got a helper spirit, and there's so much work we could all do together."

Sometimes it was like she'd watched the Mister Rogers highlight reel from when I was a kid and PBS decided to rerun all the episodes. Mom wouldn't and couldn't understand all my anxiety about Chloe Donnelly and Gestapo.

I nodded and mumbled, "I'm still thinking about it, Mom."

"We know. We're not trying to pressure you. We love you, Chloe," Dad said. "Chin up. Things could always be worse."

And there it was. The reason none of my problems would ever be worthy of a late-night call. People had it worse, people my parents saw every single day. That's why we'd gone to Burkina Faso in the first place. "Yep, Dad. You're right. Could be worse. Love you too. I'll talk to you soon."

"We might be able to connect again on Saturday?" Mom said.

Saturday, after my former friends had all played the game without me. "Sure," I said in a tight voice.

Mom blew me a kiss and then they clicked off, and I fell back into bed, unable to sleep because I felt so bad about all my silly high school worries when real people had suffered torture in Africa.

When I finally fell asleep, I dreamed of the Mothers of the Disappeared, wandering the streets of Argentina alongside female torture survivors from Africa, calling my and Mateo's names over and over again.

21

I felt all buzzy and out of sorts on Friday, knowing I wasn't playing Gestapo and everyone else would be. I was still being frozen out by the girls, though Josh and Aiden both waved at me on my way into school. Aiden had even looked at me like he thought I had a backbone. Of course they both glanced around before acknowledging me—no doubt checking for Chloe Donnelly—but it still gave me a little lift, almost as much as Mateo's Argentina presentation had.

Melissa and I sat together again at lunch. After her catching me twice peeking at Mateo's table, she finally said, "Is there something going on with you and Mateo?"

My cheeks warmed, of course, and I immediately let my hair curtain drop. "Umm . . ."

"You don't have to tell me."

I looked outside to the warm April sunshine. It felt like our Iowa weather system had finally committed to spring. "It's complicated."

She laughed once bitterly. "Yeah, I hear that."

"Yeah? You have complications?" I leaned forward and waited for her to explain.

She took a deep breath and said, "My boyfriend is at Camp Dodge in Johnston, part of the Iowa National Guard. I don't see him as much as I'd like."

"Oh." So the guy I'd once seen her with *was* her boyfriend.

"Yeah, I know what you're thinking. I didn't expect I'd get involved with someone like him either. After my dad . . ."

After her dad was an absentee parent for so much of her life. She didn't need to say it; the subtext was clear, and we'd had conversations when we were younger about how she wished he'd quit the army and move home for good.

"But you fell in love?" I asked, pushing my hair back behind my ear. "With your boyfriend, I mean."

"Yeah," she said, and smiled. A real smile that was motivated by her own happiness. The first one I'd seen from her in a long time. "But I wasn't looking to . . . you know." She waved her hand in the general area of her stomach.

"Get pregnant?" I whispered.

"Yeah. I mean, I always thought that antibiotics screwing up your birth control pill thing was a lie. I thought your mom

279

was trying to scare us when she told us about it when we were in fourth grade. But it happened to me."

Holy crap. "You're on birth control? Does your mom know?"

My own mom would be pleased as hell if I came to her wanting to go on the pill. *It's great you're taking responsibility for your own body and choice, Chloe.* But there was no way I'd ever give her the satisfaction of that conversation, even if I wanted to go on the pill. Too complicated, too much baggage from her miscarriage still swirling around inside me, and maybe her too.

"Yeah, she knows," Melissa said. "The conversation when I asked her if I could go on it was a hundred kinds of awkward, but she didn't want me 'getting in trouble.' Not that I didn't end up there anyway."

"Probably your mom didn't think of that antibiotic thing either." Not everyone was as up on these things as my own mom.

Melissa shrugged but didn't say anything else. I had a bunch more questions, but it didn't really seem fair of me to ask them when I wasn't telling her anything about Mateo. I bit my nail and glanced at his table again. He was sitting with Josh and Aiden. Cam was most likely out in the parking lot waiting for Holly. I had no idea if Josh and Aiden had resolved their argument or not, but they seemed friendly enough. Not that

that meant anything. Hard to have a big public breakup when no one knew you were dating in the first place.

Josh caught my eye but didn't wave. Instead, he glanced to where Chloe Donnelly sat. She was looking at him, then her gaze flicked to me and she smirked. I could almost hear her sarcastic *poor Other Chloe* in my mind.

I focused back on Melissa. "I kissed Mateo," I said in a low voice. "But it's complicated because I can't be with him publicly right now."

She placed the apple she was eating on top of her lunch bag. "Does he have a girlfriend already?"

"No." God, did he? No. No, he couldn't. I'd know. "Nothing like that. I can't really get into it, but let's just say there are external forces keeping us apart."

She nodded. "I can understand that."

It was enough of an opening and I was super curious so I blurted, "Did you want the baby? Were you going to keep it?"

Melissa looked at her apple, her brown curls dipping to cover her face in her own version of a hair curtain. Her expression seemed so sad. I reached out and put my hand over hers and squeezed. She looked back up at me. "It wouldn't have been ideal, but Seth—my boyfriend—said he'd take care of us. I could finish high school and we'd get married."

It wasn't totally unusual for Grinnell. Abortions might be a big thing in Chicago, but our town had at least twenty churches for a population of nine thousand people. Finding anyone out-side "the college" who wouldn't have pushed Melissa to keep the baby would have been a near miracle.

"You could have come to me. I mean, I'm not an expert on sex or anything, but my mom . . ."

Melissa reached across the table and squeezed my wrist. "Yeah. I remember. You were so excited about that baby. So excited to have a sibling finally. I couldn't tell who was more devastated about the whole thing, you or your parents."

I blinked. "I don't remember that part. I just remember my mom being so sad, and me promising myself never to get into that situation because I hated losing something I wanted so badly. I think I even announced I was going to marry a woman and get my tubes tied."

"I remember that too. It's what led to our last fight."

"Me deciding to marry a woman?"

She laughed, but it was a little stark and bitter. "No. You getting worked up over losing something you wanted."

The moment she said it, it came flooding back to me. Thirteen-year-old me screaming at Melissa that she'd never understand caring about something so much and what it was like to lose it. And her screaming back that she wanted her dad home and every day she was certain she'd lose him. I didn't think it was the same; her dad was still alive. But now, with her across from me, I understood what was really going on. We were both lonely, and I'd torn us apart to protect myself. I didn't want to be left behind like my own mom had seemed to leave me for a while, so I left Melissa.

"I forgot about that fight. I thought we'd just sort of drifted."

"We did, but that started it. We were both really hurt and angry."

"Sorry," I mumbled. "I'm sorry I was so mean."

"Not mean. Just hurt. And I'm sorry too."

"Do you still want to marry Seth?" I asked, retreating behind my own hair so I could study her face better.

She tilted her chin up, hair falling back to reveal her for-sure-certain face, and said, "Yes. That's our plan after I graduate, even without the baby."

Which explained why Melissa wasn't cowering in the corner or dropping out of school or anything else that indicated she'd wilted beneath the town shame spiral. Gossip was still flying around about her, but she seemed oddly resolved about it and now I understood why. She had someone who wanted her. She had a certainty in front of her and it was enough.

I peeked at Mateo once more, and this time he caught me and did that little half-smile thing. I pushed my hair back behind my ear again and smiled back, all warm cheeks and no-doubt-obvious crush. It was a risk. Chloe Donnelly was probably still watching me.

Melissa shoved her half-eaten apple inside her bag and stood. "I hope whatever external forces are screwing with you go away soon. It's nice to see you happy."

I stood and gathered my things too. I didn't know what was more surprising—that I managed to look happy in spite of being ignored and hated by most of my friends or that Melissa cared that I was happy.

God, I sucked as a friend to her. And I wanted so, so much to make it right.

"I'm sorry for . . . everything, I guess. Not just the fight, but all of it. I'm glad we're becoming friends again." It was awkward and too honest, but I felt like I didn't have to worry so much with Melissa. That she wasn't judging my awkwardness. That she might appreciate my honesty.

She nodded and tossed her bag into the trash bin at the end of the aisle. "Me too. Seth's coming over to watch a movie tonight. You can come too, if you want."

Friday night watching a movie instead of playing a twisted game? Yeah. I could get behind that. "Sure. Let me double-check with Nan and Pops. Text me later and we can figure out timing."

Then I walked side by side with her out of the cafeteria and didn't bother to peek back to see just who was watching.

I stopped at the media center and loaded up on books before going home for the long, lonely weekend. I was glad I had plans with Melissa and Seth, because three nights and two days with no one but Nan, Pops, and Fox News was about the most depressing thing I could imagine. I knew I needed to have a conversation with my parents about the extension, but every time I thought about it, I felt paralyzed. I hated admitting that Mateo would factor into my decision, and there was no way I'd ever tell my mom that, but it was the truth. Which meant that I couldn't have the conversation with my parents, couldn't tell them I wanted to stay in Grinnell, until I knew how things would play out with Mateo.

When I got to my house, Mateo was waiting on the porch with a glass of water that Nan had undoubtedly forced on him. I dropped my heavy bag and almost crossed to him with my arms outstretched in a dumb romantic-movie way, but managed to fist my hands and let my hair curtain fall, then leaned against the porch rail.

"Chloe," he said, sounding part sad and part disappointed. "Your hair. You're hiding."

I brushed my hair away from my eyes and said, "What are you doing here?"

He glanced toward the big front window that Nan was peering out of with the subtlety of a bull in a china shop and said, "Can you take a walk?"

I nodded. "Let me put this inside." I slung the bag onto my shoulder and slipped in the front door. Nan jumped on me as soon as I walked in.

"You didn't say you were going to have a guest." Yep. Subtle.

"Mateo and I are going to take a walk," I said as I shoved my bag in Pops's organized closet.

"He seems . . . nice. Second time he's been for a visit," Nan said, as if I weren't keeping score too.

"Yep."

"Two times is a big deal."

I had no idea the mathematics of Nan's "courtship" tallies, so I nodded vaguely and put my hand on the door to leave.

"Mateo? Is he Mexican?"

"Oh my God, Nan. You can't ask questions like that!"

"Why not? I gave him a glass of water and invited him to wait inside."

My mom would be at her throat already, seeing the criticism behind almost all of Nan's "innocent" questions. Mom would be up on her soapbox going on about our country being founded by foreigners who stole the land from Native Americans so it's best to reserve judgment about "immigrants." But I wasn't my mom. I knew Nan was old and wouldn't likely ever change her mind. And I wasn't about to get into an argument over the "illegal aliens" and the need for even more stringent security on the Mexican border. I'd lost that argument too many times already, and I didn't want Mateo overhearing.

"It was just a question, Chloe," Nan said. "I wasn't trying to be offensive."

"Well, I don't know the answer."

Nan's lips puckered. "Isn't he a friend of yours?"

"Yes."

She tsked. "You kids never bother finding out people's stories. All this 'global community' nonsense, as if it isn't important to know someone's origins."

Knowing someone's origins had long been code in my grandparents' circle for *learning if they're the right kind of people*. I held up a hand. "Nan, can we get into this later? Mateo's waiting outside."

She huffed. "Dinner is at six thirty. Invite him to stay. I'm sure he'd tell *me* his family's story."

Heh. Doubt it.

"Sure, but he might have plans. He works in town."

"In town? Where?"

"Nan, you're being nosy."

"I'm not. I'm interested. We don't have many Hispanics in Grinnell. What do you think brought his family here?"

"Nan. I love you. You know I love you. But first, no one says Hispanics. That erases the distinct cultures of individual Latin countries. And second, how come you've never asked these questions about my other friends? How come it's only about Mateo?"

"He's the only boy you've brought around. Invite him to dinner, Chloe. I promise I won't bite. I'm interested in why he's interested in you. And excuse me, but *Latinos* normally don't marry outside their culture."

"Nan!" I huffed. "Stop. You're making assumptions on a bunch of different levels here. And we're not getting married; we're going for a walk."

"Hmm. I know. But if you like him, you need to think about these things. Not for you. You'll be fine. But is being mixed something you want for your children? Minorities have a difficult life, and it would be very hard on you to watch your children suffer."

I blinked. I felt like I was in another dimension. Somehow Nan already had me married to Mateo and having mixed children, who would apparently "suffer."

I didn't say anything for a full minute, then finally mumbled, "I'll invite him to dinner. He probably can't come, though."

"You won't know until you ask."

I envied Nan's simple view of the world sometimes. It was such an easy leap for her to trust Fox News and our pastor and not worry about anything else as long as we all maintained the status quo. Mom would say it was the privilege of being a white woman in a first world country that appeared to back her 100 percent. I suspected it was more the privilege of age and ignorance. Which maybe was unkind, but no less true.

Mateo looked at me when I stepped back onto the porch but didn't appear to have overheard Nan. He didn't say anything until we were at the bottom of the driveway headed downtown.

"I've got to stop by Beau's to get my paycheck. Do you mind?"

"No."

Another five minutes of silence and I started to bite my nails. I glanced at Mateo, who raised his eyebrows at me, so I dropped my hand from my mouth.

"Are you just going to be all quiet?" I blurted. "I'm not sure how to do this."

"How to do what?"

"I don't know. Be . . . whatever we are."

He took my hand, not even flinching over the fact that it had just been in my mouth and I hadn't used any hand sanitizer yet, and said, "You're worrying too much. I'm not thinking about any of that stuff. I only wanted to see you."

My stomach got all fluttery and warm, and I had to suppress this weird feeling like I needed to pee really bad. "I wanted to see you too."

He leaned in and kissed me, but it wasn't a long, tongue kiss, which was probably for the best, because Nan's friends would definitely call her if they spotted me tongue-kissing a guy on Fifth Avenue.

I followed Mateo into Beau's, him still holding my hand *like we were a real thing*. I excused myself to go to the bathroom, and when I came out—not having to pee that bad after all—Mateo was talking to Josh with a serious expression on his face.

"What's wrong?" I asked.

Josh offered me a sad smile and said, "I tried to bail on the game, and then Aiden's parents got an envelope in the mail with pictures of him and me together."

"Oh my God. What?"

Josh smoothed his hand over his shirt. "It's okay. I mean, it's not great, obviously, but Aiden's parents were surprisingly cool about it. They're worried about him. Us, I guess."

"Did he tell them about the game?"

Josh shook his head. "No. He's trying to minimize damage, keep it contained to his parents, so that it doesn't go public and hurt his chances getting into the Naval Academy."

Josh's voice cracked a little, and I ached for him. For how hard it would be to have a boyfriend who had to keep you a secret. I glanced at Mateo, then turned back to Josh. "What are you going to do?"

Josh looked down. "I told Chloe I'd play after all."

Defeat poured off him, and I reached a hand out to squeeze his shoulder. "I'm so sorry, Josh. Thank you for trying. I wish there was something . . ."

Josh shrugged. "We're figuring it out."

Mateo glanced between the two of us, then touched my hand and said, "Be right back."

The second he was gone, Josh smoothed out his shirt again and said, "I'm sorry for how shitty things have been for you this week. I feel like a huge dick for ignoring you. So does Aiden."

"I know you think you have no choice, but you don't have to play."

His lips went tight, making his skin paler and his freckles more obvious. "You know we do. If it was just me . . ."

I sighed. "Yeah, I know. It's Aiden, and his future." I let my hair drop. "So, um, is everything okay with you guys?"

I didn't know how to explain I'd overheard their fight without feeling like the creeper Eve accused me of being.

Josh lifted a shoulder. "I guess, all things considered. It's stupid, but Chloe Donnelly helped clarify some stuff for us. I mean, we're sort of debating how our future is going to go, and I thought we wouldn't . . . Well, it doesn't matter. Seeing you this week, all alone and left out, and then having her send those pictures to Aiden's parents, it made us both realize some stuff. We're not letting her tear us apart. We've got a plan."

Before I could ask what he meant, or even get excited about the possibility of Chloe Donnelly maybe getting what she deserved, Mateo returned and took my hand again. "All set."

Josh fist-bumped him and said, "See you tonight, man." Then he turned to me and said, "You too."

I didn't want to remind him he wouldn't be seeing me because I was *all alone and left out*. No sense coming across like a pathetic loser when it was the first time Josh had spoken to me in a week. Instead, I said, "I'm really sorry again. Please tell Aiden I hope it all works out."

He nodded, and I let Mateo guide me out of the restaurant while Josh headed back toward the kitchen.

"Do we need to stop at the bank to deposit your check?" I asked Mateo.

"Not the bank. I get my check cashed at the Western Union at Hy-Vee, but it's fine. I'll do it later."

Not the bank. Of course not the bank. What was wrong with me? He wouldn't have an account there. They probably asked for Social Security cards and a bunch of paperwork Mateo didn't have.

"Sorry. I didn't think," I stammered.

"S'okay."

We cut down Fifth toward Broad Street. Already a few pickup trucks were scooping the loop, the promise of another boring Friday night making me think again how much I couldn't wait to get out of this town. Mom's organic coffee shop used to be around the corner, but a restaurant was there now. Nan and Pops said it was a "college" restaurant, which meant a foodie menu and empty tables except for during parents' or alumni weekends.

The silence between us didn't seem as awkward with my hand engulfed in Mateo's. Mostly I was thinking about Josh and Aiden. "Did you know about them?"

Mateo nodded. "Yeah. Saw them once after an away game at the beginning of the season. They didn't see me, and it wasn't really my business. Josh told me about them a few weeks ago."

I'd never have guessed Mateo knew anything. Maybe his own secrets made him fiercely protective of other people's.

We turned down Sixth so we were skirting the edge of the college. I saw Burling Library and felt a little sick.

"I'm going to ask you something, Chloe, but I need you to hear me out before you say no," he said, his voice soft and low.

My stomach tightened. "Yeah?"

"Promise?"

Part of me wanted to tell him I'd never say no to whatever he asked of me, but the more sane side of me understood the danger of the unconditional yes. Especially after the past few weeks.

"Okay," I said. "Ask."

But of course, typical Mateo, he didn't say anything until we'd passed the fancy dining hall, walked another block, and he pointed to a pickup truck parked on a side street. It was similar to all the ones that scooped the loop, only slightly rustier and older.

"Whose truck is this?" I asked as he manually unlocked

293

the door and guided me onto the bench seat inside. His hand on my back felt warm and slipped low enough for me to hold my breath. But then it was gone and he was circling to the driver's side.

"A friend from the farm. He asked me to pick it up for him," he answered when he got in.

The farm where his parents worked. Where he presumably lived. A million questions popped into my brain about what Mateo's life was like outside of school and baseball and Beau's, but I couldn't ask any of them because he locked the doors and slid over the worn vinyl bench seat to me. He wrapped an arm around me and I thought there was no moment more perfect than this.

Mateo was such a smooth kisser, as if it didn't require anything of him, as if it was an extension of him; even though I was pretty sure he liked kissing me. He took his time and didn't seem at all self-conscious of who or what was around us. I was more confident now, pleased about my third make-out session in a week with someone I could trust. In this moment the ground beneath me felt solid, as if being with Mateo made me believe in myself, believe in us.

When his hands got involved and my shirt came off, I barely paused except to fumble for his shirt too, stretching out the hem as I pulled too fast to get it off. I felt every place he touched me. Every. Single. Place. And for a few minutes it was incredible.

But then I came back into me. I tried to pretend I wasn't thinking about my overly oily skin when his hands cupped my face, or the way my boobs were obviously smaller than expected once my padded bra came off, or that someone might peek in and see us. I tried to channel *the physical present* like Mom used to say when she was doing yoga, but it had slipped away. I was in my head because I'd never done anything like this with a guy, and even though it felt good, I still felt the unescapable me-ness in everything. Which was . . . disappointing.

I was ready to give up, but then it changed again. This time because *he* changed. All his smoothness started to unravel and he was fumbling and more awkward, and I was so grateful for it I let go of all my hang-ups and allowed myself to feel excited about all the newness again. I didn't hate myself for giving in and letting go because it was obvious he wasn't disgusted by me. He liked me and was right there with me. And when he slipped his shaky hand between my thighs, over my jeans, and pressed, a weird noise came out of my throat and the feeling of needing to pee overwhelmed me.

I pulled back. "I have to go to the bathroom," I blurted. "Sorry."

Mateo looked shaken and flustered—*flustered!*—and raked a hand through his hair, laughing a little. "Didn't you just go?"

"Yes," I admitted. "But being with you makes me have to pee." Stupid honesty. Stupid blurting mouth.

He laughed a lot more this time. "Chloe, you're pretty perfect."

Perfect. Not perfectly boring or perfectly uninteresting or perfectly gross. *Perfect.*

Putting space between us had helped the pee thing, so I inched back more and squeezed my thighs together like I used to do when I was "tickling myself" as a little kid. But that made the pee thing start again and now I wondered if it wasn't a pee thing at all. If it was just feeling good between my legs like Mom used to tell me was normal and okay. If it was like the loofah on my clitoris and accidentally maybe having an orgasm.

My cheeks burned and I tugged my shirt on, not bothering with the padded bra as there was no need to put a fine point on *that* humiliation. "What did you want to ask me?" Yes, good, deflect, deflect, deflect.

He shrugged his shirt on, then linked our hands together again. "I want you to play Gestapo tonight."

"What? No. No. Absolutely not."

"You said you'd listen before saying no."

"When I thought you'd ask something reasonable."

"Chloe."

Crap. This was his big favor—throw me back into the sixth circle of hell with a girl who hated me.

I sighed and fished around for my bra, tucking it in the back pocket of my jeans. "So explain."

"The guys and I have a plan. We've already talked to Eve and Holly. We're going to win the game. Four platinum favors from Chloe Donnelly. Four guarantees of her silence and we'll be safe. All of us."

I couldn't stop the snort that escaped my mouth. "You're going to win? That's your plan?"

"Yes."

"Was this Cam's idea? A little revenge on the girl who had him on his knees?"

He looked at me curiously, then said, "No. It was mine."

I shook my head. "What would ever make you believe Chloe would stick to her platinum favors? I mean, sure, I thought of it too—for about a minute—but the more I consider what she's done and what she knows? No way. She threw that bone in front of you because she wants to ensure you'll keep playing. Four platinum favors wouldn't stop her from squealing to anyone who'll listen. Look at what happened with Aiden's parents."

"You're wrong. Look, you said it yourself, she wants to ensure we'll keep playing. It's all about the game for her. Gestapo is somehow this sacred thing. Everything she's done has been about winning and continuing to play. She wants the platinum favor."

Which begged the question of who she wanted it from and what exactly she wanted. If Cam on his knees was just part of the game, what would the prize for her be?

The game helps me be less alone because I get to know people. Chloe Donnelly had said that to me, but was it really as simple as that? Would she go to all this trouble to be less lonely? Would her platinum favor also be *stay with me?* And would Mateo be the one she asked? Mateo who she knew too much about, who she pretended belonged to me but then kept to herself as much as she could in Spanish class. And the way she'd looked at him that day in the media center? My guts churned. It was Mateo. He was her endgame.

"You seriously think you can shut her down by winning? Think about the kind of damage she could do. What she's already done. Is it worth the risk? I mean, it's not just you, it's your whole family."

He pulled me closer and wrapped his arm around me. "If it wasn't about the game, she'd already have used everything she has against us. I wouldn't even be here having this conversation with you; my family would've ghosted. But she only used the information she had when Josh backed out. She wants us playing. I'm sure of it.

"Come on, Chloe. We don't have anything to lose. She's holding all the cards right now, and the only way to get them back is to win."

I turned to face him and his arm dropped. I linked my hands together to stop me from biting my nails. "I can't believe you think it's that easy. Win and all your secrets will be safe? Really?"

"She's seventeen, not thirty-five and working for the FBI. What else could she want? I've listened to her all week. It's the game. That's what she cares about."

I didn't believe it, not really, but he made a good point about her already having spilled their secrets to everyone if she'd wanted to do real damage. Still, whatever she was after in terms of platinum favors made my stomach hurt to think about. Particularly as my mind insisted on recasting Mateo's face onto Cam's as he knelt at her feet last week.

"I still don't get why, though? What is this game buying her?"

Mateo shrugged. "I don't know."

"Maybe she met Cam at summer camp when they were fifth graders and he was mean to her and this is her way of getting back at him?"

Mateo looked at me like I was nuts. "Chloe."

"Or maybe she's a student from the college and this is a sociological experiment about how obsessive teenagers can be?"

"Chloe, stop," Mateo said, his voice low and gentle. "We're not going to figure out her motives. Just . . . please play the game tonight. I need you there. It's the only thing I can think of that might stop her. Please, Chloe, please." My whole life I'd never forget Mateo's voice and how he said my name and *please*. God, he made everything inside me grow so warm.

"Mateo," I whispered back. "I . . ."

"If we have three of the four letters, we're almost guaranteed a win. We can figure out the word. Eve and Holly are on board. They have a stake in this too. Please. We need you."

I shook my head. "She probably won't let me play again. She froze me out with everyone this week. Why would she take me back?"

He put his hand on my thigh and squeezed. "She'll let you play. She'll love it. She's mentioned it a bunch of times to me this week—speculating about how long it'll take you to come crawling back. It'll feel like a victory to her, you groveling to play again."

"I'm not groveling."

"I know you don't want to, but still. You were the only one she couldn't break with secrets. She wants you to *want* to come back. To tell her she was right all along. It shouldn't be that hard to talk yourself back into the game."

I almost told him the only way she'd want me back would be so she could watch me lose Mateo to her, but it felt stupid and needy and nothing Mateo would be interested in hearing.

"Trust me," he said.

I wanted to ask Mateo just how much he knew about everyone. I wondered about all the back-channel conversations he'd had to orchestrate this plan. But asking him meant telling him everything *I* knew and just how I came to know it and I wasn't prepared to do that.

"This all feels very high drama for Grinnell."

He laughed once. "Maybe. And maybe she doesn't even completely understand what's at stake for us, but it doesn't really change things. Chloe, my family, I keep thinking maybe I should tell them everything. But we'd have to leave. They wouldn't want to risk it. I need this chance for us. For you and me."

My heart flipped. "I know. I know." I released a long breath. "You'd still have to figure out the word. Three letters isn't a for-sure win. And she'll probably pick an anagram."

He grinned wide and leaned forward to kiss me, all sure of himself again. His smooth varsity kisses felt good even if I missed the desperate, unhinged side of him. Finally, he pulled back and said, "With you playing too? I have to believe we'll win. I'm not giving up on hope."

Then all my misgivings went out the window because he pulled me onto his lap and fumbled to get my shirt off again and unbuttoned the top of my jeans, his kisses growing sloppier with each press forward. And it turned out I didn't have to pee after all, that it was the other thing.

22

Mateo left me at the end of my block at six o'clock, claiming he needed to get the truck back, but I guessed it was more likely he was ducking the dinner invite from Nan. She didn't hide her disappointment when I walked in the door alone.

She eyed me throughout dinner—pork chops and applesauce—and Pops grumbled more than usual, but he didn't point-blank ask me what was up with Mateo. Nor did Nan speculate more about any possible future children of ours. Thank God. Instead, they grilled me about my decision to join my parents in Burkina Faso. I fidgeted in my seat, not only because I hadn't come to any decision, but also because my bra was digging into my back since I'd accidentally twisted the strap when I was trying to rehook it in the truck right before Mateo dropped me off. Adjusting it would only lead to a third-degree grilling I wasn't interested in, so I let it be.

After I did the dishes, I put on my most neutral face and said to Nan, "I'm going to Melissa's to watch a movie tonight."

"Melissa McGrill? The pregnant one?"

"She's not pregnant."

Not anymore.

Nan tilted her head. "Is that why you were acting all out of sorts at dinner? Were you afraid to tell me about these plans? I thought it might have been because of that boy."

I didn't even really consider Nan's disapproval of Melissa, but I was glad it worked to my advantage, even as I simultaneously felt crappy that I'd have to bail on my plans with Melissa and Seth.

"First, don't call him *that boy* as if he's carrying a terminal illness. His name is Mateo. And before you started fretting over our future half-Mexican babies, you were actually excited that I was spending time with him. Second, you haven't been the nicest to Melissa at church, so I think it's only fair you make up for that by letting me watch a movie with her."

My words came out too sharply, and Nan flinched a little. I instantly regretted my tone. Part of returning to Grinnell when my parents stayed in Burkina Faso was this unspoken contract that I wouldn't give my grandparents a hard time. For all that my parents were constantly at odds with Nan and

Pops's politics, it was a gift having them agree to keep me, and all of us knew it. So I almost never snapped at my grandparents, but the game was stressing me out.

Nan crossed her arms and straightened her spine. "I'm looking out for your well-being, including monitoring the influences around you. That's what family does. That's what I told your mother I would do when she asked me to look after you."

My shoulders slumped. "I know, Nan. I'm sorry. I didn't mean to snap."

"*You* wanted to live here with us."

I nodded and felt my chin tremble. "I know. If you don't want me to stay . . ." I looked down, unable to choke out the rest.

Nan sighed. "Of course we want you to stay. I didn't mean to imply we didn't want you. This isn't your fault."

I shrugged. Honestly, it actually was. My fault for not being able to cut it in Burkina Faso, and begging to come home. My fault for being afraid of too many things, because my fear had proven such a roadblock in my parents' efforts to save the world. My fault for being the child who survived but was a disappointment rather than the baby who was full of potential but had died. *We don't always get what we want, Chloe. But maybe sometimes what we get is the right thing anyway.*

"So can I go to Melissa's?" I asked in a quiet voice.

Nan tsked. "Where's Eve? You haven't seen her in a while. She has that good Lutheran mother."

I rolled my eyes with a ridiculous amount of exaggeration, knowing it drove Nan bananas when I donned my petulant-teenage-girl cape and hoping it'd diffuse my sharp words from earlier. "Melissa's mom goes to church too. You've seen them there."

"Fat lot of good Pastor John has been for *that* family."

"Nan," I said, my voice more of a plea now. "Melissa doesn't really have anyone. Isn't this what grace is supposed to be?"

"The Lord is in charge of grace. It's not up to teenage girls."

"Nan," I pleaded again. I couldn't believe I was begging to fake-hang-out with a friend. Nan would go ballistic if she knew about Chloe Donnelly and the game.

"Fine, but Pops will wait up for you. No drinking or vaping or doing molly or whatever it is you kids do these days."

An unexpected laugh burst from my mouth. *Vaping? Molly?* In an actual display of granddaughter affection that I instigated, I hugged her. "Nan, you have to stop watching *Access Hollywood* when Pops is playing bridge with his pals. It's given you a skewed perspective of the world."

"Nonsense," Nan replied, shaking out of my hug. "I watch for the celebrity outfits."

I squeezed her shoulder. "Thanks," I said. "For everything."

Nan smiled. "God, family, then everything else, Chloe. Those have always been my priorities, and I'm too old to change them."

"I know, Nan. I know. I love you."

I grabbed a hoodie from the closet but didn't bother changing my clothes otherwise. First, because Nan would get suspicious of an outfit switch only to watch a movie with Melissa. And second, because my clothes apparently didn't factor in much when it came to Mateo's interest in kissing me or my ability to fluster him. My cheeks heated as I thought about all the stuff we'd done in that truck, how anyone could have peeked in but somehow it didn't matter because it all felt so good. It probably was considered PDA, which until now seemed horrible and show-offy. I wished I had someone real to tell about it, but Eve and Holly were out of the question, and explaining getting fingered to Melissa seemed awkward times a million. We weren't at the stage where we could talk about that kind of stuff.

Pops stood at the door as I headed out. "Watch movies with your friends here next time, doll. I'll make snacks and tell old-man jokes."

He laughed and for a second I considered saying something to him, explaining about Gestapo and Chloe Donnelly manipulating everyone. The thought of having Pops to work through with me what to do was so appealing, but then I remembered Mateo. Pops might not be as vocal as Nan, but he certainly had thoughts about the undocumented. *Stealing American jobs.* So instead, I hugged him too, and said, "Sure, Pops. Next time."

He held on to my arm for a second and said, "Make good choices, Chloe doll."

It was something my mom would've said, and for the first time I understood how she could be the child of these two. All three of them loved their family and valued integrity—the problem was they couldn't agree on what exactly that meant.

"Okay, Pops. Love you." Then I hugged him again and headed out toward the college campus.

A weird calm settled over me as I got closer to Burling Library. I didn't bite my nails or let my hair fall in front of my face. I walked with purpose and a certainty that, no matter what, everything would be resolved tonight.

Chloe Donnelly didn't even look surprised to see me when I stepped into the pool of light by the library. She wore a purple dress with large outer pockets that matched the ring on her right-hand finger, and her hair was pulled back in a scarf that looked exactly like the one she'd stolen for me, the one that was still tucked away in Pops's tidy closet, waiting to be returned or paid for. She was even more ghostly pale under the glow of the library lights. Her blue eyes shone in victory as soon as she met my gaze.

"Well, well, look who decided to turn up. Isn't this pink?"

I didn't even glance at Mateo before I answered, the calm burrowed so deep inside that I didn't need his reassurance. "I was wrong, Chloe. I'm sorry. I still want to play."

Her eyes lit up even more, but she adjusted the scarf on her head completely casually. "You think it's that easy?"

Of course it wasn't that easy. She wanted to make me beg and she wanted to gloat.

"I'm sorry, Chloe," I repeated.

I could see the anger in her face. My simple apology was ruining this for her. "Try harder. That's not going to work."

"Well . . ." I glanced around. "You don't seem to have another girl to play in my place tonight, so we could stand here and have it out, or you could take the high road and forgive me now so we can get the game started."

She shot a look to Mateo but he didn't react. He looked at me as if I were just another girl. For a second I felt his coldness cut through me, but then I remembered the afternoon and how his hands got shaky and he had to catch his breath after kissing me.

"Don't you want me to be around to see you win your platinum favor?" I hedged. Mateo glanced at me in confusion, but Chloe Donnelly stared at me as if I'd just planted my surrender flag at her feet. I'd been right, her platinum favor 100 percent involved Mateo. Probably Mateo naked. I shut the door on that image and focused.

Cam stepped forward, a layer of disgust on his face that overshadowed his usual boredom. "Just let it go for chrissakes and let's play the game."

For a second I felt bad for him, for his small life filled with detention and post-lunch make-out sessions with his girlfriend. For his grudging promise to Holly of "no more girls" that made me wonder if he'd fooled around a lot, and why. He was never going to leave Grinnell, no matter how often he took off in his car. High school was probably going to be the best time of his life. He'd be stuck in this town till he became like one of the old guys Pops hung out with at the farm store. Cam was nothing like his brother. All that wasted singing talent he'd never do anything with. Aiden would give up everything to get out of here, but not Cam. Too lazy or too defeated. It was sad, really. But before I could spend more time on the pity train, I shook myself and remembered how easily he dropped to his knees in front of Chloe Donnelly, and all my compassion stalled out.

"Cam's right," Mateo said. "Let's just play."

It was a risk, Mateo taking my side. And I wondered if he'd pay for it later, but Chloe Donnelly huffed and said, "Fine." Then she pointed at me. "But you and I need to hash a few things out before we get back to school on Monday, Other Chloe."

I faltered. *Other Chloe.* I'd almost forgotten after a week of near silence. My gaze darted to Mateo, who gave me an imperceptible nod. I shrugged and pulled out all the stops on my confidence. "Whatever. I'll hash it out with you tomorrow. You can come over and I'll put on a full show of groveling. Okay?"

Tomorrow might suck. Agreeing to a weekend of possible misery and kissing butt was a gamble, but maybe the outcome of tonight would prevent it. Maybe Chloe Donnelly's wings would be clipped.

"Okay. Fine," she sneered. "Then you can help me plan out my platinum favor." She tilted her head slightly toward Mateo and I wanted to barf, but I nodded like I'd already given up in defeat to her.

Eve and Holly both looked slightly relieved when I joined them, and it helped me feel more sure of my decision to play again. Mateo clearly had talked to them. And while I wasn't 100 percent certain the guys would win, I did feel confident this was the last time any of us would play. Cam and Chloe Donnelly made a big show of stepping away from the group to write their words on slips of paper. She put her folded paper in her large pocket and I caught Mateo's gaze as it lingered on the pocket. I hoped he wasn't contemplating looking for her so he could steal it. He glanced at me and shook his head slightly as if to assure me.

Chloe Donnelly rejoined us and practically snarled a *K* at me when she gave me my letter next to the front door of Burling. I offered a benign smile and nodded. A couple of college students pushed out of the library doors and looked at us with a *Can we help you?* stare, but they didn't say or do anything.

"Back here at ten thirty," Chloe Donnelly said when we all circled up again. "Make it pink, everyone."

Make it pink? Pink. That stupid word. I wouldn't have put it past her to have made up the slang. And when once I'd thought *pink* sounded trendy and elite, now it sounded silly.

Holly whispered in Cam's ear and then kissed him. For a moment after he stepped back, the sleazy gross version of him slipped away and I saw his scared and vulnerable side. The Cam who'd been devastated to lose the student council election to Aiden in elementary school and couldn't hold back his tears in class. The Cam who sang "40" as if he really were waiting for God. The Cam who said *It fucking kills me when you cry* to Holly. He wore the same identical face I'd seen on Aiden when Josh suggested maybe he shouldn't go to the Naval Academy. Maybe the two brothers had more in common than their looks.

But then the vulnerability was gone and Cam's smirk was back. He tapped Holly on the butt in this really obvious way. God, he was so messed up. Then he slapped Aiden on the shoulder and said loudly, "Aiden, try to find a *girl* this time."

Chloe Donnelly grinned and Josh flinched, but neither Eve nor Holly seemed to understand the dig, which meant the secret had stayed with his family. I looked at Mateo, but he didn't react to Cam's words. Instead, he was watching my face. I thought he might have winked before he turned away, but I couldn't be completely sure and it didn't really matter. After tonight he'd be able to wink at me whenever he wanted.

I zipped my hoodie up and fisted my hands in the pockets, ready to go. I headed in the direction of East Campus and didn't bother looking back. The college was eerily quiet, and I wondered if there was some big campus event that kept everyone inside. When I was younger, my parents told me constantly about all the great opportunities the college gave to its students. They called me a "Grinnell Chip" as if I was guaranteed to follow in their footsteps. I'd dodged the conversation, continued to dodge it, even as graduation loomed a year closer and I'd have to tell them eventually. There was no way I was staying in Grinnell. The school might be acclaimed as the "Harvard of Iowa," but I wasn't intending on sticking around to find out.

My phone buzzed with a text when I was halfway to the JRC, going a longer roundabout way to get there. I pulled it out and saw Melissa's name.

So are you still up for movie night?

Guilt swamped me, but I shook myself. Eye on the prize. I barely hesitated when I typed back: Something came up. Can't make it.

She didn't respond and I felt like crap all over again. She was probably my only real friend in the world right now, and I hated that I was blowing her off for this. But the memory of Mateo's hands and kisses and the way he guided my hands and whispered, *Please, Chloe*, in the truck was enough to tamp down my regret. I was doing this for him. I promised myself I'd make things up to Melissa at lunch on Monday. I'd sit with her even if I was invited back with Holly and Eve.

It had only been maybe fifteen minutes, but my finger lingered over Mateo's contact information on my phone. I could call him. He'd make me feel better about all of this. He'd remind me why we had to play. But then I thought better of it. I didn't want to risk it. He might be with Chloe Donnelly—God, I hoped not—and it wasn't worth ruining his plan. I'd wait until he reached out to me for my letter.

23

Holly and Eve were sitting outside the JRC when I walked up. They must have gone directly there through the middle of campus instead of taking the long periphery way like I had. They were both dressed less scantily this week—Holly in a longish jersey dress, cheaper looking than the one from Tillys, and Eve in a tank and skinny jeans. At least they didn't look alike, except for their charm bracelets.

The inside of the JRC was definitely less active than it had been last Friday, at least from what I could see through the glass windows. I approached Eve and Holly on the bench outside with sure steps, that calm still soothing me as if I had nothing to lose—maybe pure BS, but I went with it.

"Are you talking to me now?" I asked, which was a bit hostile, but it had been a very hard week.

Eve looked guilty for about five seconds before she shrugged and said, "As long as you're playing the game."

"What the hell? You guys told me you were going to quit last week. What happened? You totally choked and left me hanging out to dry. And then you blew me off all week."

Holly sneered, "Well, Other Chloe, not all of us are as squeaky clean as you. Some of us don't really have a choice about the way our lives play out."

What did that mean?

I took a deep breath and considered walking away from them, texting Mateo my letter, and washing my hands of the whole thing, but then I saw Holly's mask drop. For a few seconds she let everything she was feeling show on her face, the same way she had in the bathroom that day. And finally I understood that she was really scared. As scared as everyone else.

"What does she know about you?" I asked, my voice going soft the way Mateo's did when he'd asked me to play the game again.

The silence between us was deafening. The stubborn way Holly held her head made me sure that whatever it was fell in the category of "not my business." But then Eve nudged her and after a second Holly's shoulders slumped. "Okay. You need to swear not to say anything. The *only* reason I'm telling you is so you get how important the game is. How essential it is for the guys to win and go through with Mateo's plan so we can end it."

"Okay, I swear."

Holly tipped her head back and stared at the sky for a second before zeroing in on me. "My dad is in prison for possession of narcotics."

I blinked twice. "Holy shit. Are you serious?"

"No, Other Chloe, I'd joke about something like that. Jeez. Of course I'm serious. And I don't really want to go into details, so don't ask."

Except I couldn't stop myself from blurting, "Must have been a lot of narcotics for him to end up in prison on a first offense."

Too many episodes in junior high of *Law & Order* seemed to have stockpiled all these dumb facts in my brain that I blurted out when I was feeling vulnerable. I knew it was a nasty and horrible thing to say considering Holly had just told me this big thing, but I was apparently still bleeding a lot of hurt from the crappy silent-treatment week—and frankly mediocre year—she was partly responsible for.

She skewered me with a look. "Excuse me?"

I took a deep breath and mumbled, "I'm sorry. That was uncalled for."

"It was," she said, and glared at me, not saying anything else.

My mind flipped through the right thing to say, but I was still processing. Chloe Donnelly knew Holly's dad was in jail, when it had managed to stay under everyone else's radar. Did she manipulate Holly's mom too, in order to find out? No, I couldn't buy that; she was seventeen and there was no way. Maybe his arrest was in some public record somewhere? "How long is his sentence?" I asked Holly.

"What part of *don't ask* is hard for you to understand? God. Money has been tight, okay? Not that it's any of your business."

My brain was spinning spinning spinning with questions. What did *money has been tight* mean? Was money tight because he was in jail? Or had money gotten tight so he took to dealing? What were the narcotics he was arrested with? Around here, I'd guess either meth or some sort of dirty heroin mix. I opened my mouth, but Holly narrowed her eyes into arrow points of rage so I shut up.

"Anyway," she said, after I'd blinked out of our staring contest, "Chloe knows about my dad and threatened to tell everyone. And that's not exactly information I want getting around school."

I shook my head. "God, I'm sorry. She's horrible. Seriously, she's the worst person. I can't believe you all can stomach sitting with her at lunch. And how does she know this stuff about everyone?"

Holly raised an eyebrow. "What stuff?"

Crap. Crap, crap, crap. I waved vaguely. "Everyone's secrets. I mean, that's why the guys want to win, right? To protect their secrets?"

"Mateo said it was to protect *our* secrets. That their platinum favors would stop her from using anything against us. What secrets do the guys have?"

My heart sped up and sweat started to gather in my armpits. I wanted to maintain my calm, but it leeched out of me when I realized I couldn't spin knowing the guys had secrets in any way that didn't make me look really bad. And suddenly, all the stuff Eve had said about me watching seemed even worse than just being creepy. It seemed pathetic. As if I had no life so I had to go around spying on other people's.

No.

No no no. I was trying to get a life. The thing with Mateo was real and he needed me to help him. I felt a little bad that Holly thought the guys would use a platinum favor to protect her secret, but maybe Cam would. Maybe the Cam that hated to see Holly cry was willing to demand Chloe Donnelly's silence.

I cleared my throat and deflected. "Why do you think she still wants to play the game so badly? She's got to know all of us hate her because of it, right?"

"I don't know," Holly answered, slouching enough from her usual dancer grace that I knew she was really messed up about the game too.

"She told me sometimes she feels really lonely because her parents aren't around much," Eve offered.

"So she forces people to hang out with her by manipulating them with a game? That seems . . . weird," I said.

"Maybe we're all on some reality TV show none of us but Chloe knows about?" Holly said.

I tried not to roll my eyes. "I'm pretty sure it wouldn't be legal to film us without our permission."

Eve's eyes got wide. "Maybe she's planning on turning Gestapo into some sort of online video game that someone like my brother would play obsessively, and she wants to see if it works in real life first?"

My mouth turned down. "So she's a tech genius playing a live-action role-playing game? That seems really far-fetched."

We were silent for a while, all trying to figure out just what the game bought Chloe Donnelly. A breeze kicked up and Eve rubbed her bare shoulders. I sighed. "Look, let's just find the guys and stick with the plan to end this thing."

Holly pulled out her phone. "I'll text Cam."

"No!"

Holly looked at me and arched her penciled-in eyebrows. "Excuse me?"

"He might be with Chloe. We can't risk her seeing a text or knowing about Mateo's plan."

Holly rolled her eyes. "Paranoid much?"

I probably was, but I couldn't shake the feeling that Chloe Donnelly seemed to have eyes everywhere.

"Just search for him. Find him and give him your letter face-to-face."

"Fine," Holly said, then started to leave. When she saw Eve wasn't following her, she stopped and turned back. "Are you coming?"

Eve shook her head. "I'm going to look for Aiden. It'll seem more realistic if different guys get our letters."

Holly narrowed her eyes for a second, but then said, "Whatever," and flounced away, all dancer huffy, her perfect posture back again.

I waited for Eve to take off too, but she lingered.

"I'm sorry I didn't back you up last week," she said, after the silence between us had gotten heavy and awkward. She sounded a little sad, and the apology felt genuine, like the Eve I used to know before Chloe Donnelly or even Holly came into our sphere.

"Why didn't you?"

"I got freaked out. Chloe knows something about everyone and . . ."

"And?"

She stared at her feet. "Look, I know you think I'm hooking up with Cam, but I'm not. I really didn't know it was him that night."

"I know you didn't, but then after school that day . . . I mean, you got in his car. I saw you."

She looked back up at me, eyes blinking with tears. "You have no idea the pressure I'm under. It's worse than it's ever been. My dad is always on me, always bugging me about school and homework and starting to think about college and making sure I'm *living up to my potential*. It's like he's got nothing better to do than give me a hard time. And he's got my mom involved too. She makes me sit at the kitchen table every day after school doing homework, but I hate it. It's like too much of the semester has passed and I don't know what I'm doing. I can't focus."

My heart squeezed a little. The last time I'd seen Eve like this was when she'd pushed her brother, Jamie, on the sidewalk too hard and he'd fallen and broken his arm. She'd felt horrible and deeply ashamed.

"I didn't realize it was that bad with your mom. I know she's very involved with school stuff, but she used to write you notes to excuse you if you were overworked."

"My dad put an end to that. Now they're all over me because junior year is so important grade-wise on college applications. You don't get it because your parents aren't even here. They're not hovering or constantly on you."

No. They weren't, but Eve had no idea what she was talking about. For as much as her mom was a hoverer, she'd chosen to be *here*. When Eve got mono last year, her mom pulled all these strings to get her homework waived and extra time to finish her projects. My parents couldn't do that from Burkina Faso, and they wouldn't waste their time on it if they could. Instead, they'd tell me again to come live with them and be unschooled.

"You're right," I said, my voice as emotionless as I could make it. "My parents aren't here."

Eve sighed. "I mean, I know it sucks for you only to see them at Christmas and during the summer, but, overall, you're really the lucky one."

That was how Eve saw me—as the lucky one? I wanted to smack the stupidity out of her. "I don't get why you're saying all of this to me. What does this have to do with not quitting the game, or whatever you were doing in Cam's car?"

Eve shifted from foot to foot. "It's just, I was getting behind in English, all my classes really. My mom keeps checking to see if I've turned in my homework. Every day online. And she's always hovering over me to make sure I'm not cheating or pla-giarizing or whatever. I have so much work to do still. I thought Cam might have something to help me pull a few all-nighters to catch up."

I blinked for a second, then the pieces clicked into place. "Drugs? You were buying drugs from Cam?"

"Yeah."

"Did he get them from Holly's dad?" I asked, my random brain deciding to skip over the more obvious questions.

"What? No. Holly doesn't even know he sold them to me."

I wondered how Holly was going to rationalize the drug-dealing part of Cam, considering the situation with her dad. Maybe she'd cry and make him promise to stop, but what did Cam's promises really mean? As far as I could tell, he only cared about himself.

"I can't believe you," I said, blinking at this girl in front of me who I didn't even know anymore.

"God, Chloe. Stop being so judgy. I needed them."

Freshman year in health class, Eve and I had sat across the room from each other. We'd rolled our eyes through the ragingly unhelpful sex ed unit, and we'd both cried during the unit about suicide and self-injury—though we'd never known anyone who'd killed themselves and hadn't yet met the kids who were cutters. But during the drugs and alcohol unit, we'd texted each other throughout each class.

I don't get how our school thinks this will stop anyone from drinking. As if there's anything else to do in Grinnell.

I hadn't been drunk yet at that point, but I wanted to impress Eve, even though I was certain she hadn't been drunk either.

Totally. This is so worthless.

A minute later she'd texted again.

Drugs are stupid, though. I mean, not pot, obviously. But the rest of them? Who wants to be some tweaked-out freak who doesn't care about anything but themselves?

It was strangely prudish of Eve, who even then was immensely curious about so many things. But I'd agreed with her about drugs, which I had to admit was another thing that had always scared me a little. There were so many unknowns, too many things that could go wrong.

"So you went with Cam to buy drugs from him?" I said. "Even knowing about Holly's dad being in prison for them?"

"Well, I didn't know then. And anyway, this is totally different. It's Ritalin, not heroin. And it's not like I'm a user and Cam is my dealer. He just had some extra. It was *one time*, but Chloe saw us, and later she showed up at my house asking questions. I thought she was being cool about it, giving me advice and stuff. I didn't think she was digging. And it was only a bottle of Ritalin!"

"Ritalin that you're probably snorting and hasn't been prescribed to you," I snapped back.

I sounded prudish and judgmental, like the churchy girls who took "purity pictures" with their dads in this slightly gross way and then posted them online. But Eve had become someone I didn't really like anymore. Someone who bought Ritalin to snort so she could pull all-nighters. And standing there in front of the mostly deserted JRC, it occurred to me that we wouldn't be able to get past this. Not just because of the drugs, but because she had turned into a person I could never respect.

In a way, it was almost a relief knowing this would probably be the last night we'd ever hang out. We'd veered off each other's courses a while ago, but I'd kept hoping we'd come back together. Now I was no longer interested in all of that. Mom was right, an empty house was better than one filled with toxic people.

"Why are you telling me this?" I asked, sounding calm and resigned.

"I . . . I wanted you to understand. Maybe Chloe wouldn't use it against me. But with what she's done to everyone else? I couldn't quit the game. You have to understand. . . ." But then she faltered as if she, too, realized we'd never be friends again.

I lifted a shoulder. "Maybe Chloe will tell your parents about the Ritalin and maybe she won't. I get that you don't want your mom finding out, but it seems like the best way to prevent that is not to do it anymore and get rid of the bottle. Then she'll have no real proof."

She got angry then. Eve angry, which had always come on hard and fast and with little warning. "You're such a self-righteous bitch. I can't believe we were ever friends. No wonder your parents let you come back here without them. They were probably grateful to be rid of you."

Ouch.

Then she stomped toward the other side of Eighth Avenue, screaming every swear she could think of.

Her words about my parents stung, not only because I'd secretly thought them myself, but also because Eve had thought them too. Did everyone think my parents were better off in Burkina Faso without me?

My parents missed me. I *knew* they missed me. But were things easier for them in Burkina Faso when I wasn't there? I thought about those first two months, how difficult it'd been for my parents to juggle establishing the school and managing me. I'd been a brat and couldn't adjust to our new life. And even though I knew they didn't want me to go back home, I also knew they couldn't have done all they'd done with me there. I was too much to handle.

My body felt as if it were being pummeled from the inside. A sob caught in my throat and escaped, and then another, and then another. I choked them all back. I pulled my phone out of my pocket with shaky hands. I let my bitten-down thumb hover over Melissa's name and then finally pressed call.

"Melissa," I said when she answered, my voice raw and scratchy.

"Chloe? What's wrong?"

I wanted to ask her if she thought I was too much as well. If she thought parents would give up on their kids because they were disappointed with what they'd become. If parents thought sometimes it was easier not being around their kids. But then I remembered her dad and how he'd barely been around for most of her life and I stopped myself.

"Chloe?" she said again.

I pressed end and powered my phone down, then sat on the steps outside the JRC and finally let myself cry for real, not holding anything back. Letting pain swamp me until I couldn't see and could barely breathe.

24

I wasn't sure how long I sat there, it seemed like hours, but crying always felt like that. Every time I thought I was pulling myself together, a new wave of loneliness and grief overwhelmed me.

A hand on my shoulder startled me from my crying jag. Melissa. And behind her a guy with close-shaved hair who looked at me as if I were an animal at the zoo he'd never seen before. Not repulsed by me, just wide-eyed and curious. This must've been Seth, her boyfriend. He looked vaguely familiar from the first time I'd seen her with him forever ago, but I'd lived a hundred lives since then.

"I figured I'd find you on campus. I thought you weren't playing that game," Melissa said.

I blinked and wiped the snot from my face. Blinked again. "How do you know about the game?"

She sat next to me, and Seth stayed standing, his hands in his pockets and his posture ridiculously straight. He almost looked like he was Secret Service for Melissa.

"Everyone knows about the game, Chloe. It's Grinnell. You think something like Gestapo is going to be kept under wraps? I'm just surprised more people in this dumb town haven't asked to join you."

My body went numb at the idea that everyone was speculating about this, about me. I tried to channel my mom and not care what other people were saying behind my back, but I couldn't. I didn't want to be the subject of the rumor mill. It was bad enough knowing people gossiped about my absentee parents.

"Why didn't you say something earlier?" I asked.

She shrugged. "Because I was waiting for you to mention it. I figured you'd tell me when you were ready to talk about it. I invited you over tonight to give you the out."

Being friends with Melissa was so relieving. I didn't think I deserved the comfort of her, but I wasn't going to turn her away because of my own insecurity. She didn't seem mad I'd kept things from her, not like how Eve always got snippy if I did something fun without telling her or inviting her along.

"I'm sorry I didn't tell you."

"I guess you had your reasons."

I nodded. "It's a big mess. I didn't want to play again, but

Mateo needed me to because . . . well, it doesn't matter. I'm supposed to be looking for him."

Melissa released a long exhale. "Chloe, listen, this girl, the other Chloe, she's not what she seems."

I let out a bitter laugh. "You mean she's not a lying, manipulative bitch?" I slapped a hand over my mouth. My mom would freak if she ever heard me say something like that about another girl.

Melissa laughed, the full open laugh she used to have when we were kids. "No, she is that. But I don't know how much of her story is true, whatever she's told you. I work in the school office a few mornings a week, doing a bunch of shredding and collating for the teachers. They haven't gotten Chloe's records from her old school. And she's got a bunch of excuses every time Ms. McVoy asks her about it."

I scrunched my face. "Really? Well, are they legit excuses?"

"Maybe, but Ms. McVoy has tried to call her parents a bunch of times and they've never answered or returned any of her phone calls."

I frowned. "Yeah, that's kind of shady."

I'd never been to Chloe's house. I didn't even know where it was, which was pretty unusual for Grinnell. I didn't know if Holly and Eve had been there, but I felt like if they had, they would've bragged about it. Said how "pink" it was and how it was too bad I couldn't have come too. She'd asked if I could sleep over last week, but that was before everything got messed up with the game. And she'd even implied maybe I'd be sleeping at Mateo's. It was possible she didn't ever plan on having me over.

"How much do you really know about Chloe Donnelly?" Melissa asked.

I shrugged. "She said her mom's a prof in Iowa City and her dad works in a law firm in Des Moines. I didn't look it up or anything. I mean, why would I? Why would she lie about that?"

Melissa glanced past me at Seth. He was still standing guard. He raised a shoulder. "Could be a fake identity, or a plant," he said. "Like a 21 *Jump Street* sting."

My mouth dropped open. "Are you serious?"

Seth shrugged again. "I don't know. Look her parents up."

Melissa pulled her phone out and googled Professor Donnelly at U of I. "I don't see anything on the website, but if she's new, they might not have updated it with her information yet. Or maybe she doesn't have the same last name."

"Probably we'll have the same problem finding her dad. And Donnelly isn't exactly an obscure name, so there's no guarantee if we find it, it'll be him. It's not Smith, but still."

"True."

"If this whole thing is a sting operation, what's her endgame? A petty drug bust in Grinnell, Iowa? Feels a little weak."

Seth frowned. "Maybe it has to do with the college. She wanted you to play here, after all."

I studied him. He had one of those chin dimples that made guys look younger than they are. I must have been staring at him too long because he tilted his head and raised his eyebrows as if asking, *Do I have something on my face?*

I stood and held out a hand. "I'm Chloe."

Seth grinned—a cute boyish smile that made me see part of why Melissa was into him—and shook my hand. "Yeah, I caught that. Seth. I'm Melissa's."

Not Melissa's boyfriend or fiancé or significant other or boo, just *Melissa's*. My gut tightened in envy. I wanted to belong to someone like that or have someone belong to me.

"It's nice to meet you. Sorry I bailed on you guys earlier."

"Melissa was worried about you," he said. A definite reprimand.

"Sorry," I said again, then shoved a finger in my mouth and started peeling at the cuticle.

"My gran used to say biting your nails would cause a tree of dirty worms to grow in your stomach."

I dropped my hand and reached for my sanitizer in the pocket of my hoodie. "That's gross."

He grinned. "Yep. But it got me to stop doing it."

Melissa stood now too. "I knew you two would like each other."

Seth wrapped his arm around her and pulled her close so she tucked into his armpit. "You should come watch a movie with us, Chloe. It'd make my girl happy."

The *my girl* had a slight twang, and it made me wonder if he'd grown up in the South.

"Yeah, Chloe, ditch this game and let's do something normal. Dari Barn is still open so we can grab some scoops on the way."

When we were little, we always called our ice-cream treats *scoops*, no matter what we were ordering. Even when we both religiously spent a whole summer eating only peanut-butter-cup cyclones, we told our parents we were getting scoops.

I wanted to hug Melissa for making me remember how easy it had been then. How drama-free and simple. But she was still tucked into Seth, and the fact was, nothing was simple for me or her any longer.

"I want to go with you," I said, but then I shook my head, acceptance and defeat churning like a gross cocktail in my stomach. "But I really can't. I need to finish this game. It's complicated, and I have no idea if any of it'll turn out, but I can't bail on Mateo."

I willed her to understand. To see that me and Mateo were a little like her and Seth and that we weren't going to give up on each other. That I wasn't going to give up on him. That he wouldn't "disappear" if I was looking out for him. That he wasn't better off without me.

Melissa grabbed my arm. "Chloe, I think you should come with us. I have a really bad feeling about this. You don't owe it to anyone to keep playing."

But I did. I owed it to everyone, to all the people whose secrets I'd been collecting and keeping—even if I didn't have any plans to disclose them. Whether I wanted it or not, my friends were trusting me to help them get out from underneath Chloe Donnelly. Though if Seth was right and it was some kind of sting, four platinum favors were definitely not going to help any of us.

I had to believe it wasn't as nefarious as that. We were in boring Grinnell. This wasn't a terrorist plot or some kind of DEA operation. That stuff didn't happen here. And I believed Mateo: Chloe Donnelly was just obsessed with a dumb game. That's why she told Aiden's parents about him and Josh. She needed Josh to keep playing. No amount of *CSI* or *American Crime* was going to make me think this went any deeper than a girl who spent way too much time gathering high school gossip.

"It's going to be fine, Melissa. Let's hang out tomorrow, okay?"

Melissa exchanged a nervous glance with Seth.

"Really," I said, reaching out to squeeze her hand. "Trust me. It'll all work out."

I hoped I sounded more confident than I felt. She stared at me for another thirty seconds then nodded. For a minute I thought she was going to hug me, but then she linked hands with Seth and told me to text her when I got home later.

"It was good meeting you, Chloe," Seth said.

"You too. I hope I see you tomorrow also."

I didn't know how that worked, if he stayed with her when he wasn't in Johnston or what, though I couldn't imagine Melissa's mom going for sleepovers. Of course, how much worse could it get than an unplanned pregnancy?

"You will," he answered, no hesitation.

They walked away, and my heart squeezed when I saw him lean over and kiss the top of Melissa's head.

I want that.

25

Even though the night felt like it was going on forever, it had actually only been an hour since we started the game, so we still had another hour and a half until it ended. I needed to find Mateo and give him my letter.

I headed toward the East Campus dorms, powering on my phone, and it immediately pinged with a text.

Mateo: Meet me outside Herrick Chapel.

My stomach swooped and I switched direction. I tucked my hands in my hoodie because the night had gotten cool and breezy. I tried not to wonder what Mateo had been doing for the past hour. It didn't matter. I was meeting him and this was all going to work out. I pushed away all my doubts and walked faster past the science center toward the other academic buildings and chapel. My parents had gotten married in Herrick

Chapel. They said it was only right since that was where they fell in love—getting to know each other more as they protested William F. Buckley Jr.'s convocation speech.

I felt raw and way too exposed as I rounded the corner to the chapel steps, but everything eased in me when I saw Mateo standing in the doorway with his foot holding the door open.

"What are you doing?" I asked.

"Waiting for you. Come on."

I slipped behind him into the dimly lit chapel. "How did you get inside? Herrick's supposed to be locked at night."

"It's locked now," he said, tugging at the door handle until it clicked. He pulled me forward for a kiss. Kissing Mateo was like having the best day in the world, over and over again. I lost all sense of time and my body got all warm and felt heavy and light all at once.

"My letter's *K*," I whispered when he finally inched back.

He laughed. "Not exactly what I was kissing you for."

"Yeah, I know. But I wanted to make sure you had it. Did the other guys get Eve's and Holly's letters yet? I should've asked the girls for their letters when I saw them, just in case they couldn't find Cam or Aiden or Josh. I didn't think. I should've given them my letter to give to the other guys too. In case I didn't find you."

He tucked my hair behind my ear. "I would've found you. I would've come for you."

It sounded both incredibly sweet and incredibly dirty, and I wasn't sure which way I should take it, all the contradictions around Mateo too much for me to stay on any real solid ground for long. Was it always going to be like this with him? I wanted to ask, but it would end up a blurt about whether he thought about me like I thought about him, so I swallowed my worries and deflected. "So did the guys get Eve's and Holly's letters?"

"Yeah. Cam texted. *P* and *I*."

I blinked away the fuzziness from the kiss and being so close to Mateo, and tried to focus on what Chloe Donnelly's word could be. *Pick*? *Pike*? "Oh. Oh, no way," I said as soon as it all clicked into place.

Mateo shook his head but grinned, having figured it out too. "*Pink*. Of course. I should've figured. Stupid and obvious. Not even an anagram. It's almost like she wants to lose."

"Or she's so sure of herself and her girls that she isn't worried about how obvious it is."

He slid his hand to my waist, his thumb slipping beneath my shirt to rub my hip. "Probably that. Though she was stupid to trust you girls. Not after only knowing you three weeks."

"She knows secrets about Eve and Holly too," I said. Though I didn't want to get into the prison thing or Eve's Ritalin usage.

He didn't ask, which was classic Mateo, never one to gossip. Instead, he put his other hand on my hip and said, "She doesn't have anything on you, though. My sweet, honest girl with a big heart. *My* Chloe doesn't have secrets."

Why did every dumb line sound perfect coming from him? Everything I would've scoffed at if Eve or Holly had said some guy fed them seemed genuine from Mateo. As if what he said took him by surprise, like he was a blurter too. I loved the idea that I could unhinge this boy, make him blurt. It made me seem powerful, the same as when his hands shook and he became breathless and flustered in the truck with me. Not giving me a line. Not pulling a varsity move. Just being him. It was maybe better than how Seth had said, *I'm Melissa's.*

"Did that sound cheesy?" he asked. "That *my* Chloe. Sorry. It was . . ."

I grinned. "No. It's okay. I liked it, which I probably shouldn't say because . . ."

Because it was possessive and I wasn't someone's anything; I was my own person, and, and, and . . . But all my mom's judgy feminist criticism dissipated in my mind. *My Chloe* sounded perfect to my ears because it meant someone thought I was special enough to be his. Mateo was taking a risk for me. He made me feel like I was worth it. As if the cost wasn't too high. As if I was the first person on his list instead of the last.

"So what are we doing here?" I asked, glancing toward the altar, a piano in the middle next to the pulpit that made me think there'd been a concert earlier. "Aren't you worried we'll get caught?"

"Cleaning crew left about twenty minutes ago. That's how I slipped in. Doors won't open up again until the morning."

The dim light and the echoing way our voices bounced off the pews and the stained-glass windows made me feel as if time had stopped. Like we were in a sort of dreamworld where nothing could penetrate the walls around us. A strange hazy glow and Mateo's smell and warm breath heating up the skin on my face and neck.

Mateo took my hand and led me to the small balcony. Track lighting along the walls guided our path. I didn't know if they always kept the lights on in Herrick or if Mateo had figured out how to work them, but I was grateful to be able to mostly see him, even if it was all angles and shadow.

The chapel was like most churches in our town, nothing hugely special about it, the altar and the pews and a big pipe organ and stained-glass windows portraying Biblical figures. But my parents had told me about all the people who had given convocations there over the years, and it was overwhelming to think about the history of the place. As if the powerful words from each presenter had seeped into the walls and made every pew, every candle, every pipe from the organ come alive.

I stepped lightly walking up the stairs, not wanting to interrupt the silence and sacredness of the space. I'd seen my parents' wedding photos taken here: Mom in a simple yellow dress and Dad in khakis, a blue shirt, and a wide red tie that matched the carpet. My parents told me they didn't do anything fancy for their wedding because they were broke and every extra penny was saved to set up my mom's organic coffee shop. But they looked happy in the pictures. The only other time I'd seen them that happy—not weighted down by all the trivialities of Grinnell life or a baby they couldn't have—was when they'd told me we'd been accepted into the Spirit Corps.

Mateo directed me to a pew near the front of the balcony and then slid in next to me. I suddenly felt all shy and awkward and nervous about what we were doing. It wasn't the church so much as it was the quiet, the space being ours until we had to return to the game.

Mateo wrapped his long fingers around the top of the pew in front of us. No dirt and nicely trimmed nails. Probably his parents' hands looked like they worked on the farm, but Mateo worked at Beau's and his hands were a little rough but clean. I noticed a tiny burn scar on his wrist from what I assumed was a too-hot pizza pan and touched it with my finger.

"I brought you here because I wanted to be with you. We have time before the end of the game and who knows what's going to happen later. But I wanted to see you and hang out with you. This seemed . . . I don't know, kind of the perfect place." His voice echoed around us, and because of the chapel or because it was him, it felt grave and important.

I nodded, then leaned forward and kissed him again. I wanted to get lost in him, to forget about the game and Chloe Donnelly and my tears over my parents and just think about him. His mouth and his lip ring and his hands and his skin.

He drew back from our kiss and said, "Are you still scared, Chloe?"

"No," I whispered. "Not with you."

I didn't ever think I'd be this girl. In my wildest imaginations about Mateo over the past year, I couldn't believe I'd be the one to take off my shirt and bra first. To help him pull his shirt off because I wanted to feel his skin against mine.

We were both in deep. I could tell by how shaky his hands were and how he wasn't nearly as smooth and coordinated as the first time we'd kissed. He was fumbling, like he had in the truck earlier. Coming undone in the same way I was. Everything I'd been afraid of for so long seeped out of me until my mind wrapped itself around a want I couldn't ask for but felt desperate to have. Mateo. Mateo. Mateo.

He pulled back a few inches and looked at me like I don't remember anyone ever looking at me. Like he was the lucky one to get to be there with me. Like he wanted me as much as I wanted him. "Chloe," he said.

"Yeah?"

"Would you let me?" His hands moved to the button of my jeans. "Could I be your first? Could we . . . ?"

The logical side of me wanted to say no. This was going ridiculously fast with us and we were in the middle of a game that could have terrible consequences. But the logical side of me was outside of this space. Only my heart was here now, pumping double time at the way he'd asked me. It was a plea and a prayer and a question all tangled together, and I was ready to hand him my unconditional yes. Almost.

"I'm not scared," I said again. "But sex is kind of a big deal for me."

He nodded, all serious face. "Yeah. It is for me too. I've never . . ."

"Wait. You haven't?" God, for all his varsity kisses, he was a virgin, same as me.

"No. We'd both be having our first time together."

I took a breath. "Together?"

"Yeah. And it would mean something. It *does* mean something. *You* mean something to me."

My heart beat even faster. I breathed through my nose three times, then licked my lips and whispered, "Okay."

"You sure?"

I nodded. "Do you have protection?" Because for all that I was doing something daring and a little dangerous and very unlike me, I was never going to give that up.

He pulled out his wallet and held up a square foil. "Cam's safety condom."

I hid my face with my hands. "Oh God. I'll die if he knows we used that."

Mateo tugged at my wrists. "Hey, hey. It's me. I wouldn't say anything. You *know* I wouldn't say anything. This, now, it's just you and me, okay? Tell me you want this."

I shoved my fears into the back of my mind and reached out to touch Mateo's cheek. "Yes," I breathed. "Yes. Yes. Yes."

Then I helped him slide off my pants and lower me from the wooden pew onto the red carpet. Thousands of student feet had walked over this carpet and I was about to lose my virginity on it. We were about to lose our virginity together on it. I almost laughed at the absurdity. But I didn't, because this was my first time and, finally, I knew it was right and I had nothing to be afraid of.

Mateo shifted and my logical brain tried to bust back in. I was doing this, and dreamworld or not, there were some things to address. Mom had lectured about "first times" enough that I didn't expect a lot on the physical front. My big O in the truck earlier was a surprise, and it was a lot bigger than anything I'd ever accidentally done myself, but Mateo had good hands and I had always been sensitive down there. Still, I had every expectation that sex would hurt, that I would likely bleed, and that he wouldn't last long. All of

Mom's "sex-positive education" and her insistence on "owning your orgasm" couldn't really undo what I'd learned from overheard girl conversations in school or even speculated about with Eve, and the essays in the first-time book I'd read were too varied to be of much help on the "what is this going to feel like" front.

I shut my eyes for a second and willed my logical brain away. This was Mateo, who I wanted so much I couldn't imagine anywhere else I'd rather be. This was the boy who made my whole self shake and tingle, and feel like I had to pee.

"Open your eyes, Chloe," Mateo whispered. I peeled them open and looked.

He moved between my legs and slid his pants and underwear down. I'd seen a penis before—thanks, internet—but not in real life. I'd felt Mateo through his jeans earlier, but it looked different up close. Sort of red and a little angry looking.

"You're circumcised," I blurted, then wanted to die.

He laughed. "Yeah. So?"

I was completely exposed, all naked on the red carpet with only my fingernail-bitten hands to cover any of me. I wanted to either get to the sex so my dumb logical brain would stop interrupting or snap my legs shut. But my brain refused to let go without an explanation. "You're from Mexico. I thought the rates of circumcision in Latin countries are really low."

He gaped at me.

"God. Sorry, my parents are really into different cultures. I know a lot of weird facts."

Oh, jeez. I hated hated hated my mouth's refusal to ignore my brain.

He raised an eyebrow. "You really want to get into a discussion about this right now?"

"No. God no. Sorry, you're right. Go ahead."

I tried to relax, but I must have looked all contorted because Mateo put his hand on my thigh and said softly, "We don't have to. I don't want to pressure you."

"No. I want to. With you. First time for both of us."

"You're sure you're not scared? *I'm* a little scared."

I laughed and something in me eased. Then I whispered, "You're sure no one can come in here?"

"Positive," he said, then bent his head and shifted it down. Down, down, down, past my stomach. My legs snapped together, and he said, "Ow."

"Sorry. God. I'm sorry. This isn't going well. I'm so sorry. But not that, okay? You don't have to do *that*. Prep me or whatever you think you're doing. It's fine. Just, you know, go ahead with the main act."

He laughed again and moved up to kiss my stomach and the top of one of my boobs. "For some guys, going down on a girl *is* the main act."

It was a line. It had to be a line. I couldn't forget how Cam had said Chloe Donnelly tasted like old Miracle Whip and if what I'd overheard in gym class was anything to go by, guys did not like putting their mouths anywhere near the vulva.

But he looked down like he was interested in seeing me. Which made my whole body feel like it was on fire, though if it was from embarrassment or desperation, I wasn't totally sure.

"My mom told me not to shave because you need pubic hair in evidence collection kits, but Eve said every girl does it so I did." Oh God. It was the worst blurting I'd ever done. My logical brain had rocketed into overdrive in a mortifying way. I slapped my hands over my face and hoped for a heart attack so I could die right there on the floor. Right there on the crappy red carpet, which no longer seemed to be full of history but more the location where I'd be mocked for the rest of my life. *Do you remember that girl who was trying to lose her virginity but messed it up by talking about rape kits? Isn't this where that "shaving girl" cock-blocked some poor guy with her own stupid, blurting mouth?*

I expected Mateo to at best laugh and at worst say he wasn't going to have sex for the first time with such a blurty freak show after all. But he peeled my hands away and kissed my face in a bunch of different places, over and over. Cheek, jaw, forehead, nose, eyelids. "I like you so much, Chloe," he said. And he repeated "so much" with each kiss.

I eased my legs open again. He picked up the condom he'd

set to the side, and because I'm me and couldn't stop, I took it from him and rolled it on.

He watched my hands and then laughed once in this kind of throaty way. "You sure this is your first time?"

"My mom made me watch videos about how to put these on right. Most condom failures happen because they aren't put on properly. Or they're old and break."

Mateo grinned and kissed all the places on my face again. "I think I'd like your mom."

"Yeah, maybe. But she can be a bit much."

"At least she didn't make you practice on a banana."

I grinned, feeling at ease even though this conversation was going nothing like I'd ever imagined. "That'd be a waste of a condom and a banana."

He laughed and then, without any fanfare or real warning, he pressed in. *I* was having sex, with no real plan or long, drawn-out discussion or presex conversation with my friends or my mom. I was doing it. For Mateo, for me, for us. God, the things I was willing to do for him, the things I would give up for him.

Where the hell was my logical brain now?

It was pretty much shut down because having sex with Mateo actually felt good. Really, really good. There was no burning sensation or tearing or feeling like I was going to split in half. There was just wet and warm and . . . oh.

"The pee thing is back," I gasped, when his hips pressed in a little more and he reached down to touch my clitoris.

"What?"

"Oh. Oh." I didn't know what to do or say. This was different from in the truck, different from the loofah. My body got super tight and tense and then I was twitching, twitching, twitching, which I definitely had never done like this before, and clinging to him and whispering his name. And maybe it sounded like a plea to him too because he started moving faster and felt bigger, which was confusing but I couldn't register any of that.

After what felt like an hour of me twitching but was probably twenty seconds, he paused and pressed himself up in a sort of half push-up and said, "Did you . . . did you just come?"

I slammed my eyes shut. "Yes," I whispered.

"Chloe."

I peeked one eye open and he looked so happy and pleased. My heart flipped over, fully in control now. My logical brain had been orgasmed out of me completely. Mateo kissed my face again, the same pattern he'd done the first time. Cheek, jaw, forehead, nose, eyelids. But now his hips moved as he kissed me, and he whispered, "Thank you, thank you, thank you," with each kiss. Finally, he jerked and shuddered, and it was done.

He laugh-groaned after a few seconds. "I didn't know it was

going to be like that. That was . . . pretty great." Then he pulled out of me and tied up his condom full of what seemed like an ungodly amount of semen—Mom had trained me not to say things like *cum* or *jizz* or *love custard* or *man batter* or whatever other gross words guys used. He held it awkwardly because there wasn't exactly a Kleenex around or a wastebasket.

"I guess you came too, huh?" I said.

Then we both laughed for a long time and he put his tied-up condom on the edge of the pew while we started tugging on our clothes. Mateo ran down to the bathroom to get toilet paper, then wrapped the condom up and wiped off the damp spot on the pew.

It was sleazy and furtive and a little bit gross, but I'd had sex for the first time in the church my parents had gotten married in. And I wasn't afraid or anxious, because it was Mateo's first time too. And he made me feel like I mattered.

I followed Mateo downstairs where he tossed condom-filled toilet paper into the trash and washed his hands. Then he brushed my hair behind my ears and said, "That's the best time I've ever had in church. It was totally pink."

I swatted him and said, "You're so ridiculous."

He smiled at me, his lip ring glinting and his eyes full of warmth. I wanted to tell him I loved him. I wanted to thank *him* for making sex better than I could have imagined. But my logical brain had pushed its way back in, and the game and stupid

Chloe Donnelly and a tiny prickle of worry about whether the condom might have failed were all in the way of my heart truth.

We stood at the chapel door and Mateo kissed me again. "I'm going to go find the guys. We've got about a half hour till we need to meet at the library. Give me a three-minute head start in case anyone is around."

I nodded. "See you back at the library."

"Yep. It's almost done."

Then he slipped out of the chapel, leaving me alone. I wanted to hold on to the magic of the past hour just a little bit longer, and gather myself together. I felt lighter, in that way when you're trying to solve a difficult precalc problem and after trying it a dozen different ways, you finally get it. And I wondered if sex was always going to feel like that, or if it was just sex with Mateo.

I brushed my fingers over my lips and smiled. Then I took a deep breath and pushed out the door of the Herrick Chapel entrance and straight into Chloe Donnelly.

26

"I need your phone," she said from the top step outside the chapel.

"Excuse me?"

"I need your phone. I'm supposed to check in at home."

Dumbly, I pulled my phone from my hoodie pocket and handed it to her. I watched her thumb swipe and then flip through something. The glow from my phone lit her face and made her eyes look weird and ghostlike. She smiled, then handed me back my phone.

"I figured it was Mateo. You look deflowered. I hope it was as good for him too," she said, crossing her arms.

I flinched. "You were reading my texts?"

"You're so quick, Other Chloe."

I didn't want to give her any kind of power over me, and

I wasn't ready for a conversation. Particularly not with her. I gathered as much of my courage as I could and said, "Did you need something or were you just spying and being creepy?"

Her eyes flashed. "Yes, Other Chloe. As a matter of fact, I was hoping you'd explain to me exactly why you decided to play after all."

I shrugged. "These are my friends."

She laughed in this cruel, sneering kind of way. She looked a little unhinged, her pupils blown out like she was on drugs. Her pretty white-blue eyes had taken on a strange, slightly possessed look under the street lamps. "They are definitely not your friends. If you've learned anything over the past few weeks, I'd hope that it was at least that."

What could I say? She wasn't wrong. I shoved a finger in my mouth, and she laughed again. It was like pinpricks on the base of my neck. I dropped my finger and said, "What in the hell is wrong with you? Don't you care about anyone but yourself?"

"No. I don't. I really, really don't."

"Then why bother with us? With this game?"

"Because I was bored."

I blinked, her voice echoing in my head. "That's it? You started all of this? You played Gestapo because you were bored? That's . . . cruel."

"So?"

Fury burned in my stomach. "All this stuff you've done, all these lives you've tried to ruin were because you were bored? Do you even know how that sounds?"

She smiled and all the wrongness about her was more obvious than ever. "Yes. I do. And Mateo's little plan? His idea to 'take me down'? That's not going to stop me. You think I care about the guys' asking me for a platinum favor? You think I'd give in over that? Stupid girl. Stupid people, all of you. Don't forget, Other Chloe. Cheaters automatically lose."

Oh God. Oh God.

"No one will play with you anymore," I whispered. "You can't make them."

She adjusted the blue-green scarf at her neck. It looked exactly like mine. "You have no idea what fear will make people do. Look at the world you live in. You'll see."

"You're such a huge bitch," I said, my voice tight with anger. "You're the worst thing that ever happened to any of us. You can't keep doing this. We'll tell. Everyone will tell."

She stepped back. "Poor Other Chloe. So much to learn still."

Then before I could say anything else, she turned and headed back toward Central Campus. I wanted to scream. I wanted to shout every horrifying word I could think of at her. This wasn't a girl with low self-esteem who just needed someone to befriend her. This was a girl with no feelings at all. I slumped down on the sidewalk and took several breaths. She knew about Mateo's plan somehow. I felt sick and so, so defeated. A small part of me must have thought it actually might work. But now? I couldn't imagine a way out of this for Mateo, for any of them, really.

I sat there for ten more minutes until my butt got too cold. I walked around the back of the arts building toward the library, trying to figure out how I'd tell Mateo what happened. My mind couldn't conjure any ideas to protect him. I wanted my mom and dad. I wanted them to tell me what to do, to tell me how to get out of this.

Mateo was already there when I got to the library, and the guys had huddled. I heard Cam laughing and even Aiden and Josh seemed more at ease, like that first time when we'd played a practice game on Pearl Street and it didn't mean anything. I hated that it was going to be ruined. I knew I should say something before Chloe Donnelly got there, but I couldn't force myself to speak. The numbness from earlier seeped in again, but now it felt different, not like strength but like I'd lost everything.

Mateo glanced at me and smiled, and for a second warmth bloomed inside of me. We'd still be a *we*. I'd figure something out. I had to. I couldn't let go of everything that had happened in Herrick Chapel. A spark lit inside. Mateo and I would figure something out *together*.

"Where's Chloe Donnelly?" Holly asked.

"Don't know," I mumbled.

Eve eyed me, tilting her head like she was trying to figure out a difficult puzzle. Too many things happened during the game and I couldn't imagine how I looked from the outside. Sexed up? Defeated? Determined? As unhinged as Chloe Donnelly had looked twenty minutes ago?

I stood for a few minutes, working up the courage to pull Mateo aside. Still not sure how he'd react if I singled him out in front of everyone. I knew I should tell everyone about Chloe Donnelly knowing the plan, but I couldn't. Too afraid they'd think I told her. Too afraid that I'd bear the brunt of their defeat.

By ten forty-five, when Chloe Donnelly still hadn't shown, everyone was pissed.

"Jesus, she's fucking late and she doesn't even have a phone. This is probably another game she's playing. I'm not giving this cunt more than another five minutes," Cam said.

"God, you're a douche," Aiden said. "Seriously. What is wrong with you?"

Cam glared at him. "I'm done with this fucking girl and her games. Pretty sure I'm not the only one."

"You know you're not," Aiden said. "But ease up. We're almost done."

Only, as more minutes passed by, Chloe's absence didn't feel like part of her game. It felt like a problem. Five minutes

356

later Aiden stepped forward and said, "Has anyone seen her tonight?"

Silence. Finally, I stepped forward and said, "I saw her a little after ten outside the chapel."

Cam looked pissed. "And you're just mentioning it now? Jesus. You could've said something."

"Sorry," I mumbled.

Mateo's face went a little pasty. "What did she say?"

I shook my head, defeat dragging over my skin. "She knows about your plan. I don't know how. But she said cheaters automatically lose."

"What?" The starkness on his face gutted me. "Did anyone tell her?" Mateo asked, looking at everyone. I glanced around too, but they all looked innocent. Except for Eve.

My eyes went wide. "Eve?"

Tears filled her eyes. "I didn't realize. I mean, I just . . . I thought if she knew I was on her side, maybe I could talk her into easing up a little. Maybe I could convince her to let it all go. Forget about it."

Rage burned inside of me. "You're that insecure? You want everyone to like you that much? Even a girl who is ruining all our lives?"

"It's not like that," Eve said, brushing away the tears and looking to Holly, who'd stepped back from her. Holly, who glared at Eve as if she didn't even know her.

"It's exactly like that," I snapped. And for a moment I saw in Eve everything I'd been feeling the entire year: the desperation to keep her as a friend, the need to be important to someone, the insecurity of thinking I wasn't enough. And a whole new perspective clicked into place. Eve was climbing rungs. She'd upgraded from me to Holly, and now was upgrading from Holly to Chloe Donnelly. As if it would somehow be able to buy her a sense of place in the long run.

The truth about the loneliness of girls hit me like a truck. How much we were all willing to give up just to mean something to someone. Me with Eve, Eve with Holly, girls with guys, all of us in one way or another with Chloe Donnelly. And then when we thought someone actually cared about us, it turned out it wasn't enough. It would never be enough. I glanced at Mateo. Was he a way for me to feel necessary? Maybe it was more than that. Maybe he was the way for me to find that on my own.

Aiden sighed, all the palpable defeat pouring off everyone reflected in the sound. But then he squared his shoulders and said, "We need to look for her. Let's split up. Guys will take South and East Campus, girls take from the library and the academic buildings to North Campus. Everyone keep your phones on. We'll circle back here in thirty minutes to see if she's shown."

"We should blow this off," Cam said.

But Aiden shook his head. "No. We gotta find her and make sure she's okay. It's the right thing to do."

"She's probably at some campus party, ruining the lives of college students," Cam mumbled.

Josh snorted. "Probably. But Aid's right. We need to find her and deal with all of this."

We all mumbled an agreement. Nan and Pops were expecting me home soon. But I couldn't bail. Mateo skimmed his fingers along mine as he passed me on the way to East Campus. A little tingle fizzed up my arm, and I felt the same happiness I'd had in Herrick. As if all this dumb stuff was just a detour we needed to take in order for me to be me and for the two of us to be *us*.

"I'll talk to you later," he whispered. "We'll work it out."

I nodded and hoped he believed in me, in us. "I'll help you get around her. You're not on your own," I whispered back. But the starkness in his face hadn't completely gone away. And for a second I thought of the Mothers of the Disappeared. Then I recalled what I'd done in Herrick Chapel, how exhilarating it was, but also how dangerous. What if I got pregnant? I shook my head. We'd used a condom. I wasn't going to get pregnant. Mateo and I would be fine. This would all be better tomorrow, when the game was over, Chloe Donnelly was stewing over her defeat, and Mateo and I could figure out our future.

I followed behind Eve and Holly, scanning everywhere for Chloe Donnelly's light-purple dress.

"I can't believe she no-showed," Holly complained, pulling her hair up into a makeshift knot. "It's like she knows we're done with all her crap and is refusing to let the game end because she's so obsessed with it. Whatever. I don't care. Even if the guys lose for cheating, we're not playing again."

I snorted. "That's ironic, considering you could have ended the game last week."

She glared at me. "I told you why I couldn't."

"Nothing's changed. She still knows your secret."

"It's different now. Because all seven of us know what she's about. And we're not letting her get away with it. It'll be our word against hers." She gave Eve a pointed look, and Eve nodded, repentant.

I wasn't sure how different it really was. But none of it mattered anymore. I couldn't believe I'd ever thought of any of these girls as my real friends. All the secrets and lies were exhausting. Who would care if Holly's dad was in prison? It didn't have anything to do with her. And Eve was being stupid about the Ritalin and stupid to think Chloe Donnelly was a friend worth keeping. Mateo was the one I needed to protect. He was the reason to shut Chloe Donnelly down.

I continued to scan the area, but while I did, I imagined my plans for the next day. First, I'd talk to my parents, tell them I wanted to stay in Grinnell, ask them to come home instead of extending their Spirit Corps assignment. I could be brave and ask for that. Then I'd call Melissa and meet up with her and Seth. Maybe Mateo would want to come too. I'd get to hang out with a real friend and it'd be easy and fun, even if the two of us were the biggest outcasts in school.

"Oh my God." Eve stopped suddenly and I bumped into her.

"What?"

"Look." She pointed to a bench in front of one of the academic buildings. I leaned forward and peered into the dark where her finger was directed. Then I saw it, a blue-green scarf—Chloe Donnelly's scarf. It was crumpled on the bench and covered in what looked like dark paint but what all of us must have realized was blood.

I pulled my phone from my pocket with trembling hands and said, "Text the guys to get over here. I'm calling nine-one-one."

The guys showed up a few minutes before the police did, and in those few minutes the weight of what I'd done was written all over Mateo's face. Mateo's beautiful and now panicked face.

"I can't stay," he whispered, pulling me away from where everyone else was arguing over what the hell had happened.

"What? Why?"

"I can't get involved with the police. Not with my status. You know I can't. It's too dangerous. I have to skip."

"Oh God, Mateo. I'm sorry. I didn't think. I just saw her scarf and the blood and I didn't know what else to do."

"Chloe," he said, kissing my forehead. "It's okay. You did the right thing, but I can't risk this. My family . . ."

Of course he couldn't risk it. I knew that. But the thought of him leaving me pierced through me. I wanted to cling to him and ask him to stay, beg him. I released a long breath. I needed to pull myself together, think of him first, what he needed.

So I nodded, tears brimming. "I know. Of course you can't risk it. Will you stay in Grinnell? Lie low around here?"

He looked broken and trapped. Stupid, stupid, stupid Chloe Donnelly. She ruined everything. Though even as I thought it, I felt terrible. Something might have happened to her. God, what was wrong with me? I was a self-absorbed brat.

"I don't know if I can stay. I need to talk to my parents. I have to disappear for a while until they find Chloe."

Neither of us said what we were both thinking—the only way he'd be able to come back was if they found her and she was fine. An open missing persons case that Mateo was even peripherally involved with would close the door on him ever returning.

"They'll find her. We'll find her. She might've cut herself

and left the scarf there. She's probably at home getting herself patched up. She just doesn't have her phone so she can't tell us."

But the explanation felt flimsy, especially since I'd seen her an hour before. Why would she leave her scarf? What could have happened to her that created so much blood but wasn't really bad?

Mateo kissed me again and whispered, "I love you."

My heart slammed in my chest, and then shattered.

He kissed me again, so soft and heartbreakingly perfect. "I'll reach out as soon as I can. But the less you know about where I am, the better."

"I love you too," I choked out, tears falling hard and fast now.

He tucked my hair back, squeezing the nape of my neck, and said, "Bye." Then he took off in the opposite direction of the street, back through campus. I watched until he was too far and too hidden by the shadows for me to see him any longer.

"Where the hell is Mateo going?" Cam said when I rejoined them, mopping my face with my sleeve.

"He's looking for Chloe," I said, though it was a stupid lie. No one could really believe it.

"The cops are here. See? He should let them handle this." Cam pointed to where two police cars rolled up along the street.

Four officers got out of the cars and approached, not rushing, but even the fact that there were four officers meant they took my 911 call seriously.

"I'm Officer Martin. We received a call about a missing girl. Which of you called? What are we looking at?" the first officer said, an extremely thin, slightly older guy with sharp eyes and short white hair.

"I called. Our friend disappeared," I said. "We found her scarf there." I pointed.

The one female officer walked over to the bench with the scarf on it but didn't touch it. "Looks like blood," she called out. "We'll need to bag it."

The first guy signaled to the two other male officers, and they went back to their car. They got in and started talking to someone on the radio, though I couldn't make out what they were saying with the windows rolled up. Officer Martin pulled out a pen and small pad of paper, almost casual, like there wasn't a missing girl he should be searching for. Then he said, "All right, let's hear what happened. Why don't you start by telling me what you were doing here tonight."

27

We ended up at the Grinnell police station, which was only a few blocks from the campus, but they still shoved the six of us in the backseat of the two cars and drove us over. We shuffled out of the cars, all quiet and sober-scared. On our way in, we walked past three statue-plaques that I'd never looked at up close and couldn't make out in the dark, and then we were ushered into the station itself.

We had to sit in the seats in the front until our parents—or in my case, grandparents—showed up so we could be interviewed individually. We were the only civilians in the station and even though there was a low hum of activity, I could see this place wasn't really hopping during the night shift.

I'd hoped we could have been out looking for Chloe Donnelly, but apparently it didn't work that way. As soon as we'd started talking to Officer Martin all at once at the place we'd found the scarf, he'd decided it was too much and we needed to be interviewed. Which meant pulling Nan out of bed at almost midnight and having her show up to the station "without her face on," clucking at the officer in charge of the desk.

When he placated her and said they were interviewing all of us one at a time and I'd be next, she sat back down and asked, "What were you doing, Chloe? You told us you were at Melissa's."

"I lied," I said. I had no energy for spinning anything. I was out of sorts about Chloe Donnelly, wondering if this was all part of her plan. And selfishly, I was devastated at the loss of Mateo. I kept glancing at my phone, checking for texts, but it was silent.

On the seats across from us sat Cam and Aiden and their parents. They barely said hello to my grandparents, dropping their usual friendliness to focus on the twins. Their mom's big voice echoed in the mostly empty space, interrupting everyone's conversations with the same questions over and over again, though she mostly only directed those at Aiden. "What do you know about this girl? Does this have anything to do with the envelope we received?" she asked for the third time, and for the third time Aiden shrugged and said nothing.

Cam leaned forward, his elbows on his knees. "We don't know anything. She's new at school. We don't know where she is or what's happened to her. We've barely even spoken to her."

I noticed Cam didn't address the envelope question, but I didn't know if it was because he didn't know about it or if he was trying to protect Aiden in front of all the other people in the room. It was almost too easy how Cam lied and it made me suspicious of him, especially remembering the way he'd called Chloe Donnelly a cunt. But truthfully, I was suspicious of everyone, except Mateo, who'd been with me most of the night and who had a lot to lose if the police started sniffing around.

Thinking about Mateo made my throat get choked up all over again, so when one of the criminal investigation officers ushered a stone-faced Holly and her mom out and asked me and Nan and Pops to follow him into the interview room, I couldn't do anything but nod and shuffle behind. We passed a nearly hysterical Eve on our way in, and I ignored the glare her mom was giving me as if I was somehow responsible for all that had happened. Her mom had mostly only ever tolerated me—me not being a joiner in the myriad Booster activities available at our school—but there was no doubt in my mind that I'd never be invited over again for Rice Krispies Treats or whatever else she was baking.

Pops had been quiet since I'd first seen them at the door of the police department. He hadn't even said hello when he saw me, just hugged me unbearably long and said, "Oh, doll. I'm sorry." I didn't even know what he was apologizing for.

The criminal investigation officer introduced himself as

Officer Kay, a chubby guy with thinning hair and almost no chin, and pointed out two seats at the table. Nan sat next to me and Pops took a chair on the side by the door.

"We're not at the point of issuing an Amber Alert because we don't have any witnesses who saw the girl being abducted, but we're still questioning students at the college. When was the last time you saw Chloe Donnelly?"

I swallowed past my thick tongue and said, "Um, right around ten o'clock, when the game was still going on."

"The game. Gestapo, right?"

"Gestapo?" Nan said. "What's that?"

"Um, it's sort of like capture the flag," I explained.

Nan tsked beside me but amazingly didn't say anything beyond a quickly muttered, "Movie at Melissa's, my fanny."

"And you've been playing Gestapo for a few weeks?" Officer Kay asked.

"Yeah. Chloe introduced us to it. I wasn't going to play it after tonight, though."

Officer Kay scratched the stubble on his chin with his pen. "Yeah, that's what you all seem to be saying. Interesting. Do you know where Chloe lives?"

"No, I've never been to her house. I know her dad's a lawyer in Des Moines and her mom's a prof at U of I."

"Yeah, well, the thing is, we're having a hard time verifying all of that."

I looked down, the sensation of duplicity I'd first started feeling when I'd talked to Melissa and Seth even more prominent now. Though it seemed less like a *21 Jump Street* sting and more like something else, darker and creepier.

"That doesn't seem to surprise you much," Officer Kay said.

I swallowed and met his gaze. "I ran into a couple of friends tonight who made me wonder if she wasn't telling the whole truth about who she was. And when I saw her earlier, she seemed out of sorts. I'm not sure any of us knows her that well."

"Was?" he asked, barely looking up as his pen scratched along the yellow-lined legal pad in front of him.

"Excuse me?"

The pen stopped. "You said *who she was* as if she's no longer with us. Do you have reason to believe Chloe Donnelly is dead?"

"Honestly, Officer Kay," Nan said, her voice steely and sure. "She's seventeen. It's clear she doesn't know anything. Where are these questions going?"

Kay ignored Nan and said, "Chloe? You were the last one to see her. Do you have reason to believe Chloe Donnelly is dead?"

Did I? I didn't know. The scarf and the blood and the reasons why any one of the people playing that game would want her gone permanently, did those things all mean she'd been killed? "No," I said. "I don't know why I said *was*. Maybe because there seemed like a lot of blood on the scarf? She left me at Herrick Chapel. I don't know where she went after that."

I was digging myself into a bigger hole and I hadn't even done anything wrong. But the entire place made me nervous. When we were little, I'd visited the police station with my Girl Scout troop and imagined the police were all heroes, but now I was terrified.

"We're trying to find out exactly who Chloe Donnelly is and where she might've gone. Unfortunately, your friends explained she didn't have a cell on her."

"No," I confirmed. "She used mine earlier tonight."

His brows went up. "Did she call anyone?"

My cheeks burned hot. "No. She was reading my texts."

He nodded. "You have the phone with you?"

"Um, yeah." I pulled it out of my pocket and reluctantly handed it over to him once he'd donned rubber gloves. He pulled a plastic bag from his desk and dropped the phone in.

"We'll get it back to you as soon as possible. If she touched it, we might be able to get a fingerprint from the case. We'll grab your prints before you leave so we can rule those out."

I forced myself to choke down a protest. How could Mateo reach me if the cops had my phone? I didn't want to make them suspicious, but at the same time I couldn't be without it. Mateo needed a lifeline.

"If you're just looking for prints, can I have my SIM card?" I blurted.

Officer Kay studied me. "You sure she didn't use your phone to call or text anyone?"

I nodded. "Yeah. I'm sure. You can check my call records if you want."

Oh God. Would he see Mateo's name? I was so not smooth with all of this. And I hated that I felt cagey and guilty because I wanted to protect Mateo.

"Nah," he said. "Let's see if we can find out who this girl is first. You don't need to pull your SIM card. It really won't take long for us to see if we can get a print. I'll call the guys in now."

He made a call and two officers came in and took the phone. "It should be a few minutes. Why don't you tell me about your conversation with Chloe."

"I don't really know what to say. She knew we all wanted to be done with the game. She was angry and said we were cheating. She read my texts and knew. . . ." I didn't want to mention what she'd said about Mateo and deflowering.

Officer Kay made a note on his yellow pad, then said, "Tell me more about the game."

I squirmed. Not exactly the reprieve I'd hoped for. I was sure he knew about the game, but he wanted to hear me explain it. In front of my grandparents, who would be mortified. I'd never wished my parents were with me more.

I cleared my throat and explained the rules as succinctly as possible. I pretended I didn't hear Pops's murmured "Oh no, Chloe doll" from the corner. I couldn't decide what was worse, the "clarification" questions from Officer Kay while I explained or the grilling I would no doubt have to go through when I got home.

"And why had you decided tonight would be the last time you played?" Officer Kay asked when I was done explaining.

I had been trying to stay perfectly still, but I couldn't stop my hand from moving to my mouth for a quick cuticle rip. Kay didn't say anything, just waited for my answer.

"Chloe Donnelly knew a lot of secrets about everyone," I finally said. "And we didn't want to play with her anymore because of it."

"What sorts of secrets?"

I waved a gnawed hand in what I hoped looked sort of dismissive. "Dumb high school stuff. You know, everyone has stuff they're embarrassed about and don't want their friends to know about. We were just sick of her using that against us to try to win."

"And yet you played tonight? Why?"

It was the perfect opportunity to come clean about Mateo's plan, but I couldn't make myself say his name. I didn't want him to be any more exposed than he likely already was. I'd become tethered to him, I realized. And tonight after what had happened in Herrick Chapel, I suspected there would be no disentangling us. I couldn't give him up.

In the end, it didn't matter. Officer Kay let his question go unanswered and instead asked, "What can you tell me about the whereabouts of Mateo Vallera?"

"He didn't do it," I blurted.

Officer Kay stopped writing again. "And what exactly is *it*?"

"I don't know. Whatever it is that you think happened to Chloe Donnelly. You think something happened to her, don't you? You haven't found her and that's why you're asking us all these questions," I practically shouted. Hostility and fear poured off me in a dangerous concoction that must have made me look incredibly unstable.

"Chloe," Nan said, gripping my forearm with the slightest dig of her nails. "Stop. He's trying to do his job. He's looking for a lost girl. Trying to figure out who she is and where she could be."

I heard the fear in Nan's voice, the worry, and then I remembered. Mom and Dad's senior year at Grinnell, a friend of theirs had gone missing on her way to Iowa from Chicago. The whole campus canvased the highways. The internet wasn't like it was now, so they had to do sort of a search and rescue. Only there wasn't a rescue, just a dead girl found a few weeks later in clothes that weren't her own. It shook everyone on campus and in town. They never found the guy who did it.

"I don't know where Mateo is," I said. "I was with him most of the night. He didn't see her. I was with him almost until the time you showed up."

Officer Kay didn't look surprised. Someone else must have already told him about Mateo bolting moments before the cops arrived. It looked bad for him. I knew it did. But I was 100 percent certain that if something had happened to Chloe Donnelly, Mateo wasn't responsible.

"And why do you think he left?"

I gnawed my thumb cuticle and let my hair curtain drop. I glanced around the room as I chewed. The walls had safety posters on them, and in the corner was one of those watercoolers with the plastic-cup dispenser attached. I spit out a piece of my cuticle and Nan tapped my wrist with a murmur of disapproval. I released my thumb. I didn't know what the right thing to do here was. All the secrets and lies were weighing on me like a boulder, but when I considered blurting them all out, I couldn't do it. My mind kept flashing to Mateo kissing my face and saying, *Thank you, thank you, thank you*. Telling the truth would guarantee me never seeing Mateo again. And it would likely put him and his family on some sort of list. I had to hope they'd find Chloe Donnelly and all of this would go away.

"I honestly don't know why he left," I said, and felt Nan sag beside me as if she was relieved I wasn't mixed up with him. But the silence coming from Pops was like pinpricks along my skin. I didn't dare look at him.

Officer Kay looked disappointed, but he flipped to the next page of the yellow pad and started writing again. "Why don't you tell me what you do know and review for me again what exactly happened when you saw Chloe at ten o'clock?"

I ended up giving Officer Kay the bare minimum of information. Once I'd lied about why Mateo had left, it was easier to lie about what I knew about everyone else. The weirdest part was that he didn't seem to be bothered by the game. He didn't ask questions about neo-Nazis or why everyone would play a game with potentially dangerous information-gathering tactics. It was almost as if he'd heard of the game before. Or that it was *normal* kid stuff, all in good fun.

Instead, the officer kept asking whether anyone would have a reason to harm Chloe Donnelly, and the truth was that everyone did. But, of course, I didn't say that. He kept putting a fine point on me being the last one to see her, but I didn't get the feeling he thought I was responsible for her disappearance, even as evasive as I was.

I'd known these people most of my life, and I'd only known Chloe Donnelly three weeks. The answer to her whereabouts in my mind lay more in the lies she told us about her parents and her life than in any secrets we were keeping.

When the questioning was done, Officer Kay stepped out for a few minutes and came back with my phone. He handed it over and said, "They got a few different prints. It'll take a bit of time to process and see if we can find a match for her in our system. We'll let you know. In the meantime, we do know her mom is definitely not a professor at U of I, and if her dad is a lawyer in Des Moines, he doesn't go by the name Donnelly."

I wondered if she'd even ever lived in Chicago. Her stories had seemed so unbelievable, sort of show-offy in a way, but I'd thought she was just exaggerating, not making them up altogether.

"Make sure to have your prints taken before you leave so we know which ones might be hers. Anyone else touch your phone?"

I shook my head.

"Okay then. We'll be in touch."

When I got home from the station, I went to my room and logged on to my computer, setting my phone next to me. If Mateo were going to reach out, I wanted all channels open to him.

I stayed up till nearly dawn, staring at the pale-yellow walls of my guest room, but Mateo never called or sent me a message. I fell asleep as the sun rose, trying to ignore the ache in my heart, and wishing that wherever Chloe Donnelly was, she'd be found soon.

I woke to murmurs from Nan and Pops in the living room. It took me a few seconds, but I realized they were on the house phone with someone. Nan and Pops had this annoying habit of constantly both getting on the phone no matter who was calling.

At first I'd thought it was because Pops didn't trust Nan to get the details of something right. But then I realized it was Nan who was always screaming at Pops to pick up the other extension, as if she didn't want to be bothered with relaying to him any relevant information and he should just fend for himself.

"I don't care what it costs. She's your daughter and it's time to get back here to parent." Nan's voice rang out, sharp and clear.

I froze. They were talking to my parents, no doubt giving them all the details of what happened. And evidently my grandparents were done with me, done with letting me stay with them, done with being stand-in parents. I couldn't blame them really, middle-of-the-night calls from the police, a missing girl, and a game that would have been every adult's worst nightmare.

I covered my face with my hands and tried to breathe. My parents would come home. They were allowed a two-week leave of absence during their two-year Spirit Corps assignment. They hadn't taken it because I had always visited them. But they would come home. It was part of the deal when I'd asked to stay with Nan and Pops. My grandparents were allowed an out clause. My parents would come if my grandparents said it was too much, and they'd collect me up to be unschooled in Burkina Faso. There would be no stopping them from extending if I was already living there.

But I didn't want to go to Burkina Faso. Not now. Not when I had Mateo and Melissa and only one year of high school left. I put my pillow over my head and let them finish the call. When the murmurs ended, I hauled myself out of bed and got dressed. Then I shuffled into the living room, ignoring Fox News and trying to gather myself together.

"I don't want to move to Burkina Faso permanently," I said, less of a blurt and more of a statement of fact.

Pops's face crumpled. "Oh, sweetheart, we don't want you to move either."

I sat next to him and put my face in his chest, smelling his always-fresh shirt collar. "Nan said . . . ," I started.

"She said *they* need to come home. Not to bring you back with them, but to return to Grinnell for good. They've done enough with this save-the-world nonsense. They're neglecting their daughter right now and you need them."

"I have you," I tried, but Pops laughed and I laughed a little too.

"We're old. We feed you and watch shows with you, but we're not your parents. We had our time. This is their job. Their *first* job. Your parents know that. Your mother thought she could do everything: save the world, save herself, turn you into a little mini version of her. But it wasn't right. We told her that when you asked if you could come live with us. She wasn't going to let you, you know. She thought we might talk you into staying with her, but I told her, *Charlotte, she's not your project. Let her be a kid.* I know she wanted you to change your mind every time you visited them, but I'm glad you didn't. You're a teenager and you should be allowed to go to high school in your own town. Your parents need to come home."

I nodded but couldn't agree out loud. I'd been holding it inside me so long—the shame of wanting Mom to care more about me than about escaping her depression through work with struggling girls in a third world country, the selfishness I felt every time I'd emailed asking them to adjust their schedule because I was with my friends and didn't have time to webcam with them, knowing how hard that was for them, and even the guilt I felt for being heartbroken over Mom's miscarriage, as if the baby had been a little bit mine too.

"Thanks for saying it, Pops, but if you don't want me here, then I'm going to end up in Burkina Faso."

Nan came in. "Horse pucky. You need to tell them you don't want to go. Your parents aren't monsters; they're misguided about their priorities. If you tell them the truth, they *will* hear you. But you're going to have to be brave enough to tell the truth. Your mother will always try to fit a square peg into a round hole if someone doesn't stop her. You're going to need to be the one to say you don't belong in Africa."

I shook my head. It was a conversation I didn't want to have. I wasn't up for disappointing my mom or for the blanket of guilt I would feel knowing they'd left before they thought the community was ready. "They have good priorities."

Nan hmphed, but Pops said, "You need to stop worrying about this, doll. Nothing is going to be decided today. You have other things you should be thinking about."

There was a sharpness in Pops's voice when he said *other things*, and I suspected he was very aware of how I'd omitted a few things from my interview with Officer Kay.

"Yes," Nan said. "The police called. They don't have any leads yet, but they want us to come back later this afternoon. They have a few more questions."

"Did they say what time we're supposed to be there?"

Nan arched a brow. "You have plans?"

I swallowed. I'd been thinking about it all night. I wanted to go to the family planning clinic in Newton for Plan B. The condom hadn't broken, but I thought maybe I should be preemptive just in case. "I need to run a female errand," I said, hoping Nan's fussiness would keep her from asking questions.

"You can take my car while we're at the Hy-Vee. The police want us there by three."

I nodded, and Nan wandered into the kitchen. Pops patted my knee. "You think the things you know aren't going to help find that girl, but they could. Police need to have all the information to do their job. You never know what could be helpful."

I shoved my pinkie into my mouth, but there was no more

nail sliver to bite off. Yesterday's interview had left my hands in terrible shape. And I had to go do it all over again. I couldn't give Mateo up, not yet. Not when there was a chance that Chloe Donnelly would turn up and Mateo could come back.

"I told them everything I know," I said to Pops, trying to sound as genuine as I could.

Pops shook his head. "I don't think you did. A girl is missing, doll. Think about it. I know you'll do the right thing." He squeezed my shoulder and left me to stew.

I went to my room and saw a text on my phone. My heart skipped when I saw Mateo's name.

We're heading out of town. Getting a new number. I'll text as soon as it's safe.

My lungs froze. I was crushed. Devastated. I wanted to ask him to wait, to tell him she might still be found, but I knew how selfish that was. I texted back, not even certain he'd see the message if he was getting a new number, but I was hopeful he hadn't switched his SIM card yet.

I didn't say anything about you to the police. I love you.

I waited for what seemed like hours but was maybe five minutes.

I love you too.

28

I held out in saying anything to the cops through the weekend, sticking to my same vague answers. They were increasingly frustrated with each interview, which made me think they weren't getting much information from anyone else, either, and they hadn't yet gotten a fingerprint match. I didn't know if they were hunting for both Chloe Donnelly and Mateo, but I continued to assert he couldn't have been involved with her disappearance because he'd been with me almost the whole time, which wasn't completely true, but it was enough. I had no idea what anyone else had said because I didn't hear from any of them all weekend. I was nauseated from the Plan B or maybe from my overall nerves and spent a lot of time in bed.

At first I was pissed at Chloe Donnelly, sure she'd somehow orchestrated this like everything else in the game, but as

Sunday turned to Monday, my anxiety ratcheted up and my guilt overwhelmed me.

Every cuticle on my fingers was a bitten and bloody mess by the time I got to school. I'd put on leggings and an extra-large hoodie, going for comfort, and left my hair down and in front of my face. Approaching school felt like walking onto a battlefield with no weapons and no armor. I knew Grinnell; there was no way all that happened with the game and Chloe's disappearance hadn't been running through the rumor mill since Friday night.

I stood outside school, hiding behind my hair curtain and wondering if anyone would talk to me today. Maybe I was the only one of us who'd even be at school. But then I saw Cam's car pull into the parking lot, and he, Aiden, and Josh all got out.

The three of them walked by me with only Josh looking at me—an expression of wariness on his face. He seemed almost afraid of me. What the hell? Did they think I was somehow responsible for this?

I followed them inside but stayed far enough behind that they didn't see me. At the T in the hallway, Aiden reached out for Josh and gave him a quick kiss before turning in the other direction.

A part of me softened when I saw it. No matter what had gone down over the weekend, it seemed that a decision had been made between them. Maybe Aiden's parents had helped push that decision along. Maybe they thought it was better to tell the truth. I didn't know what that meant in terms of Aiden and the Naval Academy, but still, I was glad they didn't have to hide anymore. No one around them seemed to react to the kiss, but I thought it was because they were all in a state of unease around us. I expected a million questions, but I didn't expect people to be *scared* of us. It was as if we were surrounded by barbed wire.

I didn't see Eve or Holly all morning, but the fear radiating off people didn't go away. Even my teachers didn't look me in the eye.

I stepped into the cafeteria at lunch and Holly approached me. "Come on. We're meeting in the media center."

I followed her out, relief flooding through me. At least there was a *we*. Though I was disappointed the *we* was comprised of only me and Holly.

"Where's Eve?" I asked.

"Her mom wouldn't let her come to school today. Of course. Too much trauma for her poor little baby girl."

Whoa. Holly could be bitchy, but I'd never heard her sound so obviously envious of Eve. I peeked at her wrist—no charm bracelet. "Your parents wouldn't let you stay home today?"

Then I winced because I realized there was no asking her dad anything. Holly glared at me. "Nice. Would you care to dump any more salt in the wound? Maybe mention the number of people Cam has been hooking up with in the past month?"

"Sorry," I mumbled. "So Eve doesn't need to be here for . . . whatever we're doing?"

Holly tipped her chin and shook her head. "Not for this. But if we need her, we can call her from the media center."

When we got there, the guys were already on the couches in the back. A few other people lingered, but most of them were up front at the checkout desk. Holly and I slid on the couch across from the guys. Cam was wearing the hoodie Aiden had on the night of the first real game. The hoodie he'd used to convince Eve he was Aiden.

Cam looked directly at me and said, "Why don't you tell us everything you know."

The same suggestion Officer Kay had been bugging me with all weekend. My mouth dropped open. "Excuse me?"

Cam looked cool and confident and a little mean. "We're all walking around here like we're suspects in a murder case and you seem to be the one the cops keep pulling in. Just like you were the last one both Chloe and Mateo talked to. So tell us what you know."

My cheeks burned. "I don't know anything. I didn't do anything to Chloe. The only time I saw her was when she told me she knew about Mateo's plan."

Aiden stared at me from his spot next to Cam with a hard expression. It was his soldier-serious face. I wondered again about the Naval Academy. If his involvement in all of this compromised his chances. "Where's Mateo?" he asked.

"I don't know."

"Come on, Chloe," Josh said, his voice softer and more of a plea. He looked more disheveled than I'd ever seen him. Not exactly wrinkled, but more a little unhinged, his hair spiking out and greasy like he'd forgotten to shower. "You were with him most of the night, right? Officer Kay said you were with him."

I nodded. "Yeah. But I don't know where he is. Honestly." Mateo had saved me from lying to the police and my friends about that, and I was grateful.

"Do you know why he took off?" Josh again.

I didn't know what to say. It was one thing being vague with one police officer, but pinned by the stares of four friends was a different thing. I slipped my hand into my hoodie pocket and clung to my phone. The *I love you too* text I'd read over and over this weekend gave me the strength I didn't think I could otherwise muster.

Aiden leaned forward, his elbows on his knees and his face almost slack in defeat. "Chloe, come on. This girl, this game, it's cost us a lot. All our futures are on the line here if they can't find her. You think people are afraid of us now, just wait. We'll all be implicated in this. There is no way out but the truth."

It was something my parents had said more than once in my life—something Pops had said yesterday in front of the police station before telling me my parents were getting on a plane from Burkina Faso. Would they be able to take me back with them if I was implicated in a girl's disappearance? How long would the police keep looking for her before the case went cold?

"I don't think Mateo did it," Josh said.

"He didn't. He couldn't have. I *was* with him almost the whole time." I swallowed back my misgivings about this lie. I didn't know where Mateo had been that first hour, and I hadn't seen him for a while after he left Herrick. It was something I'd worried about over the past few days. But I couldn't believe he'd done something to Chloe Donnelly, not after he had sex with me in Herrick Chapel, which was the only time he *could* have done anything to her. His involvement made no sense. I'd convinced myself over the weekend he'd spent that last half hour after I'd seen her waiting at Burling for the guys.

"The whole time? Really?" Cam asked, and goose bumps sprung up along my neck.

"Yes. And we don't know if there even is something to worry about with Chloe Donnelly. She could be—"

"You stupid bitch," Holly snapped. She'd been uncharacteristically silent this whole time so her harsh words made me flinch. "You think she's okay? Seriously? Did you know they found her purple ring? All the way on the other side of campus.

Traces of blood on that too. She disappeared *three days ago*. Tell me you're not this stupid."

I was a stretched rubber band finally sprung. "Shut up, Holly. Just shut up. You *know* all the secrets she was keeping. You didn't hear her at the end. Completely nuts and unwilling to let any of us out of playing. Don't you think it's possible this is part of the game too?"

Holly looked at me in disgust. "No. I don't. Not when there was all that blood on her scarf. Not when they found her ring too. Why would she fake a disappearance?"

"I don't know."

"Maybe you know more about her disappearance than you're letting on. Maybe it does mean something that you were the last one to see her," she said.

I felt like I had been slapped. I'd been waiting for the accusation, almost the whole weekend, but coming from Holly it was even worse. "Do you really think that? How could you? Why would I do anything to her? *She* was the one messing with everyone. I bet she's responsible for all of this."

Holly shook her head. "Maybe in your twisted mind that's how it went, but for normal, nonstalkery people, most of the time what you see is what you get."

Only that's not how it was most of the time. I knew it wasn't. Even as I saw the faces around me, expressions ranging from frustration to fear to fury, I knew that what you saw barely scratched the surface of what you got. Aiden and Josh's secret relationship. Cam and his unexpectedly beautiful voice. Holly and her need to be loved as if she had something to prove to her incarcerated father. No one would see that on the surface.

"I don't think . . . ," I started.

"You know, Other Chloe," Holly spit out, "Chloe Donnelly wasn't the only person holding on to everyone's secrets."

"What's that supposed to mean?"

"You know exactly what it means."

Oh God. They really did think I was somehow involved. I couldn't meet their gazes. I stared at my hands fisted in my lap. *Please let this all be a nightmare.*

Josh sighed and I looked at him. "I know you didn't do anything, Chloe. You don't have something like that in you. But you have to help us."

"Where the hell is Mateo?" Cam said, each word punctuated with venom and desperation.

"I don't know. He didn't do anything to Chloe. He just couldn't stay around, okay? It was too dangerous for him to be implicated in this," I blurted.

The moment stretched out before us—a pause loaded with questions and speculation.

"Too dangerous? Why?" Josh said, his voice soft again. "Did he do something?"

I shook my head.

Josh leaned forward. "Chloe. It's important. If he's got a criminal record or something . . ."

I shook my head again. "He's undocumented," I whispered. "He had to leave or he could've been deported."

My shoulders slumped. I was broken. There was no way one of them wouldn't tell the police now. Mateo would never be able to come back. He'd be on a list, in an even more precarious situation. I'd never see him in Grinnell again.

The whole place grew silent, almost as if the other students at the front of the media center were listening in and speculating themselves. Aiden finally cracked the quiet between all of us. "You need to tell the cops. They're looking for him because they think he's hurt Chloe. They're looking for the wrong guy, wasting time on nothing."

"He'll never be able to come back," I said, lacing my gross, bitten fingers in my lap. I felt raw and damaged, all of me on display just like my chewed-up cuticles. "They'll hunt him down. He'll be deported."

Josh reached out and squeezed my left wrist. "Maybe one day you could go to him. Even if he can't come back here. But you have to tell the police. Mateo will be safer if they're not looking for him as a crime suspect. If they realize why he left had nothing to do with Chloe Donnelly."

I shut my eyes and considered his words. Oh God. Oh

God. Oh God oh God oh God. Josh was right. My silence even now was putting Mateo in more danger. Why hadn't I thought of that? I stumbled as I slid out of the booth. "I have to go."

Josh nodded and I didn't wait for anyone else's approval or good-bye. The last thing I heard as I pushed my way out of the media center door was Cam saying, "If Mateo or Chloe didn't do anything to her, then where the hell is Chloe Donnelly?"

29

Officer Kay wouldn't talk to me without a guardian present, so I had to wait in the main area of the police station for my grandparents to arrive. The burnt-coffee smell didn't hide the tinge of bleach permeating the station. My shoes stuck to the ground as I lifted my toes up and down over and over. My fingers hurt too much for me to bite my nails, and my stomach was a mess from the combination of anxiety and anticipation.

I pulled my phone out and looked at Mateo's *I love you too* text again. There was no way he still had the same number, but I tried texting him again anyway.

I'm telling the police everything. It's the only way for them to stop thinking you did something to Chloe Donnelly. To stop searching for you. I know you can't come back, but I would come to you if you wanted. I know it's dangerous, but I would go with you anywhere.

I didn't receive a response and the hope inside me dimmed. I wasn't being practical. Wanting too much like I always did. He'd said he was getting a new number. But why hadn't he texted me from there? Was it because he suspected the police were monitoring my phone? Were they? Was that why they didn't hang on to it after they'd gotten fingerprints from it?

The main door opened and I looked up, ready to see Nan's disapproving face. But it wasn't my grandparents. It was my parents—Mom's worried face contrasting with Dad's confident everything-will-be-all-right expression. They looked like they had no business being in the States, even their clothes seemed coated in the handmade otherworldliness of Burkina Faso. Mom's hair was graying, more obvious now that I saw it in real life, and Dad was tanned in a way that was unintentional and a result of time outside in the direct sun. I stood and stumbled into them. Tears rushed down my cheeks as soon as I felt their arms around me.

Mom was crying too. "Oh, Chloe, it's going to be okay. We promise. It'll be okay."

It was, as Nan would say, *a piecrust promise*, but it still felt so good to have them there that I hung on to it anyway. I wasn't alone. I. Was. Not. Alone.

"Mr. and Mrs. Sanders," a voice said.

My mom released me. "*Ms*. Davis-Sanders," she corrected, and I almost laughed. So very much my mom, even now. Even in this place where she so obviously didn't belong.

"Er, yeah. Well, you and Chloe can follow me."

Mom led the way, following the young officer back to the interview room, as Dad wrapped an arm around my shoulder and whispered more reassurances.

Officer Kay was sitting inside, his shirt buttoned tightly at his no-neck, but his face didn't reveal anything. "Chloe, have a seat. I understand you have something to tell me."

The interview took almost an hour, Kay repeating questions over and over, almost to test the strength of my answers. I couldn't really blame him. I'd evaded him all weekend long. Now I told him everything I knew, everything I'd seen, even what had happened between me and Mateo in Herrick Chapel. I had to tell him that because a part of me thought maybe Mateo's used condom could verify my truth and assure the police about his lack of involvement. My voice croaked when I suggested it.

"Yeah," Kay said, itching the back of his neck, "we probably don't need to go hunting for that."

It was embarrassing and I kicked myself for every dumb crime show I'd ever watched. My parents stayed gratefully mute through most of the interview, only intervening to ask if I wanted some water or something to eat or to use the restroom.

It was a relief to say it all out loud. I was humiliated, but I also felt like I was "cleaning up the emotional house," as my mom would say. Other than learning Mateo was undocumented, Officer Kay didn't appear surprised by everyone's secrets, and I suspected I was the only one who'd held out about them over the weekend. Mostly they *were* dumb high school secrets and not anything anyone could get in trouble for, except for maybe Cam and his side job of dealing Ritalin to Eve. But they probably wouldn't even pursue that. It wasn't like he was a real dealer, just selling his own prescription to a friend.

At the end of the interview, Officer Kay said, "We found a match for her fingerprints. A few of our guys are investigating her last known address and seeing what they can find. At this point, we're not completely ruling out foul play, but we're fairly certain this was some sort of catfishing scheme."

My jaw dropped. "What?"

"A catfishing scheme. Do you know what that is?"

"Yes. I mean, I think I do. It's sort of a made-up identity thing, right?"

"Yeah."

"Why would she do that?"

"Hard to say," he answered.

The shock of hearing this gave way to anger. I pursed my

lips and took a slow breath through my nostrils, trying to calm myself down. "Why are you just telling me this now? Why did you let me go on and on?"

Officer Kay didn't look the least bit repentant. "You had information. And it is still illegal to live in this country without paperwork, so we'll need to contact the proper authorities to look into Mateo Vallera. Overall, it's best to get as many facts as possible if we want to close a case."

"Close a case?"

He nodded, then opened his file folder and pulled out a piece of paper. It was Chloe Donnelly's mug shot. "I mentioned the catfishing scheme. We've already confirmed with the school that this was the girl posing as Chloe Donnelly. She's nineteen. We had her prints in our system on a shoplifting charge from last year. The blood on the scarf was animal blood. We think she faked her disappearance."

My hands shook as I held the mug shot. I almost didn't recognize her. Her hair was longer in the picture, and she had acne across her forehead and cheeks. Her blue eyes looked duller in the picture too. I took a deep breath and read the words beneath the picture. *Lauren Klein.* Her name was Lauren Klein. Not a Chloe at all.

A strangled sound escaped from my throat, and my mom leaned forward and gripped my free hand, squeezing and murmuring that I should take deep breaths.

I saw spots. The entire house of cards tumbled before me. Oh God. Everything Chloe Donnelly had said was a lie.

I walked on numb legs out of the interview room. I was completely spent and still reeling from the fact that we'd been catfished.

Mom squeezed my shoulders and said, "I guess we have a lot to discuss."

"Yeah." I released a breath.

"Gestapo, Chloe? Really?"

"I know," I whispered. "It was stupid. I just . . ."

Mom waved a hand. "Wanted to fit in. Yes, I was a teenager too once. But don't you see? That's how it all starts. You're forced to get in line and be someone you're not, or you're forced to leave. Look at Mateo."

"I know, Mom."

"Do you, Chloe? Really?"

I blinked back tears. "I lost him. Because of this game and this girl. I could have said no to playing and I didn't until it was too late. And now my heart is broken. So could you ease up for a minute here? I know more than you can imagine."

Her eyes softened. "I'm sorry, Chloe."

I met her gaze and then my dad's. "I don't want to go to Burkina Faso. I want to stay here."

"Chloe, we can't live without you for another year. And

Nan and Pops can't—" Mom said, but I held up a hand.

"I don't want you to extend. I want you to come home in a few months like you planned. Like you promised."

"Chloe," Mom said, but Dad touched her shoulder. The soft look she gave him almost gutted me. They were closer now, closer than they'd even been before. As if sharing all that they had over the past few years had solidified their connection forever. Not that I ever doubted them as a couple, but now I wondered how I'd fit in to that. I knew they missed me, but was I enough for them to stay?

"Maybe she's right, Charley," Dad said. "Maybe we should reconsider extending. The village will be okay, I think. We'll do the best we can to set them up. There'll be other Corps volunteers. We're needed here. You told me you couldn't stand being without Chloe much longer. If she wants to stay . . ."

I could see the argument forming in Mom's mind—all about responsibility and what we could do for the world and how I should make my mark alongside them—but I shook my head.

"Mom, please. Please. I'm your daughter. Your only child." It was the first time I'd pleaded with her like this since I'd asked to come home. I remembered what Nan had said about Mom forcing a square peg into a round hole until someone told her to stop. I let out a long breath. "I don't want to go to Burkina Faso with you. It's not for me."

Her shoulders slumped a little, but she nodded. "We'll figure it out. We'll talk and figure out a plan that we're all happy with. Let's go. Nan and Pops are waiting for us."

Melissa was sitting on the bench outside the police station when we came out. She was wearing a National Guard shirt and leggings, her hair in a messy ponytail. I blinked in surprise.

"What are you doing here?"

"You could've called me this weekend, you know," she said by way of hello.

I should have. I was so worried about Mateo and lying to the police, I'd never considered reaching out for a friend.

I nodded. "I'm sorry."

"Are you in trouble?" she asked.

I released a long breath. "No. I don't think so."

Dad stepped forward and squeezed my arm. "We'll meet you at the car." Then he turned to Melissa. "It's good to see you again, Missy."

"No one calls me Missy anymore, Mr. Sanders."

He laughed. "Okay. I guess I have a lot to catch up on."

Then he and Mom walked toward the car, heads together like always. They were a good couple, always had been. I didn't know how to find my way back to them. Especially now. But maybe if they stayed, maybe if they started to listen to me more, we could figure out a way back to one another.

"I like Seth," I said to Melissa when I turned back to face her.

She laughed. "Oh, Chloe. Of all the stuff to say."

"What? He's cute and he's really into you."

She patted the bench next to her and I sat. "So, do you want to give me the thirty-second version of everything?"

I shook my head. "No. You deserve more than that. Come over later, okay? Dinner's at six thirty."

She nodded. "Yeah. I remember. Your grandparents used to invite me over after church when we were in elementary and they had those big family dinners."

A spike of guilt pierced through me. I wanted to be a better friend to Melissa. I wanted to be everything that Chloe Donnelly could have been if she hadn't lied and turned us all against one another. I wanted to be everything Eve could have been if she wasn't so insecure. I wanted to be everything Holly could have been if she didn't have to carry the weight of her father's choices. I silently vowed to be my best self for Melissa. And maybe for me too. "Thanks for coming."

She grinned. "Thanks for reaching out to me."

"I think you were the one who reached out to me."

She raised a shoulder. "Yeah, I did. It's good to have you back, Chloe."

Then I hugged her and she hugged me back. Not totally fixed, but better now. I squeezed her one last time, then stood and headed to the car, checking my phone again in hopes maybe Mateo had responded to my text. I wanted to tell him about the catfishing. I wanted to tell him he was okay, maybe not completely okay but not being actively hunted as a murder suspect. I wanted to tell him Chloe Donnelly's real name was Lauren. I wanted to tell him I had Melissa now and things were going to be better. But there were no texts or calls from him. Just multiple texts from all the others who'd played Gestapo, asking for updates. I powered my phone off and slid in the backseat of Pops's car. They could wait. My parents were home and I had a friend coming over who maybe could help me find Mateo. Mateo. *Mateo, Mateo, Mateo.*

I powered my phone back on and looked at his *I love you too* text again. Then I looked at my last unanswered text to him. I typed another one, just in case.

Mateo. It's all okay, I think. Please reach out. It's going to be okay. We'll figure something out.

Epilogue

"What do you mean you're not charging her with anything?" I said to Officer Kay a week later.

"We don't have anything to really hold her on. I mean, sure, presenting fake identification to the school, but that's really not a lot and not worth pursuing. She lied. She played a game, made up an identity, and lied to all of you."

He tapped the folder in front of him as if that was the end of the story. I stared at him. I'd been waiting to hear more about Lauren. Waiting to find out anything, and today, finally, I'd gotten a call. She was fine, alive, living in a small apartment with her mom just off of I-80. Her mom had no idea about any of it. She'd been homeschooled through high school and had told her mom she was working when she'd been at GHS. Apparently, she was a genius with computers and incredibly bright, but her mom claimed Lauren had some mental issues that kept her from being able to live on her own.

"Isn't there a catfishing charge?"

He shrugged. "No. She didn't really do anything illegal, beyond pretending she was a student. No one was hurt, no crime was committed."

I felt like I'd been gutted. No crime? Mateo was gone. Mateo had disappeared and hadn't texted me again. Whether it was because he thought he was a suspect or because his parents forced him to cut ties knowing that they'd never really be safe here, I didn't know, but I was lost. Lost and heartsick and broken.

"So she's getting away with all of it?" I choked out.

He shrugged again. "I'm sorry, Chloe."

"Why would she do this? I don't understand."

"Like I said before, we don't really know. Maybe she was bored, maybe she was lonely, maybe she wanted to be someone else for a little while. Her mom did mention mental issues. From what I gathered, Lauren had done a pretty extensive amount of research on the internet about the school. She'd practically made a job of it."

"Is that how she knew everything? All our secrets?"

He sighed. "Maybe. Maybe she just listened really well, overheard stuff. It's not like she had to do any real schoolwork while she was there. You'd be surprised how easy it is to gather information about people. All this stuff online that people post on their social media accounts. It doesn't take a lot to piece together entire lives. I tell my kids all the time to be careful of what they post, but what are you going to do? Everyone does it."

"Mateo," I whispered, slumping in the chair across from his desk.

"I really am sorry, Chloe." But he didn't sound that sorry. He sounded like he was judging Mateo, like *Mateo* was the criminal here, and not Lauren Klein.

I nodded numbly and stood up. Officer Kay cleared his throat. He tapped the folder twice, meaty fingers putting a fine point on its contents. "Lauren works third shift at the Kum and Go on Tuesdays and Thursdays."

"The Kum and Go? Seriously? You said she was a genius with computers."

"I also said she had some mental issues. Who knows with kids today. But yes, according to her mom, she works third shift at the Kum and Go."

I looked at him for a long time. He was giving me a gift, an opportunity, and I should be grateful. Maybe he did realize what she cost me after all. But did I want to see her again? I stared at my hands. I hadn't bitten my nails for a week. Not since my parents had been home, trying to orchestrate the transition of new volunteers to move into their village in

Burkina Faso at the end of the summer and committing to stay in Grinnell with me until I graduated.

"I don't know what to say to her."

"Tell her how you feel. Tell her what her lies did to you."

"She won't care. You should have seen her that last night. She's unstable. This thing she did, people don't just do that. Not normal, compassionate people."

Officer Kay nodded. "Maybe not. And maybe it wouldn't mean anything to her if you confronted her. But maybe it'll mean something to you."

I told him I'd think about it and walked out of his office. My entire body felt out of sorts. My head was heavy with defeat and my heart hurt from missing Mateo. It wasn't fair that I only got him for such a short amount of time. It wasn't fair that he and his family had to set up in a new place, had to start all over because of Lauren Klein. I never even got the chance to meet any of them.

I checked my phone again, just like I'd been checking every ten minutes for the past week. Nothing. No calls, no texts, no Mateo. I'd been searching the internet with no luck. I'd taken to sending texts daily to his old phone number, knowing he wasn't getting them but not having any other way to reach out.

Please tell me where you are.

We'll figure out a way to meet.

I hate being without you.

I love you.

I love you.

I love you.

I got into Nan's car and drove to the Kum & Go. It was hours until the third shift started, but I didn't care. I stayed in the car, texting my parents that I wouldn't be home until very late. They didn't ask questions. They didn't realize they should; it had been so long since they'd had to actively parent. The learning curve was steep, but I thought they'd get it right eventually. Their hearts were in it completely. They just had to match the round peg with the round hole. I went inside and got a crappy burrito that ended up smelling worse than the cafeteria ones and some Vitaminwater. Then I got back in the car and waited.

At ten forty-five I saw her. She looked smaller somehow, less extraordinary. She was wearing cheap jeans and a bright-pink Kum & Go polo shirt. Pink. Of course. I stared at her and it was as if she felt me because she turned. Her eyes went wide when she saw me, the bright-blue coloring still the prettiest part of her. She stood her ground and lifted her chin, the flickering fluorescent street lamp making the moment almost scary. For a second I saw the Chloe Donnelly who had co-opted my life. Who'd somehow found me and decided to play a game with me and my friends. Who'd taken on my name and driven the boy I loved into hiding. Hate zinged through me. I put my hand on the car door handle but then paused. I leaned forward and her Chloe Donnelly face crumpled. She looked down, her shoulders curling in on themselves. When she looked back up, there was no one but homeschooled Lauren Klein in front of me. A too-smart girl who worked at the Kum & Go and was so bored and unhappy and heartless she invented a life and sought out a group of people to mess with.

Sadness slipped inside of me. I wasn't certain what had led her to this, but a tiny part of me almost understood, not the heartlessness but the unhappiness. It was the same part that understood Eve and Holly and how much they were willing to sacrifice in order to be loved. The same part that had been nearly overwhelmed by my own bone-deep loneliness this entire year. I released the door handle and started the ignition. Then I put the car in reverse and pulled out of the parking lot without looking back.

Acknowledgments

I first came up for the idea for this book in 1998 while I was hiking with my dear friend Emily Bergl. It took two hours of intense conversation to iron out a plot. And twenty years to get it right. This book has been through an obscene number of drafts, three agents, and more beta readers than I can possibly mention here. If you've known me in the past twenty years, we've probably talked about this book and you've maybe even read a version of it. Thank you, everyone, for being part of this journey.

Mountains of gratitude to Liesa Abrams and the rest of the team at Simon Pulse. Liesa is an amazing editor-partner, and our conversations about this book, about condoms and orgasms and the difficulty of being a girl, are some of the best I've ever had with anyone in this industry. Your notes were exactly what this book needed to turn it into something authentic and full of heart. I'm so glad you told me I didn't need to add "jazz hands."

To Barry Goldblatt, thanks for saying, "Yeah, I like this one," and for generally championing all the parts of me. You've always been very good at looking after me and I'm more grateful than you can possibly know.

To Jolene Perry, Rhiannon Morgan, Carrie Bouffard, and Carrie Mesrobian: You have all been so involved in this book from the start that it probably feels like it's your book. Make no mistake, it belongs to you as much as it does to me. Thank you for every minute you spent drowning with me in this. I hope you feel like all your hard work paid off and that I've taken your wisdom and done right by it. I love you all very much.

Special acknowledgment to Dr. Danny M. Cohen for numerous conversations and sensitivity discussions about Jewish plight under the Gestapo, to Silvia Lopez for expertise on the undocumented, to Ally Beckman for her help with Burkina Faso and NGOs, to Scout Slava-Ross for being my Grinnell College student on campus who walked through the game and corrected geography stuff and offered general Grinnell insight. And to Molly Campe, whose enthusiasm about all things Grinnell made me finally figure out that the heart of the book wasn't in the game but in the location.

This book is in part a love letter to Grinnell, Iowa, and while I did my very best to make it as close to accurate as possible, I hope readers will forgive some creative license. To the GHS staff and students in particular, thank you for allowing me to turn your school into what I needed it to be for the purposes of this story.

Last, but certainly not least, thank you to my family. You have stuck with me throughout this writing journey, and I love you so much for your unending support. Julio, Jojo, Bijou, and Butter: Nothing could make me prouder than calling you mine. You're my first, last, and everything.

Check out another compulsive read
from Christa Desir!

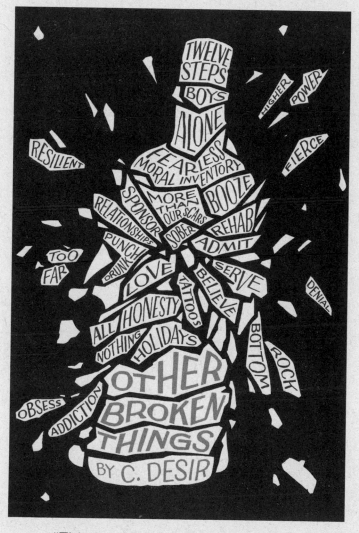

"This book is a blinding beauty."
—**MARTHA BROCKENBROUGH**, author of
The Game of Love and Death

Chapter
One

I'd cut a bitch for a cigarette right now. Unfortunately, I'm sandwiched in the car between inflatable Santa and inflatable Frosty and the only person within striking distance is my mom.

"You sure you don't want me to come in?" she asks as she tugs at her hand-knitted red-and-green striped hat. Mom is the mascot of the holiday season. Pretty sure she pees eggnog and her armpit odor is peppermint scented.

"It's a closed meeting, Mom. I told you that. Only the alkies get to go. Not their moms. Plus you've got to finish decorating."

My fingers curl in and out of my palm. Someone at the meeting has to have a smoke. *Has to.*

"I was looking online. There are some open meetings in the city. I could go with you to those."

I wave my hand. "Mom. Stop. I'll be fine. I went to a meeting every day in rehab. I know the drill. Pick me up in an hour."

I shove Frosty to the side and push open the backseat door. Yes, I'm in the back. Like a toddler. The passenger seat has been taken up by inflatable Rudolph. I slide out and Mom turns down "Feliz Navidad" long enough to call out to me.

"Proud of you, Natalie. You've got this."

I wave again, resisting the urge to give her the finger, and turn away so she doesn't see my eye roll. Mom's obviously fit time in her busy holiday schedule to read some of the *Big Book*—Alcoholics Anonymous's bible to getting my shitty life together, told through a series of steps and stories of pathetic losers just like me. Jesus.

The brown building in front of me is nondescript with the letters SFC on a plaque in front. As I step up to the door, my hands shake a little. Not from the DT's—you need to be way deeper down the rabbit hole than I ever got for delirium tremens—but from the whole business of it.

AA meetings are a requirement. Three times a week until I'm three months sober and then twice a week until I'm six months. Six months feels like for-fucking-ever at this point, but honestly, a month ago, six hours felt the same.

I pause outside the door and stare at the sign taped to the front. Meeting times, plus a plug about movie nights and a Sunday-morning pancake breakfast. There are three meetings every day. I can't imagine going to that many meetings in a day. What the hell for? How many times does someone need to hear the Serenity Prayer?

I slide my hand in my coat pocket and finger the card inside. *Go in, zone out, get your card signed.* Drawing in a deep breath, I push through the entrance and am immediately hit by the smell of BO and burned coffee. I blink my eyes a few times to adjust to the light and see I'm in a hallway. A door on my right says FELLOWSHIP MEETING ROOM.

Another breath, this time through my mouth so I don't have to deal with the BO stench. My heart is beating pretty hard. Even more than the first time I got in the boxing ring, a million years ago when I thought things were different.

There's a long mirror on the side of the door, like we some-how might feel the need to check our appearance before going in to confess our drunken transgressions. My ridiculously curly hair is pulled back neatly in a band, my slapdash makeup job is miraculously holding up from this morning, and the rest of me looks Abercrombie solid. This is definitely my 12-step best, so I'm not sure why I'm stalling.

Somehow, walking into a meeting room felt easier at rehab. Probably because I had a nurse escorting me. I squeeze my eyes shut and grip the knob, pulling open the door. Wishing with everything I have for this not to be real.

The room smells too. Different, though. Like musty books and defeat. Yes, defeat has a smell. A distinct cigarette smell, with zero traces of alcohol. An old woman near the door looks up and smiles a little at me. A quick scan around the room shows three black dudes in conversation around the big table, an obviously drunk or hungover Hispanic dude with his head leaned against the back wall, and a white guy talking to a woman with red hair and a scowl on her face. The white guy looks up when I enter and nods at me.

No beaming smiles or welcoming committee here. No one's happy to see me. They're all dealing with the same shit. I'm another soldier who's been drafted into the army of addiction. Hardly cause to celebrate. On the plus side, from the look of things, there's no way anyone here is going to be digging that deep into my business, which means I won't have to think—something I've gotten excellent at in the past month.

I unwind the scarf at my neck—hand-knitted by Mom, of course—and plop into a chair at the table. A quick glance at the clock shows I have five minutes before the meeting starts. I need to time this better. Or bring cigarettes next time so I can smoke beforehand. But I finished my last one this morning, sitting on my window ledge and watching Mom hang icicle lights. She frowned when she saw the cigarette, but didn't say anything. She's been on me about them since I got back, but she must have figured a lecture about them would have been less than welcome this morning.

The red-haired lady stands up from the table and approaches me. Ah. Meeting leader. I know by now talking to the newbies is part of their job.

"Kathy," she says, sitting in the plastic chair next to me. "First meeting?"

"First meeting here. Not first meeting ever," I mumble in response. Wonder if I could get her to sign my card now and then leave the meeting early. I give her a long look and realize she's not the type to break rules. She's got that hard-living look about her, and if she's a meeting leader, she's been in AA awhile now.

"Got a sponsor?" she asks.

"No. I'm just out of rehab."

She nods and I catch the white guy watching us. Not even slyly. Just openly staring. I have an urge to flip him off, but I doubt it'll earn me any brownie points and I have a card I need filled up.

"Take out your phone," Kathy says. I pull out my cell and she snatches it from my hand like she's going to confiscate it. Instead she presses some buttons and hands it back to me. "I'm in your contacts now. Call whenever."

"Natalie," I say.

She nods again and gets up. "Find a sponsor, Natalie. You're too young to be in here."

I almost roll my eyes, but that'd just be proving her point. I am too young. Seventeen. Way too young for rehab. Way too young for AA. It's all sort of bullshit, but to say my parents are overprotective is an understatement. So here I am. Two days out of rehab, two months after a DUI, surrounded by people who don't know anything about me, with a court card in my pocket, and wanting to beat the crap out of just about everyone.

Happy fucking holidays.

Chapter
Two

"This is the twelve thirty closed meeting of the Stevenson Fellowship Center. The only requirement for attendance is a desire to stop drinking. Calvin, can you please read 'How It Works'?"

I look at my Uggs and let the drone of Calvin's voice wash over me. I've heard the "How It Works" speech dozens of times. I could practically recite it in my sleep. And Calvin is a mumbler so it's not like I could understand him anyway. I want to shut my eyes like the Hispanic guy in the back. His mouth has dropped open slightly and he's either passed out or he's fallen asleep. For the hundredth time I think how I don't belong here.

Driving was stupid. I get that. But I wasn't plastered. I've been way drunker, and frankly, the whole thing would've been fine if I hadn't hit wet road. And if I hadn't been distracted by the shit show of my life. The "legally drunk" thing is sort of bullshit. You hit your legal limit after one drink. I've seen people have way more than that and be perfectly fine driving home. It's all a scam between insurance companies and the government to squeeze more money out of the working class. I'm not saying people should drive loaded, but seriously, three drinks is hardly shit-faced, despite what a Breathalyzer might say.

The topic for the meeting is the Second Step: *Came to believe that a Power greater than ourselves could restore us to sanity*. Cue zone-out time. The higher power thing is a really big part of AA. At first I got into all sorts of arguments in rehab about how scientifically, God just isn't possible, but I quickly realized that wasn't getting me any closer to being released or convincing my therapist that I'm fine. So now I tune it out and nod when other people talk about their spiritual awakening as if it isn't all a big fat crock.

As the three black guys drone on about getting right with God, I examine the room. The main wall behind Kathy has huge signs on either side of the door. The Twelve Steps on the left, the Twelve Traditions on the right. I still haven't exactly figured out the Twelve Traditions. Seems like it was sort of slotted into the program so people didn't turn AA into a moneymaking organization. Fools.

The rest of the room is brown paneling and bookshelves filled with self-help books and framed pictures of guys who were presumably important to the AA organization. I don't have the first fucking clue who any of them are, though I guess one must be Bill W. The giant clock on the wall draws my attention and I count seconds along with it as the old woman who smiled at me when I walked in starts to talk about medication and the Good Lord. Fifteen, sixteen, seventeen, eighteen . . .

The room has gone quiet and I look up to see everyone staring at me. Crap. I blush a little as the white guy shifts forward in his chair and drops his hands on the table.

"My name is Natalie, and I'm an alcoholic."—"Hi, Natalie."—"Grateful to be here today. I think I'd prefer just to listen." I've said this more than a dozen times over the last month. It's a mantra as much as anything else in my life. And it gets me out of having to share anything. I couldn't do it all the time in rehab, because my therapist sort of caught on to it, but I did it as much as I could.

The white guy has tats on his knuckles. I notice the letters of *KILL* on the left one. And some weird symbols on the right one. This is unexpected, as the rest of him looks pretty clean-cut. As clean-cut as you can look in AA. Jeans without holes. Flannel button-down over a long-sleeve white tee. Clean-shaven. Blond hair that isn't too long or shaggy. If I had beer goggles on, I might say he's a Bradley Cooper look-alike. And no dark shadows under his eyes. He's been sober awhile, I'm guessing.

The rest of the meeting carries on, but I don't listen to anyone. There's a thin strip of windows above the bookshelf and I mostly stare out at the gray sky. In the end Kathy lets us go early—which never happened in rehab—because no one else has anything to say. We circle up and I find myself holding hands with the white guy—Joe, I think—as we say the Lord's Prayer together.

My gaze stays too long on the *KILL* on his knuckles as the group chants, "Keep coming back. It works if you work it . . . sober." Everyone else has let go of each other and started to disperse.

"Can I get my hand back?" Joe says, and I drop it like I've been burned. God. What the hell is wrong with me?

"Nice tat," I say with a smirk.

He nods. "Saving up to get it removed. Or get a new one put on top."

I wrap my scarf around my neck. "Trying to get your outsides to match your insides?"

He shakes his head in this way that reads like he's disappointed in me. Not sure what the fuck for, as I haven't done anything as far as he knows. "Dry drunk?"

"Huh? What's that?"

"You know . . . the people working the program because they have to. Sober because someone told them to get that way. The ones who relapse the fastest."

My mouth drops open. "Fuck off, dude. You don't know anything about me."

Kathy comes over then and nudges Joe. "Leave Natalie alone. She's here. That's what matters."

He shakes his head again and zips up his coat. "I'm going out for a smoke. I'll see you."

"Yeah. You coming to breakfast on Sunday?" Kathy asks.

"Nah. Can't. Gotta do a work thing. You'll need to cover

it." He trains his eyes on me and for a second I think I see concern. But it's masked right away into indifference. "Come back, Natalie. Even if you don't believe it. It might sink in eventually."

I nod and shove my hands in my pockets. I finger the court card and wait for him to leave, but he lingers just long enough that I get pissed and pull out the card anyway. He's fucking with me and I frankly don't care. I push the card at Kathy. He scoffs and heads out the door, muttering.

"Can you sign my court card?"

To her credit, she doesn't even bat an eye. "DUI?" she asks.

"Yeah. Like I said, I'm just out of rehab. Now I've got six months of meetings and community service."

She grabs a pen from the basket full of two-dollar donations and signs the card. "Rehab your parents' idea?"

"Yeah."

She hands the card back to me. "You're lucky."

"Hardly."

"Least you got someone who gives a shit enough to help you get sober."

So, huh. Kathy isn't going to treat me like a kid. Maybe she's my ticket out of this place.

"Well, that might be overstating things," I say.

She shrugs. "Your folks drive you here?"

"Yeah."

"There you go then."

I almost tell her I don't really fit here. I almost tell her I'm not an alcoholic. I almost tell her this is all bullshit, but I decide against it. For some people all this stuff means something. They become addicted to meetings in the same way they became addicted to booze or drugs in the first place. I saw a ton of kids in rehab on their third go-around who were all gung ho about meetings, and it didn't take me long to realize it was just replacing one thing with another. Therapy and group became their new drugs.

Personally, I'd take booze over sharing bullshit feelings any day, but who am I to burst someone's bubble? So I nod at Kathy and thank her and tell her I'll see her again.

"You got my number. Use it," she says to my back as I'm walking out.

"Sure thing," I call to her.

I pull out my phone and delete her contact info before I'm through the front door.